"Just one more chapter" ↱

FROM RAGS

Suzanne Wright

The characters and events portrayed in this book are fictitious. Any similarity to real persons, living or dead, is coincidental and not intended by the author.

Original Version Copyright © 2012 Suzanne Wright
10th Anniversary Edition Copyright © 2022 Suzanne Wright

All rights reserved. This book or any portion thereof may not be reproduced or used in any manner whatsoever without the express written permission of the publisher except for the use of brief quotations in a book review.

ISBN: 9798438955702
Cover design: J Wright

For Alice. We miss you.

PROLOGUE

Jaxxon, age fourteen

"B-but...but...but—"

"Oh stop snivelling, Jaxxon," snapped Leah as she zipped up her tatty old duffel bag. "You should be happy for me. I'm finally getting out of here. I'm going to have my own place."

Jaxxon Carter, who was curled up on her bed, watched as her older sister stretched her long, lean body, looking much like a contented cat. "But—"

"Oi, what did I just say? Stop with the snivelling!"

Jaxxon took a deep breath and wiped her tear-stained cheeks with her sleeve. But she could feel more tears brewing. "Will you come see me sometimes?"

Leah snorted. "How can you even ask that? You know I'll be busy going for auditions and stuff." A self-satisfied smile surfaced on her face. "Hey, just think, you might see me on T.V. soon, singing and doing concerts."

As usual, Leah's squinty hazel eyes – so very different from Jaxxon's own huge, brown ones – shone with confidence. That was one thing that Leah had in abundance, though sometimes Jaxxon thought it bordered on vanity.

"Won't that make all the Foster Plonkers sorry for passing us off from house to house."

"But you'll stay in touch, yeah?" Jaxxon could hear the uncertainty in her own voice and didn't like this feeling she suddenly had that she was losing her sister for good. Maybe it wouldn't have been so bad if Leah would just tell her the address of her flat. But she was refusing to tell her and had even asked their social worker and foster parents not to reveal it to Jaxxon. Leah could be strange like that sometimes. If she thought you desperately wanted something from her, she would refuse to give it to you purely for that reason.

Leah shrugged. "What are you panicking for? In two years, you'll be out of here yourself."

That was true enough. But two years would feel like a long time to someone who was all alone. Once Leah – all she had left in the world – was gone, that was exactly what Jaxxon would be. Alone.

During the past six years, Jaxxon had watched the only people she came to care about disappear from her life. First went Mum. Suicide by heroin overdose. Jaxxon – the one who had found her mother's lifeless body on the sofa – had been eight, Leah ten. There was no dad or other family to care whether they lived or died, so into the social system they went.

It wasn't until eighteen months ago, after pit-stopping in a series of foster homes all over London, that they had come to live with the Glennon family. They weren't all that bad. Compared to some of the other foster parents, these people were eligible for sainthood. Although they were – in a word – slobs and not all that interested in what their foster children did, they didn't hit, they didn't grope, and they didn't decide to suddenly starve you for a short while for their own entertainment like the last lot had. Where the Glennons were concerned, as long as you didn't raid Gloria Glennon's stash of chocolate or help yourself to one of Eric Glennon's beloved beers, they'd practise the principle of 'live and let live'.

Still, Jaxxon knew that Leah would have, as she always did wherever they were, played up and set out to annoy them if it hadn't been for the other foster kids. The gorgeous Connor McKenzie and the geeky Roland Thompson had made the situation bearable. Both Jaxxon and Leah had had a little thing for Connor. In fact, Jaxxon had become infatuated with him and his cocky grin as only a teenage girl could. Not just because of how gorgeous he was, but because Jaxxon soon found that underneath his temper and broodiness was intelligence and even kindness.

He had always looked out for Jaxxon, always protected her, always chased off any boy within a one mile radius of her. Everyone had feared him – probably because he somehow had the look of a predator – but Jaxxon had never felt threatened by him. In fact, strangely enough, this menacing person had been the only one to ever make her feel safe – even when he was zooming her around town at top speed in a car he had 'borrowed' for the night. Although that was something he had done regularly, he had never been prosecuted as he had never been caught.

Then six months ago, shortly after Connor had turned sixteen, he had moved into a flat of his own, just like Leah was doing now. Jaxxon vividly remembered when he had kissed her the night before he left – something which had shocked the hell out of her. He had promised that he would visit sometimes and even take her to see his flat when it was fixed up, but so far he hadn't been in touch. Then three months after he had left, Roland's mother had finally sorted out her situation and taken her son back to live with her. And now Jaxxon's very own sister was leaving too. Sure, she'd have the newest foster addition, Rhona, but the girl was far from friendly and kept everyone at a distance.

"If you do get famous and stuff, how will I get in touch with you when I get out?"

Leah shrugged carelessly. "Maybe I'll phone here on your sixteenth birthday. Maybe I'll even come get you in a limo. Can you imagine the look on everyone's faces if I turned up here in a limo?!" Another squeal.

Her sixteenth birthday. It seemed so far away right now. Without thinking about it, Jaxxon reached under her mattress and pulled out the photograph that Gloria had let her have. Jaxxon stood smiling in front of the wonky Christmas tree with Roland on her right side, looking absolutely bored, and with Connor on her left. Connor was wearing that cocky grin she loved with his arm flung over her shoulder. Leah was in the background, combing her long blonde hair, glaring hard at them. She almost looked angry.

This was all Jaxxon had left of them.

"Oh when are you going to stop pining for him?" groaned Leah. "He isn't coming back. Why would he? What's he got to come back for?"

A pang struck Jaxxon's chest at Leah's words and that

condescending glare she had that could decrease a person's self-worth by ninety percent, just like that.

"Don't worry," continued Leah, "I'll tell him you said 'hi.'."

It took a few seconds for those last words to register. "What do you mean?"

She gave Jaxxon a sympathetic smile but didn't even try to conceal the insincerity of it. "Oh come on, Jaxxon, you didn't honestly think that he had any real interest in *you*, did you? Oh my God, you did. How cute. Or stupid, whichever."

Jaxxon felt as though she'd been slapped.

"He told me he only thought of you as a little sister, that it was me he loved. We did *it* lots of times, you know. He made me promise to come find him when I got out." She sighed wistfully. "Soon me and him will be living in L.A., our faces all over the magazines, I'll be recording album after album…Maybe we'll even get married. Leah McKenzie…I like the sound of it. It's a lot better than Leah Carter anyway."

In that one moment, Jaxxon almost hated her. Her *and* him. The tears gathering in her eyes were ones of anger and despair now, no longer of the fear of being alone. Why would he have kissed her that night before leaving and then told her he'd always cared for her if it was Leah he loved? Leah who he had been sleeping with all this time? "He kissed me," she blurted out.

"Well of course he did. He felt sorry for you – you were getting all teary-eyed. I was the one who told him to kiss you. He hadn't wanted to, but I thought it might stop you from snivelling. *Something you're doing again now.*"

Jaxxon squeezed her eyes shut against the pictures her mind was tormenting her with of Leah and Connor together – kissing, touching, sleeping together. And then them laughing at poor little infatuated Jaxxon.

"Well, that's me all packed." She squealed again with excitement. After casting one last look at the plain, musty smelling, mostly bare room, Leah threw her bag over her shoulder. "Gotta go."

Jaxxon tried to get up from the bed. Maybe to hug her sister. Maybe to slap her. Or maybe to follow her downstairs and wave at the front door. But it was as though her body was depleted. As though her body was downright sick of her mind ignoring Leah's hurtful behaviour, so had decided to intervene before she ran after Leah like a little lost puppy. She did feel lost, though. Jaxxon was a person who always looked on the bright side. But right now there didn't seem to be one, and Jaxxon didn't know how to function without it.

So she sat there immobile as Leah's singing gradually faded until she could hear her no more. In that moment, Jaxxon felt something change within herself; it was the same sensation she'd gotten when her mother died, and then again when Connor left. Like a piece of herself went with them, leaving gaping holes that Jaxxon suspected might be permanent.

But wasn't that her own fault for getting too close to people? Wasn't it her own fault that she was in such pain right now? It was stupid to have ever thought that Connor would want her and not Leah. Her sister was undeniably beautiful with her straight, sleek caramel-blonde hair, piercing hazel eyes, and tall, thin, lithe body. She would have the angelic look down to a tee if it wasn't for the fact that her smile always had a glint of deviousness to it.

The two sisters were practically polar opposites in appearance. Jaxxon sported a head of brown, untameable ringlets and a curvy body that she despised because of the attention it gained her. She was, to her utter annoyance, an early bloomer. Her generous-sized breasts and 'heart-shaped butt' – as the boys in school often described it – were constantly groped, even by total strangers. It hadn't been so bad when Connor was around; boys had tended to leave her alone for fear of what he would do. Things had changed drastically since he left. And now that she was without her older sister, things could only worsen.

Footsteps outside her bedroom door stole her from her thoughts. The door swung lazily open as her relatively new foster sister, Rhona, strode into the room chewing gum, and plonked herself on the bed beside Jaxxon. The smell of smoke clung to her dark skin and clothes. Jaxxon wasn't expecting any comfort from this antisocial girl who seemed to hate everyone. She didn't get it.

"So, Big Tits, how long do you think it'll be before Queen Bitch realises she lives in a fantasy land? Singer, my arse."

Jaxxon said nothing; just continued to stare at the photograph in her hand, wondering whether to kiss it or tear it up.

"You know she won't come back, don't you? She won't. They never do," grumbled Rhona. She wasn't feeling sorry for herself – simply stating what she believed was a fact.

"She's my sister."

"She's also a self-absorbed, spiteful, selfish bitch who—"

"But—"

"But nothing, Jaxxon," she said firmly. "Just because she's blood doesn't mean anything. I'll bet that girl has never done a single thing for you in her life. She looks out for number one – and number one only. Just like the rest of them. So wise up, Big Tits. And do it now. You're on your own." Just before leaving the room, she turned back to Jaxxon. "Wanna know what the trick is to getting through this shit? Never let anyone in."

Alone again, Jaxxon stared down at the photograph as she considered Rhona's departing words. The thing that had kept Jaxxon from losing herself so far and avoiding the bitterness that consumed Leah was that she rolled with the punches; just accepted that suffering was part of life. The whole 'woe is me' thing wasn't for her. After all, what was so special about her that meant she could flit through life without pain while others were swamped by it? So, she reasoned, her being alone while Leah and Connor began a life together was just something else that she'd have to accept, even though it cut deeper than anything else ever had.

Finally, with a deep cleansing breath, Jaxxon tore the photograph to pieces and slung them out of the partially open window. She wouldn't let this be an ending. She would try to, instead, make it a new start. She'd do as Rhona said – wise up and face that she was alone, but she wouldn't cut herself off like Rhona had.

Little did Jaxxon know, but as from the following day, her new start would be tainted. Tainted by violence, struggle, and even more pain. With all that would come her decision to never let anyone in again.

CHAPTER ONE

Eight years later

It was amazing how alcohol had the power to make people think they were attractive, mused Jaxxon. Or, in this case, some sort of gift to women. Thank God there was the bar to separate her from this bald, heavy-set bloke who was so drunk that both his eyes were fighting for one corner. For the past half hour, while he swayed and slurred, he had been flirting shamelessly with her. His 'come hither' smile revealed a set of Nicorette stained teeth – oh wait, it wasn't actually a full set. And 'flirting' wasn't quite accurate. Not unless you considered dirty talk, sexual innuendos, and being given flashes of body parts to be flirtatious behaviour. More like sick-minded crap.

Needless to say, she wasn't inspired to welcome him into her arms and body. Unfortunately, he just wasn't getting the message. Even the words 'get the fuck out of my face' hadn't fazed him. Jaxxon was now itching to get out of the dingy, stuffy pub – she was tired, hungry, and feeling homicidal. But she was pretty sure that Joe, the landlord of the pub, wouldn't be too impressed if his barmaid up and left. Jaxxon cast a quick glance at her quickly aging, flabby boss only to find him smiling at her in mock sympathy.

After serving another bloke – this one was smiling shyly at her and blushing like a virgin on a first date – Jaxxon switched her attention back to the pen and clipboard in front of her, noting what needed stocking up on, and all the while wondering how she managed to attract oddballs and plonkers. Not that there was much chance of her being approached by someone who might spark her interest in here. The pub didn't exactly appeal to the youthful. In fact, looking around at the punters, the place looked like a bloody nursing home.

The bald weirdo was now suggesting a 'fuck festival' with him and his five friends – all of who shared two things in common. One, they were over the age of fifty. Two, they had beer guts. She respectfully declined, but his persistence earned him a 'sod off you sick perv' from her. Still, he was unfazed.

Then he leaned across the bar, and by the look in his eyes, Jaxxon knew he was about to touch her. Jaxxon and 'touch' didn't go well together. "Don't dare," she warned. He ignored that warning and abruptly reached out and squeezed her breast painfully hard. Pure reflex, she gripped the pen tightly and stabbed the web-like skin between the thumb and forefinger of his roaming hand – not enough to draw blood, but enough to wrench a cry of pain from him.

"Hurts like fuck, doesn't it," she said through gritted teeth. "Don't ever touch me again."

The creepy old sod actually grinned at her. Apparently pain made him horny. Oh great – now, in his drunken mind, she had just flirted back. No doubt he would have stayed exactly where he was, hoping for more, if his friend hadn't dragged him away.

Joe joined Jaxxon's side, chuckling. "Another satisfied customer."

"He's one sick bastard."

"Sick bastards love you and your mean-arse streak."

"It's not mean to be honest and straight with people or insist on them not being perverted."

He nodded toward a particular table not far from the bar where a pair of bashful-looking blokes sat, dressed in leather. "The two submissives are here again. They still want you to be their Dom?" Joe chuckled again.

"You enjoy all this far too much."

"This place used to be boring 'til you started working here. It might help if you didn't look even spicier when you're fuming. It seems to get their blood running."

"You say all the right things," said Jaxxon sarcastically.

"Oi, if I gave you a compliment or any sweet words, you'd laugh in my face – just like you do with all the others."

He was right there, which, she supposed, was why she had never been with a truly decent bloke. Somehow, she always ended up with controlling, clingy weirdoes. It seemed like 'nice' blokes were often too intimidated by her take-no-prisoners mentality to even approach her.

At the same time as the door flew open, a gruff voice rang out,

"*Jaxxon!*"

Sigh. She had actually expected her twat-of-a-neighbour earlier. He must have taken longer at his drug dealer's flat than she'd anticipated. "Yes, Sean, what can I get you? Budweiser? Guinness? Cyanide?"

"Where is she?" he demanded as he stood opposite Jaxxon, panting like a Bull Mastiff.

"She?" enquired Joe.

Sean looked at him, wearing a bitter smile. "Imagine my surprise when I get back to my flat to find *no* Celia, and *no* kid. Gone. Clothes and all."

"Good," said Jaxxon. "All's going to plan then."

"You helped his woman run off?" asked Joe, not all that surprised or bothered.

Jaxxon held up her hand. "Correction: I helped a beaten, mistreated, petrified woman and a bruised, starving, frightened little girl have a new start somewhere away from this threat to their lives and sanity."

"You interfering bitch," growled Sean.

"What can I say – it's a gift."

"You put ideas in her head. Celia wouldn't have left me like that."

"No she wouldn't have," agreed Jaxxon. "She was too scared to take a piss without your say-so."

"Where did you get the idea that you had the right to stick your nose in?"

"I'm sure Jesus said something about loving thy neighbours."

He spread his hands over the bar, his face contorting as his anger intensified. "Where's Celia?"

Jaxxon noticed the tear in the arm of his jacket and smirked. "So you tried to break into my flat and ended up being used as a chew toy."

"That dog is a hellhound."

"A much loved hellhound. And I better not get back to find your blood all over the carpet of my flat." She had found the beautiful Great Dane, Bronty, about a month or so ago lying in an alleyway covered in bites and scratches. Without hesitation, she took him back to her flat and got to work on his injuries. From that point on, Bronty had seemed to decide she was his, and had remained with her even once he was fully healed. Since then, her flat hadn't been broken into even once.

The first time her flat – which was more or less one single room – had been 'visited', she had been both shocked and enraged. But soon she got used to these regular 'visits' from who appeared to be mostly drug addicts looking for money. Occasionally, they took some of her underwear, too. It was difficult to experience any anxiety over it anymore. How could she feel territorial about a place that was not 'home', but merely shelter? Besides, Jaxxon didn't have much by way of possessions that she could call her own, especially not anything of worth.

She would never forget the day, about three months back when she got back to find that not only had her flat been broken into, but the culprit was still inside. Not an addict looking for something they could sell, but a twelve year old boy, looking for food. Little David revealed that although he lived with his mum in the flat above Jaxxon's, the woman was hardly ever home; when she was, she barely took any notice of him.

Despite his insistence that he remain with his mum, who he was very protective of, Jaxxon might have contacted the authorities if she hadn't known from personal experience that going into care didn't mean you would be any better off. So she had taken him to meet a friend of hers who worked in the bakery at the corner of their street. Nora had told him that if he came each day just before closing time, she would give him any pastries or other foods that were left over. Thank God. Jaxxon made a mental note to check on him later.

"Where are they?"

Sean's growl snatched Jaxxon from her thoughts. She groaned. "Are you still here?"

"I won't ask you again."

"I'm curious, Sean, do you even know how old your little girl is? What date her birthday is? What her favourite food was to eat – when you bothered feeding her, of course." If the man had truly known anything about Celia and their daughter then he would have known about Celia's sister, who lived a few towns away. And if he had then suspected that that was where they were, he would have been right.

Sean leaned across the bar, his face becoming an ugly shade of purple, his bloodshot eyes bulging. "You've always looked down your nose at me."

"Now really, Sean, you make it impossible not to. You're an abusive, twisted, weak little twat, who enjoys trying to assault young girls in his free time."

His smirk was crooked and callous. "You'd know all about that, wouldn't you?" So close, he'd come so close to having that delicious body once. Even though it had been eight years ago, Sean could still remember how arousing she'd looked in her school uniform that day. And just how much more arousing she'd looked when he and his friends were tearing it off her. *So close.* "I'd told Nick you wouldn't just lie there, shaking with fear, and not fight back. McKenzie had taught you better than that – before he went off and became famous as a Formula One driver, that is. If Nick had listened to me and tied you up like I told him to, I reckon that afternoon in the alley would've turned out very differently."

"Such a shame." She didn't let it show that the memories were grating on her control, or that the mention of Connor, however fleeting, had brassed her off.

"You think that what we had in mind for you that day was bad? You think that what I did to Celia and the kid was bad? It will be *nothing* compared to what I do to you if you don't cough up what I want to know. Oh yeah, I'd have a lot of fun with you. Even more fun than what I had with that little daughter of mine."

Sick, perverted, evil bastard! Anger made her quick; without thought, she grabbed a fistful of his greasy dark hair and slammed his face down hard on the bar. Once. Twice. Three times. "You ever even *attempt* to touch me with these paedophilic hands of yours and not only will I castrate you but I'll ram your balls up your arse when I'm done." She released his hair with a shove.

Although Sean, steaming with infuriation, quietly made his way to the door with that stealthy walk he had, she wasn't mistakenly under the impression that that was the end of the matter. She was right.

"Don't be surprised if Don decides he wants his rent money early," he yelled as he reached the door.

Ah, yes. She had the company of her Wookie lookalike landlord and his grubby paws to look forward to later, when he came asking where his rent money was. It wouldn't take much convincing from Sean to make Don be awkward. It was even possible that Wookie Don would repeat his cheeky offer that Jaxxon could pay her rent with her body. She'd just have to knee the perverted old fart in the balls like she did last time.

Sean began, "And another thing—"

"Oh, for the love of God, why don't you just piss off out of here!" A moment after a scowling Sean had left, she heard Joe groan loudly.

"What?"

"There's an old man over there who's been watching the whole thing, and rubbing his crotch like crazy at the same time."

Oh bloody wonderful. Another sick perv.

Richie eyed the masturbating old age pensioner with the same disgust as the young barmaid and the landlord. Not that Richie blamed him for being affected so strongly by the barmaid he had heard being called 'Jaxxon'. God, no. This girl was a walking wet dream. He was willing to bet that she could make even a gay dick rise to attention. She was unique. Fresh. And exactly what he had been scouting for. The tabloids would love her. He could have her on billboards all across the country.

Christ, it was difficult not to be mesmerised by her. She didn't even seem to realise how she naturally commanded the attention of those around her. He doubted she was aware of just how sensual her every move was, either. The fluid, graceful way in which she conducted herself was almost feline. The inner strength she had was so apparent that it was like she wore it. Yet, there was no conceitedness about her; she wasn't gazing around to see who might be looking at her, and she wasn't dressed to impress. She just *was*. And that was enough for any man to want her.

There was also her beauty. No, 'beauty' wasn't the right word. 'Beauty' seemed to imply a certain degree of innocence. This young woman's appearance was not in the least bit angelic. That face, that body, that sultry voice…It was a package meant to tempt a man to sin.

When looking at those long, wild, chocolate-brown ringlets, a man would only think of fisting his hands in them while covering her mouth with his own. When gazing at those large, wild, brown eyes framed by a thick set of eyelashes, a man would want nothing more than to see them glazed over and dreamy after an orgasm. And those lips…Christ, it was as if they had been purposely designed to service a man's dick. The smooth olive skin would beckon even a priest. What's more, she wasn't wafer thin like most of the girls he worked with. No. This girl had curves in all the right places. Very nice set of breasts.

When her emotions were running high, it was impossible to look away from her. Anger was a good look for her, making her unique eyes feral and become somehow hypnotic. There were no real words to explain it. Whatever it was, it made his dick twitch. Just like everything

else about her.
Sinful. That was what she was.
Just what he needed.

Jaxxon had long ago noticed the long-legged, sandy-haired bloke who was sat in the far corner, alone. She had also noticed that his eyes seemed to follow her every movement. She was used to being stared at in this place, though she could never, for the life of her, fathom what it was that people thought was worth staring at. She blamed the big breasts, and the fact that she was usually the youngest female in here.

However, this bloke looked at her differently. Like he was studying her. Like she was some kind of weird artefact that needed to be carefully appraised. She didn't like that. Although he was dressed as casually as all the other punters, there was something about him that suggested he somehow didn't belong.

When his eyes met hers, Jaxxon raised a brow questioningly. Her philosophy had always been *if you have something to say, say it*. In response, he mimicked her movement. His expression seemed to be daring her to approach him and act on her agitation. She merely snorted. He was very much mistaken if he thought that a little staring would unnerve her – when you worked in a dodgy place like this, you had to learn to get used to it pretty quickly. Maybe he would have had a chance at unnerving her if he was dressed in leather like the submissives…Why were they even still here?

Throughout her entire shift, his gaze remained settled on her. Though it hadn't made her nervous, it had made her downright irritated. Still, she had ignored the out-of-place ogler. No, not ogler. His gaze was studious. When he was the last punter to leave, Jaxxon had expected him to approach her. But he didn't. He went to Joe. For a moment, Jaxxon wondered if she had gotten it wrong; if it had been Joe that he was concentrated on all along. Quickly, she discarded that notion. No, she had *felt* his gaze.

"Jaxxon," called Joe. He didn't speak again until she reached his side. "This punter here would like to speak to you."

"Yeah, so?" It wasn't exactly unusual for one of the oddballs drinking here to want to have a 'chat' with her – something they considered preliminary to the sex they also had planned. It came with the barmaid territory. It was a wonder she hadn't succumbed to the urge to murder any of them.

"*So* he's paying me one hundred to *accommodate* a ten minute talk with you, and I'm really fond of money so—"

"One hundred…to talk?"

"*Just* a verbal exchange, nothing more," assured the stranger in a shockingly well-spoken voice. But his words weren't comforting at all. What kind of person paid that kind of money for someone to talk to them? Why hadn't the oddball just approached her himself?

Before Jaxxon could speak again, Joe added, "And seeing as your shift hasn't technically finished yet, you can consider this a task from your employer."

She scowled at Joe, but he simply smiled, and left them to have their private 'verbal exchange'. The posh stranger instantly spoke. His voice was reassuring.

"I realise that this might be quite an unorthodox way to arrange a conversation with someone—"

"Oh really, you think so?"

He smiled. "I had the distinct feeling, after watching you closely tonight, that any attempt I made to engage in conversation with you wouldn't get me very far."

She nodded, conceding that.

"Plus, I wanted us to be able to speak privately, and I understood that it would need to be a place where you felt safe. I somehow couldn't envision you inviting me to your home, especially at midnight."

"You going to tell me who you are and what you want?" He handed her a business card which she read aloud. "Richie Moore. Moore's Modelling Agency. Partner." Jaxxon scrutinised him through narrowed, keen eyes. Maybe she could believe that an oddball recruiter might decide to approach her, thinking that they might get a shag in exchange for offering her a non-existent modelling job. But a *partner* of a modelling agency?

"You are wondering why the top of the food chain would bother personally with the hunt," he guessed. "Please allow me to explain." He perched himself on the stool beside him. "A close friend of mine runs a very successful cosmetic company, and he and I have come together on a project. A joint venture, you might say. A new range of cosmetics was designed between the two of us. A line that is dramatic and echoes a bold, yet carefree mind-set. A collection that will cater for both the everyday look, and the socialising evening. Now we are searching for the face that will set it off. When you open magazines, you have your sweet, open, angelic faces that look ridiculously happy, and you have those who have mastered the sexy, seductive, erotic look. In both mine and my partner's opinion, neither are particularly representative of true life. After all, if all people were truly so happy or so sexy, there would be no need for cosmetics or other such things."

She guessed that much was true, but she didn't comment.

"Neither look echoes the bold product line. What he and I have been looking for is someone *real*. Someone truly representative of life as it really is. And, unfortunately, life has its fair share of pain, suffering, and tests." It had therefore been Richie's idea to look in areas like this where poverty and crime was prominent, where silver-spoon lifestyles were alien. Thank God he had. "I believe that you, Jaxxon, know a depth of pain that some may never experience. I have sat and observed tonight as many others who know pain were drawn to you, as if they look at you and see another wounded soul, and your strength is like a homing beacon to them."

Homing beacon? This all sounded like psychological bollocks to her. Jaxxon gave him a sceptical look, but he ignored it.

"That kind of strength can only come from being accepting of what you have endured, and who you truly are. I like that you refuse to act as society expects you to act. You're not civil if you do not believe the person you are speaking to deserves it, you're not patient if you do not believe the person trying your patience is worthy of it. You're true to yourself, you're real. And that is what we need: someone who is bold and dramatic, just like the range itself."

Richie gave her a moment to digest all that he had said. Anyone else may have become defensive during someone's analysis of them, or argue with the conclusions of that analysis. But no, this young woman was totally accepting of who she was, and cared not what others thought. He deeply admired and respected her for it.

"As you are undoubtedly aware," he continued, "in my line of business, beauty is a large part of a model's success. You have a natural and uniquely strong glamour. Your desirability is not something that need be enhanced; your appearance is just as compelling as your character." He smiled widely. "What will be the key to your success, young Jaxxon, is that pair of eyes you have. They take on a certain intensity when you are…shall we say frustrated? They literally *smoulder*.

It is most entrancing. I've honestly never seen anything like it. I'm sure we can somehow manage to frustrate you a little during the photo-shoot."

The latter sentence distracted Jaxxon from contemplating whether he was a little nuts and had missed his medication. "Photo-shoot?"

"Yes, I'd like you to come and meet my business partner, have some test shots, and then together we can go from there if this is something that we would all be happy with."

Jaxxon might have sent him on his way with a snort and an insult if it wasn't for the fact that her instincts seemed to like him. She trapped his gaze with hers. "You're really who you say you are?"

Richie wondered if she had any idea just how enthralling her gaze could be. Like she was literally yanking the truth from his soul. "Indeed I am."

"This isn't some kind of scam?"

"No, it is not."

"You are honestly considering me as the face of your new cosmetics range?" She didn't hide how idiotic she found that idea.

"Yes, I am."

"You're not a fruitcake?"

Richie laughed. "I understand this may seem a little surreal. I don't suppose opportunities like this just crop up all the time."

He had that right. It was certainly not every day that someone like her was approached by a modelling agency, and then be told that she was super because she was sort of damaged and rude. It would have made sense for her to be experiencing some kind of shock at this moment. However, Jaxxon had long ago concluded that life had so many twists and turns that trying to anticipate anything in life would be downright stupid. 'Expect the unexpected' – wasn't that what they said? She still lived according to the theory that it was best to always roll with the punches. And as punches went, this risk wasn't even a slap. It wasn't as if she had anything to lose.

And yet, for her to reach for this opportunity would make her feel somewhat of a fraud. Sure she knew suffering and pain, but so did a gazillion other people; it made her nothing special. "Listen, if what you're looking for is someone who's experienced real pain then you should go further down the poverty drainpipe. Plenty of people have been through worse than I have."

"True, but the depth of your pain is not the main factor here."

"And I really don't get this 'entrancing', 'compelling' crap that you're saying about me."

Richie's lips curved into a smile. He liked that she wasn't vain. "That is merely a matter of self-confidence. We can work on that."

"The trouble is…you're not really considering what you'd be letting yourself in for. Something tells me I'm not the kind of person you're used to having around you."

"How so?"

She crossed her arms over her chest. "I'm not friendly or polite."

"Most pleasantries, pleases, and thank-yous are insincere, I find."

"I don't smile much."

"Your intensity is what I like."

"I don't pose, and I don't know how to strut – nor would I want to learn."

"Has nobody ever told you that there is an effortless sensuality to your movements?"

God, this bloke was persistent. "I don't work well by myself, or as part of a group."

"Then you'll be dearly frustrated, which will very conveniently bring that incredible spark in your eyes for the photos."

"I wouldn't think twice about hurting someone who tried to touch me if I felt I needed to."

"I shouldn't worry about that – you're scary enough to make people hesitate to touch you anyway."

"I curse like a sailor."

"We can always say you have Tourette's syndrome."

"Even someone with Tourette's syndrome would be wide-eyed by some of the things that come out of my mouth."

He shrugged. "That is simply because you are an expressive person. There is nothing at all wrong with that. It is part of what makes you so intense and puts that look in your eyes."

"So, basically, what you're saying is that you want me as the face for this range of yours because I'm a bitch who doesn't care that she's one?"

He grinned at her opinion of herself. "Even bitches can get a break in life."

CHAPTER TWO

A week later, Jaxxon found herself standing outside Westwood Studios shaking her head, and wondering what the bloody hell she was doing there. *Her* a model? Compelling character? Entrancing eyes? What a load of old shit. Richie had to be some sort of fruitcake if he really believed all that. She was just a person, the same as everybody else. She didn't see anything special when she looked in the mirror. For the life of her, she couldn't figure how being a bitch would land her a job. Particularly a modelling job.

Even if Jaxxon had thought 'big' in terms of her future, modelling would never have held any appeal for her. Nor would fame. Fortune might be nice. Or at least enough for her to move out of that shithole that Don had the nerve to call a flat, and to escape the crap situation that she was currently in. But modelling...She couldn't see how she could pull it off.

So then why was she standing there?

Two simple reasons: Firstly, curiosity. Wouldn't it be nice to just go in there and have a peek into that world? Secondly, she had never been one to miss out on an opportunity, even if the outcome wasn't likely to be in her favour. Jaxxon was pretty certain that when she got in there and dazzled Richie's friend with her lack-of-charm, she would be thrown out without so much as a pat on the head. But the fact was that she needed to get out of that mangy flat, so why not go for it?

Had Leah ever been to a studio like this?

No, she wouldn't think about Leah. Just like Leah didn't think about her; she couldn't possibly think about her, considering that Jaxxon hadn't seen or heard from her since that day Leah left her at the foster home alone. Shrug. Sometimes people who you loved just didn't love you back, even if they were supposed to. Thinking about it or dwelling over it only wasted minutes out of your life. What was the sense in doing that?

With a clear mind and a loud sigh, Jaxxon allowed her curious side free rein, and was soon in a stylish, bright reception area facing an extremely pretty redhead. Jaxxon would have shot her a brief smile if she wasn't staring at her as though she had walked in with dog shit on her shoes. It seemed that the redhead didn't approve of Jaxxon's casual look — a simple black t-shirt and dark blue jeans. It was a proper Ugly Betty scenario.

"Whoa, tone down your cheeriness," said Jaxxon with heavy sarcasm. The redhead forced a smile, though it seemed to kill her.

"Good morning and welcome to—"

"Yeah, thanks, I'm supposed to be meeting Richie Moore at nine." That was ten minutes from now. With a twist of her over-glossed lips, the redhead consulted the fancy computer which Jaxxon knew cost more than triple her own yearly expenditure, including food, rent, and clothing.

"Mr Moore and Mr Miller," muttered the redhead to the computer.

Jaxxon thought she sounded a mixture of impressed and bitter.

Mr Miller had to be the friend Richie talked about. *Hang on a sec...Miller? Miller as in Ollie Miller, the make-up artist on all the commercials for Storm Cosmetics?* Bloody hell. Jaxxon wasn't big on make-up, and only really bothered with mascara, but even she knew who he was. Not that she'd ever been able to afford any Storm stuff, so she couldn't say whether they were any good or not. But *God*, they were international best-selling products. Well, this might turn out to be an interesting morning.

"Jaxxon Carter, I presume?" said the redhead. "If you take a seat, someone will be down shortly to escort you to see Mr Moore and Mr Miller."

Jaxxon nodded and slouched into one of the seats. She noticed that apparently her attire wasn't appreciated by the girls seated around her — particularly the one beside her, who was wearing something that may as well have been a flannel. They all looked at Jaxxon as though she was a failed science experiment or something, though they were quick to look away if Jaxxon even *half*-scowled at them. Inside, she was smiling. If her casual appearance made them feel uncomfortable, they had to lead very sad lives.

It was something like five minutes later when she heard her name being called by a familiar voice. Lifting her head, she saw Richie heading towards her grinning. She could only guess from the whispers and looks of shock on the other girls' faces that it wasn't commonplace for him to come and personally greet whoever he had an appointment with.

There was an incredible amount of awe and devotion on the face of the girl seated beside her but Richie didn't spare her a glance, just as he hadn't the others. Jaxxon murmured to her, "You should have worn your jeans." Then she rose from her seat and made her way to Richie. "Hi."

"Very nice to see you again, Jaxxon." When she simply nodded rather than return the sentiment, his grin widened. "I like that you don't tell people what you think they want to hear. It's very refreshing. Now, let me introduce you to my business partner, Oliver Miller."

After a short elevator ride and a series of lefts and rights that made Jaxxon feel as though she was in a labyrinth, they finally reached a very contemporary office. Ollie looked up from the computer as they entered. Up close, he resembled Bob Hoskins. Used to Richie's gentle, eloquent voice, it was slightly surprising to hear Ollie's rough and deep cockney accent.

"Alright, luv, you must be Jaxxon."

Unlike Richie, who was all suited-up, Ollie was dressed in a pair of jeans and a thin sweater. Oh yes, she and him would get along just fine. "Yep."

"Odd name," he mused, "but I like it. Unique. Memorable. If someone was to refer to 'Jaxxon, the model', there wouldn't be much mistaking who they were talking about."

Richie and Jaxxon both took a seat opposite Ollie as he leaned forward in his chair, fiddling with his pen. A lot of girls had walked through that door, but none had done so without looking a bag of nerves. The one in front of him was as cool as a cucumber; someone who believed they had nothing to lose. For her not to be twitchy and jittery at the thought of what she could gain, she had obviously entered that door believing the answer would be a resounding no. "So," he finally said, "you want to be a model."

"No," she replied honestly. "What I want is a better job and better life than what I've already got so I can get out of where I'm living before I end up bashing my landlord's head against the toilet that he denies needs fixing. Richie just happens to have come along at the right time. I'm not one to look a gift horse in the mouth, even if I'm not all that keen on the horse."

Ollie smiled approvingly at her before looking at Richie. "You're right, she's very different."

"I'll give you the same warning I gave Richie Rich," said Jaxxon. "I'm not easy to have around, you'll never find me full of the joys of spring, and I don't mince my words."

Ollie's smile widened. "Then I think you'll find that you and I have a lot in common. How old are you?"

"Twenty-two."

"Older than I usually like, but not too old. Especially since you look around eighteen anyway, and our range is aimed at young women. Ever done any modelling work before?"

Jaxxon shook her head. "In fact, I don't really like cameras much."

He laughed silently as he made his way around the table to stand in front of her. Just as he raised his hand to touch her face, Jaxxon reflexively raised her own to block his move.

"Jaxxon has a slight aversion to touch, especially when it comes to strangers," Richie quickly explained.

Ollie supposed, judging by the kind of background she had, that she hadn't known much gentleness in her life; that perhaps she had even encountered much roughness. It would make any touch seem too intimate. Dropping his hand, he said, "Could you please slowly move your head from side to side for me. That's it. Like that."

Studying her face very closely, he was pleased to see that it was almost completely symmetrical. Not too long, not too round. Full, sensual lips. Well-proportioned nose. Perfect lashes and brows. No blemishes, moles, or spots. Her skin was practically flawless, and her bone structure made her a photographer's dream. It was a wonder no one had snapped her up before now.

"Lovely. Now, what we'd like is to take you down to one of the studios for a few test shots. As Richie explained to you, he and I have joined together on a project, and we are bringing out a whole new range of cosmetics. We intend to call the range *Allure*. If today goes well, it may be that your face will be what sells those products."

Jaxxon couldn't imagine her face inspiring anyone to buy anything, but she'd let these poor sods figure that out for themselves after the test shots.

"So, let's get you down to make-up, and then after that, you'll be brought to one of the studios where we'll be waiting."

It sounded so much like an order that she could only reply, "Copy that."

After an hour of being handled by make-up artists, hairstylists, and wardrobe assistants, Jaxxon was ushered over to a mirror. She had expected to look extremely different, to not look at all like herself, but that wasn't the effect at all. She was still in jeans and a t-shirt, although both were skin-tight, and the t-shirt showed off her cleavage. Her curls had been smoothed with some kind of serum that didn't take the wildness away but hid the split ends and made it look as though it had been polished. Her face had been treated with a minimum amount of make-up — apart from her eyes, which had been mascaraed to death, and her lips which had been heavily coated with a rich cherry gloss.

The studio she was then escorted to was nothing like she had pictured. It was massive and almost perfectly square. Everything in it was either black or white. The walls, floor, seats, and even the small, simple kitchenette were white. The ceiling, cameras, lighting equipment, laptop, shelves, and the mirror frames were all black. Weird, but not in a bad way.

Standing near the kitchenette was Richie, Ollie, a tall shaggy-haired bloke, and an equally shaggy-haired teenager. All turned and appraised her from head to toe and then toe to head. "What?" she snapped, uncomfortable under their scrutiny.

"Perfect," said Ollie. "It's you, but with everything enhanced." Seeing the surprise on her face, he added, "I don't want to turn you into someone else, Jaxxon. I want your identity just as much as I want your appearance to represent the new range. Now, meet Tony. You've probably worked out that he's a photographer, going by the fact that he's holding a camera. He also has massive shares in Storm Cosmetics. The young lad behind him is his son, Ant. He's also his apprentice."

"Very intense," commented Tony as he once again appraised her.

She was getting a little sick of being called that. "Can we get this over with? I've been pampered and groomed like a bloody poodle, so I'm not in the best of moods."

Richie smiled in amusement. "If you're already frustrated, this should make things go quite quickly and smoothly."

As directed by Tony, the pushy photographer — who she was pretty certain had been instructed to purposely irritate her — Jaxxon stood on a small platform with her back straight, one shoulder slightly down, neck arched, head tilted to one side, lips parted, and staring into the camera. He was talking *at* her, not *to* her, and it was cheesing her off. His barking earned him a lot of expletives from her, which seemed to amuse them all to no end.

"Well, as I live and breathe," drawled Tony as the three blokes and the teenager examined the test shots. "Would you look at those eyes. The *heat* in them. It's like the look of primal lust you see shooting out the eyes of a jungle cat or something."

Richie pointed at him, smiling. "Exactly. I couldn't think of any words to describe it."

"I've truly never seen anything like it."

Ollie was shaking his head in disbelief. "The look shoots through you like a spear, doesn't it?"

Tony nodded. "What's amazing is that it's *all* eyes. Her face is completely expressionless. She's not scowling or snarling or frowning; it's all coming from the eyes."

Jaxxon was getting rather sick of being spoken about like she wasn't there. "Well?" she demanded, hands on hips. "Can I get down from this sodding platform now or what?"

"Congratulations," said Ollie in a smooth voice as he shot her a wide, excited smile. "You are now the face of Allure Cosmetics."

Two Months Later

At forty years of age, and after twenty-four years in the cosmetics industry, Ollie was no stranger to campaign launches…but this was like no other. Oh everything was normal in terms of schedule: there had been no delays, and the reporters were waiting patiently in the elegantly prepared convention room of the five-star-plus hotel for the speakers to introduce the face of Allure. Everything was normal in terms of the preparations – the presentation platform was all set up, the impeccably packaged Allure products were on display in a neat yet arty arrangement, everyone was where they were supposed to be, and everything was ready for the Launch Party that was due to start shortly in the ballroom of the hotel. But what he saw when he walked into the upstairs suite where Jaxxon was being 'groomed', as she called it, knocked him for six.

Usually, he would have to make an entrance with a booming voice to attract the attention of all the people nervously fussing and busy-bodying around while obsessing over every little detail of the model – hair, make-up, clothes, posture. But in this suite was total silence. Not only that, but there weren't make-up products lying here, there, and everywhere. Not one soul in the room was standing. His instinct was to seize up – something had to have gone wrong. But it wasn't a mortified or nervous silence.

His eyes were quickly drawn to the stunning young woman perched on the arm of a bulky chair. She was dressed in the stylishly casual D & G outfit that was designed especially and exclusively for her: a pair of sea-blue, skin-tight jeans that were a kind of velvety denim, and a light-lemon V-neck top that casually drooped at one shoulder. They hadn't wanted her in an extravagant dress as that just didn't suit her character – which was just as well, because she was refusing to 'look like an ornament' anyway.

As casual as her outfit was designed to be, it was still chic and cutting-edge, and it highlighted each of her sinful curves. That, along with the subtle yet eye-catching use of Allure products on her face, had Jaxxon looking as glamorous as all hell.

"You alright?" Jaxxon asked Ollie, who seemed a little odd at the moment.

"Just wondering why there's a deathly silence in here."

"I haven't threatened them with the loss of important body parts, if that's what you're wondering. They're fine, watch." Then she smiled as she sang the nursery rhyme, "If you're happy and you know it, clap your hands."

There was then laughter and clapping. Ollie could only shake his head and chuckle.

"She told us to put everything away," said Louisa as she gazed at Jaxxon fondly.

Ollie found that he hadn't been able to look at Louisa very long without laughing since Jaxxon had pointed out that she had a Morticia Addams vibe about her. Jaxxon hadn't been poking fun or making an insult, it was purely an observation. Louisa even agreed with her. Ollie did love her bluntness.

"Yes, because there was a bloody self-correction epidemic going on," said Jaxxon. "They were all done with the grooming *ages ago*, but kept coming back fixing what didn't need to be fixed, and seeing mistakes that weren't even there. Then Louisa nearly had a panic attack when she discovered that I hadn't been exaggerating when I said that, no matter what brush or gel or spray she used, these curls of mine always did their own thing."

"That's what I like about them. They're wild, like you and those eyes of yours."

Just then, Richie appeared behind Ollie and tensed. "Is something wrong?"

"Jaxxon insisted we pack up our stuff, and just sit and relax," said Kieran, the chief make-up artist. "We've been talking about that new soap on telly about Scousers. Did you watch the first episode last week?"

Richie stared at the young woman in awe for mastering the art of calming the team. She had won people over so effortlessly, even the rather antisocial wardrobe assistant. "Who sent the flowers?"

"Oh, they're from Tony and his wife," she said. On the day that Ollie and Richie had chosen her as the face of Allure, Tony had insisted on giving her a lift home after the photo-shoot. Then he had seen the block of flats she lived in, and turned right back around, refusing to let her go back there. After much disputing, Tony apologised for his daddy approach and, in a much gentler tone, offered for her to *rent* – because she refused to stay there for free – the annexe of his house.

Only when he agreed that she could bring Bronty was the deal sealed. Both he and his wife were trying to discourage her from getting an apartment and to stay in their annexe, but Jaxxon had been looking forward to having something that was *hers*. Plus, as much as she adored Lily and Tony, they tried to baby her through the process of going from one lifestyle to another. The gentle approach wasn't Jaxxon's way. She wanted to face all the sudden changes head-on, and find her own two feet.

"Now remember, Jaxxon," said Ollie in a serious tone, "because your name was leaked to the tabloids, they'll have done some digging and will know a bit about you. There's a good chance they'll shoot some questions at you that you might find uncomfortable."

"You mean about my past. Personal stuff."

He nodded. "If there's anything you don't feel comfortable answering, just signal to me by tucking your curls behind your ear, and I'll tackle the question for you."

Richie shot her a reassuring look. "I'm sure you'll be fine, but I know this is all new to you so if at any time you feel overwhelmed, just signal to me by joining your hands behind your back."

"Jesus, you're making this sound like a covert operation," said Jaxxon. "I take it you're here to take me down now." She would never have admitted it, but she was so nervous, she was close to shaking.

"Indeed we are," confirmed Richie, ushering her out of the room. The entire team wished her good luck and told her how amazing she looked – something he very much agreed with. Something that he was sure the entire world would agree with.

Once they reached the convention room, Ollie – as Chairman of the cosmetics house – and Richie – as vice president of it – took their places on the presentation podium, keeping Jaxxon hidden behind the curtains at the rear of it. The two men each made a speech about the innovative and stylish Allure products themselves, and revealed that the release date was exactly three weeks from this day. Then, after indicating the free samples around the reporters, Ollie introduced 'the face of Allure.'

Ollie watched as Jaxxon – in that natural, catlike grace that she had – came to join them at the front of the podium. She was as breathtaking and mesmerising as always, and received a massive, welcoming applause. She didn't smile and pose for the flashing cameras, just as he knew she wouldn't. But she wasn't distancing herself from these reporters; it wasn't an act of ignorance. She somehow managed to make eye contact with each person in the room, as if she was acknowledging them. Didn't everyone enjoy the idea of being acknowledged by a woman so entrancing and captivating? More amazingly, all this was done on a subconscious level on her part. She clearly had no idea of the kind of effect she had on others around her.

It wasn't long before questions were being shot at her from all angles. The first few were benign and related to the campaign, her contract, what was happening next, and the designer of her outfit. Then, of course, the subject of her past was brought up. At first, it was relatively simple questions, but then a particular question made Ollie tense, even though he had been expecting it.

"Is it true, Jaxxon, that you spent the majority of your childhood in foster care?" one reporter asked.

"Yes," Jaxxon answered simply and clearly. There was no shame or discomfort in her tone, and she noticed that that seemed to have surprised people. Why should she be embarrassed?

"And is it true that your mother committed suicide?" the same reported asked.

"Yes," she said just as clearly and, still, with no shame or embarrassment.

Then a question was fired at Richie from a different reporter: "The rumour, Mr Moore, is that you discovered Jaxxon when she was working in a run-down pub."

Richie smiled. "It's always a surprise when a rumour is true. In this case, yes."

After another series of questions at Richie, a new male reporter asked him: "Did it not concern you that her poor upbringing might make it extremely difficult for her to deal with a lifestyle that is at the other end of the spectrum? That perhaps she might find the pressures hard to bear?"

"You know, I really don't like it when people talk like I'm not there," said Jaxxon with a sigh. "Here's something for you all to jot down on your little pads: a crap upbringing doesn't make someone weak, it makes them strong or how else could they get through it? I've never liked that people seem to think that anyone who's been brought up in care are *destined* to lead a life of poverty and crime. It's postcode lottery."

"I hope this shows those prejudiced people and those who are brought up in care that it doesn't always have to work that way," said Richie.

"That they might find themselves a fairy Godmother" – the reporter gestured at Richie, smiling – "and have a happy ending?"

"Oh no," Jaxxon quickly objected as she heard the reference to Cinderella. "If you're hoping to find that, despite my background, I'm some kind of lovely young lady who birds tweet at, prepare to be disappointed. I'm a moody cow and I know it. This isn't a Cinderella story; this is more like Harry Potter and the Gob of Ire."

Ollie had to admire her straightforwardness, and it seemed like everyone else did as well. They chuckled and smiled, and were totally taken in by her and how refreshing she was. More questions were fired at her, but she handled them all with the same ease and bluntness as she had the others. Oh he could see she was still frustrated. The trouble was that her frustration only seemed to please the reporters, bringing that feral gleam to her eyes. He was truly proud of her. He was also relieved to see that she might be able to handle how being the face of Allure was about to catapult her to the peak of success.

He hadn't mentioned to Jaxxon that he was a little concerned about how some might treat her at the Launch Party. There were some guests he knew of who would enjoy flinging a few degrading insults at her — things meant to eat at her confidence, or belittle her, or test her responses — with jealousy and prejudice, of course, being the main motives.

He couldn't visualise her crumbling, but he had to remind himself that this young woman came from nothing, and was about to enter a world where people competed over who had the biggest yacht or wore pearls and sapphires. He wondered if Jaxxon had any real concept of how famous this was all going to make her. As from tomorrow, her life was going to be dramatically different.

"One last question," a reporter quickly shouted as the presentation ended.

Jaxxon groaned inwardly. This was something like the sixth time someone had launched a 'last question' while they were trying to leave, and she was getting cheesed off now.

"We've noticed that hair care products are included in the beauty range, which isn't usual. Any comments on that?"

"Yeah," answered Jaxxon snappily. "Lather, rinse, repeat."

CHAPTER THREE

Connor McKenzie stood in the living room of his London apartment, can of beer in hand, wondering if all blokes had this much trouble getting a woman to listen up when he said no he did not intend to marry her. He'd left L.A to get some space when it seemed that he couldn't shake her off, and what had she done? Flew all the way to London to have the exact same conversation they'd had a dozen times before.

Oh she could hear him alright when he said no. Plain as day. He'd learned over the past three months that her hearing was selective. Oh that wasn't all. He'd also learned that she had planned to accidentally-on-purpose become pregnant. What exactly had she thought it would achieve? That it would trap him into a committed relationship? Although he didn't want kids, he'd have played some part in their life, but it wouldn't have made him walk down a bloody aisle.

Another thing he'd learned about this woman was that it was her who had been spreading rumours to the tabloids that he had proposed to her and that they were getting married in eight months' time. His best mate, Dane, had showed him one of the cheesy headlines: *Anita Donovan is the* formula *that tamed the womanising Formula One driver, Connor McKenzie.*

His life would be a lot simpler if he knew how to make women understand that if he fucked them, it did not mean that he cared about them. That for him, sex and love were two different things, and it was possible to have one without the other. It was well-known that he'd never had a committed relationship and that he didn't want one. It didn't seem to matter that he was honest with every woman from the start. For some unknown reason, they all got this daft idea that *they* would be the one to change him. Hence, why there was a very disappointed American woman behind him, who was trying to pluck at heartstrings that he didn't have to manipulate him into giving her what she wanted.

"Connor," she intoned. "Don't you think we owe it to ourselves, after everything we've shared, to give it another shot?"

Owe it to themselves? Everything they'd shared? They had only been seeing each other for a few months for nothing more than sex. Where did she come up with this dramatic tripe? It sounded like something right out of a corny romantic film. It probably was, actually – she'd starred in enough of them.

"Connor, talk to me." Anita was close to snapping; she felt helpless for the first time in her life. Since the day she was born, she was granted practically whatever she wanted. Having famous actors for parents, her acting career was given a huge jumpstart, and things had always come easy to her. Connor was the only thing she had ever had to truly work for. He hadn't fawned all over her, or been anything like the respectful guys that she was used to who showered her with affection and gifts – which was why she had wanted him so badly. What she hadn't banked on was that once she had him, she would have to work to keep him. Three months she had lasted…and now she was about to lose him. She was about to know the feeling of failure.

She *had* to make him realise how good they looked together. They were so different it was laughable, but that was what made them fit. She'd had the sheltered, silver spoon lifestyle, whereas Connor had spent his childhood in foster care in London. Yet two years ago, at just the age of twenty-two, he had become the youngest Formula One driver in the world.

Where she was blonde and pale and blue-eyed, he had coal-black hair and the darkest eyes. The tabloids had long ago dubbed her 'angel face', due to her innocent features and small, delicate figure. Nothing angelic about Connor: he wore either a frown or a cocky smirk, and he was anything but delicate with his athletic build and those muscles that were so defined they rippled beneath his clothing as he moved.

The tabloids loved her 'sweet disposition', her apparent vulnerability, and that unworldly smile she was a master at showing the cameras. Connor, on the other hand, had a raw, animal magnetism about him. He oozed power, strength, and danger – making him just as intimidating as he was sensual. It was as though he had been created purposely to seduce. And seduce he did, though he didn't have to invest much effort into it. How many women had she had to fight off during the last few months? God, they even flirted with him in front of her as though she wasn't even there.

It was those contrasts between them that made them perfect for each other: they balanced each other out. Why couldn't he see that? Okay, so they might not love each other, but he didn't want love anyway. Maybe he had a point when he said that he wasn't a fashion accessory for her to hang off her arm, but lots of famous people married to keep the tabloids talking about them. "Okay, Connor, if you need some more time before we get married, we'll wait."

"Anita, Anita, Anita." He swerved to face her. "I need you to listen very carefully, because repeating myself over and over isn't something I enjoy. Are you listening? I. Have. No. Intention. Of. Ever. Getting. Married. *Ever.* Did you hear that? Let the words settle into your brain. Absorb the information. Accept it. Go home."

"Maybe in time you'll change your—"

"Oh for Christ's sake."

She shook her head, panicking now. "Connor, honey, listen. I'm sorry if it seems like I've been pushing you, it's just that I love you—"

"Leave, Anita."

"—but if marriage really isn't what you want, it doesn't mean we have to end things, we can still be together." *And then I can wear you down with time.*

"Anita..." It was a warning.

Desperation flooded her veins. She was not only going to lose him, but her pride. Everyone expected them to get married after the rumours she'd spread – her parents, the media, her fans. She had even been in touch with the personal assistant of fashion designer, Donna Karan, about a dress. *And* she'd chosen her Maid of Honour, who had excitedly accepted the position. God, how embarrassing was it going to be when everyone heard about this!

She didn't even have time to buy; Connor would still go to that stupid charity event in a week's time, and he wouldn't go alone. Once the paparazzi saw him with another woman, the whole world would know about their separation. Why couldn't he see how good they looked beside each other?

Seeing her magazine on the table next to her purse, she quickly snatched it, opened it on a particular page, and then slapped him in the chest with it. "Look."

Humouring her, Connor glanced down to see a photograph of the two of them together outside a restaurant. "And the significance of this is…?"

"We look perfect together! Everybody says so!"

"I don't care what anyone else thinks." With that, he flung the magazine at her feet, and gave her his back as he began to walk away.

Then he froze, his body having caught up with his brain. Slowly he turned and looked down at the magazine on the floor, convinced that he couldn't have seen what he thought he had. He was aware that Anita was still rambling on, but her words didn't register. Tentatively, he picked up the magazine, and flipped it over to look again at the front cover that he'd had a fleeting glimpse of only seconds ago.

And there she was. Looking back at him with an intensity that reached out and plucked at his soul. Those eyes, they had always gotten to him. They had a way of entrancing you, imploring you, making you a willing captive.

Jaxx.

His chest tightened and his lungs burned. Suddenly the magazine felt like an extension of his hand. He honestly didn't know how he was going to put it down. He found himself rubbing those lips of hers with his thumb, remembering the one time he'd kissed her. How her mouth had tasted. How he had wanted to do so much more to her but had stopped himself because of her age. She might not have looked, or behaved, or thought anything like a fourteen year old girl, but that was what she'd been, and he'd been sixteen.

A barrage of random memories hit him. Her burying her face in his chest to hide how hard she was laughing when their drunken foster father slipped on the ice, chasing after the dog that had snatched his last beer. Her trying to convince him not to hotwire *another* car, and then purposely triggering the alarm when he 'wouldn't see reason'. Him teaching her self-defence moves after a gang of boys cornered her in the girls' toilets at school – the same gang of boys he had later beaten the crap out of. Her yelling at him to stop feeling sorry for himself or she'd squish his balls with her foot. Him sitting playing with that head of chocolate-brown ringlets, while listening to her defend Leah for the umpteenth time instead of seeing the lying, attention-seeking bitch for what she was. He remembered exactly how her hair had felt between his fingers.

Christ, how had he subconsciously managed to train his brain not to let him think about her? Now that the dam had been broken, the memories and images of her pelted him. It was almost like his mind was punishing him for trying to box her away into a corner.

He suddenly became aware that Anita was tugging on his arm and barking his name. Screeching something about he'd regret this, and was the face of Allure about to be his next victim? He didn't look at her. He couldn't move his gaze from those brown, feral eyes. Nor did he want to. "Out," he insisted in a calm yet lethal voice that no one had ever ignored. Except for Jaxx. She had snorted at his temper and flipped him off.

Hissing, Anita stomped toward the door. As she reached it, she turned to scream an insult at him, thinking he would at least be watching her leave – hopefully having some regret shining from his eyes. But he was still staring at that picture of Jaxxon Carter – a model who, in just the space of three months, had become widely known and desired. And now she was Anita's intended replacement. *Not gonna happen.*

Once Connor was finally alone, the slamming of the door echoing in his ears, he grabbed another beer, and parked himself on the couch – all the while still holding that magazine while Jaxx's eyes held his. It was only then that it occurred to him to wonder what the bloody hell she was doing in a magazine. No, not in a magazine, *on* the front cover.

If there was one thing he would never in a million years have anticipated, it was Jaxx becoming a model. Oh she had the figure for it; she was even more stunning now than she'd been as a teenager. The early bloomer had obviously never stopped blooming. Christ, if his dick was twitching just from her picture, he had no damn doubt that it would harden to the point of pain if he saw her again in real life.

When, not 'if', a part of him insisted. Yeah, he had to see her again; had to see this person who had seen good in him when he hadn't seen it in himself, who had somehow burrowed her way into his soul without her even realising it.

But what if she thought his contacting her meant that he wanted some kind of relationship? He'd admitted to her before he left that he'd always cared about her, so he wouldn't blame her for thinking that he now wanted to act on that. He'd have to make sure she understood that it wouldn't happen – he still had no intention of doing the whole kids and marriage thing, and his career came before everything.

Who would have thought that his stealing a Ferrari one night would have led him on the path to where he was now? Instead of prison, he had ended up in the Ferrari young driver development programme. It had been the first time that someone had ever offered him a chance to be more than what he was, and he had gripped that opportunity and latched on tight. Not once had his grip ever loosened, and he had all the trophies to prove it.

He reckoned that Jaxx would love to hear about the championships he had taken part in, would want every little detail. Would throw herself into his arms the minute she saw him. He wouldn't mind finding out about her new life. Just a little get-together to catch up. Maybe they could then meet up now and again as mates. Yeah. He liked that idea.

"Oi, Jaxxon, have you seen this?" chuckled Ollie as he placed an open magazine on her lap.

Both Jaxxon and the hairstylist, Louisa, glanced at the article that was actually an interview with a popular London rapper. Included were a few photographs, one of which featured Jaxxon talking not so civilly to him at one of London's most exclusive bars. Underneath the photograph was the quote: *'Five seconds in her company and she told me to sod off or she'd shove my balls up my arse. I think I'm in love.'*

Jaxxon sighed and threw the magazine back at Ollie. "Another oddball," she muttered.

"So what did he do that prompted you to threaten his livelihood?"

"He asked to buy me a drink."

"And that was a problem, was it?"

"He didn't ask *me*, he asked my breasts, and then drooled on them – literally. That was just the last straw for me. He'd been horrible to Anna when she tried talking to him. Trust me when I say, it had been in his very best interests to get out of my sight."

Though Jaxxon had never been one to develop close friendships, she spent a lot of time with one of Richie's models, Anna. The slender copped-haired girl was just eighteen but looked more like fifteen, and she was not even the slightest bit streetwise. She might as well have had a piece of paper attached to her back that said, 'Bully me, it's fine.' This wasn't a good thing for a party animal, so Jaxxon often joined Anna when she went clubbing to keep an eye on her. The girl was just so delicate and trusting that it was actually frightening.

"Very protective of Anna, aren't you?"

She shot Ollie a pointed look. "Don't pretend to be surprised by that. I knew what you and Richie were up to when you introduced me to her. The pair of you knew how much that girl liked going out to the clubs and bars, shaking her bloody shimmy, and you figured that she was a great way to get me out and about and under the watchful eye of the media."

Ollie smiled in surprise. She was just too astute for her own good. "We've told you it's important that the magazines and papers get glimpses of you. They'll just make stuff up anyway if they don't."

"Is all that talk about you and that footballer true?" asked Louisa.

"Footballer?" Jaxx frowned.

"Yeah, Matt Watson."

"What was said?" Jaxxon never read anything about herself, though Ollie and Richie tried to show her articles. It was just too weird seeing herself in magazines or papers. Surreal. She still hadn't overcome getting a jolt of shock each time a picture of herself stared back at her. The biggest shock had been seeing herself on a billboard, especially since she hadn't even noticed until a young bloke called out, 'Oi, luv, is that you?'

A billboard. *Her.* Jaxxon from the dodgy part of London with her dodgy past. It hadn't taken long for the tabloids to drench up said dodgy past, but she wasn't ashamed of it. She thought it was wrong that people would stand and sneer at those who had been brought up in the system, but you didn't see them getting together to come up with a better bloody system. She was just relieved the tabloids hadn't been able to dig up all of it. There were some particular things that were better left buried.

Louisa's words took Jaxxon from her thoughts. "It said in one of the papers that you two met in a bar one Friday night, then left together, went straight to his apartment, and that you didn't resurface until Monday morning."

Jaxxon groaned. "Who comes up with this crap? Matt approached me in a bar and we talked a bit, but I was mostly trying to stop a very plastered Anna from dancing on the table. I think I intimidated him, because when he asked me if I'd be interested in going out with him one night, his words came out sounding like a jumbled, stuttering mess."

Ollie smirked. "*You* intimidating? I can't imagine anyone thinking that."

"Aren't you the funny one."

"It's those eyes of yours, they knock people off balance."

"For God's sake, they're just eyes. Everyone's got a pair."

"We've all got a pair of legs too, but I don't make money from mine the way Anna does hers." Ollie looked at her through narrowed eyes. "Speaking of body parts, how've you been getting on with your fitness regime?"

"I haven't."

"What about the diet?"

"I've already told you, I don't do gyms and I don't do diets." Exercising had a way of boring the life out of her, and dieting just made her so miserable that she ended up craving comfort foods, so it just seemed counterproductive to her.

"You don't want to let yourself go, though, do you?"

"I've got a mind to get offended here. Are you saying I'm getting fat or something?"

"It's just standard for models to keep in shape."

"Then I'm not fit for model-hood. I don't have the self-discipline for it, and, to be honest, I don't want to have it. Chocolate is my only vice, and I have no wish to give it up."

"Ollie has a valid point though," said a castigating voice that was slowly approaching. Richie.

Being ganged up on? Jaxxon scowled. "Who asked you, you poncey rich twat?"

Richie laughed. "I do enjoy your insults. It's a nice contrast from having someone trying to climb halfway up my arse all morning."

"Seriously, girl," began Ollie as he gave her a speculative look, "have you been eating those vices of yours more than usual?"

If it wasn't for the mischievous glint in Ollie's eyes, Jaxxon would have undoubtedly emptied her entire glass of water over his head. "You two are just trying to get me all worked up for the photo-shoot," she realised.

Ollie chuckled. "Did it work?" She grunted. "Good. My work here is done." He hopped off his seat. "Oh wait, we were discussing your social activities, weren't we. What I was going to suggest was that you take that footballer of yours to the charity event Saturday night."

"He's not *my* footballer."

"Yeah, but there's no reason why you can't play up to the rumours."

Louisa sighed dreamily. "That bloke is just yummy."

"True," allowed Jaxxon.

Ollie smiled. "So you'll invite him?"

"Nah."

"Why?"

"Two reasons. One, I've already promised Anna I'd take *her*. Two, what I forgot to mention when I told you about Matt approaching me was that I'd turned him down."

"Turned him down?" Louisa was horrified. "Why?"

"He seemed nice, but I couldn't be with someone who's a nervous wreck around me."

Richie sighed. "Well, that limits your choice of men in general."

Rubbing his stubbly chin, Ollie asked, "What about the rumours about you and Richie's male model, Bruno?"

"Oh Anna told me about that article, it was a load of bleeding shite. There had been *four* of us sitting at that table – me, Anna, Bruno, and that other model who's his mate…Chris, is it? Anyway, whoever took the picture zoomed in on me and Bruno, and made it look like we'd gone out on some intimate dinner as a couple."

If she remembered rightly, the article had also stated that Bruno spent a lot of time at her apartment. As it happened, only three people other than herself had ever been inside: Anna, Tony, and Lily. Having grown up in a place where you had to be cautious of who you invited inside, it was a hard thing to snap out of. She still hadn't given the place any real personality yet – unless you counted Bronty, who had claimed the sofa. She simply wasn't accustomed to having a 'home'; a place she could relax, a place she could settle into, a place that wasn't going to get 'visits' from her neighbours.

In fact, for the first week that she'd had her new car – a yellow, Audi convertible – she had been nervous as hell, convinced that it was going to get stolen. Anna had been delighted at the sight of the car, thinking that Jaxxon was now ready to fall into the glamorous lifestyle, but Jaxxon had no interest in trying to keep up with the Jones'. The only reason she'd bought her Audi was that it was a car she had always said she would buy if she had the money. Anna was also disappointed that she couldn't get Jaxxon to expand her new wardrobe with anything but casual wear. The fact was that Jaxxon loved her jeans and preferred to be comfortable, and she wasn't going to apologise for it.

"So you're set on taking Anna on Saturday?" said Richie.

"Yep. She's actually dragging me shopping after this for something to wear for it. She's so excited. You aren't really going to suggest that I ruin her year by uninviting her, are you?"

"Alright," sighed Ollie. "I'll send a limo to pick you both up from your apartment."

She suddenly felt slightly uneasy and suspicious. He'd given in way too easily, which was completely out of character for Ollie.

"Now, I really must be off. Enjoy the shoot, and be good for your Uncle Tony."

She rolled her eyes. Ollie, Richie, and Tony had all decided to elect themselves to be her honorary uncles – her input wasn't important on the matter. Feeling sorry for her for being family-less, she guessed. "For God's sake. Next you'll be calling me Annie and asking me to sing the sun will come out tomorrow."

And then, swaying gently, both men softly sang the chorus of Tomorrow in unison.

"Ollie, Rich," she said awkwardly when they were done. "Have you two ever watched that film, Brokeback Mountain?" Their scowls were priceless.

A few hours later, Jaxxon was staring at a huge designer store that Anna guided her toward. "I am *so* not going in there." It was like another world. One filled with blazers, and blouses, and pencil skirts. Jaxxon knew she didn't belong in there. Even from outside, it was obvious to her that the clothes were all…what was the right word? Sophisticated? Yes, sophisticated. And prim. And posh. All of which Jaxxon equated with boring. What's more, she could never pull off sophisticated. If she was, by some miracle, going to find a dress that fit the occasion without making her look like something she wasn't, she was not going to find it there.

"Oh come on," urged Anna. "I know you don't like getting dolled up, but it's a massive event. It's going to be chock-a-block with celebs. We need to find something suitable."

"It doesn't mean we have to go there looking like the Prime Minister's wife." A tingling sensation suddenly scuttled down her spine – her inward warning system, developed after years of having to watch her back, alerting her that someone was watching her. *Probably paparazzi*, she told herself. But this felt different. It felt *wrong*. A quick glance around revealed nothing alarming.

Anna nodded. "Alright, let's try somewhere else." Jaxxon had never been able to afford shopping sprees so didn't know the magic of retail therapy, and Anna was determined to introduce her to it. She expected it might take a few trips before Jaxxon was comfortable with the whole thing – she tended to get a little claustrophobic when there were a lot of people around her.

Jaxxon vetoed four more stores but, for some reason, had a good feeling about the fifth. So now for the next part. Go inside. Pick something. Try it on. Pay. Then get the hell out.

One chirpy, overly-attentive assistant quickly became six. Then both Jaxxon and Anna were ushered into a private room where the assistants proceeded to bring in various dresses in various styles by various designers. Jaxxon glared hard at Anna. *'Places like this serve models and celebs all the time,' she says, 'there'll be no fuss,' she says*. Anna was going to get her little shimmy kicked so badly.

The assistants kept using terms like: 'looks perfect with your skin tone', 'brings out your eye colour', 'highlights your curves'. Soon, Jaxxon was feeling overwhelmed. The idea of getting into her beloved car had never sounded better. But going home empty handed wasn't an option. Determined to not have to go to another store to endure this again, Jaxxon was resolved that she would choose something from this collection if it killed her.

She tried on a few dresses. The first made her look like a porcelain doll. The second made her look stuck up her own arse. The third made her look like a posh prostitute. But the fourth…It was an ice-blue, silk, halter-neck that was elegant yet stylish, and apparently 'clung to her like a second skin.' According to the happy assistants, the skin-clinging part was vital. Whatever. It fit, it was a nice colour, and she didn't look slutty but had avoided looking all prissy. That was good enough for her. The price was more than she had anticipated, but she would overlook that – she needed to get out of this sodding shop and *breathe*.

The good Lord had obviously been looking down on her, because Anna also selected something from this store, though Jaxxon suspected this was mostly because Anna had gotten caught up in the whirlwind of attention. The dress she finally settled on was a short, black number that complimented her long legs.

It was later, as they were tackling the pizza they'd had delivered to Jaxxon's apartment – she had managed to convince Anna that indulging occasionally was good for the soul – that she relayed to Anna the rumours about her and Matt. Amazing how a five minute conversation with a bloke in a bar had been turned into a wild weekend.

"You know, I'm surprised that anyone would even *print* that, let alone believe it," declared Anna. "I mean, *come on*, you'd eat him alive. The idea of you as a couple is just totally unrealistic. Same with Bruno. The man might be built to pleasure, but he's a walking talking teddy bear; he doesn't suit you. No, what you need is a *man*-man." Her face suddenly took on a faraway quality as she got caught up in her thoughts.

"A *man*-man?"

"Yeah, you know, someone who won't quiver before you."

"But who I can still boss around," Jaxxon quickly insisted.

"Someone who won't back down once you get started on one of your disputes."

"But who will accept that, ultimately, I will win all arguments."

"And we'll throw in a healthy sex drive for good measure. Someone intense. I just can't see you being satisfied with slow and gentle."

The sound of her mobile phone ringing broke them out of their 'Jaxxon's *man*-man' design. Tired and bloated, Jaxxon huffed with the effort of rising from the table and going to grab her phone from her handbag. The screen said 'Withheld Number'. "Hello." Nothing on the other end. "Hello." Still nothing. Jaxxon scowled at the phone as she ended the call.

"Something up with the signal?" asked Anna from the dining table.

"I've got five bars." The phone in her hand started to ring again. "Hello." Again there was nothing. "Must be the signal of whoever's on the other end." She ended the call, slung the phone back in her bag, and then returned to the table. No sooner had she sat down than the landline phone began ringing.

Jaxxon groaned as she got up to answer it. "Hello." Nothing. "*Hello.*" Still complete and utter silence. "Say something or sod off." Again nothing, so she replaced the receiver and sat back down. Wouldn't you know it, the phone began ringing again. "Oh the machine can get it. I can't be arsed getting up again, I'm too stuffed." Her whole world seemed to pause as she heard that voice…

"Jaxx…God, it's been ages hasn't it…I'm really glad you're doing well for yourself. Give me a ring and let me know when's a good time for you to meet up."

As Connor rattled off his mobile phone number, Jaxxon closed her eyes and allowed the deep, seductive timbre of his voice to wash over her. The sound should be illegal, it was like a caress. It conjured up images in her mind of his gorgeous face, his cocky grin…and the back of his body as he walked out of her life and never came back.

God, she despised him. God, she missed him. Just like that, her mind was a mess. That arsehole always had a way of knocking her off kilter.

Jaxxon had heard plenty about him over the years. It was hard not to. Most of the people where she grew up had all raved about Connor. She always got that, 'Hey, weren't you once Connor McKenzie's girlfriend? Did he dump you before or after all the F1 stuff?' That always earned them the snarl from hell.

She knew about his fiancée and their upcoming wedding too…which just made him getting in touch all of a sudden even worse. There was no way she could look at him without wanting to poke his eyes out and feed them to his fiancée. Or maybe the other way around. Maybe both. Why not?

A growl almost spilt from her throat. The *nerve* of him to phone her after eight years of nothing! What, was she considered good enough to be associated with now that she was featured in magazines like him? How could he even think she would want to see him? And he *did* think that she would. She could tell by the way he had spoken.

"Oooooh, who was that?" intoned Anna.

"Connor," replied Jaxxon without thought.

"Connor…?"

"Connor McKenzie."

Anna frowned. "Connor McKenzie, Connor McKen—" Her eyes widened. "Connor McKenzie as in Connor McKenzie the F1 driver?"

"That's the one."

"Oh my God, that man is just divine. Well, he looks like it on the photos anyway. Don't hold back, how did you meet him? And when?"

Another sigh. "When we were both in foster care." Anna's mouth dropped open. Jaxxon supposed that she hadn't kept her expression as carefully blank as she had thought, because Anna's own expression quickly became cautious and concerned.

"He didn't hurt you, did he?"

"He was my teenage obsession. Gave me my first kiss."

"Then what happened?"

"Then nothing. He turned sixteen, left, and I didn't see him again."

"So then why do you look ready to kill?"

Jaxxon swallowed back the hurt. "Probably because the night before he left, he kissed me and made out like he cared about me…when it turned out that the whole time he'd been shagging my older sister and the kiss had been a sympathy-kiss. To a teenager with the most humungous crush, that was a really big thing. And then…"

"And then…?"

No, Jaxxon wouldn't talk about all that happened after that. She never had, not with anyone, and she had no wish to. Ever.

"Are you going to ring him back?"

"No." She didn't even have to think about it. "Sometimes it's best to leave the past where it belongs. Behind you."

CHAPTER FOUR

All of three seconds had passed since Connor brought the Ferrari test driving car to a halt on the empty test-track circuit, and the very thing that he had been trying to gain a reprieve from – for even just a short time – came rushing back to the forefront of his mind. Jaxx.

Nothing had succeeded in making him numb from the frustration and confusion that came with the fact that she hadn't phoned him. Granted it had only been four days since he had left a message on her machine, but he knew she was in London, so she would have heard it by now. Jaxx didn't play games, or make people sweat, or put them on hold. That meant that she had, either, changed dramatically over the years into a creature that more resembled her sister, or she simply did not wish to see him.

That's fine, the proud side of him thought.

But it wasn't fine. How could it be fine when one of the very few people in the world you had ever cared for suddenly didn't want to know you? And it wasn't just anyone, it was Jaxx – the only person he had ever valued, ever trusted, ever let his guard down for after what happened with his biological family.

And then you left and never went back to her, a voice inside him whispered.

Was that what this was about? Fuck, she could never imagine how difficult it had been to leave her that day. He had felt like he was abandoning her. And when he had looked at her puffy eyelids, her forced smile and her wobbling chin, it had immediately made him think of when his mother had dumped him and walked away. Suddenly, he had felt no better than that cold-hearted bitch.

Promising Jaxx that he would go back to see her had been wrong and stupid; it had been the only time in his life when he had ever told someone what they wanted to hear. For his own reasons, he had stayed away, reminding himself that she had Roland and Leah. She wouldn't be alone, wouldn't have to know what 'alone' felt like.

He left the cockpit and removed his helmet. Circling his head on his shoulders, he groaned. His Saturdays were usually spent on his aerobic conditioning. His physical fitness was imperative; only during a marathon did a person's heart rate go high for such a long time. Normally on Saturdays he would either go swimming, or running, or cycling. But today he had needed greater speeds.

Speed was his tonic. Always had been. When he was driving at 200mph and hitting forces of more than 5G, he actually felt at peace. Because they were the moments when he actually felt in control of his life. Even cramped, boiling hot, having his movements constricted by straps around the crotch and chest, while his heartbeat reached approximately 170 per hour and his blood pressure could increase up to fifty percent, Connor never experienced a more undiluted sense of freedom.

Also, with his concentration solely on steering the race car, all his senses at their peak alertness, that was a time when Connor could totally and utterly shove all other thoughts away. Even Jaxx. But only for a short while, it turned out. His mind was now again hooked on trying to work out her sudden indifference to him. And he was pissed off to no end.

Maybe he should just let it go and continue to stay away. It was obviously what she wanted. Maybe he should just be content with knowing that she was doing well, that she was happy. What else was there to know anyway?

Fuck. He knew he wouldn't be able to do that, just as he knew deep down that it was reasons other than curiosity that made him want to see her. If he didn't have to go to the charity event later tonight, he might have found himself hunting her down to demand to know what her problem was. He would give her until the morning; if she still hadn't responded to his message by then, she would find that the next one wasn't so friendly.

It was as Jaxxon hopped into the white limo that she realised why Ollie had caved so easily about her taking Anna as her guest to the event. Sitting there, looking equally surprised, were Bruno and Chris. Both were also looking very smart and appealing, and yet her body was not at all interested. She was concerned that she might be turning into a eunuch.

"Oh my God," gasped Anna, surprised but delighted. "You never said we were going out as a foursome." She gave the Latino looking Chris her best flirtatious smile.

"I take it this is Ollie's doing," said Bruno, grinning and running his hand through the sandy hair that tickled his cheekbones.

Jaxxon sighed. "Apparently he didn't like that we hadn't all paired up, so decided to take matters into his own hands. Crafty sod."

"Do we tell the driver to stop?" asked Chris, wondering whether Jaxxon would be annoyed enough to chuck him out if he didn't offer in advance.

She thought about it for a moment. "I say we just forget about pleasing everyone else and sweating about what the tabloids might print, and just go there as the mates that we are."

"I'd go for that," said Bruno. As much as he would have liked there to have been more between him and Jaxxon – who wouldn't? – he had heard her tell Anna often enough that she wasn't interested in getting involved with anyone just yet. He understood. She needed time to get her head around all the changes that were suddenly happening in her life.

"Same here," said Chris. He noticed the hurt on Anna's face. "You should probably know that I'm gay."

Her eyes almost popped out of their sockets. "Wow, really?"

Bruno saw that Jaxxon and Anna were now giving him an odd look which he easily interpreted. He quickly lifted his hands up, palms out. "No, Chris and I are not a couple. Just mates. And when I say mates, I mean friends. As it happens, I'm hoping to corner my ex tonight. She's been texting me and phoning me the past couple of weeks, talking about us getting back together. She doesn't know I'm coming tonight."

"I'm hoping to find myself a nice, rich actor," sighed Anna dreamily.

"That won't happen unless you learn not to faint when they get near you," Jaxxon told her. Anna always became very intimidated in the presence of celebrities.

Anna bounced in her seat. "I know, I know, but I just get all tongue-tied, and it's like the blood just leaves my head."

"In Bruno's case, the blood all rushes to a particular body part, giving him the hard-on from hell," chuckled Chris.

"I don't know what you're laughing at," snickered Bruno. "You're as bent as a boomerang and yet you only ever seem to attract women."

Chris frowned. "What's with the stubbly face?"

Bruno scratched his chin self-consciously. "Just thought I'd try out the rough look."

"You're not pulling it off. Your face…it's too *pretty*."

"*Pretty*?"

"Boys, boys," soothed Jaxxon. "We're here." The venue – a five-star hotel – was huge and impressive. Again, Jaxxon got that sense of not belonging. Never would she have imagined setting foot in a place like this. Just like she never would have imagined being asked for autographs or photographs – mostly, though, being renowned for telling people to sod off meant that she didn't get too much of that. It was something that she suspected would always feel weird to her, just like the special treatment she received and the invites to parties of celebs who she'd never even met.

More shocking was that she'd actually been asked to feature on a reality T.V. show, to go to various castings, and been asked several times for interviews. Ollie and Richie didn't mind so much that she refused, as they thought it went in her favour that she was mostly a mystery. Besides, she was busy enough already – another thing Ollie and Richie liked.

What did Jaxxon like most about her new life? Not the attention, or the fancy car, or the designer clothes, or the constant mingling with celebs. It was the financial security; the fact that she didn't have to fret every day about whether she'd make her rent money, or afford enough food to last the week. What's more, not only did she feel as though she was finally in control of the direction her life was taking, but her life was actually taking a direction instead of her just plodding along. She was still adjusting to that, but it was an adjustment she was gladly making.

Still, though, a conflicting cocktail of emotions assailed her as she hopped out of the car and into the lights of dozens of flashing cameras – awe at the grandness before her, awkwardness at entering this other world, and also dread at having to be around people who were, for the most part, condescending to her. It wasn't the fact that they were celebs that had Jaxxon rumpled, it was the judgmental looks and the smiles that were so sickly sweet they were simultaneously acidic. Where Jaxxon had grown up, if you had something to say you said it. In this world, it was indirect insults and whispers behind your back. Groan! Not that everyone was like that, but the ones who were just grated on her nerves. Jaxxon swore that she would never allow herself to become so used to luxury and money that she was snobby and narrow-minded.

Basking in the attention, Anna took her time heading through the break in the gang of reporters, posing and smiling and blowing kisses. Chris waved like he was royalty. Bruno just nodded and smiled with his hands tucked in his pockets. Jaxxon might have given a fleeting wave if the lights weren't getting on her bloody nerves. It occurred to her that the frustration would leak into her eyes and give the reporters what they wanted, so at least Ollie and Richie would be happy with any photographs printed.

The questions being yelled were just as frustrating: Were she and Bruno an item? Would she care to comment on the rumours about her and Matt? Who designed her dress and where was it flown in from?

Jaxxon groaned aloud. "What's the point in answering any of your questions when you'll only print whatever you want anyway?" She had meant it as an insult, but it seemed they all thought it was rather funny.

As soon as they stepped inside and Jaxxon realised how huge the place was and how many celebrities were about, she reached for a very nervous Anna. "You'll be fine."

"My God, Jaxxon, there's Stuart Nolan!"

And so it begins, thought Jaxxon.

After they had each been greeted by the celebrity host, Bruno went off searching for his ex, and Chris went off to find himself some meat for the evening – as he so oddly put it. Jaxxon and Anna tried the 'mingling' thing, but soon names and faces became blurry, and Jaxxon felt dizzy with it all.

The attention was unreal; it was as though every move she made was watched, every word she said examined, every expression she wore scrutinised. And then there were the randy bastards who kept giving her tits-to-toes inspections and then gazing into her eyes. *Just goes to show oddballs are everywhere.* Mostly, Jaxxon just glided through the crowds murmuring soothing words to Anna who was, by that point, almost bouncing off the walls with excitement. "Christ, Anna, breathe. You're going to hyperventilate."

"I'm sorry, but it's just so…wow. Aren't you even a little bit excited? I mean, come on, Jaxxon, you've had enough celebs flirting with you like crazy and you haven't even blushed."

"Anna, they're just people. Same as you and me. Just because I get to occasionally see them on the big platinum box in my apartment doesn't mean they deserve to be worshipped like gods. Granted, most of them have worked hard to get where they are, but so do plenty of other people. Just because *their* job doesn't get them on the big box doesn't mean they're worth any less than anyone here, does it?"

Anna inhaled a long breath, steadying herself. "You're right. I know you're right. I shouldn't let them scare me."

"No, you shouldn't."

"They're just people, same as us."

"Exactly."

"Oh my God! Isla Merrick and Jonathan Griffith are on their way over!"

Jaxxon groaned. Starry-eyed Anna was back.

"The face of Allure," drawled the curvy auburn-haired actress.

Jaxxon resisted the urge to scowl. Isla's greeting had been pleasant, but there was a clear undercurrent of that good ole condescension. The tall, immaculately groomed film producer wore a flirtatious grin that topped anything she had ever seen before now. Instead of it making her blood rush, it made her skin crawl.

"Jaxxon, isn't it?" he asked.

She nodded then gestured to the giddy girl beside her. "This is Anna Lawson."

Isla and Jonathan both smiled at her, deepening Anna's blush until her face glowed like a neon sign.

"My God," said Anna, "I'm a massive fan. Of both of you."

Isla peered around and then zoomed in on Jaxxon. "Looks like you lost that model boyfriend of yours."

"Can't lose what you don't have."

"Oh, you two aren't a couple then?" asked Jonathan.

"Mates."

Isla looked at her with sympathy – false sympathy. "Don't take it too much to heart that he's not looking for more than friendship with you."

Jaxxon had to again resist scowling. Isla *knew* that was not what she had meant.

"Move on to different pastures," continued Isla. "They might not be greener, but there's no dignity in chasing after someone who isn't interested, is there?"

Anna gasped. "It's not Bruno, it's Jaxxon. She's always getting the come-on from blokes, but she's too picky."

It was said with such affection that, even in this situation, Jaxxon found herself smiling.

"Still," began Isla, "beggars can't be—"

"It won't work, you know," said Jaxxon in a bored, flat tone. "Trying to make me feel small…It won't work. I feel sorry for you if you have to put other people down to make yourself feel big." Isla guffawed, but Jaxxon could tell that her directness had put Isla out of her comfort zone.

"Sweetheart, if you're such a sensitive person then fame *really* isn't for you."

"Sensitive?" Jaxxon smiled. "No. You see the thing is, *sweetheart*, unless insults come from someone who I care about, I really couldn't give a shit about their opinion. It's the fact that you're trying so hard to get at me that I don't like. If you can't handle frankness, then having a conversation with me *really* isn't for you."

Merely a second after her last word was said, a tingly feeling spread down Jaxxon's spine and the hairs on the back of her neck stood on end. Someone was staring, and staring *hard*. There was nothing about it that felt threatening, it was just intense. She resisted the urge to look – if she'd managed to land herself an extremely intense admirer, she didn't want to give him any encouragement.

Just as Jaxxon was about to drag Anna away, her attention was snagged by the loud snickering of a dark-skinned, busty woman who was shrugging her way through the crowd. Jaxxon recognised her to be a chat-show host.

"Well if it isn't Crystal Marsden." Isla's smile was deceivingly friendly.

Crystal halted in her stride and glared at the actress. "Don't bother, I don't have time for backstabbing over-actors, or" – she looked at Jonathan – "failing producers, or" – she switched her attention to Anna – "little—"

"Hey," snapped Jaxxon. "Not a word about her."

Crystal inhaled sharply, a look of surprise on her face. "I'm supposed to bow down to the face of Allure, am I?"

"I don't care whether you bow, clap, or flip me off. But you leave

Anna be."

Scrutinising Jaxxon with her eyes, Crystal placed her hands on her hips. "You know what they say – you can pamper a poodle, but it will still be a dog."

Jaxxon was pretty sure she had never heard anyone say that before. As backward insults went, that one was crap, but whatever. "If that's the best you've got in your locker, your imagination can't be up to much."

"Face of Allure you might be, but remember this: you'll always be a product of the failed social system."

Jaxxon pinned the much-too-talkative snotty cow with a glare that she knew had to be shimmering with all the exasperation she was feeling. She guessed it was the same look that Richie, Ollie, and Tony claimed put people in a thrall, because the snob seemed mesmerised. Good, at least she would definitely be listening. "Here's something for *you* to remember: you might have been born into money, but you came out of a vagina the same as everyone else. Popping out of one that's rich doesn't make you anything but lucky, or susceptible to being stuck up your own arse. Whichever."

With that, Jaxxon pulled Anna further into the crowd. Again, her spine tingled and the skin of her back was almost burning. She wasn't sure how much longer she could resist swerving around to see who the hell was staring.

"Bloody women," grumbled Bruno as he very abruptly appeared at their side. "No offense," he added quickly.

"What's up?" asked Jaxxon.

"My ex."

"She didn't come," guessed Anna, her voice sympathy itself.

"Oh she's here alright. With someone else." Anna gasped. Jaxxon winced. "They're looking really cosy."

"Maybe you should talk to her," said Anna. "It might just be for show – you know, like Ollie wanted you and Jaxxon to play up to the rumours."

"I thought of that, but after talking to her, I learned that it's not so innocent at all."

"Boyfriend?" guessed Anna.

"Fiancé."

Again Anna gasped as Jaxxon winced. Jaxxon knew from experience that finding out someone you cared about actually cared for someone else…it was like being gutted.

"You can't let her see she's got to you like this," insisted Anna. "Her or him."

"I agree," he said.

Anna spoke in a conspiratorial whisper. "You should find yourself a beautiful girl in here, and flirt outrageously with her right under your ex's nose. Show her she's not the centre of your world."

"I was thinking exactly the same thing." He looked at Jaxxon, his expression a plea.

Jaxxon understood immediately. "You want to use me to make her jealous?"

"I just don't think it's fair to use someone who doesn't know that I don't really have any intention of acting on what—"

"I get it, I get it." Jaxxon sighed. "Well, I am pretty bored…"

Instantly Bruno threw an arm around her, but it was an embrace full of gratitude. Jaxxon managed to refrain from wincing at the physical contact. "So, I'm thinking that we basically just keep murmuring in each other's ears, and laugh now and then at absolutely nothing…?"

Anna giggled. "You two look so cute."

The first thing Connor had felt on spotting her was shock. It was not at all an easy thing to shock someone who had seen the unexpected so many times in his life. It had just never occurred to him to even wonder if Jaxx would be at the event. He'd have to get used to the fact that she was now part of the celebrity world. A world that had him gritting his teeth and rolling his eyes a lot of the time.

It was an instinctive reaction to want to go to her, but he'd resisted – taking a moment to drink her in as she talked with that pain-in-the-arse actress and producer. Gorgeous. Entrancing. In that dress and with her hair gathered up, tendrils dangling around her shoulders, she had almost everyone admiring her. Not that she noticed. So she still didn't see how attractive she was. Still didn't realise what she did to people. In Connor's opinion, with her uniquely enchanting appearance and her incredible inner strength, there was no one to equal her.

Mine.

The thought came from nowhere and everywhere. He shrugged it away, wondering what was wrong with him. He wanted her, yeah, but only in a physical sense. In which case, he had to ask himself how he could honestly have thought that he could meet up with her as a mate and expected not to want a little more. He didn't have an answer. Apparently his brain was a bit scrambled tonight.

Just as he had been about to approach her, a bloke had appeared who was now touching and whispering to her. A feeling so black and unfamiliar that he didn't at first recognise it travelled through his veins like wildfire – jealousy. He tried to shake off the odd feeling, but couldn't. At that moment, he didn't know what he wanted to do more – yell at her, or fuck her within an inch of her life. He supposed that his anger over the situation was hypocritical, considering that he hadn't come alone either, but this intense feeling of possessiveness had driven out all rational thought.

Almost as if she had felt Connor's gaze boring into her, Jaxx turned her head. The second her eyes met his, a raging need slammed into him with the force of a freight train. What passed between them as their eyes locked was a frighteningly fierce and primitive need. He felt stripped bare under that powerful, smouldering gaze, but he didn't try to hide anything – not even his feelings of possessiveness or jealousy. He doubted that he could have done anyway, it was all too potent.

He picked up on her surprise…and something he hadn't expected to see: anger. There was something else as well, but she had suppressed it too quickly for him to process it. She was holding back? Oh she had a lot of explaining to do.

Watching as Jaxxon and who she quickly recognised as Connor McKenzie locked gazes, Anna wondered if they were aware that the people in close proximity to them were caught up in the spell as they watched the intense, silent exchange. Wondered if, like her, those people all felt like voyeurs and yet were too mesmerised to look away. Cameras were soon clicking as the sexual tension just kept on increasing.

His eyes still holding hers, Connor slowly made his way toward Jaxx, doing his utmost best to contain his jealousy-induced rage. He could have sworn she looked a little nervous for her ponce of a boyfriend. Good. So she remembered exactly what he liked to do to any male who went near her.

On reaching her, he stood still for a few seconds, just breathing in her amazing scent and enjoying the simple fact of being close to her. Then he leaned in and gently kissed her cheek, not hesitating to invade her personal space; communicating to both her and her ponce that he had every right to. A small part of him pointed out that he actually didn't have such a right, but again the possessiveness drove out the thought.

"Alright Jaxx," he said in a low, intimate voice. He didn't acknowledge the ponce or it would have given him the impression that Connor thought him important enough to notice.

Why did he have to be so gorgeous? Jaxxon inwardly moaned as a profound yearning rushed through her. Everything about the bloke was dark; his eyes, his hair, his masculinity. Still, it all called to her. The good Lord had been having a very creative day when he made Connor McKenzie and, to her annoyance, she was more susceptible to his appeal now than what she was before.

The young teenager in her who had been infatuated with him thrilled at his presence and wanted to fling herself in his arms. But Jaxxon quickly shut the door on that traitorous part of her and withstood the power of the caress in his voice — which was helped along by how annoyed she was that he spoke *so* intimately. It was a clear message to anyone close enough to hear that they were already well-acquainted. More specifically, it was designed to encourage Bruno to back off. "Connor," she greeted simply.

Yes, she was angry, Connor realised. There was no hint of it in her expression or tone, but it was made apparent by her indifferent reaction to him. A reaction he knew to be faked. Connor gave her a look that said she looked good, knowing better than to give her a verbal compliment as they made her feel uncomfortable. "How've you been?"

She shrugged a little. "Alright."

Noticing that the ponce was still lingering too near her for his liking, Connor hovered over her a little, bringing them both into their own private cocoon. "I never thought you would ever be interested in modelling. You don't even like cameras. But I can't say I'm surprised that you're good at it."

"Thanks." She wondered if Connor was aware that she knew what game he was playing. What she didn't understand was why he was playing it. She didn't need a big brother to chase away the boys anymore. Equally confusing was the undisguised lust in his eyes, a lust that had intensified with every step he had made towards her. The sexual tension was so thick, it was almost visible. But it wasn't real on his part, she knew that.

Maybe he was still intent on playing his other game of leading her to believe he wanted her. The stupid sod obviously didn't know that Leah had told her all about the two of them. And to act like this when he had a fiancée for God's sake!

Her one-word answers were starting to rile him, but Connor held himself in check. Clearly if he wanted to snap her out of her attempt at indifference, he would have to skip straight to the point, give her a push. "I left you a message."

"Yep."

"You didn't phone me back."

"Nope."

"Why?" She shrugged again. He allowed a small amount of his frustration to leak into his voice. "Jaxx, why?"

"I'm trying to make a fresh start, forget about my past. You're part of that past."

Connor smirked. "That's bollocks."

"What?"

"I said, that's bollocks." He only leaned forward very slightly, but the level of sexual tension rocketed. "You've never run away from what you've been through. If you don't want to see me, you must have a reason for it."

"Don't think looming over me will intimidate me, McKenzie."

He had to smile at that. She had often called him by his surname when he ticked her off. "Just tell me what I want to know, Carter."

An outburst was on the tip of her tongue: *'You want to know what reason I have for not wanting to see you? Take your pick – there's the fake kiss, there's what happened between you and Leah, there's the fact that you have a fiancée, oh and let's not forget that after you left and never came back, everything went to shit and you weren't there!'* But before she could say a word, a pale, slender arm threaded through Connor's.

"I've been looking for you everywhere," said the tall, slim blonde to Connor, all the while looking at Jaxxon.

So this is the fiancée. Jaxxon waited for him to at least acknowledge the woman on his arm, maybe even introduce her, which would be painful, but she'd grin and bear it. Instead, he continued to stare at Jaxxon with questions in his eyes. She wanted to be away from both of them so she could alone enjoy the fantasy of slaughtering them in their sleep.

However, because of Connor's wild nature, he had to be treated like a wild animal – never show them a sign of weakness, or they'll pounce. If she were to back away now after it was *him* who had entered *her* space, he'd interpret that as her being intimidated, and that would only encourage him. With anyone else, it would be shocking that they would act like this with someone while their fiancée stood there, but Connor wasn't normal.

She suddenly wondered if he liked the idea of waving this woman under her nose. Bruno must have been thinking the same thing, or maybe it was that his ex was nearby, because he placed a gentle hand on her back. It felt supportive. Connor's eyes tracked the movement, and then suddenly he was nearer. "Any closer and you'll be wearing my dress."

He smiled, but it wasn't nice. "Nervous?"

Of course he made her nervous when he was like this. The man was a walking red button – push it and bad things happen. But she would never admit to her anxiety, just as she would never admit that the closer he stood to her, the harder it was to ignore the hunger she had for him. What concerned her the most was that there wasn't just lust and agitation in his eyes now, there was darkness there. He was on his way to losing it. She spoke in a whisper. "Why are you really in my face like this? No way is it just because I didn't phone you."

How could Connor explain to her the muddled, intense emotions that were suddenly circulating through him when he didn't even understand them himself? All he knew was that he *needed* the ponce away from her. Almost as if the silly twat was provoking Connor – or had a death wish – he whispered something into her ear. Connor couldn't contain a growl.

Jaxxon swallowed her gasp. She felt Bruno stiffen. Shit, this could get out of hand very fast. She hadn't seen Connor this territorial since that day she had been cornered at school by a gang of boys. Jaxxon very discretely used the hand at her side to lightly touch his fingers. "You need to go now," she said calmly, trying to infuse that sense of calm into him. "Normally I wouldn't give a shit where we argue, but this is a *charity* event."

Connor took a deep breath and shuddered. Her touch was like a drug. She was right, he needed to move away before he did something he wouldn't necessarily regret but that would piss her off. "I won't be far, Jaxx." Just as discretely as she had been, he ran his fingertips along her sleek, outer thigh before, with extreme effort, tearing his eyes away from her and stalking off.

Anna's mouth was still gaping open after having just watched from a front seat as the two alpha personalities clashed. Neither had shown any sign of submission or exhibited fear of the other. It was a match that might to anyone else have seemed hopeless, but Anna believed that if anyone could handle Jaxxon and her strong character, it was Connor McKenzie. A *man*-man.

Once he was gone, the sexual tension quickly dissipated, but Anna noticed that Jaxxon's agitation levels were so high that her frustration was almost pulsating in the air. There was one way that Anna could think of that would distract her best mate from everything else.

CHAPTER FIVE

With the foul odour of Anna's vomit clinging to her dress and shoes, Jaxxon was surprised that she hadn't been sick herself. Usually the acidic smell would have sent her stomach rolling. Why was it that when people vomited, there always seemed to be carrots in there? She had spent the entire night nursing a drunken Anna who, shortly before reaching dreamland, had asked – well, *slurred* – 'Did it work? Did looking after me take your mind off the race driving man?'

To think that the girl had purposely put herself in such a helpless state in the hope of diverting Jaxxon's thoughts was, in a strange way, touching. But Jaxxon was still resolved that she would kick Anna's bony backside for making herself near catatonic.

As for whether Anna's idea had actually worked...It had. Sort of. Connor wasn't a person you could easily ignore. His eyes had continued to bore into her back all evening, sending shivers, and tingles, and sensations of prickly heat down her spine. But not once had she dared to look at him. If she had, not only would there have been a very good chance she wouldn't have been able to break the eye contact, but it would have given him encouragement.

His odd behaviour had her mind reeling. A mind that was too worn out and confused to reel any longer. Now all Jaxxon wanted to do was shower, have a nibble on something bland – her stomach was not going to accept a decent meal anytime soon – and then catch up on her sleep.

The first thing she did as she entered her apartment was relieve herself of the high heels. She allowed her feet to sink into the lush hallway carpet, groaning with pleasure. Jaxxon saw that the light on the landline phone, which sat on the hallway cabinet, was flashing. No, she wouldn't check her messages. The outside world was going to be blocked out for a while. She didn't want to think or hear about *anything*.

In fact, she'd even switch off her mobile phone.

She saw the figure in her peripheral vision a mere second before she heard the voice.

"Late night with the ponce?" It was said with bitterness.

Jaxxon's heart skipped a beat and her jaw dropped – there was Connor lounging comfortably on her sofa with Bronty sprawled over his lap. The dog lifted his head and looked at her. "Traitor," she mumbled at him before turning her attention back to the intruder. "What the bloody hell are you doing here?" She needn't bother asking how he got inside. Picking locks had always been a talent of his. She noticed that he was wearing the same blue shirt and black pants he had been wearing at the event.

"I told you I wouldn't be far."

"Oh I'm sorry, I didn't realise that was code for 'I'll break into your apartment.'"

"At first I thought it was the wrong one. I had to double-check with the ever-so-responsive-to-flirting secretary of Miller. This place isn't you, Jaxx. There's not a hint of colour anywhere. Everything's white or magnolia. There's not a single thing out of place. You are *no* Mary Poppins."

"If you had a point, I missed it."

Connor leaned forward and clasped his hands together, exploring her with his eyes. That feral gaze of hers stole his breath. He was itching to touch her, hold her, kiss her, drive himself into her. His cock was fully supportive of that idea. "You're afraid to let yourself get comfortable somewhere."

"Something tells me that you didn't break in here to give me your opinion on the interior of the place."

He rose and stalked over to where she stood at the edge of the living area. "Tell me why you ignored my message."

Jaxxon crossed her arms over her chest, mimicking his confrontational stance. "It's not obvious that I just didn't have any interest in meeting up with you?"

"It's more than that. Last night, you treated me like I was a virtual stranger."

"Aren't you? It's been a long time. Things change. People change."

"I haven't."

"I have."

He shook his head. "You've clammed up a bit, I can see that. But you're still you. You're still my Jaxx," he added softly.

Infuriated by that comment, she abruptly swung one of her balled up fists into his solar plexus – a move that he himself had taught her. "Bastard," she said through gritted teeth.

At the impact of her well-delivered punch, his breath escaped him in a whoosh and his hands flew to his chest. "Bloody hell, Jaxx."

"I'm not *your* Jaxx. Never was. Now piss off out of here!" She stormed over to the kitchen area. The tap, kettle, and mug bore the brunt of her anger as she made herself a coffee – she needed to be doing something while infuriation was riding her. *Still my Jaxx?* Cheeky sod. He honestly thought that a few years of looking out for her gave him any rights to her? Now that was some messed up logic.

A moment later, her sideways vision alerted her to the fact that Connor was leaning against the refrigerator, watching her. It wasn't until she took the first sip of her coffee that he spoke.

"I'm sorry I never went back to see you."

He did sound genuinely contrite, but Jaxxon ignored that.

"I had my reasons. None of them was that I didn't care."

She continued sipping her drink as she leaned back against the kitchen counter, refusing to look at him. Because to look at him and that gorgeous face and those sleek muscles was to crave him. But she was kidding herself if she thought she could block out the animal magnetism that seeped from him, or how seductive and alluring his voice was, or how his raw masculinity was beating at her defences. All that, together with the sexual tension and her own anger swirling around her, and she was about ready to boil. *God make him go!*

"You might as well talk to me, Jaxx, because I'm not leaving."

Clearly she should have prayed louder.

He took a few steps, but didn't get too close. "Come on, don't freeze me out."

She snorted. "How can you be frozen out if you weren't in?"

"We were always close."

"Does your fiancée know you're here?"

He arched a brow. "I have a fiancée?"

"Don't muck about, Connor. I don't read the papers, but even I heard about the engagement."

"You, of all people, should have known that was a rumour. I always said I'd never get married. So did you."

"Fine. Your *girlfriend* then."

"I don't have one of those either."

Exasperated, she gritted out her words. "Well then the woman you were with last night. Your bed buddy, I'm assuming."

Connor exhaled a small laugh. "Miranda was nothing more than my guest for the evening. I took her straight home after the event, and then I came here. *You* didn't though, did you," he added curtly. "Lucky for him you didn't bring him back here."

Jaxxon shot him a scowl as she plonked her half-empty mug on the counter. "What I do is *my* business. I don't need a big brother anymore—"

"Big brother?"

"—and if you find the idea of your once-upon-a-time foster sister shagging someone a bit too much for your stomach then maybe you should keep your nose out."

He spoke in a voice heavy with disbelief. "Is that what you think? Jesus, Jaxx, where the hell did you get the idea that I think of you as a sister?" His eyes glittered dangerously as he continued, "Oh and if you don't want me to snap your ponce in half, don't ever again mention you shagging him because I'm close to losing it."

"You dare touch Bruno—"

"*Bruno*? He sounds like a St. Bernard or something."

"—and I'll kick the shit out of you. I don't need you to protect me anymore; I'm twenty-two years old."

"It was never about just protecting you."

"Yes it was, Connor. You missed your sister, and you used me as a replacement." As Jaxxon watched every muscle in his body tighten, she wondered if maybe she had gone too far by bringing up his deceased younger sister. The words had just popped out before she could stop them. But even as he advanced on her looking like a bulldog chewing a wasp, she remained where she was – unflinching, back straight, chin up.

Connor placed a hand either side of her on the counter, imprisoning her. Then he pressed himself hard against her body, snuggling his painful erection between her thighs. She gasped, and he whispered against her neck, "Still think I think of you as a sister?"

Jaxxon, her eyes wide with shock, instinctively tensed and cringed at the contact in spite of how delicious it was. Connor noticed, pressed himself even closer, and then ground against her. She hated herself for the moan that escaped her, but God the feel of him was so good; as good as his sensuality promised.

The daring, unguarded part of her wanted to strip them both of their clothes and feel his skin against hers, feel him filling her — *finally*. God knew she'd envisioned it enough times. He ground himself against her again. "Stop." No more words came to her disordered brain.

His lips trailed kisses up her throat, over her jawline, and up to the corner of her mouth. "Can't," he breathed. And he meant it. He breezed the pad of his thumb over her plump lower lip. He had always loved her mouth — so soft, and plush, and sensual.

He thought it was strange just how much he wanted to kiss her. His breathing was becoming heavy just thinking about it. He had never been big on kissing — it was just a means to an end. Other than with Jaxx, never had he had this overwhelming urge to *take* someone's lips. Once he kissed her, he would know for sure if she wanted him as he suspected she did, if she wanted him as much as he wanted her. He *had* to know.

Certain he was going to kiss her — at which point she'd lose what composure she had left — Jaxxon shoved at his chest. Unfazed and totally determined, Connor grabbed her wrists and pinned them behind her back as his lips ravished hers. She tried to resist, but he was relentless, refusing to be denied what he wanted. He tugged her bottom lip with his teeth and then thrust his tongue inside her mouth, stroking her own. That was it for her — game over, willpower gone. In that moment, his lips and tongue absolutely owned her. Branded her. He kissed her with a terrible insistence and urgency, as though he had been starved for her. All she could do was kiss him back.

Connor had always prided himself on his self-control. He might have slept with a number of women, though he wasn't as bad as the tabloids made out, but that wasn't because he had a weak will. If anything, he was choosy. A woman had to tick most, if not all, of his boxes before she even had his interest. With Jaxx, there were no boxes or ticks because with Jaxx, there was no choice. He *needed* to have her. Self-control…He had none at all where she was concerned. It scared the hell out of him.

Finally releasing her mouth, his lips travelled down to her neck. Connor licked it and then bit down hard. She shuddered. No, she wasn't immune to him the way she wished she was, and she hadn't ceased wanting him. If anything, her attraction to him was even stronger. "See – still my Jaxx."

Well that snapped her out of it. Jaxxon struggled against his now lax grasp and managed to free her hands. She shoved at him again. Still, he didn't budge. "I belong to no one. Stop with this crap and get out." She didn't look at him, afraid he would see how unsettled she was by the urges and sensations attacking her.

"You expect me to believe you want me to go?"

"Why are you doing this? You don't want a relationship, you don't want anything even remotely resembling one, so what is the point in pushing this? You can't be that hard up for sex that you'd harass someone who isn't interested."

He fisted a hand into her ringlets and tugged so she'd look up at him. "I have to have you, Jaxx. I want to fuck you so bad my cock actually fucking hurts. They might not be sweet, flowery, poetic words – the kind you'd laugh at – but that's the truth. I have to know what it's like to be deep inside you." He felt the tremor that ran through her. "You think I can't tell that you want me?" Before she could bark out a denial, he ground himself against her again and watched her bite back a moan. Then his arms were like steel bands around her, and he was kissing her again – his tongue plundering her mouth, demanding a response...

...a response that Jaxxon just couldn't give him. This was someone who had already devastated her once before, whether he knew it or not. She would be a complete idiot to set herself up for more hurt. But he wouldn't be shoved away, wouldn't free her mouth, hell he wouldn't even remotely loosen his hold on her. Desperate to be free, Jaxxon played him at his own game. She slid her hand down his chest, past his navel, and down to his cock. He groaned and pushed into her hand, and that was when she squeezed hard and twisted, eliciting a sharp cry of pain from him.

"Jesus, Jaxx," he coughed out as he staggered backwards and bent over, cupping his dick.

Her voice was deadly calm. "Playtime's over. I advise you to piss off out of here, and don't even think about coming back."

He straightened and met her eyes. For a minute, he was lost in the catlike gaze that speared him. Then he saw the apprehensiveness and uncertainty there. Clearly the whole thing unsettled her just as much as it did him. He wouldn't push it. For now. But he still had questions. "You've yet to explain your sudden change of heart toward me."

But that's the problem, she thought, *there's been no change in the heart department at all.* She forced a snort. "*Sudden* change? It's been eight years, Connor. Not eight days."

"But it's been one hell of a change, wouldn't you say? You went from caring about me to trying to freeze me out – which won't work, by the way. Christ, Jaxx, if I'm supposed to have done something to hurt you, just tell me!"

"You know, I'm pretty sure I've told you at least four times already to *get out!*"

Connor squeezed his eyes shut and massaged his temples, willing himself under control. It wasn't just his temper she was prodding, it was his dick. The angrier she got, the more she bloody aroused him. "Babe, you have absolutely no idea how close I am to the edge. Believe me when I say that if you keep pushing, my cock is just going to take over and I'll fuck the answer right out of you."

She laughed at the absurdity of his statement. "How you've even got a hard-on again after I nearly snapped it, I'll never know."

"I don't think you understand, Jaxx, I'm deadly serious."

"Yeah? Well if I were you, I wouldn't bank on getting very far. I'm a bit of an expert at fighting off overactive cocks." He went very still, and Jaxxon realised what she had just blurted out. *Shit.*

"And why would you be an expert at it?" His words were coated with menace. "For you to be an expert at it, you'd have to have had practice. And for you to have had practice, some people must have tried to force themselves on you." His gut clenched at the thought of it. Rage was practically steaming from him. He noticed that she was keeping her face carefully blank. "Jaxx, the time for holding back answers is over. Who hurt you?"

Jaxxon felt her face contort with anger. "Oh no, you don't get to waltz back into my life and return to the role of protector. You weren't even interested in my existence until I landed on Planet Celebrity. Well, I hope you enjoyed the interlude in our lack of contact because this will be the last we ever see of each other. Now get *out.*"

If Connor hadn't been so livid, he might have argued her point or insisted on staying. But he knew that if he didn't leave now, he would end up pressing her over memories that she obviously didn't want to dredge up. His voice was barely controlled. "I'll be in touch." As he reached the door, he yelled over his shoulder, "Oh and get rid of that ponce. If you want him to live, that is." The slamming of the door gave extra emphasis to his threat.

For a long moment she just stood there, trying to regain her sense of equilibrium and wondering how the hell things had gone from her finally being the dictator of the direction of her life to having that control snatched from under her. The man was like a force of nature, storming in and robbing her of her centre with his kisses and his insistence on having her, even arrogantly expecting her to ditch her boyfriend – however non-existent he was – just to placate him! And for what, one shag? Maybe two? This was irrevocable evidence that blokes really were led around by their dicks.

What was she supposed to do now? She knew he wouldn't let her rejection faze him. No. And he wouldn't proceed cautiously and gently. He would swoop in and *demand* and browbeat, and then ravish her with those kisses until he had totally worn her down. The frightening thing was that it would be so easy for her to melt into him like that, to this person she cared for in spite of herself. Especially when she had the young teenager in her revelling at how she'd just been thoroughly kissed by Connor McKenzie. That freaked her out like nothing else could.

So, basically, she would be fighting herself just as much as she would be fighting him. Yet, giving in to him wasn't an option. She couldn't let herself get involved with someone, no matter how briefly, who had so much power over her. It would be so easy for him to hurt her.

Was there a book on how to get rid of someone who didn't accept the word 'no', didn't care for other people's wishes unless they matched his own, and would laugh at a restraining order?

The ringing of her mobile phone pulled her from her thoughts. It was a 'Withheld Number'. If it was Connor, he could bet his arse she'd be hanging up. "Hello." She was surprised at how fatigued she sounded. No answer. "Hello." Just like the other day, there wasn't a single sound coming from the other end. Not even the sound of breathing.

She growled and ended the call. Bronty gave her a curious look. She was still disappointed in her traitor of a pet who had apparently welcomed that selfish, arrogant caveman with open paws. "Some thanks that is for saving your arse from death's door, Scooby bloody Doo," she grumbled.

Sleep didn't come easy, but she was thankful that she at least had two hours of it. Although things had always tended to feel better after a snooze, that hadn't worked so well this time. But with the aid of coffee, chocolate, T.V., and Bronty's inexcusable egg-smelling farts, her mind eventually became occupied by other things. Until Anna turned up at her door, her face painted with sympathy.

Jaxxon was instantly uneasy. "What?"

Anna chewed her bottom lip as she entered the apartment. "You seen today's paper?"

It was only then that Jaxxon noticed that Anna had one rolled up in her hand. "Give me the brief version."

"Okay. Well. There's a big photo of you and Connor McKenzie staring at each other all lustfully last night. The tabloids are loving this, because Connor's not one for being forward, the girls usually do the chasing. They've made it seem all romantic, saying he's been '*Allure*-d in'. How cheesy is that? Another reporter dubbed it, 'Lust at First Sight.'"

"That doesn't sound that bad. It's just general crap."

Anna's smile was comforting. "Apparently 'sources' say that even though you and Connor left separately, he was seen coming out of your apartment this morning. The tabloids have made a big thing of it. I'd say you're going to be followed around a hell of a lot for a while."

"I'm going to kill the cocky sod." She should have considered he might be seen.

"I doubt it was him who made that up." She settled on the sofa next to Bronty. "If I was you, I'd be expecting a call from him soon, though, because—" Noticing Jaxxon's odd expression, she frowned. "What is it?"

"He was here. When I got back this morning. Sitting where you are now."

Anna gasped. "Noooooo."

"Yes."

"What happened?"

Jaxxon sighed and began pacing. "I don't know what to do, Anna."

"What do you mean?"

"I mean that I don't know how to get him to understand the meaning of the word 'no'. It didn't matter what I said to him, nothing made a blind bit of difference. He still stayed, he still argued the toss about whether I wanted him, he still kissed me—"

"Kissed you? What was it like?"

Jaxxon threw her a look full of exasperation. "Focus, Anna. How do I get shot of him?"

"Are you sure you *want* shot of him?"

"Positive. Anna, he's like a bloody tornado; he whirls into your life, makes a mess, and whirls back out just as fast. I won't be used like that." It would hurt too much.

"But you kissed him back, I'll bet."

"It's a little hard to resist someone you've lusted after for ten years," said Jaxxon defensively, which made Anna smile.

"I can imagine. How long's it been since you last had a shag?"

"Too bloody long."

"Well…" Anna crossed her legs and started drumming her acrylic nails on the arm of the sofa. "I'd say go have a one-night stand to burn off some of that sexual frustration, but I know you don't do those. If Connor was anyone else, I'd suggest acting like you're in a relationship, but he already thinks you're with Bruno and he doesn't seem fazed by it."

"That reminds me, I'm going to have to tell Connor I've 'dumped' Bruno. The thought of doing what he wants cheeses me off, but Bruno seems alright and he deserves to live."

"Let me ask you a question. All the issues aside, do you want to shag Connor? It's just…last night, I thought you were going to jump each other's bones right there in front of everyone. Maybe one shag to burn him out of your system wouldn't be such a bad thing."

"Anna," groaned Jaxxon. "I want to get rid of him, not encourage him."

"I know, I know. What I'm trying to say is that you looked like you were up for it just as much as he did. If that's true and he's not going to let this go, you might end up having a moment of weakness and then you'd hate yourself for it afterwards. Why not, instead, turn the tables? Become the aggressor?"

"The aggressor?"

"Yeah."

"I don't play games."

"It's not a game," insisted Anna. "I mean *you* instigate the sex. That way, it will be on your terms, and you'll be using him as much as he's using you. You'll get him out of your system, and then you'll be the one walking away afterwards."

Jaxxon could actually see the logic in that. She wouldn't have to worry about how her will seemed to crumble when he touched her because the whole thing would have been her doing. She would have back the control that she lost over her life when he unsettled it. He hadn't just walked back into her life, no, he had barged into it. And his kisses hadn't been coaxing. Oh no. He had kissed and touched like he had every right to. That's what got to her the most – he was taking the choice and the control from her.

By later that night, Jaxxon had decided that if Plan A – getting him to go on his way without any more crap – failed to come to fruition, she would turn to Plan B: become the aggressor.

CHAPTER SIX

There would always be times when Connor questioned what exactly had inspired his mate to make him godfather of his son. He'd never thought of himself as role-model material, despite that he was admired and respected for coming from nothing and achieving what he had. Even though Jaxx had always insisted there was good in him, all he'd been able to see was a volatile temper and an overbearing nature. Then there was the fact that nowadays he had a reputation as a womaniser.

Yet, here was Dane's two and a half year old son, Little Dane, hanging off Connor's neck talking about Thomas the Tank Engine and calling him Uncle Connor. He had met Dane when he was sixteen, when they were both in the young driver's development programme. Dane hadn't had a similar upbringing to Connor, but seemed to understand him and never looked down on Connor for not coming from wealth as he had.

When Dane got married, Connor had expected to see much less of him, but Dane and Niki always invited him to visit. It hadn't escaped his notice that his godfather duties were pretty damn heavy. Sometimes he wondered if Dane was trying to domesticate him.

"Don't take this the wrong way, mate, but you look knackered," said Dane as he settled down on his sofa to watch the football match, crossing his long legs.

Connor, who was slouched in one of the armchairs with Little Dane on his lap, shrugged. "Not sleeping much lately."

"You never sleep much. But today you look like shite."

He shrugged again. "Training hard in the day and then not getting much kip in the night will do that to you."

"You're not losing sleep over Anita, are you?"

Connor snorted. That question wasn't even worth an answer.

Dane nodded approvingly, making his tousled dark hair fall over his forehead. "I never could stomach her. I wasn't really all that surprised when Niki said Anita was planning to get pregnant, thinking it would trap you. Why she thought Niki wouldn't tell me something like that and *I* wouldn't then tell *you* is beyond me."

"You're not talking about *her*, are you?" Niki grumbled as she entered the room and sat snuggled into her husband's side. She held out her arms invitingly to Little Dane, but he shook his head madly, wanting to stay with Connor. Niki had taken an immediate dislike to Anita, instantly picking up on her deviousness. She hadn't liked the way the actress clung to Connor either. It was unhealthy. But Niki had still been friendly and pleasant to keep things from being awkward for Connor. Anita, however, had read more into their 'friendship' and treated Niki as her confidant. If she hadn't, the manipulative woman might be pregnant with Connor's baby right now.

"Niki's right, she's not worth even thinking about," said Connor.

"True. Still gets my blood boiling, though." Dane had been through something similar himself. An ex of his had turned up, claiming the baby she was pregnant with was his, hoping to drive Niki away. Niki, however, had seen the crazy cow for what she was and had stuck by Dane. Paternity tests had then proven the baby wasn't his at all. To think he could have lost Niki because of some callous lies…They would never have gotten married, wouldn't have all that they had now, and Little Dane wouldn't even exist. A world without his son – he couldn't even imagine it.

"Connor, do me a favour and pass those magazines to me please. They're on the little table next to your chair." Holding out her hand, Niki waited for him to pass them over. However, he stopped still as something on the cover of one of the magazines caught his eye. He had the oddest expression on his face. "Connor?" Quickly he handed them over. Curious, she examined the cover and then smiled. "Oh I remember reading something in the papers about you and her getting together after a charity event."

"Who?" asked Dane.

"Jaxxon Carter."

Dane enquiringly raised a brow at his mate, who just nodded, verifying it was true. Dane thought it was odd that Connor wasn't saying a word and was wearing a blank expression. The girl was absolutely gorgeous; any male would be smug to have had her. And yet, Connor wasn't even wearing a very-pleased-with-himself smirk.

"She is beautiful," conceded Niki. What she wouldn't give to exchange her thick, wavy red hair for those silky curls. If she could also exchange her pale complexion for Jaxxon Carter's olive skin, she'd be a happy woman. "From everything I've read, she's a right character. She doesn't seem conceited or uppity, seems really down to earth. Is she?" When Connor simply nodded, Niki cast a confused glance at Dane, who looked equally confused.

In Dane's experience, there was only one reason why a male kept totally zipped on what was going on between him and a woman – there was a little more to it than physical stuff. He winked at Niki then signalled for her to leave the room.

"I need to phone my mum about Sunday," announced Niki. "Dane, want to come and talk to Nan on the phone?" The two year old nodded excitedly and bounded out of the room.

Dane picked up the magazine Niki had been looking at and whistled at the photo of Jaxxon Carter. "If I wasn't married, I'd happily shag that."

Connor's head whipped round. It was an effort not to growl. It wasn't unusual for Dane to comment on one of Connor's 'conquests', as Dane liked to call them, but Jaxx was anything but a conquest. "Don't let Niki hear you talking like that."

"I'll bet she was a good shag." Dane could swear Connor was grinding his teeth. "Are those tits real?" Still no response. "Come on, give me *some* details."

Connor was seriously considering punching his mate.

"I've never known you to tap a model. You always said they got on your nerves 'cause they were so vain."

"Well the ones I've met in the past were but, like Niki said, Jaxx isn't." Connor inwardly groaned as he realised he'd only gone and abbreviated her name in front of Dane.

Dane chose not to comment on how Connor had shortened the girl's name, but it wasn't easy to hide his smile. "Mate, I don't blame you for breaking your rule. If I'd had a girl like that throwing herself at me – before Niki, I mean – there's no way I'd have turned her down." He saw something on Connor's face that made his suppressed smile break free. "Oh," he chuckled. "She didn't throw herself at you at all, did she? You had to do the chasing for once in your life." He chuckled again. "Oh I like this girl. I have to meet her."

Connor scowled. "Drop it, Dane."

"Not a chance. I've been waiting for this for far too long. I intend to enjoy it."

"Waiting for what?"

"For you to get sucked in by a woman."

"I haven't been sucked in."

Dane snorted. "Sure you haven't, mate. Why chase her when you've got a line of women waiting then? Why are you so prickly about me complimenting her?"

Connor knew that he had to give him something if he was going to shut him up. He sighed. "I knew her before all this."

"Before?"

"Yeah. Before."

"You mean, like, you were together back when you were teenagers?" asked Dane. Then something occurred to him. "She's not the girl you mentioned that time I found you absolutely hammered when you were seventeen, is she? You said something about it being her fifteenth birthday, and you'd *had* to get yourself well and truly rat-arsed or you'd have gone to see her." Connor's silence told Dane everything. "Let me ask you something then. If Jaxxon Carter is that girl who was important enough to you that you would drink yourself into a stupor over her – something I've never known you to do over *anything* – and she's now back in your life, why are you sitting here with me?"

Oh Connor was deeply regretting that he was there with Dane. All Connor had really wanted was to distract himself from thoughts of Jaxx. He had managed to ruffle her on Sunday, and knew he couldn't afford to allow her too much of a reprieve or a lot of recovery time. He needed to be right there, taking up her breathing space, if he had any chance of wearing her down. However, he had also wanted her to sweat, wondering when he'd next show. Plus, a few days for her to cool off would help his cause. But thinking about her all the time wasn't helping him keep to his plan.

If he was honest, they weren't the only reasons he was staying away. It rattled him that he had such a driving urge to see her. Since kissing her on Sunday, he hadn't been able to shake the memory of how she tasted, and he hadn't wanted to. What he wanted was more. Maybe it was time to go and get it.

"Please tell me you're done 'cause I'm freezing my tits off here!" griped Jaxxon, to which 'Uncle' Tony and his small crew chuckled. It was alright for them – they weren't required to appear one with bloody nature in the chilly evening air, wearing a thin dress.

"We're done now, chick," said Tony, almost drowned out by the bustle of the equipment being gathered to be loaded into the SUV that was parked down the hill.

Literally dithering, she leaped from the fallen tree she had been posed on and dived into her coat. She saw Tony's smug look and shot him a glare that swore revenge. The idiotic man had come with the proposal of her modelling a collection of designer dresses made by a friend of his. Regardless of the fact that he was a popular designer, Jaxxon wasn't keen on modelling skimpy things that revealed her body. Her response had been 'Oh no.' Ollie had said, 'Sounds good.' Richie had said, 'I like that designer.'

Their claims that she was out-voted meant jack to her, so Tony had resorted to gambling. He had bet her that she couldn't get through a photo-shoot without swearing. Of course he'd won, so there she was in the middle of a woodland area, having spent the day posing on rocks and protruding tree trunks.

"Just think, in a few weeks' time you'll be on that tour advertising the Allure line, sunning it up in places like Miami," said Tony as he urged her to walk beside him down the hill. "You won't be shivering then. Have you thought anymore about going on that trip to Milan before you go?"

"Still undecided."

"Oh, chick, you don't want to miss an opportunity like that. Others would kill to have a famous designer release an exclusive collection for them to model in their very own name. Did they want to use just your first name, or was it your surname as well?"

"Tone, you must know by now that I'm not seeking the keys to Catwalk-dom. Strutting just isn't *me*."

"If nothing else, you can go over there and find yourself a fine, rich hubby whose life you can make miserable, even while he adores you."

"Funny, Tone."

"Did Richie tell you that FHM magazine wants you to pose for it?" he asked, smiling.

"You know very well what my response was to that. No way am I spreading myself all over a men's magazine."

Tony chuckled. "Jaxxon, darlin', blokes will wank over that body of yours whether you're in a men's mag in your underwear or not, so what's the difference?"

"I wouldn't be comfortable *on display* like that."

"Why? You've got the body for it, though I can't for the life of me figure out how you can't see that for yourself. Go on, give the men of your country something to add to their wank-bank."

She narrowed her eyes at him. "Anthony Masters, you are going to roast in the lowest level of hell."

He laughed. "Oh, speaking of roasts, Lily asked me to invite you over for Roast Dinner on Sunday again. She also asked to adopt you, but I told her that would be pushing it a bit."

Jaxxon chuckled. "I wouldn't miss one of your wife's Roast Dinners for anything."

"I'll try to make sure my son doesn't drool all over you this time. I suppose sticking him in the shed is always an option."

"I still can't believe Ant's sixteen, he only looks about twelve."

He nodded. "Don't say that in front of him. The lads have always given him grief over it. Poor bugger – when you *were* in the annexe, we swore him to secrecy so you wouldn't have fans sitting outside the house. So now that you've moved out, he told all his mates you used to live there, and they didn't believe him. He was guttered."

"Aww." Jaxxon giggled. As they continued toward the vehicles, he told her which were his favourite shots and teased her about which were most wank-worthy. She swatted his arm for that.

Jaxxon hadn't thought much of the azure-blue convertible parked next to her Audi until she saw the figure leaning against it. Her heart stuttered and her stomach knotted. It had been three days since he had 'visited' her apartment; three days during which she had wondered when he would be in touch again; three days during which, every time she had unlocked the door to her apartment, she had wondered if he was waiting inside; three days during which she had hated herself for obsessing over it all.

Connor grinned at Jaxx's scowl. He hadn't expected a warm, welcoming reception, especially since he technically shouldn't know where she was, but he wanted her to know how easily he could find her. As always, the urge to touch her had his fingers tingling. Seeing those bare legs of hers had his cock rising to attention. That scowl...Did she have any idea what she did to him?

"You gonna be alright?" Tony asked her as the sexual tension smothered him like humidity in summertime. He saw the way the F1 bloke was looking at her, and he didn't like it. People stared at Jaxxon all the time, but this was different. He made Tony think of a predator that had already caught his prey and was finding humour in watching it try to get away.

"I'll be fine, Tone," she reassured him with a nod and a half-smile. Then she stood in front of her car, keeping at least three feet between her and Connor. She could feel her body tightening with a carnal hunger. His primitive need for her was beating at her skin, making her close to vibrating with her own. He was so magnificently masculine that it hurt. As his dark, hooded eyes roamed over her, a blast of heat coursed through her.

Once they were alone, she spoke, "I won't ask how you got my schedule." The smoky tint to her voice betrayed her desire. Same way he got her phone number and address, she imagined. Ollie's secretary was obviously easily charmed.

"I'll always be able to find you, Jaxx. Remember that."

"What do you want?"

"Only the same thing I've always wanted: You."

His frank words didn't help reduce her horniness level. "I already made my feelings on that issue clear. For the record, they haven't changed. So now you can run along home."

She was so wrong. As it was, Connor was rooted to the spot by the thick and heady lust in her brown eyes. He conceded to himself that it was, in fact, possible that if he didn't get to touch her in some way, he would break down and pounce on her. He regarded her Audi. "I remember you used to say you'd buy a car like that if you won the Lotto. Ever fucked in a car, Jaxx?"

She snickered at what was more of a proposition than a question. "You really do have selective hearing, don't you?"

He shrugged. "I want you. You want me. I don't get why you're fighting it. I don't get what I've done to make you want to fight me."

"Basically, then, this is like a mathematical equation to you? 'I want you' plus 'You want me' equals 'Shag'?"

Just the way she said that last word had his cock hardening excruciatingly. He shrugged again, smirking.

"Connor," she said tiredly. "If you want sex so bad, I'm sure there are easier ways to get it than chasing after an antisocial bitch."

"I don't want sex so bad, I want *you* so bad. There's a difference."

He'd said it so resolutely that Jaxxon knew Plan A wasn't a viable option. He had no intention of letting this go, probably just because her rejection was biting his ego. Worse still, her body didn't appear to care that he could so easily emotionally scar her for life; the importance of the fact that he had already caused her pain was fading against the pressure of the mindless lust. "Alright."

"Alright, what?"

She pinned his gaze with her own. "You're right. I do want you, whether I like it or not. So" – she lazily unzipped her coat – "I'm going to take this off, then I'm going to brace myself against one of those trees behind me" – she flung the coat on the hood of the Audi – "and we'll see what you want to do about it." His eyes darkened, his nostrils flared, and his Adam's apple bopped. That seemed promising.

Turning, she advanced through the cluster of trees and over to an old oak. She stood with her palms flat against the tree and her feet a foot apart. She needed it to be like this – nothing that anyone could term romantic or loving. Out in the open, in relative darkness, facing away from him, and not even naked. It would just be sex. No emotions. No gentle shite. No flowery words. No sense of closeness. Just burning out this overwhelming need.

Connor wondered why he was standing there like an idiot when he could be touching and caressing that body that had been tormenting his every waking thought – and his dreams, for that matter. The answer? He hadn't wanted it to be this way. He had envisioned having her spread-eagled on his bed while he feasted on her and savoured every minute. This seemed too impersonal. Sordid, even. But that didn't mean that he would or could walk away. He would take her any way he could get her.

Each moment that went by was agonising for Jaxxon. Her entire body was on high alert. Anticipation was twisting her insides as she waited for him to touch her somewhere, anywhere. Just when she began to wonder if he was backing out, there was the rustle of footsteps in the grass. Hands landed on her outer thighs as a hot mouth landed on her earlobe, sucking and nibbling. His splayed hands slowly skated upwards, edging under her dress, as he trailed kisses along the curve of her neck. She nearly groaned from that alone.

Jaxxon let her head fall back on his shoulder to give him better access to her very sensitive neck. Her stomach clenched as his hands reached her thong, but instead of getting to work, they slid down her inner thighs. His movements were too slow for her liking. She would have snapped at him with impatience, but then his fingertips bit into her skin as they ascended. One hand cupped her while the other continued upwards, under her dress, and palmed her bra clad breast. A soft moan was followed by a gasp as a finger slid past her thong and between her wet folds.

"You know, Jaxx, I have to ask myself why you caved just like that." He worked a finger inside her and groaned inwardly at how wet she was; at how her muscles tightened around his finger. "You're one of the most stubborn people I know. You've fought me since you first saw me again. And up until, what, five minutes ago, you wanted to fight this."

Jaxxon was beginning to think this might not have been a good idea. Not only was his every touch sending a thundering rush of desire through her that topped anything she had ever before known, but the fact that they were outside and it was dark was only adding to the thrill. Her back arched slightly as he thumbed a hard nipple through the lacy bra. And now his finger was picking up its rhythm…Oh Jesus. They needed to get to the shagging part quickly. Why was he still talking?

"I can't work out why you just threw in the towel like that." The complete turn-around was really bugging him. If she had caved during a moment of pleasure, he could have accepted that. But for her to go from a confrontational stance to a 'shag me' position – he just didn't get it. He was about to say as much, but then that perfect arse teasingly rubbed against his hard cock. Control gone.

He drove his hand into her chocolate-brown curls, yanked her face to his, and slammed his mouth down on hers. He took complete possession of it, tangling his tongue with hers over and over and then sucking on it. As he added another finger inside her, she hummed her satisfaction into his mouth. It was going to be a tight fit. He scissored his fingers – stretching her, teasing her, preparing her. "Why the sudden white flag, Jaxx?"

"For God's sake," she snapped. The bloke never let up. "I'm horny and I want you; if that's not enough, if this was only fun when I was resisting you, then get into your car and piss off." His fingers stilled. A moment later, he withdrew them. For a second, she thought he was leaving, but then she heard the telling sound of a wrapper being torn and a zipper being lowered. Her thong went with a snap. Finally she felt the tip of his condom covered cock teasing her soaking wet entrance.

Connor caught her hips firmly and worked an inch inside her. So wet. He closed his eyes against the temptation to plunge into her. He was long and thick and she was so tight. She squirmed and her muscles clutched at him, trying to take him further inside. But he held himself immobile and tightened his grasp on her hips to stop her squirms. "Want more?"

Oh he better not be one of those people who loved to hear begging. She didn't do begging. She gave him a curt nod.

"Then tell me who's inside you."

"What?"

"I need to know you're not picturing yourself with just anyone." It bugged him that she wanted to have her back to him. "I need to hear that you know it's me who's about to bury my cock inside you and fuck you raw."

A tremor rippled down the length of her spine. "I'm not picturing anyone else."

He rewardingly pushed in another inch. Her muscles clamped down on him, practically squeezing the life out of him. "Then you can tell me who's inside you."

Swallowing her profanity, she relented. "Connor." He gave her another inch. God, the feeling of him stretching her...It tingled, it burned, it stung. It was absolutely amazing. She was sure that she hadn't accommodated someone so thick before.

"Tell me again." He didn't doubt for one minute that his insistence would have her snapping at him, but he wouldn't let her treat this as a nightly encounter with a stranger.

"Connor."

Another inch. He groaned – she was so gorgeously hot and tight around him. It was taking every ounce of his control not to fully sheath himself in one last stroke. It really didn't help that her body language was urging him to do exactly that. "Again, Jaxx."

So far Jaxxon had bit back at least a dozen curses, and even resisted the temptation to stomp on his foot, but now he was just cheesing her off. She growled. "Christ, Connor, either stop with this crap and fuck me, or sod off and I'll get someone else to take care of the itch." He stiffened and everything suddenly seemed deathly quiet. Alright, maybe that hadn't been the smartest thing to say. But he was getting on her wick, and he knew it.

She silently cursed herself as he withdrew from her. Yep, she'd pushed too far. But then he abruptly slammed into her, seating himself to the hilt. Her eyes snapped open and she cried out at the painful but so blissful invasion.

He bit her ear. "*Don't* talk to me about letting another bloke touch you." He surged into her again. "D'you hear me? *Don't.*" It didn't matter that they weren't in a relationship. It didn't matter that once the lust had burned away, they would go their separate ways. His soul had already claimed her as his a long time ago and would always see her that way, no matter where in the world she was, or who – he hated even the thought of it – she was with. The idea of another bloke's hands on her...It would always drive him to breaking point.

Jaxxon's back was arched like a bow as he plunged in and out of her with hard, fast, powerful strokes. She threw her head back to rest on his shoulder again, relishing every sensation. He nibbled and kissed and sucked on her neck. She knew he was purposely marking her, but she couldn't find it in herself to care. The concoction of heat, lust, and bliss that was blasting through her like a hot wind was so intense that it left no room for anything else. It was all simply too much. It was nowhere near enough.

"Ten years, Jaxx," he gritted out. "Ten years we've wanted this, and you thought you could ignore it?"

He was right, she acknowledged. It was always going to happen. From the moment she had heard his voice again on her machine, it was inevitable. But even if she had been prepared to admit that aloud, it seemed that she had forfeited the power of speech in favour of carnal bliss. She was adrift in the sensation of his thick, long cock pumping in and out of her. She knew that with one touch to her clit, she'd go off like a sodding volcano.

As the tenor of her cries signalled to Connor that her climax was looming, he pulled out of her, spun her round, and meshed his lips with hers. The kiss was raw and primitive, just like their joining. The second he lifted her, she locked her legs around him. Then, holding her gaze, he drove into her over and over and over, making her take everything he had to give.

Jaxxon clung to him, her nails digging into his back through his shirt. She loved the feel of him so deep inside her. But she didn't like the eye contact. It made her feel exposed, vulnerable even; she didn't want him to see the truth that this was more to her than just a shag in the dark, a scratch to an itch. She tucked her face into the crook of his neck. She was so close now.

"Look at me, Jaxx."

Oh the bastard.

"Look. At. Me." He wanted to be caught up in that feral gaze when they both came. "Jaxx."

Hoping against hope that the out-of-control sensations spiralling through her might disguise any deeper emotions from her eyes, she lifted her head. And just like that, at the raw possessiveness and fevered lust she saw on his face, a violent climax tore through her.

Connor covered her mouth with his own, capturing her scream, as his own release hit and his come exploded out of him. "*Fuck.*"

Neither of them moved as, panting and gasping for breath, they waited for the aftershocks to subside. He wanted to say something, but didn't know what. He could tell her the truth; that that had been the best sex of his life; that it hadn't been meaningless to him like every other shag he'd had; that he'd missed her *so* fucking much. But wouldn't that be the equivalent of leading her to believe that more could come of this?

Jaxxon slid down his body, not letting it show that she felt the loss of him being buried deep within her. It hadn't been as good as she'd always imagined it might be; it had been a million times better. "Not bad, McKenzie." She was going for calm, flippant, and casual. It must have worked a lot better than she thought, because his eyes bugged and his mouth drooped open. Clearly he had been hoping for a much more decent compliment.

She fixed her dress, praying her legs would support her quick exit. No sign of her torn thong. Great. Seeing that he already had questions in his eyes, she decided she'd just have to leave the thong – it was time to go.

"Not bad, McKenzie," he echoed in a tone filled with disbelief as he removed the condom and zipped up his pants. "Whoa, whoa, whoa," he called after her as she scuttled off. "Is that all you can say?"

"What do you want me to say?" She retrieved her coat from the hood of her Audi and slung it onto the passenger seat as she hopped into the car. Before she could close the door, a hand grabbed it tightly. She looked up to see him scowling down at her. "Connor, what's the problem? We both got what we wanted. We're both going home satisfied."

"So that's it? One shag and *done*?" It wasn't lost on him that he sounded a lot like some of the women he had shagged in the past.

Jaxxon veiled her relief at hearing he had more than just a one-off shag in mind. It was going to take more than the one time to rid him from her system. But she couldn't let him see that weakness. Connor was, essentially, a predator. Predators and weaknesses did not mix well.

She maintained her casual air. "Alright, look, I've got a lot on at the minute, but I don't see why we can't get together again. Phone me." With that, she snatched the door from his grasp, banged it shut, and drove off without a second look. It was the only way to keep herself safe – she couldn't let anyone in, especially not Connor McKenzie.

CHAPTER SEVEN

"Not bad, McKenzie," repeated Anna, shocked. "Oh, Jaxxon, you didn't." It had been days since she had last seen Jaxxon, and she been waiting desperately for the scoop. Whatever she had expected to hear, it wasn't that Jaxxon decided to have a rendezvous at night time in a wooded area. Brilliant. But 'Not bad, McKenzie'…Dear God.

"For all I knew, one shag was all he was after," said Jaxxon defensively, swinging Bronty's lead in the humid air. The dumb dog was fascinated with a pine comb at the moment. Each time she walked him in the park, she became more and more concerned by the fact that her dog didn't seem to do anything typical of canines. He didn't go around pissing and shitting, marking his territory. He didn't sniff everyone and everything he came into contact with. He didn't try to chase other animals. It was almost as though he had no innate instincts that told him how to behave.

"I thought I'd play it casual, so it was painless for both of us to walk away." It would never be truly painless for her, though. She knew that for sure Wednesday night.

"I guess I see your point. But 'Not bad, McKenzie'."

"At least I commented on the shag. All he did was pounce on the idea of me walking off after just the one time. He sounded like a girl, to be quite honest. I don't think I've ever met a bloke who minded being used for sex."

"So what does that tell you?"

She knew what Anna was getting at, but Jaxxon was smart enough to know that Connor would never want more than what they had now – which was very little. "That his ego is too sensitive."

Anna shook her head, smiling. If only Jaxxon could see her own worth instead of viewing herself as a moody bitch, Anna might have a shot at convincing her of what she herself believed: Connor McKenzie would never let her go, even if he didn't realise it himself yet. "When are you seeing him next?"

Tingles abruptly scurried along Jaxxon's spine, and the nape of her neck began to itch. Someone was watching her. Just like when she went shopping with Anna that time, it felt *wrong*. Like the gaze was sending a bad vibe. Still managing to hold on to the thread of the conversation, she replied while scanning her surroundings, "I told him to phone me." There were people around the park, but no one who gave her cause to look twice. Was she getting paranoid?

"He's a bloke so that could take days. They like to play it cool so they don't seem desperate, as if the way they ravish us when they *do* see us doesn't tell us differently." They both winced as Bronty tried to eat a bee. "Do you fancy trying that new bar, 'Frankie's', later?" When Jaxxon groaned, she added, "Come on, we never hit any bars last weekend."

"Only because we went to the charity event."

A loud bark had them both jerking around. Jaxxon felt her eyebrows shoot up as she found Bronty in the kind of pouncing position expectant of a lion, glaring at someone who – judging by his attire – was a jogger. She could only guess that he had given Bronty a fright when he sprung out of the trees onto their path. "Bronty, you daft sod. Sorry," she told the jogger when she approached. "He's a bit odd, to tell you the truth."

"I-it's, er, alright, he's just, er, protecting his mistress."

Jaxxon gave Bronty, who hadn't moved a muscle, a little shove. "Oi, snap out of it. And stop posing like that." She looked at Anna. "Do you think he knows he's a dog?" Anna was too busy staring open-mouthed at the jogger to answer. Jaxxon knew that look, and what it meant. It wasn't unusual for celebs to stroll about this park. But damn if Jaxxon could recognise him. She again took in his athletic build, his dark eyes, his high cheekbones, and tousled dark hair.

She also took in the fact that he didn't have an ounce of sweat on him, which was surely odd for someone jogging around, especially in this heat. And then there was the look on his face…He seemed nervous; had the look of someone who'd known exactly what they wanted to say, but been put off. Like stage fright.

"Alright, well, bye." She took a frozen Anna by the arm and guided her away. The bloke did start jogging then. Yes, she was being paranoid.

"Now that is one divine man," said Anna, finally back to Earth. "Who is he?"

Anna regarded her like she was loopy. "That's Luke Winston." Jaxxon looked none the wiser. "Don't you know who Luke Winston is?"

Jaxxon shook her head. "He seems a bit familiar."

"So he should. He was in a boy-band when he was younger and now he's an actor. Doesn't he have the most gorgeous arse?"

No, Connor does, thought Jaxxon. *Alright, whoa, where the hell did that come from?* She really did not want to end up in the state of mind where she compared and contrasted every bloke she met against Connor. For one thing, that would make her a very sad individual. Also, she knew perfectly well that no one would ever measure up to him. No one ever had in the past eight years, and that was before they'd even shagged – and what a bloody good shag it had been. She would be destined to lead the life of a spinster. Not going to happen. Yes, a night out where loud music could drown out her thoughts would do her the world of good.

Connor's muscles ached deliciously after his work-out. And so they should. He'd spent longer hours than usual at the gym – practically abusing the exercise bike, the rowing machine, and the specially designed weights that helped develop the muscles required to withstand the g-forces and racing conditions. It might look like all an F1 driver had to do was sit on their arse and steer, but there was more to it than that.

Connor had to ensure that he worked on his neck muscles as a lot of stress was put on them considering that the helmet weighed 7kg and the g-force could send his head lurching and bobbing. He also had to concentrate hard on keeping up his upper body strength, so that he could tackle the twists and turns of the speeding car and the physical stress coming from the g-force. For similar reasons, exercising his arms and wrists were important. And of course there were his legs. A driver's braking power depended massively on the strength of his leg muscles, seeing as the pedals of F1 cars were made to be stiff.

He thought it was ironic that he had trained his mind to be alert and prepared for anything – how else would he handle a speeding car and be totally attuned to every movement? – and yet the reappearance of one person in his life had thrown him completely. During training seemed to be the only time that he was actually in control of his body – a body that craved Jaxx in a way that scared him. His theory was that if his body had been well worked, it wouldn't be so unruly. So, yeah, he'd overworked himself a lot lately.

Nonetheless, whenever she crept into his thoughts, his cock roared to life. How was it possible that he thought of Jaxx so much? But, then, how could he *not* think of her? How could he not think of Wednesday night? It had felt so good to be inside her. She had been so responsive to his touch. So hot and tight around him. So gorgeous as she came, screaming.

And then she had topped it off with 'Not bad, McKenzie.'

Not bad, McKenzie?! It had been amazing, that was what it had been. He'd never had a shag like that in his life.

Then she had scarpered like the hounds of hell were chasing her. Had that been regret? Or was it that what happened had meant so little to her? That *he* meant so little to her?

Christ, why was he stressing over this? He should be glad. She was his favourite kind of woman: she understood that sex didn't mean the involvement of 'feelings', she didn't have this need to bask in the bloody afterglow, and she didn't put any pressure on him. She had just got her jollies and left, not even hinting for a compliment on her performance or if she was the best sex ever. The irony that this woman *was* the best sex he'd ever had wasn't lost on him. He wondered if that meant it would take longer for him to burn off his cravings for her.

The chiming of his mobile phone stole him from his contemplations. The name on the screen of his BlackBerry was 'Warren', an Olympic runner who had been a good mate of his over the years. "Hello."

"Connor, you busy right now, mate?"

"Just got out of the shower. About to have a beer and wind down. What's up?"

"Er...I'm at that new bar, 'Frankie's', with Clive and Mick."

That explained the background noise. "I'm not really in the mood for that tonight."

"I think you might change your mind when I tell you who I'm looking at right now. Jaxxon Carter's here, she's with the really cute, leggy model who went to the charity event with her. And, er..."

Connor's entire body tensed and his jaw locked.
"Well, that actor, Luke Winston, is hovering around her."
Little bastard.

She probably should have been politely concentrating on what Luke was saying, but Jaxxon was busy wondering if there was such a thing as Celebrity Fright Syndrome and if Anna suffered from it. She hadn't said a word since Luke had appeared at their table a half hour ago, just stared at him like he alone held the keys to the secrets of the universe. He certainly held a secret…but Jaxxon had yet to figure out what.

On the surface he seemed totally fine, and the evening had so far been alright, if you discounted the fact that he sat with them without waiting for an invitation. He didn't seem conceited, he hadn't mentioned either of their careers, and he hadn't ploughed her with extremely personal questions. They were just two people talking, which was kind of refreshing.

But something just wasn't quite right. He was so nervous, and he couldn't meet her eyes for very long. A few times already he had tried to get her to leave the bar with him. Also, he was trying to get her plastered. Poor thing didn't know she'd worked in a pub for years and could handle her alcohol better than most people – not that she wasn't the teensiest bit tipsy. The only reason she hadn't sent him away with a kick up the arse was that she was certain he'd be plastered before she was, and then maybe she could coax his big secret from him.

"Oh bugger."

Jaxxon nearly jumped when Anna spoke. So she *was* alive then. "What's wrong?"

"You're not going to like this."

As Jaxxon followed Anna's gaze, she inhaled sharply. Connor and a cluster of blokes were stalking toward their table. He was in predator-mode, it would seem. "A wolf dressed in Armani clothing." It had only taken a second of seeing him before the memory of Wednesday night was all over her. It didn't help that he looked good in his grey shirt and black pants.

As he came to stand before Jaxxon, only the mahogany table between them, there was a wordless exchange between them. His tense posture, twist of the lips, and raised brow asked if there was a reason why another bloke was so close to her that justified allowing him to live. Her shrug, casual swig of her drink, and a twirl of her ankle said that she wasn't affected by his crap and didn't have to explain herself to him.

She watched as Connor's eyes slammed down on Luke, who was settled in the bulky armchair beside where he was standing, looking from her to Connor and back again. Luke hadn't missed the 'fuck off' blazing from Connor's eyes, but he seemed to be waiting to see if Jaxxon would object to him going on his way. She didn't. She knew it was in his best interests to be out of Connor's sight. Something told her that Connor would be like this until he had tired of her. She could only hope that she had burned him out of her system before then.

Jaxxon had expected that Luke might shoot a snarl at her or Connor, but he had the oddest look in his eyes. She was sure she saw flashes of shock and betrayal, but the emotions weren't directed at either her or Connor. What was with him? Almost the second after Luke had vacated the seat, Connor flopped into it. This meant he was now directly opposite her as they stared the hell out of each other. Honestly, she felt like a cowgirl about to have a showdown.

"It's Anna, isn't it?"

Following the male voice, Jaxxon turned her head and saw what she had never expected to see: a celebrity had seated himself next to Anna, and she hadn't frozen.

"Yeah, hi," she said a little shyly. "You're Warren, right?" Of course Anna was faking her uncertainty. She knew exactly who he was – the man was a gold-medal winner, for God's sake! She had first seen him in the flesh at the charity event. He had smiled at her a few times, but they had never gotten round to talking. Probably because she had made it her business to get drunk to distract Jaxxon from Connor's antics.

"And you're Jaxxon," said Warren as he looked past Anna at the woman who he had thought Connor was going to devour in the middle of the charity event. He didn't know what, if anything, was going on between them, but he knew Connor. He'd seen how possessive his mate was of her, and he'd figured it might be best to warn him that there was now another man coming onto her. Turned out he was right to do so. He handed Connor a Budweiser, noticing at the same time that it was what Jaxxon was drinking too.

Jaxxon nodded. "And you're the one who snitched to Connor that I was here tonight." There was no way that Connor was already here when he saw her. It was obvious by the frustration on his face that he had been stewing on his emotions for a while, which suggested having dragged himself here from somewhere else.

Warren smiled at her astuteness. "What made you think it was me?"

"You're finding way too much pleasure in this awkward little situation. Plus, it gave you an excuse to hang around Anna. Upset her, you'll lose your bollocks."

She said it so matter-of-factly that he laughed. "Fair enough. That ginger one there is Clive, the tubby one is Mick. Both are my brothers-in-law."

Jaxxon nodded at Clive and Mick, who sat on either side of Connor. It was almost like they were flanking him. She smiled at that. Connor gave her a questioning look, but she said nothing. There was a long silence at the table. She realised that Anna and Connor's mates were all fixated on her and him, watching and waiting to see how this was going to play out: Was Jaxxon going to blow her fuse after Connor's display of ownership? Was Connor going to pop a vein after seeing her with Luke? She considered warning them that there was likely to be unsuitable language from the outset and scenes that some people may find disturbing.

It seemed that over the years Connor had forgotten just how often he had had to chase idiots away from Jaxx. The problem was she had a body that made a bloke think sinful thoughts. It had always gotten her attention, and always the wrong kind of attention. Boys had seemed to automatically think that if she had a body so alluring, she was some kind of seductress who was up for anything. Then there was the fact that her sister had been very loose with her body; boys had tended to then reason that Jaxx must be easy like her.

From minute one, Jaxx had brought out his primitive instinct to protect. It hadn't even mattered if the boy had seemed harmless – if he was a male and too close to her for Connor's liking then that male needed to be on his way…because she brought out another primitive instinct in him too: to possess. Every wicked curve of her body called to any red-blooded male. She was edible. And he wanted another taste. He hadn't thought of anything else since the second she drove away the other night. Having her again was the only thing that would calm the raging lust coursing through him, the only thing that would feel *right.*

Connor itched to touch her so much that he found himself tapping his restless fingers on the arms of the chair. He wanted to drag her out of there and fuck her to unconsciousness. Disliking the way she looked so unperturbed, he made sure he said something that would get him a response. "Oh there's nothing quite like finding a randy bastard sniffing around your woman."

Jaxxon looked at him with mock sympathy. "Oh Connor. How you do love to delude yourself. I'll say this one more time: I belong to no one." She was impressed at how steady her voice was, given that her insides were coiling with a vicious hunger for the raw, carnal pleasure she knew he could give her. There was no denying that his body was designed for it. She could vividly recall the feel of him, thick and hard and long, inside her. And going by the way his lips were curved into his cocky smirk, he knew that she was recalling it.

"You felt like you were mine the other night."

It probably should have bothered her that he had announced that for his mates to hear, but the world thought they were shagging anyway after what the tabloids had printed. "Sex doesn't give you ownership rights."

"My body owned yours the other night, and you know it."

It nettled her the way he said that — like she was at his mercy, like her body was his to bloody command or something. "It's so sad, Connor. The way you're being all cocky and boastful, you sound like a teenage boy who's just finally popped his cherry. It was a quickie in the woods, no need to get carried away with yourself."

"I'm getting carried away, am I? As I recall it, you were the one screaming."

"If you think that makes me anything like the other women who follow you around like you're the Pied Bleeding Piper then you're very much mistaken. And you're just as mistaken if you think I'll tolerate your possessiveness."

It was a struggle to keep his voice level. "And you're very mistaken if you think I'll *ever* be alright with another bloke being near you, let alone touching you. I see red every time."

"Try to imagine how little I actually care."

He couldn't help smiling. She was pushing him, but her ballsy responses and the frustration shimmering in her eyes only made his dick harder. It wasn't easy reining in his eagerness to have her when he could sense that she was just as affected by the sexual tension as he was. "Be as pissed off with me as you like. It won't change the fact that Wednesday night will happen again. But you already know that, don't you."

There it was again: that insinuation that she had no control over things. Fair enough, she didn't have much at all. But she knew that he wasn't as in control as he liked to think. Maybe it was time to fight fire with fire. "You know, McKenzie, these games of yours – getting my private schedule, swooping in and scaring off other blokes, breaking into my apartment – are pretty annoying. I'm not usually a fan of game playing, but I've got a good mind to make an exception here."

The calculating gleam in her eyes had him intrigued. "I'm up for it, Carter."

"You don't know what it is yet."

"Doesn't matter."

"So over-confident…" She sighed wistfully. "Anna, what time is it?"

After consulting her wristwatch, she replied, "Eleven."

Jaxxon fixed her eyes on Connor. "I'll bet that you won't last until half-past eleven to get me out of here." There was no point in acting as though there wouldn't be a repeat of the other night. They both wanted it. It would happen.

A crooked grin appeared on Connor's face. She knew just how desperate he was to be inside her again, just as she knew that turning down her challenge was as good as admitting aloud that desperation and that she had managed to splinter his iron control. She had cornered him good and proper. Pride wouldn't let him admit his weakness. "Alright."

Jaxxon sank further into her seat and shifted slightly so that her pants sagged slightly over her hipbones. Connor saw and his nostrils flared.

Anna looked at her curiously. "Comfy?"

"Oh yeah. I wouldn't normally chance this position, it makes my thong ride up my arse, but since I'm going Commando…" Connor's eyes darkened, and she smiled inwardly.

Anna laughed to Warren. "She's actually telling the truth. She never wears underwear with her low-cut pants."

"Just think," Jaxxon said to Connor, "if I'd been wearing a skirt, I could have done a 'Sharon Stone Basic Instinct' move and flashed you."

Just the thought of that had Connor swallowing hard. "Maybe next time."

"So tell me a bit about yourself, Warren," said Jaxxon.

"Er...Born and raised in London. Twenty-eight. Got five gold medals."

"What's your favourite sex position?"

Stunned, he stuttered, "I, er, I d-don't know."

"Oh come on, we're all adults here."

He chuckled. He liked Jaxxon Carter, she was good for Connor. She would never take any of his shite without dishing it back. "I like having a woman on top."

"Anna, what's yours?"

"Same, actually." She wasn't just saying what she thought might excite Warren, it was true.

Jaxxon tapped her chin thoughtfully. "Personally, I prefer being taken from behind." Someone made a choking sound. "But I do like a good shag up against a wall." She smiled at Connor, watching as his Adam's apple bobbed.

Connor took a long guzzle from his bottle. Her words were conjuring all kinds of images in his head. His cock got impossibly harder. Now all he could think about was fucking her against a wall. He was going to kill her for this. He'd fuck her first. But then he was going to kill her. He glared at her warningly, but she seemed unfazed.

"What about you, Connor?"

"You'll soon find out, won't you?" His eyes became glued to her mouth as she took a small swig of her drink and then circled the tip of the bottle with her tongue. His entire body clenched. He wasn't sure whether he wanted to encourage her or throttle her. Then she took as much of the neck of the bottle into her mouth as she could, and swirled her tongue around it before sucking it. "Bitch." He hadn't realised he'd said it aloud until she smiled smugly.

She swiped a drop of beer from her chin. "I can't believe I've just dribbled. I usually swallow with no problem."

He groaned aloud this time before taking another long, comforting guzzle from his bottle.

"Connor, have you ever wanked thinking about me?"

Half of his drink went down the wrong tube, and the other half he spluttered back up.

"That's a nasty cough you've got."

There was water in his eyes when he looked back at her. "Have you ever got yourself off thinking about me?"

She shrugged delicately as she said, "Of course. With the help of my vibrator." Hell if she had one, though she'd always been curious.

Had he been taking another gulp of his beer, Connor would have coughed that up as well. His voice was hoarse and shaky. "Vibrator?"

Anna had to hide her laugh as every bloke at the table became riveted. It wasn't just Jaxxon's words, it was those famous eyes, and that sultry voice, and the way her sensual mouth moved as she talked.

"I pushed it in and out, in and out, imagining it was you," she said in what she hoped was a hypnotic tone. At the same time, she threaded the neck of the bottle through her closed fist. "I played with my tits and my clit, pretending it was you. And I came screaming your name." She took another swig of her Budweiser. "Then I sucked the vibrator clean."

With that, Connor sprung from his chair, snatched the bottle from her hand which he handed to Anna, dragged Jaxx to her feet, and then threw her over his shoulder like she was an unruly child – all in the space of about four seconds.

"Oi!" she shouted.

"Not a word, Jaxx," he gritted out as he stalked toward the door. He had never been so hard in his life. There was probably an imprint of his zipper on his cock. It was all her doing, and she was going to see to the problem personally. He couldn't care less at the moment that he had just lost control – and with witnesses. All he cared about was having her.

Jaxxon continued to shout at him and pounded his back with her fists as he exited the bar. He didn't even slow down. Desperate times, desperate measures…She slid her hands down the back of his trousers, grabbed the band of his boxer shorts, and tugged hard, determined to give him the world's worst wedgie.

Connor stiffened, then writhed, then tried walking faster – nothing alleviated the pain, it only worsened. So this was what it was like to wear a thong. He yanked hard on her legs and slid her down his body as he reached his convertible, which was parked quite illegally to the side of the bar. He tried to fling her inside, but she took on a starfish pose, spreading out her arms and legs to hamper his attempt.

Out of patience and uncaring of anyone who might be watching, he boldly cupped her. Instantly she retracted her limbs and began sliding into the car to escape his grip. But just before he had a chance to shut the door, she snatched the car keys from his hand and scooted over to the driver's seat. As the engine roared to life, he gave her a warning look. "Jaxx." It was a warning she ignored.

Grinning, Jaxxon took the handbrake off and began driving the car at a crawling pace. She had no intention of driving away. For one thing, she had been drinking, and two, Connor would have a hernia. But the horror on his face was priceless. As he dived into the passenger seat, reaching for the handbrake, she was opening the driver's door and heading back to the bar.

As mad as he was, Connor couldn't help laughing. He put the car in park and jogged after her. He caught her easily, since she was laughing so hard she could barely move. He jerked her back against him, twirled her round, and hoisted her up, urging her to curve her legs around him. "You're a tease," he said, still laughing with her. Then he brought his lips to hers and devoured her, pressing her body close to him. She didn't fight him; she opened up to him like she was as hungry for the contact as he was. That in mind, he couldn't get them in the car fast enough.

"You taking me back to my apartment?" she asked, all innocence, as she clicked her seatbelt into place. Judging by the direction he was heading, the answer was no.

"Not a bloody chance. You're coming home with me, and you're going to do something about this hard-on that you caused and then deliberately aggravated."

"I can do something about that right now."

CHAPTER EIGHT

Before the words had properly registered in his brain, she was across his lap, and her mouth exhaled heavily against his erection through his pants. He groaned. His button and zipper were deftly dealt with and then her soft hand was fishing him out of his boxers. He sucked in a breath as she licked him from base to tip before running her tongue along the slit, lapping up the drop of moisture there. "Jaxx." Then she closed that mouth that should surely only exist in fantasies over the head of his cock, lathed it with her tongue, and sucked hard. "Jesus."

Driving one-handed now, Connor speared his fingers in her hair as she took as much of him into her hot mouth as she could. When his dick hit the back of her throat, he groaned helplessly. Just as she had to the bottle, she swirled her tongue over and under him. The breath slammed out of his lungs as she then began sucking with vigour. Had he been standing, his knees would have given out. "Fuck, yeah. That's it, babe. Just like that."

Jaxxon smiled around his dick – it was a smile of pure feminine satisfaction. With her mouth, she learned the length of him – sliding her tongue over each ridge and vein, and sporadically pausing in her sucking to lazily curl her tongue over the silky head. She fully intended to drive him to the edge of his control again. She knew that soon enough he would have his fill of her and then she would probably never see him again. That could even happen tonight. She was going to make sure that she wasn't easy to forget.

Who was it who said that reality can never live up to fantasy? thought Connor as he groaned again. Here was evidence that that theory was absolute bollocks. How many times had he imagined this? Too often, and yet never had he imagined it would be this good. He'd have loved to watch, but there wasn't a chance in hell that he was going to stop this car and delay having her any longer. He'd managed to catch fleeting glimpses, and, shit, just seeing his cock disappearing into her mouth…What he wouldn't give to have the feel of her mouth around his dick while *she* came.

Christ, she was sucking him even deeper now; gliding the flat of her tongue along his underside each time. Helplessly he began lifting his hips, surging into her mouth. And now the little witch was lightly grazing him with her teeth. "Jaxx, babe, you have to stop."

Instead of ending the torture, Jaxxon worked harder and faster, tightening her lips around him and sucking until her cheeks hollowed.

"Jaxx, I mean it, you have to stop, or I'll blow my load right now."

"Good," she hummed.

The hum vibrated along his cock, dragging at his self-control. That was it, he was gone. Fisting his hand even tighter in her hair, he lifted his hips and erupted into her mouth with a loud, guttural groan. She continued sucking, milking him of every last drop as he pulsed incessantly inside her. Then the mental bitch sat up, took a deep breath, and faced forward to gaze out the window as if she hadn't just given him the best blowjob of his life.

His half-promise half-threat came out in a gruff voice. "You should know right now that I'm going to fuck you 'til you can't think straight once we get to my apartment."

Connor wasn't oblivious to the looks they received when they hastened into his building a few minutes later. The doorman, Henry, looked at him with surprise, and then realisation and approval. Connor knew why: he never brought a woman back to his apartment. It seemed that Henry was an admirer of Jaxx's, because apparently the fact that it was Jaxxon Carter the model meant it all made sense. He wanted to tell Henry that he was only bringing her here because his apartment was nearer than hers, that it was nothing to do with the puzzling, primal urge to have her in his home.

Admiring looks followed Jaxx with every step she took. The security guards practically drooled, and even the female receptionist looked a little mesmerised. Jaxx, however, was as totally oblivious as ever to her effect on people. Two feelings battled for dominance within Connor: frustration because of the blatant ogling going on like he wasn't there, and satisfaction at seeing people want so desperately what was his.

If there hadn't been people in the elevator with them, there was a good chance that the shedding of clothes would have started then. Although emptying himself into her mouth had calmed his frenzied state, his need for her still hammered at him. So much so that he wasn't able to refrain from pressing his front to her back and reaching around to briefly cup her, loving her answering shudder. He couldn't bring himself to care that one of the blokes in the elevator had caught the movement and was staring at them, his expression hoping there was more to see. Why disappoint the man?

This time, Connor cupped a breast briefly. Jaxx, completely oblivious to their voyeur, subtly rubbed her arse against his ever-hard bulge. Connor punishingly bit her ear, so she retaliated by reaching around and pinching his arse. Had the elevator always been this slow? "We should have taken the stairs," he muttered. To the ninth floor? Not likely. He ignored the knowing chuckles of those around them.

As the doors opened at the seventh floor, Jaxxon held them open. "I'll tell you what, McKenzie, let's hit the stairs. Whoever gets to the ninth first gets to be on top."

For a second, he didn't breathe. "You're on, Carter."

Jaxxon could barely walk for laughing as Connor attacked the flights of stairs like a rocket. He must have tired of waiting, because he came back looking for her, finding her on the eighth, still giggling. He more or less dragged her the rest of the way up. They darted to the door of his apartment like they were being pursued by a knife-wielding madman…which was why Jaxxon was taken aback when he didn't jump her when they got inside.

Instead, he stood staring at her, breathing hard. As she mirrored his stance and remained rooted to the spot, a part of her brain took notes on her surroundings. The interior was exactly like Connor: masculine, bold and stylish. The place was a hell of a lot bigger than her apartment. The balcony was a surprise.

Moments went by, and still he didn't move. He was so still, it was unnerving. She realised he was trying to retain some control. But she didn't want him controlled, she wanted him the way he had been the other night. So she did what would get any predator moving. She began to back away. Sure enough, with each step she took backwards, Connor took one forwards.

When the back of Jaxxon's knees connected with something, effectively stopping her retreat, Connor was on her. His hands dug into her hair as his lips took command of hers; *taking* the response he wanted. Each sweep of his tongue against hers sent tingling sensations shooting to her clit. He took the kiss deeper and deeper, until he was practically drinking her into him. It both promised and warned her of what was to come.

Without parting their mouths, he took her by the waist and guided her around whatever had obstructed her backpedalling, and then urged her to walk backwards…maybe they took a left somewhere. When he brought them to an abrupt halt, Jaxxon opened her eyes to find herself in – no surprise – his bedroom. Like the other parts of the interior she had glimpsed, the furnishings were all modern and masculine in design. Dominating this room was a big, hulky bed fit for a Sheikh. "Do you have a crown and a harem to go with that?"

He laughed. "You won't be taking the piss out of it once you've laid on it. It's the softest thing ever." He ran a fingertip down her cheek. "Except maybe for your skin…which I haven't seen all of yet." He raised her arms above her head, and then slid his hands down her arms to her stomach. Gathering the lacy, red fabric, he peeled the strappy top from her body. "Do you have any idea how many times I've thought about stripping you like this?" He couldn't resist thumbing her already taut nipples through the lacy bra. Tonight there would be no bra between his hands and those breasts that taunted him. He unclipped the offending contraption and whipped it from her. The breath left his lungs in a whoosh. Perfect, plump, high breasts with puckered tips greeted him.

"Jaxx," he breathed. The pants needed to go now so he could finally have her naked in front of him. When he let them pool at her feet, he groaned. "You weren't lying." Commando. And bald. Jesus Christ. "Lie on the bed."

Having kicked off her shoes, she sensually climbed onto it with a catlike grace and sank back into the mattress with one leg out straight and the other bent at the knee. He swallowed heavily at the inviting, erotic, cock-torturing sight. Yes, this was how he had envisioned it would be: Jaxx laid out for him to explore and tease and pleasure until she sobbed for him to be inside her. Was that why his need for her was so great, because he had wanted and imagined having her for so long? If that was true, then maybe once he had lived out this very fantasy he could let her go, maybe—

"Your turn to strip," she announced, snapping him from his thoughts. Jaxxon was only barely resisting the urge to shyly shield herself from his heated gaze. Or to reach out and drag him to the bed. Either would do.

"Not yet."

"I'm not being naked here all by myself, McKenzie. Get your kit off now."

Aroused by that assertive tone, he smiled and slowly shed his clothes until he stood completely naked before her.

Jaxxon's mouth went dry at the vision in front of her. There didn't seem to be a part of that blessed body that wasn't toned. She loved that although he was muscly, he wasn't stocky or beefy. No, he was just right. Better than just right. He was the personification of power and raw masculinity and, for tonight at least, he was all hers. His dick was, as usual, standing to attention. And what a dick it was. Looking at it now, she was amazed it had actually fit in her mouth. Involuntarily, she licked her bottom lip. It was possible that Connor groaned, but she was too engrossed at the sight of his tempting cock to pay much attention.

"Jaxx?"

Her eyes remained glued to his dick. "Hmm?"

"Jaxx, my face is up here."

"And your point is?" He laughed, and then his face was suddenly in front of hers and his body pressed down on her as he kissed her wildly. She went to curl her arms around his neck, but he took her wrists and placed them above her head.

"No touching me yet. It's my turn now. Keep your hands here." This kiss was a goodbye kiss, because it would be a while before he was back to ravish those talented lips. He wanted to know this amazing body better than anyone ever had, better than even she knew it. With his hands, mouth, tongue, and teeth, he proceeded to explore and pay homage to every inch of her, purposely skipping her main erogenous places. He discovered other erogenous zones that he tormented and teased.

He also learned other things. He found that her neck was so unbelievably sensitive that he could have her bowing from the bed by just exploring that alone. He discovered that licking the length of her spine could make her shudder, laugh, and moan all at the same time. And he also found that if he took too long to "get to the good parts", a string of curses would emit from her.

"For God's sake, Connor, will you leave my fucking belly button the fuck alone and either move up a fucking bit or down a fucking bit!" A moan of relief spilled from her when *finally* his hands possessively closed over her breasts as his mouth landed on a nipple and latched on tight. His hands massaged and kneaded while he suckled on the bud and plucked at it with his teeth. Jaxxon moaned again as she felt a climax building. The bastard had subjected her to a sensual assault, rendering her a bomb waiting to go off.

He lifted his head and pinned her with a look. "Don't come yet."

"Like I can help it!" He smiled, and it was too cocky and smug for her liking. "Oh you think this is funny, do you?" She curled her hand around his dick and stroked him. When he groaned, she mimicked his smug grin.

Connor placed her hands back above her head. "I told you, no touching me yet. You had your fun in the car."

"I also made you *come*." He kept backing off every time she came close to the edge.

His smile transformed from cocky to wicked. "You're right. I'm being selfish. You want to come, I'll make you come." He slid down her body, nipping and sucking just because.

One lash of his tongue to her clit had Jaxxon's body bucking. His fingers parted her wet folds and he blew out a long breath, making her entire body quiver. Then he swept that tongue between her folds and swirled it around her clit. She was lost.

"You taste so good," he groaned. Pinning her restless hips to the bed, Connor feasted on her — lapping, suckling, licking, nipping. He continuously flicked the bud with the tip of his tongue, loving the sounds she made. He couldn't resist biting it gently. Then he plunged his tongue inside her, and stabbed over and over.

"Oh my God," she rasped. Unconsciously, she grabbed his head but he gently slapped her hands away and mumbled, 'Above your head.' The vibrations of his words rocketed up into her core and sent sizzles through her body. As he alternated between stabbing his tongue and swirling it around, wringing moans and gasps and words of encouragement from her, she held onto the headboard to anchor herself. He had totally overloaded her senses…and now he was doing something else oh so clever with that seriously talented tongue of his. Tremors were racking her. She was so close yet so far, because he was dragging it out. "Connor," she said in a cautioning tone.

"Just a little longer, babe." He couldn't get enough of the taste of her.

"No. I need to come now." His onslaught continued. "Connor."

Connor speared a finger inside her and sought her G-spot as his mouth latched onto her clit and suckled. She gave a loud cry as she came, shuddering and bucking. Her eyes were wild when she opened them again. They pulled at his soul, fired his blood, and…there was another feeling, but he didn't want to examine it.

He retrieved a condom from the bedside drawer, donned it quickly, and settled his hips between her invitingly spread thighs. Locking one of his hands around both her wrists, he pinned them above her head and began to slowly work himself inside her. It was killing him to move slowly but she was so tight, and he didn't want to hurt her more than he already was.

Jaxxon sucked in a breath as her muscles stretched to accommodate him. The pressure was unbelievably good, even with the burning. That edge of pain added to the pleasure like a cherry complemented a cake. Yes, the pain could stay. But this going slow business…that had to go. "You know, Connor, as big as your dick is, it's not really the destructive weapon you apparently perceive it to be. And I'm *no* delicate flower of the north."

"Jaxx, you're tight and I'm so hard it hurts. I want you screaming in pleasure, not pain." He added in a low voice, "I hurt you last time."

"I liked it. I even relived the entire thing with my vibrator when I got home."

He groaned and dropped his forehead to hers. "Don't start talking like that again. I'm hanging on by a very thin thread here."

She curled her legs around his hips. "If you won't snap that thread, I will."

The second her teeth sank into the flesh of his shoulder, he was a goner. "Fuck." He slammed home and his groan mingled with hers. Her muscles clamped around him, and it felt so good. Better than he remembered. Along with the pleasure was relief – he was finally inside her, finally where he needed to be. It was agony not moving. "Jaxx, you okay?"

A good word to describe what she felt was 'full'. So unbearably yet blissfully full. "Fuck me, Connor."

And there went his sanity. His control was utterly shattered – reason and rationality gone. His lips set in a merciless slash as he ruthlessly powered into her at a frenzied pace. "Is this what you want?"

he gritted out in a harsh voice.

"Yes," she hissed. His mouth took hers in a hot, urgent, dominating kiss. She returned the kiss and drew his tongue into her mouth, teasingly sucking it just as she had his cock. Logic told Jaxxon that they were as close as it was possible for two people to be, and yet her body repeatedly writhed, twisted, and arched beneath him in an anxious bid to be closer. He seemed to have the same frantic need, as his hands grabbed, shaped, clutched, squeezed, and kneaded her body like he was trying to mould her to him. It was as if they were fevered with need, drugged by each other. The tension just continued to build inside her, winding her body tighter and tighter.

Connor groaned as her nails dug into the flesh of his back. "That's it, babe, scratch me." The sweet pain had him driving into her impossibly harder, wrenching louder moans from her. He knew this was going beyond rough, but he also knew nothing could make him stop. Every nerve ending was aflame with the skin-to-skin contact. Every sense was honed on Jaxx, making him totally attuned to her, so that he knew exactly when her release was imminent before she even spoke.

"Connor," she rasped, "I'm going to come."

By then, he had already adjusted his position slightly so that he ground against her clit with every hard thrust. She was practically sobbing now. "Come for me, Jaxx. Let me feel you come." Seconds later, she shattered, screaming, as her muscles clamped bitingly around his cock, triggering his own climax. He bit out a harsh expletive as he exploded with what had to be an unnatural force.

The first thought that Connor had when his brain collected itself was: More. Inwardly, he snickered. Even after she had sucked him like a hoover, even after he had uncovered and tasted every inch of her and lived out his fantasy, he still wanted her. Instead of feeling less desperate for her, he was ready and eager for his next fix.

Conscious of his heavy weight crushing her, he rolled onto his back, taking her with him so he could remain inside her, and lazed her over his chest. Both of them were breathless, limp, and being racked by reverberations. He closed his eyes, well and truly sated.

Jaxxon was glad he couldn't see her face. She didn't want him to read any of what she was feeling. She had been apprehensive about them using a bed, worried that it might make everything seem that much more intimate, worried that she wouldn't find it so easy to keep a chunk of herself detached and safe. It turned out that she had been right to have such concerns.

A traitorous voice within her was insisting that Connor wouldn't have spent such time exploring and pleasuring her and wouldn't hold her so close if this was all physical. The fourteen year old girl in her fully agreed. That naive little girl could stop that crap right now. This was *Connor* for God's sake! It didn't mean anything that he had been so attentive. Of course he was good at sex, he'd had plenty of practice. She supposed that she shouldn't be too hard on herself – he had promised her that he would fuck her until she couldn't think straight, and that was exactly what was happening. Oh she did like a bloke who made good on his promise.

"Tell me how you got into modelling." It was good to be able to form a coherent sentence again. "I just can't picture you pursuing that kind of career."

Keeping her face buried in his chest, she responded tiredly, "Richie approached me when I was working in The Lion's Head."

"Richie?"

"Agent."

"Oh, right. Wait, The Lion's Head? What were you doing, working in that shithole?"

She shrugged. "It was a job; that was all that mattered."

"Where were you living?"

"The block of flats near the pub."

He winced internally. The whole time he'd been living the life of Riley, she had been stuck there. He would have apologised if he hadn't known she would get pissed off with him if she thought he pitied her. "I'm guessing Selfish Arse left you to be the bread winner." If there was one person in the world he despised, it was that self-involved bitch who was single-handedly responsible for Jaxx's low sense of self-worth. The only times Jaxx had ever closed her eyes to the truth were when it concerned Leah. She never wanted to see that Leah was actually a chronic liar and pathetic attention seeker, who could always be counted on to hurt Jaxx in some way. And why would Leah do that? Because she could.

Jaxxon did her best not to tense at his words, but that one sentence told her something she had secretly pondered over. Connor couldn't have seen Leah since she left care – whether it was because she hadn't found him or he hadn't responded to her attempts to contact him – if he assumed that she and Leah had gotten a flat together like they had once talked of doing. The sisters had even taken a blood oath when they first went into foster care that neither would ever leave the other. Snort.

Not wanting to talk about Leah, she changed the subject. "How did you get into F1 racing?"

"It was about three months after I left care. I was walking home from my late-night shift at McDonalds when a red Ferrari past me and stopped at some posh restaurant just ahead."

"Oh Connor, tell me you didn't."

"Of course I did. I'd always wanted to drive one and figured this was my only chance. What I didn't know was that the owner was a rally driver, and he had gone there to meet up with some mates of his who were rally drivers as well. So when I whizzed off in his Ferrari, him and his mates jumped into a Porsche and went after me. I managed to avoid them for ages but – for the first time in my life – I got caught. I was expecting to either get my head kicked in or get dragged before the plod and arrested. Instead, the owner of the Ferrari offered me a placement in the young driver development programme."

"What did he say when he found out you didn't have a license and were a self-taught driver?"

"Same thing you always said: that I could go far if I got my act together."

Jaxxon closed her eyes, feeling contentedness wash over her. Then her eyes snapped open as she suddenly became aware of two things. One, he was idly plucking at her curls the way he used to when they were younger. Two, this was becoming way too comfortable. A strong urge to bolt came over her. She moved to get up, but he held her to him. "I need to pee." She cocked her head. "That your phone ringing?"

It was. "Bathroom's through that door." He smiled as he pictured shagging her in his shower in about, what, five minutes? Digging his phone out of his pants pocket, he saw that it was Dane.

"I know it's late," said Dane, "but I figured you'd be awake."

Something in Dane's voice had Connor tensing. Even though Jaxx was in the en-suite bathroom for the moment, he went into the kitchen to take the rest of the call. "What is it?"

"I just got back from The Pool Hall about fifteen minutes ago. Guess who I found crying *fake* tears all over my couch. Anita Donovan."

Great. "I thought she went back to L.A."

"Well if she did, she's back."

"So sling her out on her arse."

"I must admit, that was my first instinct, but Niki stopped me. Something's off about Anita. She's up to something."

Connor sniggered. "She's always up to something."

"Right, and we wouldn't have known exactly what she was up to last time if she hadn't told Niki first. Niki wants to let her stay with us, play the sympathetic friend, and see if she can get her to spill what her newest little plot is."

"Mate, you don't have to do that."

"She's pretty wound up about the rumours of you and Jaxxon Carter."

Connor stiffened. His protective instincts came rushing to the surface, and all he wanted to do was drive to Dane's place and throttle Anita.

"I've agreed to let her stay a week. Hopefully Niki can come through for us again. She knows what it's like; we've been through this ourselves. And we don't want another spoilt little princess starting some shit."

When Connor went back into his bedroom, it wasn't to find Jaxx naked on his bed as he'd pictured. Quite the opposite. It seemed that she was making another sharp exit. He grabbed the shoe she was reaching for, gaining her attention. He shot her a questioning look.

"I need a reason why I'm going home?"

"You need a reason why you're rushing off. *Again*."

"Oh," she drawled as realisation dawned. "You're one of those blokes."

"What blokes?"

"The ones who like to do the leaving or the dictating when time's up. You don't like the reversal of roles. Well I'm sorry, Connor, but I didn't come here to stroke your ego, I came here to stroke your cock, and I've done that." She seized her shoe from his grip and slipped it on. "I'm shattered, and my bed is calling my name."

"There's a bed right there." He double-blinked when he realised what he had just blurted out. Jaxx looked equally stunned.

"You want me to stay the night?"

No, he didn't, he'd never spent the entire night with a woman. He actually had no idea why he was panicking – and he *was* being panicky

– about the fact that she was leaving.

Jaxxon was fully expecting the 'no' in his eyes, but it stung all the same. "If you're still horny, I'm sure there are plenty of numbers in that BlackBerry of yours."

It wasn't until she had walked past him that the implications of what she had said settled in. "Are you shagging other blokes as well as me?"

She pivoted sharply. "Excuse me?"

"You seem to think *I'd* be up for shagging other people, so I'm asking if you're doing the same." Rage steamed from him as a thought formed. "Are you still shagging that ponce? He's dead if you are." A lesser man would have shrunk away from the anger blazing in her eyes.

"I'm sick of you carrying on like this. You persist in thinking you have some kind of hold over me, when you *do not*. And why wouldn't I think you're still spreading yourself about? My understanding is that this" – she gestured from her to him – "is about strictly sex. No strings, no commitments, no questions. Are you saying you want more than that?" she asked rhetorically, wanting him to realise how he was coming across. He looked away. "Exactly. Don't expect anything of me that you wouldn't expect of yourself." With that, she swerved back around and headed for the door. She nearly jumped out of her skin when he suddenly sprung in front of her.

"Alright, what if…What if we both agree that while we're…"

Amused at his struggle to describe their lack-of-a relationship, she supplied, "While I'm your replacement shag doll?"

Connor did a double take. She had to know he'd never think so little of her. "While we're having casual sex—"

"Oh very primly put."

"—we don't see other people?" He knew he sounded *over-possessive* and unable to control his jealous streak, but it wasn't just about that. The idea of another bloke touching her made him feel sick. As he'd waited in her apartment after the charity event, and the hours had ticked by with no sign of her, he'd known she was busy with her ponce. He'd felt increasingly nauseous until he'd honestly believed he would spew up. Now that he had been inside her and felt her come apart around him, the idea of another bloke touching her was even worse.

Jaxxon hadn't expected him to say that. Not now. Not ever. It was a commitment – teensy, sure, but still one of sorts. It was a commitment that a woman wasn't even guaranteed to get in an actual relationship. Not that Jaxxon thought he suddenly cared for her or anything. She was just surprised that he was willing to go to that length not to have to share her.

He gripped her by the nape of her neck and tugged her to him. "You won't have time for anyone else anyway, not if I'm going to do all the things to your body I've got in mind."

Jaxxon relaxed slightly as he massaged her shoulders. "Alright," she agreed with a small nod. He seemed relieved. There would never have been a different answer from her, she hadn't thought of anyone else since she heard his voice on her machine. "Got to go."

As much as he wanted to haul her arse into his shower for that shag he had planned, he didn't try to convince her to stay longer. He suspected he'd already pushed her by asking her to agree to things being exclusive. The simple contact of his lips against hers had his senses hyper. "If you give me a few minutes, I can drive you." Any other time, he'd have insisted on it, but again he was conscious of pushing her.

"Thanks, but I'll be alright." Jaxxon needed to physically demonstrate to him that her small concession didn't make her another of his rats following the Pied Piper. He needed to have the memory in his head of her casually breezing out of his apartment, indifferent about leaving him behind. She couldn't afford for him to see that she did care for him. Predators and weaknesses…Disastrous mix.

CHAPTER NINE

Awkward – that about described the situation. Jaxxon supposed this was what it was like to have a father sit his teenage daughter down for a 'talk'. Only in this case it was three blokes. And they were all self-appointed honorary uncles. *And she was twenty-two years old.*

Tony, the bugger, had ushered her away from his dining table the second she had polished off the Roast Dinner á la Lily, and had urged her into a lounge where Ollie and Richie were waiting. Tony had gestured for her to take a seat, and now the three men stood looking down at her wearing anxious expressions.

Ollie slapped today's newspaper onto the coffee table in front of her. "Well, aren't you going to flick through it?"

Instead, she mirrored their posture – shoulders back, arms folded, face twisted into a grimace. She didn't need to look at the paper. Anna had raced over to Jaxxon's apartment at a very unreasonable hour of the morning to share all the details about her time with Warren – who she was now dating – and then she had produced the newspaper. There were three photos of her and Connor outside the bar: one of her giving him a wedgie while he was carrying her caveman-style, one of her running from him after she'd played a little with his car, and then one of him holding her close with her legs around his waist while they laughed.

The tabloids, predictably, had blown it out of proportion – suddenly Jaxxon and Connor were infatuated with one another and in a serious relationship: Connor McKenzie so besotted that his primal instincts have kicked in and, for the first time ever, he is territorial over a woman; hard-arse Jaxxon Carter is melting under his sensual nature and his utter determination to have her. She could only imagine what Connor must be thinking of all this. The more she thought about it, the more she became convinced that he would want to get out of this now just to set the world straight.

"Will you leave the poor girl alone," griped Lily, her face a mask of frustration, as she barged into the room. Her short sandy-blonde hair bounced with her harsh footsteps.

Ollie began, "I'd heard the rumours about you and McKenzie, but I didn't think much of them until I saw these photos. Then Tony tells me McKenzie was waiting for you at the end of your photo-shoot on Wednesday like some sort of weirdo."

Jaxxon snickered. "He wouldn't have known where to wait if your secretary had any sense of discretion. A few flowery words and he had my phone number, address, and schedule."

Shocked, Ollie was about to curse loudly, but then he narrowed his eyes at Jaxxon. "Don't you change the subject. We're talking about you and McKenzie."

"I already know what goes where and that babies aren't made in a factory, so we really don't need to have 'the birds and the bees' chat."

"I want to know exactly what's going on with you two."

She shrugged. "I'm using him for sex." She heard Lily chuckle.

"Going by the loved-up expressions on that last photo, the tabloids have a different theory."

"And like most stuff in the tabloids, it can be filed under 'fiction', or 'complete shite'."

Richie smiled gently. "We just want to be sure that you know what you've got yourself into. Connor McKenzie might be handsome and successful but he's also—"

"A good shag," she finished. "That's all I need to know. And anyway, you and Ollie have spent the past *how* many months jabbering on at me to get in some kind of high profile relationship, and now that the tabloids think I'm in one, you're fuming?"

Ollie waved his hand dismissively. "McKenzie isn't like Bruno or that footballer. He isn't some brave yet ever so foolish soul who'll be intimidated by you and do as he's told. He's a law onto himself. I don't like that this bloke who's never chased after a woman has been on your case. He even carted you out of a bar over his shoulder."

"Is this about you not liking him?"

Sighing, Ollie shook his head. The way she looked smitten with McKenzie spooked him. He needed her to understand what was to come. "The reason the tabloids are all over this is because you're both liked by the public for being people who don't live to please others. You're entertaining because when you're angry you show it, when you've got something to say you say it, if you don't want to smile for the cameras you won't. You're not interested in putting on an act for everyone, you're *real*. And now you're together – or so the public believes – embarking on an exciting, spontaneous, no-holds-barred relationship; something most people dream of having themselves."

"I know *I* do," grumbled Lily for which she received a frown from Tony.

"Throw in the fact that most blokes would happily be Connor McKenzie and most females would happily be you, and you've got a very nice following of fans," said Richie.

"They will follow your relationship like it's all a soap opera," continued Ollie. "That means that when it ends, it'll end with the world watching. And believe me, luv, it *will* happen, and it'll be nasty. You won't get a happy ending from him – just ask his past lovers."

Tony held his hands up in a helpless gesture. "We don't want you to be one of the multitudes of girls who have fallen for him only to end up broken."

Ollie nodded. "You won't get to keep your pain private, no, because the world will be watching."

"You've said that already," said Jaxxon in a bored tone. "And for the record, I know that he doesn't do committed relationships. Do you know why that's okay? Because I'm not looking for that. So you can simmer down and breathe, Captain Cautious."

But Ollie couldn't simmer down at all. He didn't want to see this girl, who he instinctively knew had already been through enough, to have to go through what was inevitable if she didn't end things with McKenzie now. He wiped his face with one hand. "Why couldn't you have just picked a nice, well-mannered lad like Bruno?"

Jaxxon leaned forward in her seat. "Do you want to know what nice, well-mannered Bruno said to me when he was plastered at the charity event? He said that I was even more gorgeous than his dick, and that if I was hungry, I could always put my mouth around it."

Everyone but Ollie burst out laughing. "W-well," stammered Ollie, "like you said, he was plastered." He wasn't going to get through to her; he could see that. At least they had the tour coming up soon. That would get her away from McKenzie for a while. Maybe she would see things more clearly with him far away, or maybe McKenzie would meet someone else while she was gone and this could be over before it got any worse.

Jaxxon stretched. "Well, as fun as this has been, I must go." She stood and joined her hands as if in prayer. "I promise to file away all your advice, Papa Wolves."

As she drove back to her apartment, she tried not to think on that advice. Tried really hard. But Ollie had got her thinking. She'd known that she could never come out of all this emotionally unscathed. But she hadn't given much thought until now into how she would be put under a microscope, having every expression scrutinised and dissected. She wouldn't be allowed to wallow and heal in peace. The public would know the full extent of her pain. And, therefore, so would Connor. That was something she really hadn't banked on.

Was Ollie right, was it better to put a stop to all this now?

She wasn't sure that she could. Her yearning for him was just so strong. Even if she did try to end it, she doubted Connor would accept that yet. Not when he'd proposed that they didn't see other people – that wasn't a sign that he was looking to put an end to this very soon. If he wanted to contest her decision to finish things, he wouldn't need to browbeat her. No, all he would have to do was show up, nothing more. As soon as he was in close proximity to her, what was left of her willpower would totally crumble. How sad was that?

So what now? she asked herself as she pulled up outside her apartment building.

She supposed that all she could really do was hope that after a few more close encounters, things would calm down. Obviously, she'd have to promise herself that when it was over she wouldn't curl up like a foetus and pine away. She would do what she'd done when she was fourteen and realised he wasn't coming back; instead of treating it as an ending, she'd look at it as the beginning of something new.

There was another promise she had to make to herself: if she suddenly developed stronger feelings for him, she would put a firm stop to their arrangement. She couldn't be with someone, in any capacity, who she loved who didn't love her back.

It was as she locked the car that she saw the slip of paper jammed behind one of the windscreen-wipers. She pulled the paper free to find that it was actually an envelope with her name on it in capital letters. Once in the empty elevator, she tore it open and unfolded the white, plain paper inside. Only two words were written on it in black ink. 'Die Bitch'.

Oh. Well that was not what she'd expected. She got letters from nutters all the time, but never one that was malicious. It shouldn't have spooked her. Words were just words. But a chill still passed through her, as if the paper was stained with the malice and spite that had seeped from whoever scrawled those two hateful words. Resolved that she wouldn't let some fruitcake unsettle her, she rolled her eyes, sighed, and balled up both the piece of paper and envelope. *The 'bitch' part I can agree with*, she thought with a smile.

She was just feeling a teensy bit more relaxed when the elevator doors opened and she saw that someone was crouched on the floor next to her door. For a reason she didn't understand, she was wary of this woman. As Jaxxon got closer, she saw the look of hopelessness on her face and how she had an arm curled around her stomach. When Jaxxon stopped in front of her, the woman peered up and smiled. It was a sweet, innocent smile…but there was a falsity to it.

"You must be Jaxxon."

The American accent surprised her. Was she supposed to know who this woman was? Her expression said *she* thought so. Jaxxon searched her memory. Yeah, the woman was familiar. A celebrity. If she had to guess, Jaxxon would say she was an actress…?

"My name's Anita," she said sweetly. "Anita Donovan."

Now Jaxxon remembered her.

"I'm Connor's ex-fiancée."

That she hadn't expected.

"Can I come in? I think we should talk."

Her voice and smile were so sweet and pleading and friendly…and yet Jaxxon had no inclination to agree. Her instincts were going off big time here; they didn't like this woman. It was a lot to do with that smile. It was beautiful and pure, yes, but there was that tiny curve to her lips on one side that suggested mischief and cunning. She had seen a similar smile on someone else. Leah. "We can talk right here. But make it quick."

Anita flinched. "You don't like me very much. I can understand. No one likes their boyfriend's exes, do they? But I needed to see you." Gingerly she rose from the floor.

Jaxxon eyed the beautiful woman with a degree of resentment. She had touched Connor – that was all it took for Jaxxon to dislike her.

And claiming to be his ex-*fiancée*...She may be his ex-bed buddy, but nothing more. She waited patiently for Anita to speak.

Anita twiddled her fingers, making a show of being nervous and feeling a little awkward. "I'm pregnant," she lied well. She waited for a reaction. There wasn't one. "The baby's Connor's," she added, just in case Jaxxon was missing the point. Still no reaction. "I thought it was only fair that you knew." She gave a sad, low laugh. "He wouldn't have told you, not until his hand was forced." Finally Jaxxon responded. With a nod. *That's it?*

Fairly pissed off about having to stand there while someone told her a barefaced lie and fully expected her to buy it, Jaxxon dug her keys out of her black, leather bag. "See ya."

"Wait, please, wait," said Anita quickly. This really wasn't going how she'd planned. Jaxxon was supposed to gasp in horror at the news, feel jealous and envious and have an instinctive reaction to want to break it off with Connor.

"Sorry, was there something else?"

Yes, why aren't you reacting like a normal person?! Anita flashed her that famous, angelic smile that had made her billions. "I just want to be sure you're okay. I know it's big news."

"Oh I'm sorry, I'm being rude, aren't I. Congratulations on your fictional pregnancy!" With that, Jaxxon swung the door shut on Anita Donovan's face.

What a bloody day.

The only explanation Connor could find for Dane's behaviour was that he was determined to terminate their friendship. Why else would he have spent their entire tennis match repeatedly commenting on Jaxx's body, *and* on everything Warren had told him about last night, *and* on what was printed in today's newspaper?

'Infatuated', 'besotted', 'territorial' – the tabloids had made him sound like he was...What was that term? Pussy whipped. And it wasn't great when it was broadcasted that you were in a serious relationship when you didn't even believe in the concept.

In his experience, any type of relationship was fickle and unstable. His father proved that when he turned into an abusive alcoholic and, with one single act that Connor never allowed himself to think about, ruined the lives of those around him. His mother also proved Connor's theory when she abandoned him because her new boyfriend didn't want another man's kid around. His aunt proved it when she refused to take him in even though she was the only other family he had. All those foster parents proved it when they passed him around like a parcel.

His impression of people was that their own wishes always came first; that no one could be truly counted on or be truly trusted, and they could all drop people so easily. That was why he lived life the way he did.

Dane had been having a whole lot of fun teasing Connor that Jaxx was his Niki; the woman who would end his 'wayward ways' and have him walking down an aisle and being a daddy. Connor wasn't sure whether he wished that was true or was relieved that it wasn't.

He'd made the decision at just nine years of age to never have any of that. For all he knew, Jaxx felt the same. She had always said when they were younger that she could never see herself getting married. She could actually be as anxious as hell right now because of what the tabloids had printed. He doubted it. She had never much cared what other people thought of her. But what if she looked at that photo of them both looking all cosy and lovesick and panicked that he might want more? She had never explained exactly what her own reasons were for why she didn't want anything more than casual sex between them. But how did he ask about those reasons without sounding like he was hinting for more?

As he sat in the car outside the gym, waiting for Dane, he took his BlackBerry from his pocket. Maybe if he phoned Jaxx, heard her voice, he could put his mind at rest. He would rather see her, but after asking her to agree to them not seeing other people, he didn't want to do anything that might make it seem like things were now more intense — she would probably bolt. Usually he waited a few days before getting together with her again, so he would do the same this time. Still, a phone call couldn't hurt.

"Hello."

Connor tensed. She didn't sound her usual self. There was a mixture of annoyance, fatigue, and fretfulness in her tone. "Just checking to see how you are."

"Why?"

Was that suspiciousness in her voice? "Because the tabloids printed an awful lot of crap and I wanted to make sure it hadn't cheesed you off too much."

"Oh. Like you said, it was just crap. Look, I've got to go."

"Why?"

There was a huffing sound. "I don't need to explain myself if I want to end a bloody phone call." Then the line went dead.

He stared at his BlackBerry, stunned. No one had ever hung up on him before. And what the hell had he done other than ask why she had to go? Had he been right when he speculated that she might be spooked by that photo and was ready to end things? Not a chance would he let her do that! He was surprised by the vehemence behind that thought. Of course they would end it *eventually*. Just not yet. He wasn't ready yet.

Dane hopped into the car and looked curiously at Connor, who seemed annoyed with his BlackBerry. "Can't you get a signal?"

"She put the phone down on me."

He didn't need to ask who Connor was talking about. At any other time, he would have smiled at the situation. "I'm not surprised." Connor's glare switched to him. "Niki just phoned me. Anita walked through the door ten minutes ago. Apparently, she went to see Jaxxon." A string of curses flew from Connor's mouth. "Jaxxon didn't mention it over the phone?"

"No," Connor bit out. Why hadn't she told him? Was that the reason for her mood? Given everything that was going on, there was a very strong chance that she was going to end it between them. Shit. He took off the handbrake, whizzed out of the parking space, and sped onto the road, heading to Jaxx's apartment.

"I take it you're not dropping me off home first then."

"If I get anywhere near your house, it's highly likely that I'll barge in there and strangle that bitch."

"Oh. Good choice then." Dane wished that his best mate wasn't living in a world of delusions. The real reason he was speeding straight to Jaxxon's apartment was that he wanted to check on her. Dane would do exactly the same if it was Niki. He'd been trying to make Connor see the truth, but he was starting to think that it wouldn't happen until Connor was ready to face it.

What concerned Dane was that it could take his stubborn mate a long time to face facts. Jaxxon Carter was a stunner; she had plenty of blokes admiring her wherever she went. If Connor took too long, he could lose her to one of them. Dane didn't want to see that happen to this person who had done a lot for him over the years.

If it wasn't for Connor, Dane's son would never have survived his birth. Niki had abruptly gone into labour when Dane was miles away. Connor had whizzed round to get her, and then whizzed her to the hospital. The doctors had told them that if she had arrived any later, Little Dane would have been stillborn. Never would he forget what Connor had done. It made Dane feel like crap when he was stood in a room with his family while Connor stood alone. Even with his newest conquest hanging off him, he always looked alone. If Jaxxon Carter could change that, Dane wanted her to stick around.

Jaxxon growled for, like, the tenth time in the past fifteen minutes. *Why was it that when you wanted to be alone, you became popular all of a sudden?* Her phone had been like a hot line since she walked through the door. First it was Ollie, who was oh so sorry if he had seemed abrupt and overwhelming earlier. Then it was Richie with the same apology. Next was Tony, who also apologised for the lecture but then went on to *repeat* the lecture. Jaxxon had hung up. Following that, Anna had called – she was going for a meal with Warren and had an overpowering urge to share her excitement with Jaxxon. Then Connor…who she really hadn't wanted to speak to while her brain was so scrambled.

She was certain she didn't have the willpower to follow Ollie's advice and eject Connor from her life, and she was heavily irritated by this. Damn the sod! If he hadn't turned up, they would both be fully functioning people operating on a strictly normal level as opposed to being dominated by a lust so consuming and controlling that it bordered on an obsession.

A hot bath had seemed the best idea to help her relax. For the first time in her life, she had tried bath salts and candles, and the soothing bubble bath that Anna had given her. Until today, Jaxxon hadn't actually known that it was possible to get the simple running of a bath totally wrong. The candles wouldn't stay alight, the different scents didn't gel, and the bubble bath hadn't produced more than ten bubbles. Needless to say, she hadn't stayed in it for very long and had come out more stressed than what she was before.

No sooner was she towel-dried and wrapped in her silk, black robe than there was a knock at the door. Absolutely fricking fabulous. It didn't take a genius to work out that it was Connor. She didn't have the energy for him and his oppressiveness right now. But wasn't this her own fault for hanging up on him? She couldn't exactly ignore the knocking. He'd either keep it up until she answered or pick the lock.

"Hi," her visitor said nervously as she opened the door.

Not Connor. And had she looked through the peephole like she usually did, she would have known that, and then she could have ignored the knocking. "Bruno."

"I know I'm probably not your favourite person right now, but can I come in?"

While she was only wearing her silk robe? Not bloody likely. "I've only just got out the—"

"Two minutes. Please? I promise I won't make any more lewd suggestions."

She had to smile at that. "Alright." He didn't sit down, which made her a little uneasy.

"First, can I just say sorry again for last weekend? I know it's no excuse but I was absolutely smashed and—"

Jaxxon held a hand up, deciding to put him out of his misery. "Bruno, I've heard a lot worse than that over the years. I know you were rat-arsed and messed up over your ex."

He winced and tucked his hands in the pockets of his navy jeans. "That's the thing…"

"There's a thing?"

He sighed. "I was fuming with my ex, yeah, but that's not all it was, Jaxxon. That's why I'm here. It's not going to come as a surprise to you that I like you. As more than a mate."

Actually, it did. She couldn't remember him ever being flirtatious or making hints.

"Jaxxon, I work with beautiful people all the time, but you're different…There's no vanity, you don't look down on people, you don't take it all too seriously. You had me roped in from the start. I didn't do anything about it because when I first met you, things were crazy with your new job, and I knew it had to be hard for you adjusting to everything. I figured that what you really needed right then was a mate."

And he had been a mate, she remembered. Always quick to offer help or advice or...well, anything. But she had been determined to find her own two feet. Still, why tell her this now? "Bruno, I don't understand what you're hoping I'll do with this information."

"I'm not expecting anything. I know you're with McKenzie. I saw the photos." It had hurt to look at them, and it was then that he'd realised exactly how much he'd come to like her...and what a dick he had been for not telling her. "I want you to know that when McKenzie's out of the picture..." He trailed off again, realising how corny 'I'll be there' would sound. He was striving for another way to term it when there was a harsh knock on the door.

"Jaxx!" The voice was demanding an immediate response.

"Oh bloody brilliant." There she was in her slinky robe with Bruno in her apartment with her. No prizes for guessing how this was going to play out. And, to be fair, why wouldn't Connor think something was going on? It wasn't going to occur to him to think through it logically – especially when he thought Bruno was her ex. He was just going to immediately assume the worst and react like a crazy person. "Don't try to tell him nothing's going on, it'll only wind him up more if you speak, and he'll pounce on you like a rabid dog."

"I'm not scared of him, Jaxxon," he said, snickering.

She gave him a pointed look. "Then more fool you." As she had anticipated, Connor barged right in. Then of course he turned to ice when his eyes settled on Bruno. "Connor—"

"What is he doing here?" It was only then that Connor got a proper look at her. And what she *wasn't* wearing. A red mist seemed to fall over his vision. Rage was pumping through his veins and his lungs felt ready to implode. His stomach was twisting and knotting and his gut burned. His entire body ached with the need to lash out. He heard a voice behind him say 'Oh bugger' and realised Dane must have followed him instead of waiting in the car. Connor didn't even bother looking, he only had eyes for the ponce...who he was about to kick the living shit out of. With. Pleasure.

"Connor, before you turn Hulk on our arses, listen to me." She put as much authority into her voice as possible, but it wasn't enough. "*Connor!*" When he started toward his target, she threw herself directly in front of this certifiably insane bloke and did the only thing she could think of to distract him. She whipped her robe open. It worked. His eyes dropped down the length of her body. She knew it would only distract him momentarily, but that moment to insert some semblance of rationality into him was all she needed.

"Now listen to me," she insisted calmly as she re-tied the robe. "Yes, there's a bloke in my apartment and, yes, I'm only in a robe…but you and I made an agreement, Connor. You know me. Would I go against that? Would I have made it if I never intended to keep it?"

No, she wouldn't have. Not Jaxx. Another woman, maybe. But not Jaxx. A part of Connor knew that. A part of him knew that it wouldn't make sense for her to let him in without hiding the bloke if she really had anything to hide. A part of him registered that although she was naked under that robe, the ponce was fully dressed and didn't have the look of a man who'd just had the best fuck ever – and he would have done if he'd had Jaxx. But his brain was spitting images at him of her and Bruno together, and it was making him want to kill. His fists were clenching and unclenching and he was grinding his teeth.

"You best think through that haze, McKenzie, 'cause I'm not being held responsible for something that didn't happen 'cause of what *other* people have made you think about human nature!"

That had his eyes snapping back to her face. Then he saw the strain there. Not just at how he was acting now. She was stressed and tired and he was just making it worse by insulting her like this. His distrust, how easily he found it to believe she would do this, wasn't just offending and annoying her, it was hurting her. He recognised something else too: how he acted now would determine whether he was welcome to ever walk through her door again.

CHAPTER TEN

Taking a long, deep breath, Connor threw an arm tight around Jaxx and pulled her hard against him, aligning her body to his. The feel of her calmed him like nothing else could.

Bruno saw the question in McKenzie's wild eyes and shrugged. He wouldn't let him intimidate him. Jaxxon needed someone strong. "I haven't got an innocent reason for being here, if that's what you're hoping for. The truth is…I came here to tell Jaxxon that I care about her." He heard a groan come from the bloke by the door. It was a sound that said 'you are one stupid sod.'

Connor snickered. "Oh you did, did you?" If Jaxx hadn't been right there, he would most likely have charged at the silly little twat.

"You don't have to worry," Bruno spat bitterly. "She hasn't chosen me over you. But I didn't expect that she would, and I didn't ask her to. I just wanted her to know. By all means stand there looking smug, but let's not forget that once this big passion you've got between you has fizzled out, you'll drop her like a bad habit. It's what you do. Something I'd never do to her."

Connor wanted to growl that it wasn't like that; that he cared for her. But the ponce was right in a way, wasn't he? Nothing changed the fact that when the out-of-control need had been satiated, he would finish it between them. The situation was still the same whether he was doing it coldly or not. He understood that the ponce wanted him to feel like this; wanted to show Jaxx that Connor wasn't going to deny it so that she wouldn't be fooled. One more push – that was all Connor needed – and he'd be on the ponce no matter what Jaxx said.

"And who knows, maybe Jaxxon and I will have that passion as well. It's not always something you know at first glance."

As the ponce's words sank in, a frown surfaced on Connor's face and he glanced at Jaxx. If the ponce wasn't sure there would be any fire between them, they couldn't have slept together, could they?

Jaxxon shrugged as he arched a brow enquiringly. "You're the one who said it, not me."

She was right, Connor realised. And he understood exactly why she hadn't corrected him. Jaxx didn't explain herself to people, and she especially wouldn't have explained herself to someone who had acted the way Connor had. Besides, he wouldn't have believed her anyway, he'd have thought she was just trying to placate him or protect the ponce.

He returned his eyes to the ponce and it was as though he was looking at him for the first time. He didn't see a rival or a threat anymore. He saw a pretty boy who hadn't even been able to bag Jaxx before Connor was in the picture. A deluded hopeful, he decided. "You could never handle Jaxx."

Bruno ignored him and spoke to Jaxxon instead. "You know where I'll be when he does to you what he always does to women. Whether you want me as a mate or more, I'll be there."

A little touched by the sincerity in Bruno's voice, and full of a newfound respect for him for standing up to the red bull beside her, she smiled. "Thanks, Bruno."

"*Thanks, Bruno?*" echoed Connor as the ponce left. She would honestly go running to him?

Jaxx arched a brow and a hip. "What? You thought that once we were done, I was going to lie on the sofa in my pyjamas blasting 'All By Myself' and cry my aching heart out?" A laugh from behind her stole her attention. "You must be…?"

"Dane," he said, chuckling. "I'm a mate of Connor's."

"Jaxxon," she returned.

"Nice to finally meet you." He thought she was even more stunning in person.

Shaking his head to rid himself of thoughts of Jaxx going running to the ponce to experiment on whether or not there was anything between them, Connor held her slightly away from him to establish better eye contact. "Why didn't you tell me she came to see you?"

She didn't need to ask who he meant. "How do you know about that?"

"My wife told me," explained Dane. "Anita often confides in Niki. She's actually been staying at my house."

"My condolences."

"It's to keep an eye on her," said Connor. "She likes to play games and she's obviously playing them now. What did she say to you?"

Sighing, Jaxxon flopped onto the sofa. Bronty didn't look too pleased by that. "She said she's pregnant with your baby."

"The bitch!"

"I thought it might be something like that," muttered Dane. He knew there was no way that it was true that she was pregnant. Anita would have been shouting it from the rooftops if it was.

Connor perched himself on the edge of the coffee table, facing Jaxx. He held her hands. "Babe, listen, Anita was planning to try to get pregnant, but when I found out I got shot of her, so whatever she says—"

"Oh I didn't believe her," laughed Jaxxon.

"You didn't?"

"You honestly thought I'd fall for it? Thanks a lot."

"Well she *is* an Oscar Award Winning actress."

"And she does have that innocent butter-wouldn't-melt-in-my-mouth smile perfected," grumbled Dane as he relaxed into one of the plush chairs.

Jaxxon snorted. "Just because someone has an innocent smile doesn't make them innocent. I know that better than most people."

Connor started at that. Was it possible that Jaxx had finally seen through Leah? Come to think of it, Jaxx hadn't mentioned her, and he hadn't seen her at the apartment. It could be that she had stayed behind in the flat the sisters had rented together, unable to be happy for Jaxx. Or maybe they had fallen out at some point. "So you're alright?" Connor couldn't believe that she wasn't ranting and raving at him for bringing a crazy person into her life.

"Why are you fussing?"

"You put the phone down on me."

"And I'll probably do it again."

Dane laughed. "You should've seen his face. I thought he was gonna smash his phone."

Connor ignored him. "What did you say to her?"

"I congratulated her on her 'fictional pregnancy' and then slammed the door in her face."

A huge smirk filled with pride and amusement spread on Connor's face. *That's my girl.* Before he could say anything else, a knock sounded at the door. Jaxxon rose to open it but he tugged her back down. "You're totally naked under that."

"As the day I was born," she verified, smiling.

"So you're not going to the door. *I'll* see who it is."

Not liking his harsh tone, she snatched her hands from his and rose to her feet. "I know you don't think I'm going to stand for your crap. Either sit or, I swear, I'll take off the robe."

"Please Connor, I beg you, don't back down," joked Dane.

Connor didn't find it so funny. While he was busy glaring at Dane, Jaxx was looking through the peephole.

As much as she felt like enough people had glimpsed her almost naked today, she wasn't going to ignore Anna. She nearly knocked Jaxxon over as she dashed inside, looking fretful.

After assessing Jaxxon from head to toe, Anna raised a brow. "You been having a tumble with Connor?"

"I wish," grunted Connor. It was tormenting him that her naked body was so close yet so far. All he would have to do was loosen that tie on her robe…

Anna blushed. "Hi. Didn't see you there." She turned back to Jaxxon. "I've phoned you, like, a gazillion times but you didn't answer. When you didn't phone me back, I thought I'd check on you."

Jaxxon suspected that Anna had also intended to share more information about her and Warren and was gasping to reveal it. But, obviously, she wasn't going to do it with Connor and Dane there – neither of whom made any move to leave. "How was the meal?"

"Gorgeous. Warren's waiting for me in the car."

"She's seeing Warren?" Dane asked Connor.

"Who's he?" asked Anna. Before anyone else could speak, there was another knock at the door. Anna let Warren in.

Connor sniggered. "Maybe we should just invite the neighbours in as well so they can see you naked."

"Sorry," said Warren, though he wasn't if this was winding Connor up. "I saw your car in the car park and figured you were with Jaxxon, so I came up to say hi."

"Hi," returned Connor then made a gesture for him to leave. He couldn't wait much longer to whip that robe from her body.

Warren laughed. "Alright then. Jaxxon, nice seeing you again, even if it was brief. Dane, want a lift home? Something tells me Connor isn't leaving just yet."

Once they were finally alone, Connor pulled her to him and scrutinised her face. "You sure you're alright?" He certainly wouldn't be if the situation had been reversed.

"I'm insulted that you think I'd be shaken by some pathetic cow's lies."

That comment got him thinking about another pathetic cow. "Have you heard much from Leah since you moved here?"

She stiffened. Faking indifference, she replied, "Why do you ask?"

"It's just that you haven't mentioned her at all. You two had a falling out?"

Jaxxon left his embrace and, purely out of the need to fidget, went to the kitchen to boil the kettle. "I haven't seen or heard anything from her since the day she left care."

That had him frowning. He would never have imagined Leah actually leaving Jaxx behind. "At least you had Roland."

She sighed. "He left a couple of months after you."

The truth hit him like a blow to the gut: all this time, Jaxx had been alone.

"Want one?" She gestured to the coffee tin. He shook his head. "I would've thought you might have heard from Leah," she said casually as she prepared a cup of coffee she had no intention of drinking.

His frown deepened. "Why would I have heard from her?"

"Just before she left, she mentioned you'd told her to find you when she got out of care."

He was just about to pounce on that comment when two things registered that unsettled him. She wasn't looking at him; hadn't since he'd first mentioned Leah. Also, although her face was blank, she had swallowed heavily twice now – a movement that, coming from Jaxx, hinted at pain. He suddenly had a very bad feeling. "Jaxx, what else did she say?"

A long pause. "Enough."

"Define 'enough.'"

"Oh don't make me say it, Connor," she said as she leaned back against the counter, coffee in hand. "It makes me sick just thinking about it."

Yep, the bad feeling was justified. He closed the distance between them and placed a hand on the counter either side of her, caging her in. "*What* did she say?"

Jaxxon met his eyes. "That you loved her, that you'd been shagging her."

He slammed his hand on the counter. "I don't know what I'm more pissed about: that she could want you to believe something like that, or that you actually do believe her!" He twirled around to face the wall, taking a moment to try to regain his composure. He was livid.

"Why wouldn't I believe her?"

He turned back to her. "Oh I don't know, *maybe* because when a chronic liar tells you something so farfetched, it's reasonable to consider that just maybe they're talking drivel!" He laughed a totally humourless laugh. She truly believed he could do that? It explained why she hadn't wanted to phone him after he left her that message asking to meet up.

"It wasn't farfetched. It made sense."

"Tell me you didn't just say it made sense."

Resisting the urge to pour the coffee all over him, she placed it on the counter. "It made me remember all the times she'd whisper stuff in your ear and you'd never tell me what she said."

"It was always a bit graphic, and I knew you'd be upset if you knew how much she used to come on to me."

"And the times when she'd phone, asking you to pick her up, and off you'd go."

"Because she was your sister, otherwise I wouldn't have given a crap whether she got herself in shit!"

"And I'd never met a boy who didn't want her, and she was your age."

"She was a pain in the fucking arse!" he spat, getting more livid by the second. "I absolutely despised her! I wouldn't have touched her with someone else's dick, let alone my own! Christ, Jaxx, how could you not know that it was *you* I cared about?!"

"Really?" she said sceptically. "*If* you cared about me back then, it was as a sister."

"Then why would I have kissed you the night before I left if that was all it was?"

"Other than that one time, never had you kissed me or even hinted that you looked at me differently, so is it any wonder I find it hard to believe there was more to things?!" *Especially when you never came back like you said you would*, she refrained from adding.

"We were only young and you were two years younger than me! Unfortunately, it was hard to remember that – you were a *very* early bloomer and more mature than anyone I knew! I didn't dare touch you because I knew I wouldn't have stopped and you'd have ended up losing your virginity very early!"

"Yeah?!" she yelled back even louder. "Well maybe if you'd had the bollocks to act on what you say you wanted, I wouldn't have lost my virginity to—" Jaxxon stopped dead, swallowing back the rest.

Connor took a long, calming breath. "Jaxx...finish that sentence." If she told him she'd been raped, he wasn't sure what he would do – other than hunt down and gut the sick bastard. But he had to know. It was one of those things that would be worse not to know the truth of.

"Go, Connor." Her voice was toneless, dead.

"Not a chance. Finish that sentence."

At the sharpness of his tone, Jaxxon's blood boiled. He wasn't asking, he was demanding. Like the information was rightfully his to know and she was disobeying him by withholding it. There was no sensitivity there or any respect for boundaries. "You are one selfish, inconsiderate arsehole."

"Why do you hold back from me?"

"Why do you have this insane need to know everything?"

"You never used to shut me out like this."

She growled. "Can't you just accept the fact that my business isn't yours to know?"

"Like it or not, your business became mine the minute you let me inside your body."

"You're wrong there, McKenzie."

"Tell me why you're holding back, why you're shutting me out!"

"Why would you want to be let in?"

He didn't have anything to say to that. He shouldn't want to complicate things any further and yet, at the same time, he wanted to be important to her; someone she trusted and confided in like she used to. He wanted to be to her what she was to him.

"Why would I *let in* someone whose part in my life amounts to using me to satisfy his sexual urges?"

That stung. It belittled what was between them...but it was the truth, wasn't it? "Fine." He stalked toward the door. "I'll phone you next time I get one of those *urges*, shall I?" he added bitterly before slamming it.

It was after at least forty-five minutes of Anna sitting on Jaxxon's sofa, telling her all about her nicely developing relationship with Warren, that Anna realised something: Jaxxon was hurting. The girl always kept her pain hidden so well. Anna might not have picked up on it had it not been for the fact that when she asked what time Connor had left, Jaxxon had winced ever so slightly. And didn't that make Anna feel like absolute crap!

Here she had been sitting, announcing how fantastic things were going and how Warren treated her like a princess…and the entire time, Jaxxon was in pain over a certain F1 driver. Not once had Jaxxon looked envious or bitter, or even attempted to change the subject. On the contrary, she had shot plenty of questions at Anna, wanting every detail she could wring from her and then being so amazingly chuffed for her. She was just *the best* in Anna's opinion.

"Okay, what's he done?" asked Anna gently.

"Oh let's not talk about me and Connor. I'm not spoiling your good mood."

"Jaxxon, please?"

Humungous sigh. "It's not so much something he's done. It's just that…sometimes I just feel like he wants too much from me. First he wanted me to agree not to see anyone else, then he's complaining that I don't 'let him in' and share all my past with him. And you know what really gets to me? When he *does* want to see me, he doesn't phone – he just shows up and expects me to accommodate him. Even worse, I do. I can't help it; it's like I've got no willpower when it comes to him. I'm just his beck-and-call girl and I hate it, but I can't seem to fight it."

Anna nodded. "I was in a situation like that once. It scared me when I realised I always put my life on hold just in case he phoned. I'd be ready to drop everything if he wanted us to meet up – I literally didn't feel like I had a choice in the matter, it was like I was obsessed. But he never used to give me any indication of when he'd phone next, and we never did anything together other than meet and shag. I was like a doormat, I felt so weak…I almost hated myself. And him for taking me for granted. So you know what I did?"

"What?"

"Went abroad." When Jaxxon's eyebrows rose, Anna nodded. "I didn't tell him I was going. I didn't have to because we weren't serious as far as he was concerned. So when he next phoned and realised that I was out of the country and that, yes, I was going to have a life outside of him – that I wouldn't always be dropping everything when he phoned – it made him do a double-take. Then, suddenly, he stopped taking me for granted and shaped up."

She let Jaxxon consider that for a minute before adding, "I think you should do the same. That way, the next time Connor phones, you'll likely be abroad – it'll shock the life out of him that will – so you won't have to worry about trying to resist his offer because it just won't be possible to see him. With all that distance between you, it might make you feel stronger. And it'll teach him a couple of things."

"Like what?" Jaxxon was starting to like Anna's idea.

"Well, he'll learn that he won't always know where you are, even with your work schedule. He'll also learn that if he really wants to see you, he's going to have to do better than just materialising out of thin air or you might not be available. And it will serve to remind him that you have a life that exists outside of him that he can't always invade when he pleases."

Oh Jaxxon was really, really, really starting to like this idea. This was what she needed: some distance between her and Connor, a way of stopping herself from running into his arms when he next turned up out of the blue. It would also be a change of scenery. As it was, Jaxxon had never been abroad in her life.

"And I'll be coming," Anna quickly added. "A girls' holiday, just the two of us having a laugh and mellowing out."

"Aw, Anna, you don't have to do that. I know you're enjoying spending loads of time with Warren right now—"

"All the more reason to go. It'll teach him exactly what it will teach Connor."

Jaxxon couldn't stop a wide smile from creeping onto her face. "Where were you thinking?"

Leaning forward in her seat, Anna returned Jaxxon's smile. "Ever been skiing?"

CHAPTER ELEVEN

Is this who the Eastenders' character Ian Beale is based on? Jaxxon wondered as the cockney bloke in front of her heading for the Bunny Hill again shot her what he seemed to think was a come-get-me smile – it actually came across as an I-am-so-creepy-so-stay-away-for-your-own-safety grin. He was obviously one of those blokes who had a wealth of experience in the art of freaking women out. Oddball.

She knew he didn't recognise her or Anna as celebrities. How could he when they were each snug in several layers: long thermal top and bottoms, an additional long-sleeved t-shirt, a fleece sweater, ski jacket, ski pants, ski socks, neck warmer, helmet, goggles, a pair of waterproof winter gloves, and ski boots. It gave them an anonymity that they needed right now. The fact that Jaxxon was a female was apparently all that was needed to inspire him to flirt so sleazily and poorly.

Only an hour after Anna suggested the skiing trip, they had booked their one-week holiday over the internet. In fact, they had booked a flight for the following morning, completely disregarding both their work schedules. Although Ollie hadn't been thrilled, when Jaxxon mentioned that it was just them, no Connor, he had all of a sudden become very accommodating and supportive. Even to the extent that he offered to take Bronty in while they were gone.

Due to Anna's love of alcohol and vibrant night life, they had settled on staying in Méribel, France – the centre of the Three Valleys with Courchevel and Val Thorens on either side. There, the revelry could start as early as late afternoon within some bars and could carry on until ridiculous hours of the morning. In addition to that, Méribel had 150km of pistes, a few decent snow parks, and lots of non-ski activities.

Earlier – literally two minutes after arriving at their chalet – Jaxxon and Anna had had a little something to eat, and then wrapped up warm in the clothes they had bought on their emergency shopping trip the night before.

If they hadn't been so excited about hitting the slopes, it would have been a struggle to leave their chalet. It was amazing. Contemporary. Spacious. Lavish. Jaxxon's favourite room was the living area which featured two leather sofas, a coffee table that was actually a varnished sledge, an open fire, and a 42' flat, wall-mounted widescreen T.V-DVD with UK Freeview and cinema surround sound. Happy days.

There was a very large, modern kitchen – all marble and chrome and immaculately clean – a dining area with an oak table and chairs to match the solid oak flooring that ran throughout most of the chalet. There were six bedrooms, all en-suite – yes, they were being greedy booking something huge for just the two of them, but they were determined to get something spacious…and that was exactly what they got.

Naturally she and Anna picked the most luxurious bedrooms; both had a gigantic sumptuous bed, modern furnishings, a wall-mounted flat screen T.V., a separate area for dressing, a balcony, and a stylish, pristine-white en-suite bathroom that had heated flooring. There was even a garage for their rented car. And then there was the icing on the cake…a Jacuzzi hot tub and sauna inside *and* outside. The views from the south and west facing terraces and balconies were absolutely breath-taking.

As they had ventured out to rent some ski equipment and arranged a beginner's lesson, Jaxxon had soaked it all up – the ambience, the ethos, the views, the comfort, and the idyllic blend of mountains and snow and the beautifully blue sky. Little by little, all the tension had left her body and been replaced with excitement and anticipation. Although Anna had been skiing before, she didn't consider herself above intermediate level and hadn't wanted to leave Jaxxon, so she came along to the lesson. After going over the basics with them, the instructor decided they were ready to try the Bunny Hill. Although they had fallen a few times, the instructor thought they were brilliant because neither feared falling so were quick learners.

"If he smiles at you one more time, I'm going to whack him with my ski pole," said Anna, gesturing to the Ian Beale lookalike in front of them. "He's severely creeping me out." She shuddered, and it wasn't from the cold temperature. "Not that I'm at all complaining, but why did you slap his helmet?"

"He said he loved my voice and asked if I worked for a sex hot line."

Anna gasped. "The cheeky git!"

"Want to see me ski backwards?" he asked.

"Nope," replied Jaxxon as Anna said, "Not even a little bit."

He didn't seem deterred, not even when their instructor, Todd, directed an impatient glare at him. Jaxxon might have snapped at him if she hadn't been distracted by the cute sight of a bunch of kids snowballing-to-death someone dressed up in a reindeer suit. She remembered the time she had been in a military-type snow fight with Leah, Roland, and—

She let the thought stop right there.

The Bunny Hill, Jaxxon soon discovered, was a small slope that had a chairlift to take them to the top. As they waited in the loading area, she saw that Anna was nervous. "What's up?"

"I don't like these things. There was a rope tow when I last used a Bunny Hill. The first time I went to a beginner's hill and used a chairlift, I couldn't pluck up the courage to push myself off." And then she had been embarrassed as shit when someone from Ski Patrol stopped the lift and helped her down.

"That's because you didn't have me to bitch-slap you into moving your arse."

Anna laughed. "It might actually come to that." Even with Todd's encouragement, Anna found herself fidgeting apprehensively. Side by side, she and Jaxxon waited for a chairlift to come around and then, holding both poles in one hand, smoothly sat on it, allowing it to take them up. Like Jaxxon, she kept the tips of her skis pointing upwards as they ascended. "Bugger, bugger, bugger," she chanted nervously.

"Anna, do you really want to go home and tell Warren you got stuck on a moving couch?"

That was all the motivation Anna needed to straighten her shoulders. As she had told Jaxxon, it kind of intimidated her to know that Warren was an Olympic medal winner. She had never been into sports, and even though she was a celebrity the same as him, she wasn't doing a job that meant she represented her country or that people looked up to her. Mostly people just drooled over her. She didn't want Warren to think that that was all there was to her; that they couldn't enjoy the same things.

As he had told her that he loved skiing and would love to take her himself some time, she was determined to get some practice in so that she didn't make a fool of herself. Anna told Warren about the holiday but swore him to secrecy; he was not allowed to tell Connor a single detail. He swore he wouldn't. In fact, it didn't take much convincing. He seemed to like the idea of Connor being subjected to a little torture. Those boys loved winding each other up. Only one thing concerned her: Warren was a very bad liar.

"Remember," said Jaxxon as they neared the unloading station, "point your skis forward and push away as the chair goes around." After wincing at the sight of the creepy sod on the chair in front making a daring jump off the chairlift and ending up colliding with another skier, the pair glided off the lift and to the side, clear of the upcoming chairlifts.

Anna made a rejoicing sound. Funny how being set on impressing your boyfriend could make you face your fear. At last they came to the slope, and just in time to watch the creepy bloke do an elaborate toss over and become closely acquainted with a tree. She flinched at the spectacle. "Do you think that was an attempt at suicide?"

Jaxxon shrugged. "If it was, it was ill thought out. Someone should have told him a run-up is always advised. On a lighter note, it's our turn."

"Right, you go first."

Remembering all that the instructor had told her, Jaxxon ensured her hands were through the straps on the poles which she held at her sides. She bent her knees, and leaned forward slightly – careful not to lean too far forward or else her skis might get all squirrelly. Then she assumed the 'pizza' position, keeping her skis pointed together and heels pushed out to make a wedge with an open point.

She drunk in the view, admiring the enormous mountains and hills and trees, and the way it looked as though a soft white marsh-mellow blanket covered everything. After taking a moment to appreciate the weird, nerve-wracking yet exciting feeling of being poised on the edge, she slowly began sliding down the slope. To pick up a little speed, she narrowed her pizza position, loving the liberating feeling that came with the descent. Knowing that she could easily fall was unsettling but, at the same time, made the whole thing even more exhilarating. All of a sudden, she felt invigorated.

As Jaxxon reached the bottom of the slope, she widened the angle of her position, which finally brought her to a smooth halt. But she didn't express her delight with herself until Anna reached her side, also having executed a smooth slide down. They giggled like a pair of kids in a playground, overwhelmed by exhilaration and relief and a delicious adrenalin rush.

"Well done," praised the creep as he appeared out of nowhere. "You're both naturals at it. Looked like goddesses the way you did that so gracefully."

And then he made the biggest mistake of his life: he attempted to touch Jaxxon. Having reached her limit with the randy bastard, Jaxxon leaned toward him slightly. "Do you see this pole? If you don't stay out of my face, I'm going to rip you another arse hole with it. Understand?" He gulped and nodded before awkwardly skiing away.

Anna sighed in relief. "Thank the Lord for that."

After a few repeats at a smooth glide down the Bunny Hill, Jaxxon and Anna tried doing turns during their descent. When Todd eventually decided that they were ready to try a beginner's hill, they went for a little something to eat and drink to boost their energy levels before then hitting the other slopes.

By the time they were ready to head back to their chalet, Jaxxon found that although she was physically exhausted, having used muscles that she hadn't known she had, her mind was energised. The whole experience was so strange…like being in some kind of suspended reality. With all the breath-taking views, the snowy mountains, the cold crisp air, the wintery trees, and the luxurious chalet, there was nothing to remind her of home. She found that she could literally forget everything – her stresses, her problems, even the rest of the world.

With each day that passed, all those pressures eased more and more.

Connor grunted and slapped down the set of cards. When did he get so bad at poker? Probably about the same time that he started abusing the test track and overdoing it at the gym and walking around with a permanent hard-on. All of which was brought on by the reappearance of—

No, no, no. He wasn't going to think about Jaxx.

But, then, he didn't really have to think about her for him to undergo any torture. It was now four days since he had last seen her. It was five days since he had last been inside her. He had planned to give it at least seven days before seeing her again, purely to prove to himself that he didn't need her so badly, but he wasn't sure he was going to last much longer.

The fact that he was spooked by how he was absolutely addicted to her wasn't so important now that the raging need was taking over again. His dick was hard and hurting like a twat. Worse, he didn't feel whole. In short, his mind, body, and soul were pining for her. He knew it. He ignored it. Or, at least, he tried to. And the harder he tried, the rottener things got.

Once he had calmed down after their argument, he had started to feel like a right bastard. In truth, he had been angrier with himself than with her; maybe it could be said that he had created this situation. If he had gone back to see her at least once, he would have seen that she was alone and hurting over Leah, and he could have done…well, he didn't know what exactly, but he could have done something. Then maybe she wouldn't be closed off from him the way she was now. Now he knew why she wanted things to be nothing more than casual.

Despite how painfully horny he was, not once had Connor been tempted to relieve the ache using anyone else. Obviously he would never have given in to any such temptation if there had been one. The point was that there had been no temptation. There was one thing he had come to understand in the past few days without her: it wasn't lust that had consumed his blood, it was Jaxx. That was why he couldn't escape from the need to see her, or be with her, or be inside her.

In sum, she had bloody ruined him. He belonged to her as much as she belonged to him, and it terrified him. When she eventually walked out of his life – even the thought of that had his gut twisting – he wouldn't be whole ever again. And yet, he knew he couldn't keep her. She would never settle for someone who couldn't fully commit to her, and even if she was prepared to try it, he would never let her. She deserved better than that. She deserved to start the family she had grown up without.

For the first time, he wished he had more to offer someone. All he could really do was make the most of the time he had with her. With that in mind, he had to question why on Earth he was sat playing – well, losing at – poker and not spending time with Jaxx.

Decision made, he went into his kitchen to phone her mobile. No answer. He tried her home line. No answer. He tried her mobile again. No answer. He tried her home line again. No answer. Half an hour went by and nothing. No answer from either phone, no returning his calls, no answering the voicemail messages he'd left. Unfortunately, Ollie had gotten himself a new secretary and she was not easy to charm like the last one, so that got him nowhere.

"Oi, Warren," he said, a thought forming. "Where's Anna tonight?" Because wherever she was, Jaxx was likely to be close.

That had Warren licking his lips nervously. He'd been dreading that Connor might ask him about Anna in case he accidentally said too much. "Oh, er, she's, um, in…Europe."

Connor frowned. *Europe? Hmm.* Had to be a modelling thing. He was sure he'd heard Jaxx say something about Anna going to Paris and Milan a lot. He checked his BlackBerry again – still no messages.

"Waiting on a phone call?" Dane tried to hold back his amusement. It was obvious that Connor had finally cracked and wanted to see Jaxxon again. Warren had told Dane all about the holiday and how Anna had sworn him to secrecy. But Warren forgot to do one thing: he forgot to make Dane swear to keep it secret from Connor.

Dane had absolutely no intention of withholding the fact that Jaxxon was in a whole other country, where males of all ages could flock around her, and there wasn't a thing Connor could do about it. He was going to go off his rocker. Boy, this was going to be so much fun.

Connor said nothing to Dane's question and shoved his BlackBerry back into his pocket. A few minutes later, he fished it out again and went to the bedroom to try Jaxx's mobile again…still nothing. Home line…still nothing. Secretary…still not charmed. He growled. Jaxx didn't play 'ignore the ring tone'. She'd sooner answer it, tell him to sod off, and then hang up if she didn't want to speak to him. In which case, he had to assume that she hadn't seen his attempts to contact her.

He should be able to shrug and think 'she'll phone when she can.' But wondering when, exactly, he should expect a response was bugging the life out of him. Was this how she felt when he didn't give her any idea of when he'd next be in touch? On re-entering the living area, he caught the latter part of Dane's sentence:

"…doesn't bother you she's on holiday without you?"

"Who's on holiday?" When Dane and Warren exchanged an odd look, Connor frowned.

Warren cleared his throat. "Anna."

"Oh, so it's not some modelling job she's away doing?"

"No," said Dane. "A last minute booking wasn't it, Warren?"

"Er, yeah."

Dane folded his arms across his chest. "I'm surprised you didn't go with her, even if three is a crowd."

"Another time, I will." Warren sighed inwardly. He wasn't going to pull this flippant act off – not while Dane, whatever his game was, seemed like he intended to let it slip to Connor that Jaxxon had gone with Anna.

"I wouldn't like it if it was me," said Dane gravely, shaking his head.

"It's just a holiday, she's not relocating."

"Yeah, but still…Just the idea of Niki that far away from me…I think I'd lose my head."

"How far away are we talking?" asked Connor.

"France." Warren inwardly winced as he realised he'd revealed a detail of the holiday.

Dane *tsk*ed. "It's still a foreign country, which means it'd be too far away for my liking. Even worse, the French are supposed to be right smoothies. And women love those European accents, don't they?" He sighed. "Personally, I'd be a paranoid wreck."

"I trust Anna." That hadn't stopped Warren from worrying, though.

"Yeah, but do you trust the smoothies around her? That's the question. You told me Anna loves her drink. One weak moment, one very smooth smoothie…" Dane jiggled his head. "At least she's not on her own and there's someone to make sure she's got her wits about her."

Connor was starting to feel as though he was missing out on something important.

"What about you, Con?" asked Dane. "If it was Jaxx, would you be alright with it?"

"Did I say you could call her Jaxx? She's *my* Jaxx, she's Jaxx*on* to you." Then it occurred to Connor that Dane had spoken in a very odd tone. Suddenly, as snippets of the conversation flicked through his mind, it all came together. He took a deep breath, determined to maintain his composure. Then he slowly turned his head to look at Warren, who was looking awfully nervous. "Warren, who's Anna on holiday with?"

"A mate," he said flippantly.

"Would that mate be Jaxx?" His voice was deceptively patient. Warren's twist of the lips and hesitation to speak told Connor what he needed to know. "When did they leave?"

"Monday morning."

"*Monday morning?* What, and you never thought to tell me?" When he heard Dane chuckling quietly, he rounded on him. "You've known all this time as well, haven't you?" The chuckling stopped.

"No need to have a panic attack," said Dane. "They'll be back on this Monday coming."

"*Monday.*" He couldn't wait that long to see her. Nor did he want to. What he wanted to do was grab her, yell at her for sodding off like that, and then shag her senseless.

Dane kept all amusement from his manner. "Now, see, you haven't really got a right to go all nuts, have you? Okay, so Jaxx – sorry, Jaxx*on* – didn't tell you she was going on holiday. Should she have to tell someone who only shows up when he feels like shagging her?"

Connor knew what Dane was getting at, and he knew he was right, but it still didn't take the sting away of her buggering off without a word. "Where in France?" he asked Warren.

"Oh I can't pronounce it."

Dane laughed. He had to admire Warren for his never-ending loyalty to Anna's promise.

"Is it in the North, South, what?"

Warren scratched his head. "Um…"

"Is it near Paris?"

"I'm really not comfortable with these questions."

Connor pinned Dane with his serious gaze. "You know where, don't you?"

"Come on mate, don't get yourself all worked up. She's probably not into the French accents." It was killing Dane not to laugh. "It's just the tourists you've got to worry about. You can't blame them if they try sniffing around her. I mean, come on, you would have. Even believing she was in some high publicity relationship with an insane twat, you'd have still tried your luck. I bet you're glad you and her made that agreement to not shag other people. Tell me, though, did you specify if kissing or touching or oral sex was allowed?" Connor growled. Dane faked a horrified gasp. "Tell me you definitely specified no anal sex."

As much as Connor knew that Dane was trying to get a rise out of him, he couldn't help but give it to him. The idea that she was so far out of reach…"How would you like it if it was Niki, eh? If I knew where she was and wouldn't tell you?"

Dane smiled. "Ah, but Niki's my wife. What is Jaxxon to you again?"

Completely exasperated by his two mates, Connor dug the heels of his hands into his eyes. "Alright," he bit out. "You've made your point, Dane."

"And what point is that?"

It made him ache to say it. "I haven't got any rights over her, and I haven't got the right to know everything that goes on in her life. There. I said it. Now where is she?"

"I'm not so sure I'm comfortable passing on this information."

"Dane…"

"Not until I at least know what you're going to do with it."

"Only the same thing that you'd do if it was Niki."

"Now hang on a minute," Warren quickly interrupted. "You can't go over there and butt in on their holiday." But he saw by the determined expression on Connor's face that that was exactly what he was planning to do.

"I'll tell you what," Dane said to Connor, "I'll tell you where she is if you admit why it is you want to see her so bad."

"This isn't some game," retorted Connor.

"If you can't admit it to me, how are you going to admit it to Jaxxon? She doesn't strike me as the type of person who'll be okay with you turning up like that just for a shag, or to prove the immature point that you can always find her. If she thinks that's the kind of crap she'll have to put up with, she'll end it right there. So, get some practice in, admit why you want to see her so bad."

As a last ditch effort to find out her whereabouts without putting himself out there, Connor looked at his other mate.

Warren shook his head. "I happen to agree with Dane."

"Well?" Dane raised his brows, waiting.

Connor sighed. "Do you have to be such a twat?"

"It's genetic, sorry. Do you want to know where she is or not?"

He slumped onto the couch and covered his face with his hand, sighing again. When Connor finally plucked up the nerve, he released his face. "I miss her, alright."

"And not just shagging her?" Dane wanted Connor to hear himself say it aloud.

"No. Although I do miss that. I miss *her*. Happy now?"

"Méribel, France."

"She's gone skiing?"

"I'm not sure where exactly they're staying, but Warren knows."

Warren groaned. Why oh why did he mention the holiday to Dane? "Anna's going to have my balls for this."

Dane smiled. "Well it seems to me, then, that you should go with him. You're both going to have a lot of explaining to do. Might be best to have each other to lean on for strength."

Warren shook his head at Dane. "You're loving all this, aren't you?"

"I told the pair of you that I would get you back for the shite you pulled at my bachelor bash *and* my wedding night. Oh and let's not leave out the stuff you put in the best man's speech just in case Niki didn't already know I'd been a bit of a slut in the past. Excuse me for finding some sweetness in revenge." He smiled, unashamed. "Go on then, get your arses on a plane, and go see your girls."

At the risk of entering the world of stalking, Connor immediately booked a flight to take him to Jaxx.

CHAPTER TWELVE

Crap! Crap! Crap! The word circulated around Anna's brain as she read the two text messages that Warren had left for her. The first was sent five hours ago with news of his and Connor's pending arrival and the time of their flight. The next was to announce that they had arrived at France 'safely' – like she cared about that part – and would be there in something like forty-five minutes. He had sent the last one *thirty-five minutes ago*. If only she had checked her phone when she first got back instead of now just before they were going out again!

Crap! Crap! Crap! To think she'd been worried about impressing Warren! It turned out that he was going to be the one having to do the impressing, because unless he had some way of getting back in her good books, she was going to do a Jaxxon on him: she was going to kick him in the balls.

Not five minutes ago, Anna had been thinking about just how great Jaxxon was doing with some space away from Connor. The past few days had been such a laugh. Hitting the slopes. Going dog sledging. Almost getting a concussion while ice skating. Drinking until all hours of the morning – well, that was mostly just Anna. Gulping down all that gorgeous French wine and cuisine. Abusing the hot tub and sauna. Trying to talk French and failing miserably. Not once had they mentioned Connor or anything else stress-related since they arrived. And now, thanks to the big gob on her boyfriend, the perfect holiday was going to be tainted.

"Have a guess who has left over a dozen messages on my phone," said Jaxxon as she entered Anna's room.

Anna's eyes widened. "Saying what?"

"Just that he wanted to meet up, completely unaware that I'm not even in the country." The thought of that made Jaxxon smile.

Anna winced. Crap! Crap! Crap!

"I'll phone him after we've been to the restaurant. Come on or we'll be late for our table."

She considered telling Jaxxon about their soon-to-arrive visitors, but if she did that then the person getting yelled at would be her rather than the two arses who were truly at fault. All Anna had done was trust her boyfriend with a secret.

Grudgingly, Anna sent a message to Warren, strongly advising him and Connor to unload their stuff while she and Jaxxon were out. She contemplated telling them to wait at the chalet, but then she decided it would be better for Jaxxon to first see Connor while they were in public. Anna figured that Jaxxon might very well go ape shit, so if things were going to be smashed, she would rather it wasn't anything from their chalet. *And, who knows, maybe the fact that they were in a public place would make Jaxxon contain herself.* Of course it wouldn't.

Twenty minutes later, they were at the front of the queue within the restaurant, which was one big posh bugger in Jaxxon's opinion. The walls and ceiling were covered with oak wooden slats that matched the oak-brown floor tiles. It might have made Jaxxon feel like she was in a box if the ceiling hadn't been so high. The fantastic part was that one side of the two-floored restaurant was all glass.

Anna tried not to fidget and squirm, but how the hell was she supposed to remain calm? Those two idiots would have unpacked their stuff at the chalet by now and would be here any minute. There could be bloodshed. She saw that while Jaxxon was busy admiring the interior, the maître d' was gaping at her in a way that suggested he knew who she was. A few moments later, they were seated at one of the best tables near the glass wall. Considering that their booking had been last minute, it was obvious that this table hadn't been reserved for them. It was a circular table, she noticed. Good, because soon they would need to cram two other people on it.

"I love it when this happens," said Anna, referring to the special treatment. Even better, they were presented with a complimentary bottle of red wine when handed their menus. Immediately she poured herself a glass. She needed the calming effects of alcohol.

Jaxxon looked at Anna curiously. "Are you alright?" The girl was chugging down that wine like it was the drink of eternal life. Come to think of it, she had been restless since before they left and had been nibbling on her lip like she did when she was dreading something.

"Of course, why wouldn't I be?"

"Anna, what's going on?"

"Just remember that I love the bones of you, I really do." She poured herself some more wine. *Holy Mary Mother of God, keep her calm, I'm begging you?!*

"Anna, make sense."

"And don't forget that violence doesn't solve anything. Well, it doesn't solve everything."

"Why would I be inspired to become violent?" And that was when she felt it – tingling down her spine as the hairs on the back of her neck stood on end. Ever so slowly, she turned her head. She vaguely registered that Warren was chatting to the maître d'. Most of her attention was taken up by the figure beside him that, as always, had the most overwhelming presence…and was staring right at her.

An oppressive sensual hunger struck her, and desire instantly began to course through her body, heating her blood and twisting her insides. Even while she was mad as hell at him, she wanted him. What cheesed her off more was that a part of her was glad to see him.

The instant Connor spotted her, he felt like he could breathe again. The knot in his stomach untangled, and the ache that had been throbbing in his chest for days stopped abruptly. But the throbbing in his pants didn't ease one bit. In fact, it worsened as need assailed him violently. She was his addiction, and going cold turkey had left him a mess. Seeing her eyes alive with fury only served to make his cock harder.

Anna observed as Jaxxon and Connor's gazes met and, instead of the verbal and physical explosion she was expecting, there was that same electrical exchange of pure, primal need between them that she saw at the charity event. Just like then, the people around them were caught up in the moment, in the excess sparks of desire that surrounded the couple. It was there and then that Anna came to a conclusion about Jaxxon and Connor: as much as their craving for each other was primitive and raw, their connection couldn't be on just a physical level. A link that intense couldn't only survive on sexual hunger. It would need the involvement of the mind and the soul just as much as the body.

Jaxxon continued to hold his eyes as he stalked toward their table at a casual, non-threatening pace. He stopped before her and slowly bent down, pressing the softest lingering kiss to her lips. She wondered why she hadn't slapped him yet. She wanted to. Really wanted to. But instead, all she seemed to be doing, despite her anger, was devouring the sight of him. Their gazes remained locked the entire time that two more chairs were added and Anna and Warren took positions on either side of her, almost as if protecting her and Connor from each other. That left him opposite her, which made it easier to snarl at him.

Anna, scowling wildly at Warren, spoke first. "We were just about to order starters before you interrupted our meal and, also, our holiday."

Warren gave her a pleading expression. "Look, how about we enjoy the meal and then we'll talk about it when we get back to the chalet?"

"Translation: let's not argue in public?"

Back to the chalet? Jaxxon held back a growl. So not only had they interrupted the holiday, they were planning on staying. And in *their* chalet. For them to have gotten inside it, Anna had to have left the key for them somewhere outside. Jaxxon would deal with her later. When she was sure she could speak without the sound being animalistic.

"Garlic bread," drawled Warren. "Haven't had that in a while. What about you?"

"The soup," Anna said through her teeth. As much as she was glad to see Warren, she wanted to throttle him right now. So far, there had been no outburst from Jaxxon. When she was silent, it wasn't a good sign.

Warren turned to the lump of stone on his right. "Connor, what do you want for starters?"

"For starters…" He hardened his gaze on Jaxx. "You can tell me why you left for France without even a goodbye."

Hoping to distract Jaxxon from giving Connor a very heated response, Warren quickly turned to her. "And you, Jaxxon? What're you having?"

Only one thing had stopped her from lashing out at Connor after his remark: she knew that was what he wanted. A reaction would show she was ruffled, unsettled. She wouldn't give him the satisfaction of seeing her lose it. She was resolute on keeping her rage controlled. But that didn't mean she was going to sit and have a civil evening with him. She consulted the menu. "I'll have the 'Get over the Fact that My Business Isn't Yours, You Prick'."

"I had to find out days later from Dane," said Connor. "My two best mates knew exactly where you were, but I was purposely kept out of the loop."

She could almost believe he was genuinely hurt by that.

"You couldn't even manage a text message to let me know you were going away for a week? All you would have had to do was press a couple of buttons. Wouldn't have even taken you two minutes."

"You're going on at me about the simplicity of text messaging when you've just flown all the way to France to argue with me?"

"Oh I don't just want to argue with you." The implication was in his voice, in his eyes.

"Do you always follow your bed buddies abroad?"

Warren nearly choked on his wine, but no one at the table seemed to give a shit.

"You're not my bed buddy," said Connor quickly.

"Oh?" She arched a brow. "Then what am I?"

You're mine, he found himself wanting to say. He leaned forward. His tone was grave, cautioning. "Don't ever make out that I think that little of you, Jaxx."

The appearance of the waiter was welcome, giving her a reprieve from her stare-out with Connor. They all ordered their starters and main meals. Other than those coming from Warren, each order came out robotic. It was then that Jaxxon noted that Anna's mood was no better than her own. Maybe she hadn't played a part in their coming here. The poor waiter nearly jumped out of his skin when Connor growled.

"What was that for?" she snapped when the waiter scarpered.

"I didn't like the way he was looking at you."

Anna snickered. "That was nothing compared to the stares she's been getting over the past few days." Yes, she wanted to cheese Connor off just like he had cheesed off her best mate. "If you thought you being here would discourage that, I'm thinking you'll be proven wrong. Why do you think we got such a fab table? And then there's the complimentary bottle of wine. We've had a load of freebies since we got here because of how admired she is. Aw, there was this one bloke who stuck a piece of paper with his phone number onto her ski pole. And another who sang a song to her on the karaoke." She left out the fact that Jaxxon flipped him off.

Noticing that Connor was getting even more frustrated, Warren gestured for Anna to leave it there. But with a wide smile on her face, she continued. "It was hilarious when that tall, blond Viking-like bloke asked her to write her autograph on his pecks. It wasn't so hilarious when that little old man asked her to do it. She's had quite a few people come up and ask to have a photo with her. I don't know how they even recognised her with all her ski clothes on. I think a lot more would have approached her if she wasn't known for telling people to sod off."

There was a little silence then – Connor striving to remain in control, Anna trying to think of how else she could wind up Connor, Warren wishing he could get his beautiful girlfriend to shut up, and Jaxxon condemning herself for the fact that she couldn't stop thinking about that kiss that Connor had given her a few minutes ago. He'd never kissed her like that before, it was actually affectionate. And that fourteen year old girl in her wouldn't let that fact drop.

The starters came then. The silence continued as they ate. Jaxxon and Connor stared at one another while Anna glowered at Warren and he looked at her apologetically.

The way Jaxx seemed so calm and collected was nibbling at Connor, mocking him. Here he was digging deep for the strength to not drag her out of the place, make her promise never to jet off like that again, and then fuck her until she couldn't take any more. She, on the other hand, was calmly sipping her soup and her posture was totally relaxed. He wanted her as prickly as he was. "The chalet's great, isn't it. I can't wait to try out my bed." Connor held Jaxx's gaze. "I picked the room that overlooks the outdoor hot-tub." Her room.

Jaxxon didn't give him the rise he wanted. "It's quite comfy that bed. I always end up falling asleep on the couch, so you're welcome to it."

"Not joining me?"

"You came all this way for a shag? Oh, Connor, you should have just sent me a simple message saying you wanted to break off our agreement; then you could have fucked whoever you wanted right on your doorstep."

He leaned forward. "If you keep talking about fucking, I'm going to lose my composure and throw you over my shoulder again. You remember what happened last time I did that?"

Just the memory of that night, just thinking about him being inside her again, had her clit throbbing. "Yeah, I remember. It was alright."

"You're doing a lot of pushing, Jaxx."

"Oh I'm sorry, were you expecting a show of open arms?"

"I don't need your arms open, babe, just your legs."

His cocky smirk had her gritting her teeth. *I won't give him a reaction.*

I won't give him a reaction. I won't give him a reaction. But then, as if her hand had a mind of its own, it flicked the spoon in his direction; the dollop of soup splattered over his face and black shirt. The giggle literally popped out of her. Anna was chuckling too. Warren seemed an equal blend of horrified and amused. Connor, however…well, he looked like he wanted to rip her liver out and eat it.

Grinding his teeth, Connor wiped away the soup and dumped the serviette back on the table. He had told himself that he wouldn't retaliate, but she was still giggling and it was grating on his nerves. He took another bite of his garlic bread then slung it at her face. He managed to keep his laugh silent, but he couldn't stop his body from shaking. Both Anna and Warren seemed to be bracing themselves for Jaxx's wrath.

Jaxxon was totally dignified in her movements as she removed the buttery grease and breadcrumbs from her face and hair. Then, moving too abruptly for him to have prepared himself, Jaxxon snatched her dessert spoon and launched it at Connor. It hit his forehead with a thunk, which only made her chuckle again. Then he sloshed his glass of white wine all over her *favourite* cashmere sweater, hence Anna's horrified gasp, and he had more or less signed his death warrant.

Jaxxon booted him hard in the shin and simultaneously flicked vinegar and salt at him. Pre-empting what she was going to do next, Connor seized the opened bottle of wine and placed it on the neighbouring table. That just pissed her off even more. She reached onto the table behind theirs and grabbed a bottle of – aha – *red* wine. Connor warned her with a look, but she just smiled as she splashed the contents all over him. Then she slammed the bottle down onto the table and glared at him.

"You drowned me in red wine," he said disbelievingly.

"That's right, prick."

"And I reek of vinegar."

"You ruined my favourite top." She turned to Anna then. "Toilets?"

Although Anna was terribly conscious of the deathly silence and the amount of eyes on them, she didn't feel the need to shrink in her seat as she normally would have. No, it was the boys' fault and, besides that, she was drunk so for now it didn't matter. As if what was happening was perfectly normal, she casually gestured to the ladies' restrooms as she sipped more wine from her glass. Jaxxon, of course, stomped off.

As she stood examining the stains on her sweater, debating whether it could be saved or not, a string profanities flew from Jaxxon's mouth. God, she wanted to kill that bloke! It wasn't enough for him to turn up out of the blue and interrupt her holiday, oh no, he had to go and ruin her favourite top as well!

Sure, it was only a sweater, but it was the first item of clothing she bought with her first wage from Ollie. It had sentimental value. She didn't have many things that could be considered sentimental to her. She had always made a point not to have any such things, having grown up in a place where things generally weren't yours for long. Just when she tried snapping out of the mind-set of not relaxing or treasuring anything…Urgh!

If he had any sense of self-preservation, the miserable little arsehole would be scarpering out of here! At that very second, the door slammed open, arsehole barged in and locked it behind him. So he *didn't* have any sense of self-preservation.

Connor had entered the restrooms with every intention of giving her an intense verbal rollicking, but then he found her in only her bra and pants and his intentions quickly changed. He slowly advanced on her.

She shook her head wildly, gasping at the barefaced cheek of him. "Do not think you're having your way with me, McKenzie." Her eyes helplessly dropped to his muscled chest as he removed his soup/vinegar/wine-soaked shirt. She forced them back to his face. In his gaze was lust, heat, desperation, and…something else, something she didn't recognise.

"Look, you've had your fun: you've ruined my holiday, you've ruined my evening, you've ruined my favourite sweater! Just go, and don't ever come near me again."

He halted. "You think I came here to mess up your holiday? You think I would do that? That I would ever *want* to do that?"

"Yeah, to punish me for daring to go somewhere without asking you first."

"This isn't me punishing you or playing some game." Dane had been right; he was going to need to tell her the truth if he had any hope of stopping her from finishing this.

"You expect me to believe that you got on a plane and came all the way here just because you felt like a shag?"

"I came here because I missed you."

That shocked her to silence. She might have laughed if he didn't look so serious. He must have meant he missed being inside her, it had simply come out wrong. "And you couldn't wait until Monday?"

"No, I couldn't. As much as you drive me bloody mental and make me want to spank your arse, I missed you."

There it was again. "Your dick missed me, you mean."

"My dick as well, yeah." He began advancing on her again.

Completely knocked by the things he was saying, she found herself suddenly mentally off-balance and was backing away rather than standing her ground. She hadn't even taken four steps before her back met a wall. She should have been fighting him, condemning him, cursing him. But those three words had totally thrown her, especially when the desperation in his eyes gave emphasis to that claim – desperation that she could also feel sizzling in the air. He had never looked at her like that before. And so, instead of denying him, her body reacted by sending tingling sensations to her clit and releasing a rush of moisture from her core.

Connor snatched the sweater from her grip and flung it aside. Then he crammed her against the wall, his forearms resting either side of her. "And you missed me," he whispered against her neck, enjoying the feeling of her skin against his.

She snorted, hoping her voice wouldn't come out shaky with her desire. "Do you think I consider a food fight to be a mating ritual?"

His voice was low. "If I put my finger inside you right now, it would come out wet, wouldn't it?" She swallowed hard and he smiled inwardly as he spoke into her ear, "I need you just as much, Jaxx." To prove it, he ground his rock-hard erection against her. "I'm obsessed with you. Addicted to you. You're a blow to my self-control, do you know that?"

Now Jaxxon was even more thrown. His iron control was what gave him his strength against everything he had been through and had protected him from more hurt. What he was basically saying was that she had a power over him that made him vulnerable. She made him vulnerable, and yet he'd come to her.

He brushed his lips against hers. "I know you're pissed with me, Jaxx. But you don't really want me to go. What you want is for me to drive as deep inside you as I can and fuck you." He tugged on her bottom lip with his teeth. "Don't you? Here. Now. Right up against this wall." Ever since she had told him she loved a good shag against a wall, he hadn't been able to get the image out of his head. As he felt a shiver ripple through her, he raked his fingers through her hair and devoured her mouth with his.

Jaxxon felt another shiver run through her – his kiss was coated with all his pent-up arousal, but it was also a drugging kiss; something that wrenched at her soul. And she didn't have a hope in hell of fighting him. Not after his admission. But then, why fight it when she needed this too? Giving herself over to the sensations, she locked her arms around his neck and pulled him closer as she opened up fully to his kiss.

Relief surged through Connor. She wasn't pushing him away; she was being as gorgeously responsive as always. Then lust fogged his mind and all he wanted to do was lose himself in her. But not before getting reacquainted with this delectable body that was his. He roughly cupped a breast and she groaned into his mouth. He loved that she liked things intense just as he did. His mouth then landed on her nipple as he sucked and bit it through the black lace, making her back arch so that she was curving her body into his. Wanting to give her some of the relief her body was begging for, he quickly and nimbly dealt with the buttons and zipper of her pants and then slid his hand inside her thong, cupping her.

Jaxxon groaned again. How did he always manage to do this to her? One touch and she was primed for him. Sometimes he didn't even need to touch her. The sensations that he ignited were as agonising as they were pleasurable, as unbearable as they were addictive. Only he could ever do this to her. She knew that just as surely as she knew that she *had* missed him.

He burrowed a finger inside her. "So wet," Connor murmured against the lace of her bra as he added another finger. He lifted his head to watch the pleasure flit across her face as he fucked her with his fingers. Then she was practically riding his hand, frantically seeking relief. As much as he loved the sight of her like this, it wasn't enough, he needed to taste her. Abruptly he sank to his knees and yanked down her pants and thong. She stepped out of them and her shoes. Then he lifted one shapely leg and hung it over his shoulder. He swiped his tongue between her folds and groaned. Her taste was like...Fuck.

There wasn't a word to describe it. It had all his senses exploding. He'd missed it.

"Oh God," she rasped as he tortured her with sensual licks.

"Not God, Connor," he said, now flicking her clit with his tongue and then swirling around it as he dug into his back pocket for a condom. "Say it."

Why was it that he always seemed to want her to say his name?

"Say it."

She might not have if she hadn't heard the tearing of a wrapper and then the lowering of a zipper. Thank God! She needed him inside her quickly. "Connor." Then he was stood before her with the leg that was hung over his shoulder now resting in the crook of his arm. Holding her eyes, he plunged into her. A noise that was something between a moan and a sob tore out of her. For once he wasn't treating her like she was fragile, and she delighted in the burning sensation of him stretching her. "Deeper."

"Oh I'll fuck you deeper," he assured her in a harsh voice as he palmed her arse and lifted her, rearranging her position so she could lock both of those luscious legs around his waist. "But first…" He brought a hand down hard on that perfect arse.

Jaxxon jerked in shock. Did he just spank her?

"Yeah, I did. That was for just drenching me in wine and vinegar and soup." He did it again, wrenching a gasp from her. "That was for jetting off without a word and not even answering my calls." This next spank was harder, causing her to gasp loudly. Moisture flooded his dick – so it turned out that she liked being spanked. "And that was for even thinking that I never cared about you."

Just as she was about to curse the bastard, he plunged into her again, going even deeper this time. The pain was as sweet as always, making her groan and shudder. She felt his tongue lick over her pulse, and then he was sucking on the patch of skin there. She had missed his hot tongue tasting her like this, had even missed his bites. Almost as if he read her thoughts, he bit down hard on her neck.

"Ready to take all of me?" When she nodded, he gripped her hips and withdrew. Then he slammed into her, seating himself to the balls. Her muscles clamped around him like a tight fist. "Jesus, babe." He had needed this, *her*, so badly. He sought out those brown eyes that he knew would have that wild, stormy look in them. "Jaxx, I need to fuck you *hard*." His tone made it clear it would be rough and fierce.

"Good." His nostrils flared, his eyes darkened and then he was pounding into her with jackhammer thrusts. She had to bury her face into the crook of his neck to try to muffle the endless stream of moans, groans, gasps, and sobs that were literally erupting from her throat. Minutes later a huge, lingering orgasm washed over her, but he didn't stop. He continued to surge into her in that masterful way of his, building the friction within her again.

Connor knew that the press of her nails into the flesh of his back was drawing blood but, if anything, it only spurred him on. Like he needed spurring on! He was hanging by the thinnest thread but he didn't want it to end. It had scared him that she had seemed to want time away from him. He needed this; needed to be inside her; needed to hear her moaning his name, clinging to him, coming apart around him.

"Connor, I'm going to come again."

He pounded even harder, clutching her arse even tighter as he did. "Now, Jaxx."

Her release ripped through her entire body, shattering her. She sank her teeth into the juncture between his neck and shoulder to muffle her scream.

"Christ, babe," he growled as her muscles clenched around him and triggered his own forceful climax. When his brain eventually switched back on and he was finished gasping for breath and being rocked by reverberations, he kissed her gently. "Admit it, you missed me."

She tried to hold back a smile but half of it surfaced. "Maybe a bit." Though he'd confessed his weakness for her, Jaxxon couldn't bring herself to do the same. It was worth noting that if she did, he'd shit his pants, thinking she wanted more. But that wasn't her reason: she couldn't do the same because whereas he'd walk away from this unscathed, she wouldn't.

He missed her because she was his addiction – addictions could be cured. He'd walked away from her once before and been just fine. She missed him because she cared about him too much for her liking. That wouldn't go away. She knew that because she'd cared for him this much since she was twelve, even when he'd left. Still, she was resolute that if her feelings ever evolved into something stronger, she'd be gone faster than Houdini out of a knot.

CHAPTER THIRTEEN

After a shower to wash away the after-effects of their food fight – a shower during which they savoured the joys of oral sex before having another shag for good measure – Jaxxon and Connor collapsed onto the luxurious bed in the chalet. Jaxxon could only assume that they had been a little noisy because Anna was blasting one of her C.Ds ridiculously loud. Either that, or she and Warren were using the music to disguise the sounds of their own fun.

She was glad that the couple was no longer in danger of arguing. After all, it wasn't Warren's fault that Connor was a lunatic. A lunatic who had gone striding from the restrooms with Jaxxon slung over his shoulder – he'd been too impatient to get her out of the restaurant and her legs had been too unsteady after their reunion in the ladies' room to match his pace. They had tried apologising to the maître d' for the food fight, but he actually thanked them for their dispute, suspecting it would get his restaurant new publicity.

"Ow," whined Jaxxon as Connor sharply tugged her to him, snuggling her naked body into his. She was surprised when he did nothing more than hold her comfortably close and play with her wet ringlets. "How long are you staying?"

"I was thinking of leaving Monday, same as you."

So this really isn't just a stop off to get his jollies. Jaxxon couldn't decide if that was a good or bad thing. The fourteen year old girl in her was absolutely thrilled and reading all kinds of crap into it. But twenty-two year old Jaxxon knew better: it was likely that even if he had missed her, something she wouldn't have believed if she hadn't seen it in his eyes, his main reason for coming was that he was too possessive to cope with the idea of other blokes being around her without him being present. And there was the fact that he was insatiable.

"How's the holiday been going? You and Anna enjoyed yourselves so far?"

"We've had a right laugh. We've moved onto the intermediate slopes now."

"Yeah? Do me a favour: don't take it too hard when I beat your arse on those slopes tomorrow. You were always a bad loser."

"*You* were the bad loser. I remember you swiped the board when I was winning at Monopoly. That time when I beat you on the go-karts, you didn't speak to me for about an hour."

He chuckled, idly drawing circles on her back with his index finger and marvelling at how soft her skin was. "You must be thinking of Roland."

"I take it you've been skiing before."

"Not in France, but yeah. I went with Dane and Warren a few times before Dane married Niki. I'll begrudgingly admit that Warren's the better skier. You ever been abroad before?"

"No. You know, I never pictured myself going skiing."

A lot of things Jaxx said made Connor feel like he'd had a punch to the gut. He'd been abroad more times than he could count. To think that each time he had been away having a ball with his mates, Jaxx had been all alone, concentrating on nothing more than getting by…"I did very nearly come to see you once, you know." His voice was low, full of regret. "It was your fifteenth – the first birthday I'd missed since meeting you."

At the very mention of that birthday, she stiffened. "It doesn't matter." She tried to think of a subject change, but the memories of that day hit her too hard.

He felt her tense. Had he really hurt her that much? He hated himself right now. "I didn't stay away because I didn't care, Jaxx. It was just…I had this vision of going to see you and" – subconsciously he held her tighter – "you either laughing at the fact that I'd even turned up, or seeing you with someone. I'd have beaten them to a pulp, Jaxx; I wouldn't have been able to stop myself. I figured you were better off without a person like me in your life."

She was glad he hadn't turned up that day. Even though she had come to terms with what had happened, it wasn't something she enjoyed sharing, and there would have been no way of keeping it from him if he had come. But if he had just turned up even *once* before that day then so much may not have happened.

She had never truly put any blame on Connor, especially because that would mean absolving others to some extent of their actions. But if he hadn't done what he did to those boys before leaving, if he hadn't made them want revenge so badly then maybe...No. She wouldn't dwell on the 'what ifs'. Pain was just part of life.

"You're miles away, Jaxx." She tensed again, and he noticed that she was still keeping her eyes tightly shut, as if afraid her secrets might shine from them. "Look, I was wrong to expect you to tell me the ins and outs of everything. I just hated that you didn't feel like you could confide in me the way you used to. But I see that's my own fault. What I'm trying to say is that I'm not going to pressure you to tell me anything again, but if you ever want to..."

That stunned her. It didn't sound like Connor. Warily she opened her eyes...and saw only sincerity in his. As if to assure her it was the truth, he brought his lips to hers. It wasn't one of his demanding, dominating kisses. It was soft and drugging, and she felt herself relax.

"There's something I need to know, Jaxx," he said as he cupped her face. "I need to know that you believe me that I never touched that selfish bitch."

She found that she actually did believe him. Even though she hadn't allowed herself to think about him or their argument during the holiday, it was almost as if a part of her brain had been subconsciously sorting things out. He was right about her sister. Leah hadn't been able to form a sentence that didn't have some deception within it. Jaxxon had always preferred to believe those lies than believe that her sister would have this need to hurt her all the time. "I believe you." He gave her another one of those drugging kisses, this one filled with relief. Hoping to escape the subject now, she said, "I need to get some PJs on."

"You'll have my body heat to keep you warm." He dragged the pile of blankets and bulky duvet over them. "Now sleep."

Sleep? "You're going to stay with me the whole night?"

"Mm-hm."

"But—"

"Jaxx, sleep." He knew what she was thinking: that this wasn't something he did, that there were other rooms. He didn't want to properly acknowledge that he actually wanted to lie with her and simply hold her while they slept, or that he liked the idea of her being there when he woke up. He'd never seen the attraction in that before. He didn't want to explore why he did now.

With morning came the discovery of the magic of morning sex, something Connor intended to make the most of during the remainder of the trip. If he was right and Warren was itching to comment on Connor having slept in the same bed as a woman the entire night, he held himself back. Wise man. After breakfast, they all bundled up warm. There was no stopping the smile that spread on his face at the sight of Jaxx – even though she looked like she was about to go strolling on the moon, she was absolutely adorable. Amazingly, her movements were still as sensual as always.

"You're dying to laugh, aren't you," observed Jaxxon.

"What I'm dying to do is rip all that stuff off you," he said as he grabbed her waist and yanked her against him. "I don't like knowing there's that much between your skin and mine, and I really don't like that I'll have such a big job getting to your body."

"The hard work will do you good."

"It's going to be a lengthy job. Maybe I should start it now."

"Jaxxon!" Anna yelled from her bedroom. "Your phone's ringing!"

Jaxxon dashed from the living room to her own bedroom and dug deep into her bag. "Morning Oliver," she greeted as she answered.

"You know," began Ollie, "I really shouldn't be surprised to hear that you had a food fight in the middle of a posh restaurant, but I actually am."

"I take it the papers got wind of it." That was going to make the maître d' very happy.

"I'm looking at a very interesting photograph of you with a face like thunder drowning McKenzie in red wine."

Jaxxon suspected that Connor wasn't going to see the funny side of that photo having been seen worldwide. "He ruined my sweater."

"You told me it was just you and Anna going on this trip."

"That's because it was the truth. Connor and Warren paid us an unexpected visit."

"There's also a photo of him carting you over his shoulder out of the ladies' restrooms where, according to the tabloids, you both had been arguing."

"At least they thought that it was *arguing* we were doing," she mistakenly said aloud.

"What?"

Moving quickly onwards... "We did apologise to the maître d', but he was ecstatic about the idea of his restaurant getting publicity. I take it the tabloids see us as nothing more than wild animals now."

"Actually, it's gone as a positive for you."

She noticed that Ollie didn't sound very pleased. He obviously still didn't approve of her and Connor. "How?"

"Do you have any idea how many couples sitting in restaurants suddenly, for one reason or another, have an overwhelming urge to throw food across the table? They don't do it because they fear making a scene – something I wouldn't expect you to understand. They love that you and McKenzie shoved society's etiquette aside like that, and of course they like to see that you're a normal couple – as they're still under the impression it's an actual relationship – who argues just the same as everyone else. Are the boys still there?"

"Staying 'til Monday."

Ollie groaned. "I don't like that he showed up like that. I don't like this caveman crap that he pulls. I don't like that you haven't made him go home."

Jaxxon mocked, "I can't help it, Daddy, I love him, please don't make me give him up, I—"

"Alright, fine, I'll see you Monday."

When she joined Connor, Warren, and Anna outside the chalet, it was to find them studying her ski map.

Connor gestured to the all the markings she had made with a red pen. "Are all those X's the slopes you've been on?"

"No, it's where I hid the bodies."

Shooting her a playful snarl, he fisted his gloved hand in the snow and launched a clump of it at Jaxx. That sparked off a grand scale snow fight between the four of them – boys against the girls. When twenty minutes went by and neither side showed any signs of weakening, they agreed to a tie and headed off to rent Connor and Warren skiing equipment.

Jaxxon might have been a bit put out to discover that Connor was just as good a skier as he had claimed to be – confident, smooth, skilled – if it wasn't for the fact that he seemed to have forgotten she was such a quick learner. He'd therefore been shocked to see her competence level on the slopes. When she bettered his timing, it wasn't a good moment for Connor. It was a great moment for Jaxxon.

What had been even greater was seeing Anna's delight at Warren being genuinely proud of her skiing abilities. Even sweeter, although he was an expert skier he had insisted on staying with Anna the entire day on the intermediate slopes, wanting that time with her. Warren then instantly went up in Jaxxon's estimations. And suddenly, at the sight of Anna's happiness and the playful scowl on Connor's face, Jaxxon was glad that he and Warren had come.

They decided to try a different restaurant that evening, and then afterwards they went to one of the bars. It was one that Jaxxon and Anna hadn't tried yet and, to Anna's delight, was open until the early hours of the morning. Jaxxon was surprised by how stylish the interior was. Despite the massive use of colour, nothing clashed and the décor was perfect for the atmosphere. Sporadically situated around the bar were clusters of leather sofas framing artistic, white, snowball-shaped tables that had a flat surface.

It was while Jaxx and Anna were in the restrooms and Connor was at the bar with Warren that he heard a friendly male voice behind him drawl his name. Connor turned to see, just as he had known he would, a fellow F1 driver. "Kev." They slapped each other's back in greeting, as they usually did.

After Kev and Warren exchanged greetings, Kev asked, "So how've you been, Con?"

"Alright. You?"

"Great, yeah. I'm over here for my birthday. I'm having a private bash upstairs in the VIP room. You and Warren should come up."

Before Connor could respond, three women and two men surrounded Kev and he quickly began making introductions. "Connor, you know my girl, Lorraine, and my sister, Kim. Next to Kim is her bloke, Roy, and a mate of mine, Peter. And you must recognise this one." He gestured to an incredibly sexy blonde whose single had just reached number one in the charts.

Connor had seen her a few times before now. A singer. She shot him a seductive smile that was filled with sexual promises. She seemed about to say something to him – in fact, she might have done – but his focus immediately shifted to the husky laugh and the 'isn't that just bollocks?' that travelled through the door of the restrooms ahead of Jaxx.

Again he was torn between smugness and irritation when heads turned to look at her. She was looking as sinfully gorgeous as always, dressed in a black, satin dress. But once her eyes met his, he was thinking of nothing but her. As usual, his need for her hit him like a sledgehammer, stealing his breath. All he wanted to do was roll up that dress, snap her thong, and then drive deep inside her. It always left him with the same feeling: like coming home. Suddenly, he was very homesick.

As she and Anna headed toward Connor and Warren, Jaxxon sensed the sudden tension in Anna. Following her gaze, she saw a woman who was eyeing up Connor and standing a little too close to him. For once, Jaxxon didn't struggle with the identity of the celebrity. It wasn't a face you could forget. Lotti Rivers: the platinum selling solo artist known worldwide was, without a doubt, one of the most beautiful people Jaxxon had ever seen.

To her surprise, Connor snaked an arm around Jaxxon's waist as soon as she neared him, making her senses suddenly hyper, and the lust she was feeling intensified ten-fold.

"I hadn't believed it," said Kev. "Kim told me it was in the papers that you were all loved up, but I said no way."

Jaxxon wasn't surprised when Connor tensed at the word 'love'. Most males would, especially if the relationship wasn't serious. She bit his earlobe and squeezed his arse – he was then officially distracted.

"You up for it, Connor?" asked Kev, gesturing to the indoor balcony of the VIP room. "Come on, you can't refuse the birthday boy."

"Jaxx, Anna, this is Kev, a mate of mine. He's having a party upstairs."

"You should come, it'll be a good laugh," said Lotti. To Connor.

Jaxxon saw that he was intending to say no because of Lotti. As much as the last thing she wanted was to be around this floozy, she wasn't going to let it show. Not to her, not to Connor. It would reveal too much about what she felt. "Are the drinks free?" she asked Kev.

"All night."

"It would be a crime to turn down free ale."

The VIP room was similar to the floor below but the furniture was better quality and practically everything sparkled. A mix of blue, silver, and white balloons decorated the place – dozens of them were resting on a net that was hanging above the dance floor, obviously intended to shower the dancers at some point in the night. There was an extravagant buffet, but it wasn't yet open, to Jaxxon's disappointment.

She wasn't sure who was more surprised when Connor laced his fingers through hers, him or her. But he didn't release her hand as they strolled to a table and she didn't retrieve it. Not even when they parked themselves next to each other on a leather sofa. Strangely, the contact felt…nice. Of course his usual possessiveness was there in his manner, but it wasn't beating at her, suffocating her, tiring her. It made her feel safe and protected.

For a short while, Kev, Lorraine, and Kim spent some time talking to them. Jaxxon found them to be pretty down to earth people. Kev actually made her think of Roland, only he was without that geeky intelligence that she found Roland so adorable for. While the boys talked 'cars', Lorraine and Kim asked Jaxxon and Anna about modelling and Ollie.

Then Lorraine begged Jaxxon to tell her if the rumours that once circulated about her and Bruno had any truth in them. Instantly Connor, who had obviously been keeping one ear on the conversation, tugged her to him and said he wanted her to himself now. Rather than be offended, Lorraine and Kim had said 'awww'. Jaxxon didn't see what was sweet about that.

It occurred to Connor that he had been experiencing a lot of first times on this trip. Here was another: he actually felt uncomfortable by the presence of an ex-*acquaintance*. He didn't remember much about her other than her name was Elena. Or maybe it was Elaine. Suddenly, he actually felt ashamed of the life he'd led. A life that he would at some point go back to, but he wouldn't go back to it the same person. No, because Jaxx would take a chunk of him with her when she left his life, she just wouldn't know it.

Jaxxon picked up as easily on his discomfort as she did on the snarl coming from the voluptuous redhead at the bar who looked ready to gouge someone's eyes out. "I can't work out whether that snarl is directed at me or you. I take it that you were going through a period of having low standards when you shagged that one."

"I forgot how cute you are when you're jealous."

Her eyes snapped up to his. Amusement was plastered over his face. "Jealous?"

"You've got that same look you used to get when we were younger whenever the girl who lived next-door used to shout 'hi' to me. You even called her a slut for it once."

She ignored Warren and Anna's chuckles. "I just didn't like her, that's all."

"I only used to smile at her to wind you up, so I could see that look on your face that you're wearing right now."

"I'm *not* jealous. I just don't like being snarled at, which I'd say makes me pretty normal."

"Forgive me for not feeling sympathetic – I have to put up with you getting ogled all the time. Not that I blame the oglers, especially while you're in that dress that is, in fact, a creation of the Devil. Come here." He leaned in, but she shuffled to the other end of the sofa.

"No. It's about time you learned to exercise some self-control, McKenzie. Besides" – she pointed at the bottle – "I don't want to take advantage."

He leaned in again. "Have the advantage, take it, I don't want it."

"Hands off, you randy sod," she giggled. "I need a pee. I'll be back in a minute. Hopefully you'll have some self-control by then."

Anna got up to follow her but then paused as she reached Connor. Seeing that Jaxxon was out of hearing range, she said to him, "Don't give her anymore emotional bruises."

His brow creased. "Excuse me?"

Yeah, it was fair to say her words had come out of nowhere, but as she'd watched the playful exchanges between Connor and Jaxxon, she'd sensed something: Jaxxon loved him, she just didn't realise it yet. "I don't want her hurt."

"Are we really having this conversation?" Was he really being given 'the talk' by an eighteen year old girl?

"People meet her and think she can't be hurt. So did I, but I've learned that what makes her tough is that when she *is* hurt, she deals with it."

"I don't need a lesson on Jaxx, alright. I know her a lot better than you do."

"Oh so then you know why she shies away from social touches? You know why she refuses to celebrate her birthday? You know why the smell of Vodka makes her wince?" His expression asked her to verify she was serious. She nodded. "I'm just making the point that you might have known her inside out once, but you've been out of her life for eight years."

And he hated himself for it. "Has she ever...Has she ever talked to you about..."

"About whatever went on that makes her hold a huge piece of herself back from everyone?" She shook her head. "But something happened to her, Connor. Something bad, I can tell that much. I've never asked her about it. I know that if she wants to tell me, she will.

But I'm starting to think it's not something she'll ever want to tell. That's what you have to accept. You might never know."

He sighed. "Look, if it makes you feel any better and puts an end to this awkward talk, I've already told Jaxx I won't pressure her again. The…arrangement we have is simple enough, so I don't see how she can be hurt."

Anna regarded him through narrowed eyes. When she had first seen Connor acting weird and possessive with Jaxxon, she had thought it was because he wanted her to belong to him. But soon she realised that he believed she already was his. She couldn't understand how he could be prepared to walk away from someone so important to him.

"If either of you think that telling yourselves it's not a real relationship means you're emotionally protected, you're kidding yourselves." With that, she quickly made her way to the ladies' restrooms, only to find Jaxxon conversing with someone begrudgingly. Lotti spun and smiled at Anna, offering a 'hi there'. Her voice was friendly, but Anna detected an undercurrent of deviousness.

"Alright, Anna," said Jaxxon, observing her apprehensiveness. She couldn't blame her. This woman had something to say, and Jaxxon was getting brassed off with how long Lotti was taking to spit it out. "Lotti, this is Anna. She's also a model."

"I don't know how you guys do it. I'm forever getting my photo taken and it drives me insane. I could never stand there all day in various poses. But we use what God gives us, don't we, even when he doesn't give us much to work with."

Jaxxon almost growled. Although the words sounded harmless enough, there was an insinuation in her tone and gaze that said there wasn't much more to models than their appearance – something which Anna feared Warren believed. It wasn't the only buttered up insult Lotti had delivered in the past few minutes.

This was what annoyed Jaxxon so much about this world: it seemed that no one was straight with anyone and, for some reason, they seemed to think that backward insults were very clever. "You know, I heard that most singers aren't actually singing live, even when they claim to be. Is that true?" A brief, quiet laugh escaped Anna. "I suppose it must be to stop you from getting things like Laryngitis all the time."

Although Lotti hadn't yet managed to intimidate Jaxxon, she didn't let it faze her. "I'll admit my career choice isn't all rosy. It's definitely not the best lifestyle. You hardly sleep, hardly have any time to socialise because you're just constantly on the road."

"It must get a bit lonely," said Anna with fake sympathy.

"Oh yes it does. Whenever I've had a boyfriend, it's been *disastrous*. They expect to come first, and I didn't work so hard to get where I am to push it all aside like that, you know?"

Anna and Jaxxon both nodded, silently wishing she'd just come out with it.

"And you never know who's around you because they want to be, and who just wants what publicity will be in it for them if they are." Again Anna and Jaxxon nodded. "That's why I've always understood why people like Connor McKenzie and Dane Andrews live the way they do – no attachments, no commitments."

'Live the way they do', not 'used to do'. Oh. *Now* Jaxxon understood what Lotti was all about: she didn't believe that Connor had suddenly changed just like that. Jaxxon had to give her credit where it was due.

"I tried to tell Anita Donovan that, you know," Lotti quickly added.

"You know Anita?" asked Anna, barely keeping the growl from entering her voice. Jaxxon had told her before they left for France all about that nutcase.

"It was so sad how things ended between her and Connor." Lotti shook her head. "But I had warned her that it was the only way it could end if she pushed things with him."

Jaxxon forced a dramatic yawn. "Oh sorry, it's just that people who don't just say what they really mean bore me *so* easily."

For a moment, Lotti was lost for words. It wasn't often that people weren't intimidated by her, and Jaxxon Carter certainly wasn't. Now that her eyes had that famous, feral gleam, Lotti was feeling even more ruffled. Finally she collected her thoughts and straightened to her full height. "I just think you're foolish if you're anything like Anita and think that you and Connor are really anything serious. People like Connor McKenzie and Dane Andrews don't change. Take it from someone who's just like them."

"Hmm." Anna crossed her arms. "Funny you should say that…Dane's actually married now. Did you not know?" If she recalled rightly, his wife's name was Niki. Jaxxon had told Anna about how Dane and his wife had Anita staying with them where they could keep watch over the living time bomb.

Lotti sneered, but before she could think up a smart retort, Jaxxon was speaking.

"Sorry, hang on," said Jaxxon. "You think you and Connor would be a perfect match – is that what, in so many words, you're trying to say?"

"Oh no," giggled Lotti. "I'm not looking to get involved with anyone, but I'll be honest with you, I've got every intention of using him for a while once you two are over."

"You're very confident he'll want you," commented Anna.

A snicker popped out of Lotti. "Oh he'll want me."

Vanity always made Jaxxon wince. "Well don't let my presence stop you from making your intentions clear to him." She swept a hand out in the direction of the door.

"I'm sorry?"

"I'll head over to Kev and Lorraine with Anna; that'll give you undisturbed time with him."

"He's not exactly going to do anything with you here."

"You obviously don't know Connor if you think that. He does what he wants: The End. If he wants you as much as you say, you'll be taking him home with you tonight, won't you?" Jaxxon held back her instinctive reaction to slap the tramp. If she hadn't held back, it would have looked as though she was intimidated by Lotti and insecure about Connor, giving weight to everything Lotti was saying.

In truth, Jaxxon was a little intimidated. Lotti was beautiful, even if a high percentage of her was silicon. And Connor, as Lotti had pointed out, preferred his sex life to be the epitome of 'simple'. So, yeah, of course a part of her was panicking that he would take his out now, that he would say, 'It was fun while it lasted, Jaxx.'

"You're giving me permission to come onto your boyfriend?"

"Don't tell me you're not as sure of yourself as you say." As Jaxxon fully anticipated, Lotti didn't back down. She gave a carefree shrug that said 'You brought this on yourself.'

As Anna watched a hip-swaying, arse-wiggling, hair-flicking Lotti stroll out the door heading for an unsuspecting Connor, she knew that whatever he did now would decide whether he was allowed to keep both his bollocks. Oh Jaxxon wouldn't castrate him if he chose Lotti. No, she would say all's fair in love and war and wave him off. But Anna…if he hurt Jaxxon, Anna would castrate the bastard.

"Hi."

The seductive, sickly sweet voice came from behind Connor where he stood at the bar with Roy. He turned to see the sexy blonde from earlier licking her bottom lip and eyeing him as though she was a chocoholic and he was a Cadbury's Dairy Milk bar. Lotti Something-or-Other.

"I didn't get a chance to introduce myself before. I'm Lotti, Lotti Rivers."

Rivers? No, he wouldn't have guessed that was it. When she held her hand out, he just stared at it. Why did Americans always like to shake hands? He might have taken it just to humour her, but her expression, the tone of her voice, and her body language all made perfectly clear what she wanted. "I'm with someone. Which you already know."

Lotti dropped her hand but refused to drop the issue. "Yes, I've met Jackie."

He didn't bother correcting her. He would bet she knew what Jaxx's name really was.

"I was just telling her I'm a good friend of Anita Donovan." It was impossible to miss the flicker of pure hatred that passed over Connor's face. "I told Anita not to expect anything from you," she quickly added. "But she was convinced there was more to things."

Her seductive voice slithered over him. Her finger played across her impressive cleavage, drawing his attention to it. "If you have a point, make it."

She didn't let his abruptness put her off. Instead, she stepped closer to him, making sure she rubbed her breasts against his arm. "My point is that I know you like things simple; so do I. The way I see it, you and I can help each other out."

He now had a perfect view of those plump breasts. *Very* plump breasts. The word plump couldn't apply to anything else about her. She was tall and slender, and was a woman who obviously kept in shape. And yet, he wasn't interested. If there was no Jaxx, he definitely would have been. Lotti was extremely attractive and exactly the type he usually went for, but compared to Jaxx, she was as ugly as sin. There was no one who could compare to Jaxx, could ever even come close. "Like I said before, I'm with someone." He gave Lotti his back.

Had he really just dismissed her? Lotti gaped. No one had ever done that before. Was this what it felt like to be ordinary? She wasn't being rejected, she assured herself. He must be under the impression that Jaxxon would fly into some sort of rage. Lotti had heard she was temperamental like that. "You don't have to worry about *her*. She sent me over here."

That had Connor pivoting on the spot. "What?"

"I told her I was interested in you, and she encouraged me to tell you and let you decide for yourself who you wanted."

"Oh she did?" A smile crept onto his face. He could believe that. Jaxx wouldn't show weakness. Plus, she'd find some kind of morbid enjoyment in the discomfort this would put him through. After scanning the place, he spotted her chatting to Anna. Without removing his eyes from her, he began edging through the throngs of people toward her. As though she sensed his gaze, she looked right at him, and that was all it took to send a fierce, primal need rocketing through his veins, demanding release, demanding her. Not any woman, Jaxx.

There was no denying that she had utterly ruined him. She was without a doubt the most amazing creature…and he had no idea how he would give her up. That wicked smile of hers had his dick hardening to painful proportions. He crowded her body with his. "I've just had a very *un*interesting conversation with a blonde who swears you gave her your blessing to come onto me."

Jaxxon did a mock gasp. "Should I not have? I just figured it wasn't my place to warn her off when we aren't technically in a relationship."

He leaned his forehead to hers. "We said there would be no one else while we're—"

"Having 'casual sex', yeah I remember." She shrugged. "Still, it seemed only fair for you to know who's interested in you for after we're finished and you're—"

At the very idea of that, his control slipped. He grabbed her by her nape and mashed his lips with hers, thrusting his tongue inside her mouth just as he wanted to thrust himself into her body. Each stroke of her tongue against his seemed to be dragging him down deeper into that place where there was only her. He groaned. "I wish we were alone right now. Let's just go."

"No, you can wait," she laughed.

"Don't make me throw you over my shoulder again."

"If you do that, everyone will know I'm going Commando."

His eyes fell closed and he groaned again. "It is such a good thing I hadn't known before now or I'd have lost my grip on my sanity long ago. Time to go, babe."

"Can't we try reining ourselves in like normal people?"

He ground himself against her as he spoke devilish words into her ear. "I need you, Jaxx. Don't you want my fingers inside you? Don't you want my tongue licking you and tasting you? Don't you want me to fuck you hard the way I know you love?"

His whispers were making her wet. Not good. "Connor," she said in a reprimanding tone. But he kept up the whispering and grinding. "Alright, enough," she eventually snapped. He was delighted that, as usual, he got his way…which just made her want to punch him right in the face. That was up until they got back to the chalet and he did all the things he promised; then she just wanted to collapse in his arms and sleep right there like that. And she did, with him holding her to him – something he did for the remaining nights of the trip.

CHAPTER FOURTEEN

It was little more than ten minutes after Jaxxon and Connor's session of morning sex – their last ever morning sex, she couldn't help but note – was over that she heard her phone ringing. Once upright in bed, she answered, "Hello." She swatted the hand that reached around her and cupped her breast.

"I've checked your flight details," said Ollie, "and everything's on schedule, no delays."

"Good."

"The boys still with you?"

Was she being paranoid or did he not sound his usual self? "Yeah, they've managed to get themselves on the same flight as us."

"If Anna wants Warren to take her home from the airport that's fine, but I'll be picking you up." It was completely non-negotiable, his tone told her.

"Hang on a minute, what's with this abruptness?"

A short pause. "It's just important that I speak to you before you go back to your apartment."

"What? Why?" She stood sharply, bracing herself for whatever impact was to come.

"Just trust me, alright. It's important I speak to you first."

"Not good enough."

"I'll be waiting at the end of the terminal, don't dawdle."

"For Christ's sake, Ollie, what aren't you telling me?" But he was gone. Pacing the room, she dialled his number but his phone was now switched off. As was Richie's. As was Tony's. "The bastards."

"What's wrong?" It was the third time Connor had asked her, yet still he got no response. Rising from the bed, he approached her and seized her gaze. "Who are bastards, and why are they bastards?"

She exhaled slowly, hoping to calm herself. "Basically, Ollie doesn't want me going back to my apartment without seeing him first. He said he's picking me up from the airport. Something's wrong, I could tell by his voice, but he won't tell me what. Conveniently, his, Richie's, and Tony's phones are *currently unavailable.*"

He wanted to tell her it was probably nothing, but the fact that no one was willing to tell her anything until they were face-to-face with her didn't sound good. Before he could say another word, she was dragging out her suitcase and slinging her belongings inside. He tried to calm her down, as did Anna, but their efforts were futile. Connor wasn't surprised.

He suspected that Jaxx would be fine if she knew what had happened. Sure she'd be swearing and cursing all over the place, but she would be alright. It was that she didn't know what was wrong that had her like this; she couldn't deal with it because she had no idea what she was supposed to have to deal with. The not knowing was cracking her up and leaving her the space to imagine all kinds of things.

As such, neither he, nor Anna, nor Warren had been able to offer her any words that would reassure her. Her uptight, nervous mood stayed with her, which brought her problems while going through airport security. Connor was thankful that the guards were more amused than offended during the brief body search when she told them to get their grubby hands off her or they would each lose a bollock. Her mood also earned her anxious looks from other passengers. If they hadn't recognised her as a celebrity, they might have mistaken her for a suicide bomber or something.

When they finally reached the end of the terminal at Heathrow airport, Connor half-expected her to launch herself at Ollie and throttle him, going by the murderous expression on her face. Clearly Ollie was just as worried, because he immediately raised his hands in a placatory gesture. It didn't help him.

"You bastard," she hissed when she neared him.

"Shh, let's go somewhere private," urged Ollie.

"Oh not a sodding chance," she whispered abrasively. "Either you tell me right now what's been going on, or we'll be testing how well you can balance on one bloody leg because I'll have snapped the other one."

He sighed. "Someone broke into your place last night, trashed it, and scrawled words all over the walls in corn syrup – obviously hoping it would look like blood, which it does."

Anna gasped. Warren said 'You're joking'. Connor let loose a string of curses. Jaxxon just stared at Ollie.

Ollie saw the question in Jaxxon's eyes. "Mostly 'Die Bitch'."

Why Anna and Ollie thought they could talk her out of this, Jaxxon had absolutely no idea. Connor hadn't even tried; he knew that she was the type of person who didn't shrink away from the bad stuff. She faced it and then took it on the chin. That was how she got past it.

Ollie made one last ditch effort to reach Jaxxon. "Luv, I promise I'll tell you every single detail, I won't leave anything out. You don't need to do this." He didn't want her to – there was a big difference between knowing someone had invaded and wrecked your own personal space and *seeing* that defacement for yourself.

Even though he had been prepared for the scene by Lily – who had let herself into Jaxxon's apartment last night to leave her some milk, bread, and other little bits for when she got back the next morning – the mess had knocked him for six. Hell, it had enraged him and it wasn't even his apartment. She hadn't yet spoken a word since he revealed what had happened. A swearing, pissed off Jaxxon he could deal with. But this hard, mute, unreachable version of her he didn't know how to handle.

Her focus still on confronting this, Jaxxon held her hand out to Ollie for the key of the new lock he had fitted on the door. When he gave it to her with a sigh, she unlocked it and gave it a hard shove, making it swing open. The smell hit her first. Cracked eggs, stale milk, and other such crap – once contents of her fridge – now decorated her carpet. She might have gagged if she hadn't been prepared for it.

Plenty of times she had got back to her old flat to be greeted by foul odours; sometimes it was the smell of the blood of whoever broke inside, cutting themselves on the door or window in the process. Sometimes the sick buggers would even leave her a present by using the middle of her living room carpet as a toilet. So the smells she could overlook. Being no stranger to damaged belongings, she could even overlook the smashed vases and lamps and kitchen ware, could overlook the strewn of clothes that seemed to cover the floor of every room. Could overlook the overturned couch and mattress, and could shrug at the rolls of toilet paper that were scattered everywhere like garlands. It was the words smeared repeatedly all over her walls that snagged her attention:

'Bitch', 'Slag', 'Slut', 'Die Bitch'.

"How do you know it's not blood?" Warren asked Ollie as he put a gentle, comforting hand on Anna's shoulder. Warren thought she was more unsettled than Jaxxon, who looked more curious than anything else. Oh she was enraged, there was no denying that. But there was no fear there to be seen on her face.

"Don't forget I have plenty of scientists and lab technicians working for me. It was easy enough to get them to test it."

"Why didn't Lily phone the police?" asked Anna. "You said in the car that the police haven't seen this yet and that's why the papers haven't got hold of it."

Ollie sighed. "I asked her not to. I don't think we should get the police involved."

"*What?* How can you say that? Look around you. Whoever did this was sick."

"And cowardly," muttered Jaxxon.

Anna double-blinked. "Cowardly?"

Jaxxon turned to her. "Did they have the courage to come and say any of this to my face? No. Did they leave a signature? No. There's nothing big and bad about breaking into someone's place, making a mess and then running off, so it doesn't exactly strike fear into my heart. Same as with the letter."

"Letter?" said Connor, Anna, and Ollie.

"Last Sunday, someone stuck an envelope under my window-wiper. Inside was a piece of paper that said 'Die Bitch'." And in her opinion, it was too much of a coincidence for it *not* to be the same person who did this to her apartment.

"*What?*" demanded Connor, Anna, and Ollie.

"Will you all stop talking at the same time, it's freaky."

"You got a threatening letter and didn't think to say anything?" Connor wanted to throttle her. "Where is it?"

"I wouldn't exactly call it 'threatening'. Besides, it was just a little note. I binned it straight away. Come on, celebs must get things like that happening all the time."

"Indeed they do," confirmed Ollie with a sigh. "So we can assume they also did this."

Warren nodded. "And that she has a stalker."

Connor frowned, sceptical. "A stalker who doesn't make themselves known until she buggers off on holiday?"

"Maybe he missed her."

"I know stalkers are normally stealthy, but they do like for their existence to be acknowledged by who they're stalking. I'm pretty sure Jaxx would have picked up on someone following her around." The twist of her lips and the way she dropped her eyes bothered him. "Jaxx?"

She scratched her head. "A couple of times, I did get this feeling like I was being watched."

"*What?*"

"Could have just been the paparazzi," said Warren.

"I know. But this was different…it didn't feel right."

Connor resisted the urge to growl. "Jaxx, when did this happen?"

"Sometimes I'd feel it just as I was going into or leaving my apartment building. Other times, it was when I was out shopping or walking Bronty."

"And it didn't occur to you to tell me?"

"Exactly what could you have done? Besides, it doesn't have to mean anything. Being stared at and being stalked are two different things. I'm not even saying that if someone *was* watching me that they had anything to do with this or the stupid note."

Anna ran a hand through her hair in a movement that screamed 'stressed out'. "We have to phone the police, they can look for fingerprints and stuff."

Ollie sighed. "There are plenty of nutcases out there, Anna, and plenty of them fixate on someone – often a celebrity – and do crap like this. What they want is to scare, distress, and unsettle that person, to get themselves some attention. It makes them feel good, clever, and powerful. A reaction of any kind only encourages them to continue. The way I like to handle things is to clean up the mess discretely and quickly, and then keep quiet about it. The trick is not to give the nutcase what they want."

"I'm sorry, but I don't see the logic in annoying a nutcase."

"When they realise they haven't got themselves a reaction or any attention, they'll get bored and stop."

"In theory."

"I've seen it happen. Look, it's uncommon for stalkers of celebs to be violent toward them. Having said that, I still think Jaxxon should stay elsewhere for a while."

"No one's scaring me out of my apartment," Jaxxon insisted sharply.

Ollie appealed to her with a look. "Be smart, not stubborn."

"This isn't about being stubborn. It's the principle of—"

"Luv, you'll be leaving for the tour in a week, your lease ends then. Will it really make that much difference to you to leave the apartment a week early? Besides, the cleaning job will take at least two days."

"He's right." Connor stood in front of her. "I'm not saying you need to run and hide. I'm saying you don't give this person the satisfaction of getting near you. Make it hard for them."

Jaxxon could see where Connor's thoughts had led him. "It wasn't Anita."

"You think it's a coincidence that while you and I are away together *this* happens?"

Ollie frowned. "Who's Anita?"

"Oscar Award Winning Actress, Anita Donovan," elaborated Anna. "I agree with Connor, Jaxxon – it's not looking good for Anita that while the tabloids are printing photos of you and him looking all cosy—"

"Hold on a minute," interrupted Ollie. "What reason would she have to do this?"

"She didn't take it well when I ended things with her," said Connor.

"I'll bet she didn't, you're not known for your sensitivity."

"It's hard to be sensitive to someone who was planning to get pregnant with your kid to try to trap you into marrying them."

"Still, why mess up Jaxxon's apartment, why not yours?"

"Anita came to see Jaxx a few days ago and fed her some crap about being pregnant, hoping it would make her back off. Instead, Jaxx slammed the door in her face. I don't think Anita did this in a rage. I think she did it as part of a game – wanting to scare her."

"That makes sense," said Warren. "That's the type of thing she'd get a kick out of. Phone Dane and ask if she was out last night."

Ollie waved his hand. "We'll look more into who's responsible once we've sorted out what we're doing next. I still say we don't involve the police—"

"I say we do," Anna spat.

"—or we'd be giving this nutcase what they want."

"That's better than winding up said nutcase."

"Ollie's right," sighed Jaxxon. "Phoning the police will show that all this got to me and give this arsehole all the satisfaction they're hoping for. And since I can't do what I really want, which is to pound their face into the ground, I'll have to settle for cheesing them off."

Pleased, Ollie smiled and nodded. "A few things, though: if there are any more notes or whatever, save them, they're evidence – just in case it's something that ever goes to trial. If there's ever a time they contact you, wanting to meet up, the answer's always no. If you're ever cornered by them and need help, shout "Fire!" That always gets people's attention, and it's a cry for help that's rarely ignored. Change any patterns you have, and maybe use a different route to get to the studio or anywhere else you regularly go. Try not to go about alone, if you can help it. You might want to change your phone numbers as well."

"Don't you think that's all a bit extreme?"

Ignoring that, he continued, "Lily and Tony have already offered for you to have their annexe again for as long as—"

Anna held up her hand. "No, she shouldn't be alone. Jaxxon, you can stay with me."

"Anna, no, it's fine." As much as she wasn't looking forward to being coddled by Lily and Tony, she didn't want to crowd the two lovebirds and listen to them shagging at all hours.

"How about this, then: Warren and I won't do our business unless we're at his apartment?"

"Our *business*?" echoed Warren, amused.

"She's staying with me." A hush fell over the room and all heads turned to look at Connor. He felt defensive, though he couldn't explain why.

This was obviously a day for shocks, in Jaxxon's opinion. She knew why Connor was making the offer: he felt guilty because he was convinced Anita was responsible and that he had brought all this on her. Jaxxon also knew that what Connor was offering would cost him.

Having grown up in an environment where he never had much to call his own, he was territorial about whatever was his. More than anything, he was territorial over his own personal space. He would never let anyone pass the threshold of his room when they were in foster care. He didn't like to share that space that he had reserved as his own. He needed that distance, that special place where only he went, that place that nothing or no one could taint. She was still surprised he had taken her to his apartment that time. "Connor, it isn't your fault that this happened. Even if it was Anita, the blame would be hers, not yours."

"This isn't about Anita. This is about you needing somewhere to stay."

"And I can stay with Lily and Tony."

"No, Jaxxon, please," interrupted Anna, "stay with me. I'm not going to see you for ages once you go on tour and—"

Connor shook his head. "If you're going to be at Warren's a lot then she'll be alone a lot, won't she."

Anna snorted at him. "You'll be at the gym all the time, so what's the difference?"

"I'll cut back on my training hours." Again everyone's eyes snapped onto him, and again he felt defensive. "It's only for a week until the tour starts." He flippantly shrugged to give emphasis to the simplicity of it all. He could tell that Jaxx didn't buy that he was truly comfortable with this. "If you stay anywhere else, all I'm going to do is wonder where you are and if you're alright. Then I'll end up harassing you by phoning you all the time, and if you don't answer, my imagination will run away with me like yours did today – remember how you thought you'd crack up? *This* way I'll know where you are, and I'll be there with you. Most of the time, anyway."

"I couldn't ask you to cut back on your training."

"You're not. I'm saying I will. For once, Jaxx, don't fight me." For a long moment, they just stared at each other. He knew Jaxx was searching his eyes for uncertainty or uneasiness. He was confident she would see neither because there was none to be found. Eventually she gave him one simple nod.

"When you said you had to pick up a few things, I didn't think you meant *that*," griped Connor as a huge Great Dane trotted inside his apartment and settled on his sofa. Jaxx had insisted that before going with him to his place she needed to go shopping to stock up on some items and clothes, since most of hers had been destroyed. He'd wanted to go with her, but she had threatened to stay at Tony's if he was going to coddle her; after whining about it a little, he relented.

Jaxxon stayed behind the threshold and shrugged. "Bronty's mine, end of conversation." He threw her a pained look, but she saw the amusement there. Still, she didn't walk through the door. "Connor, are you sure about this? About me staying here for the week? I swear I won't get cheesed off if—" He yanked on her wrist, bringing her crashing into his chest and swung the door shut. She let her shopping bags drop at her feet as his hands shaped her.

"Why wouldn't I want this body in such easy reach for seven whole days?"

"You've just had it in easy reach for four consecutive days."

"I'm greedy when it comes to you, you know that." He regarded the bags on either side of her. "That all you got? I was expecting something like twelve bags and ten boxes."

"I don't like shopping. Anyway, I've got my suitcase of stuff from the holiday, so I didn't need all that much. Speaking of the suitcase…"

"It's in the bedroom." He swatted her arse before releasing her. "Unpack your stuff wherever you want."

"Oh, guess what, I bought some lovely little pink decorative cushions and ornamental candles and some tubs of jasmine-scented potpourri." At the look of horror on his face, she burst out laughing.

"That wasn't even funny." But he was laughing with her.

"You're so easy to wind up."

He shook his head, smiling, as she headed to his room. He was surprised at himself. He had wondered if once Jaxx got here with her stuff and it all became real, he might start regretting his decision or at least feel a bit uncomfortable. But no. Not even the sight of that huge dog dominating his sofa had him second guessing himself. He might have even been able to cope with decorative cushions for a week…Then again, maybe not.

It was while she was still unpacking that Dane arrived, paying him a surprise visit. Connor sighed at the smile that Dane was trying to hide on spotting Bronty. "Warren phoned you, didn't he?"

"Why would Warren phone me?" But his smile broke free. "Alright, Warren phoned me, and I had to see for myself if you really were being the Shining Knight."

"I think it's supposed to be 'the Knight in Shining Armour', isn't it?" said Jaxxon as she caught the end of Dane's sentence on her way into the kitchen; both he and Connor were leaning against the black, marble breakfast bar.

"Hello there, Jaxx."

Connor's brows flew upwards. "When did I say you could call her that?"

"Oh, right, yeah. Jaxx*on*, sorry." But he wasn't sorry, and Connor knew it.

"I don't suppose you know where Anita was last night…?"

"She went to bed about ten o' clock, and there wasn't a murmur out of her 'til this morning." Which meant that Dane was thinking the same as what he could see Connor was thinking right now: Anita could have gotten out of the house without them knowing and gone to Jaxxon's apartment, but there was no knowing for sure.

"It wasn't her," said Jaxxon with surety. She didn't know why she was so certain, considering that her opinion was based purely on theories. Her gut told her it wasn't Anita.

Connor threw her an impatient look. "Who else could it be?"

"Maybe she has a stalker," suggested Dane.

Jaxxon tapped his temple. "Connor, think about it: would Anita do that to my apartment, risking that you might ask me to stay with you? I seriously doubt it."

He waved away the comment. "She'd never think I'd do that."

"Well if she felt threatened enough by my being in your life to come to where I live and feed me some tripe about being pregnant, she must believe what the tabloids are printing about us being in some heavy relationship. If she believes that, then she could easily believe you might ask me to stay with you if my apartment was trashed. I doubt she'd risk it."

Dane winced. "Actually, the main reason I came here was to pass on some news that I don't think you're going to sing and dance about." He sighed. "Anita's pregnant."

Silence met that statement for a few seconds.

"You know this for sure?" asked Connor after he got over the sensation of his stomach plummeting.

"She did a pregnancy test yesterday morning while Niki stood outside the bathroom door. She never tried convincing us she was pregnant the way she had with Jaxxon. But then the past few mornings she was spewing her guts up, so she did a test. I don't have to tell you she's ecstatic. She's planning on coming to tell you tonight."

Jaxx was going to leave now, wasn't she? Connor wouldn't blame her. As soon as he told Anita she still wouldn't be getting a ring on her finger, she'd be onto the tabloids, spreading news of the pregnancy; then Jaxx was going to get caught up in the whirlwind that followed. He glanced at her and, yep, there she was putting on her black leather coat.

"Where are you going?" asked Dane.

"There's someone I need to have a little chat with."

Connor's head snapped up. "What?"

"Wait." Dane placed himself in her path to the door. "Of course you want to tan her hide—"

"Oh I don't want to tan her hide," snapped Jaxxon. "I want to carve out her heart with a burning hot knife while she's alive and screaming in agony, but that's completely off the subject. As it happens, it's not her I'm going to visit."

"Then who?" asked Connor.

CHAPTER FIFTEEN

The last person Luke Winston expected to see when he opened his front door was Jaxxon Carter. As usual, her natural allure threw him for a second. There was nothing at all revealing about what she was wearing, and yet she looked sexy as hell. He squeezed his eyes shut and shook his head, willing back his ability to speak. "Er, hi."

Jaxxon gave him a winning smile. It hadn't been difficult to find him. When he had been trying to get her to go home with him that night at the bar, he had told her about the house he owned and the name of the street. All she had had to do was look for the black Mercedes he had also told her about, and she knew exactly where to find him. "I know this is out of the blue—"

Luke cleared his throat with a deliberate cough. "It's fine. Come in." He winced as it suddenly occurred to him that the inside wasn't in great shape. The cleaner wasn't due in until tomorrow. Those thoughts ended as she strutted past — his eyes became helplessly glued to her arse. Just as he was closing the door, a hand shoved against it, sending him backpedalling.

"Winston," drawled Connor as he entered.

"Alright there mate," greeted Dane in a deceptively friendly voice.

"Oh I brought them along," announced Jaxxon before entering the living room. "Hope you don't mind."

Connor smiled at Luke. "Don't worry, we're not here to break bones. What reason would we have to do anything like that?" He gestured toward the living room. "After you."

Choosing to go with the flow for now, or until he got near his mobile phone, Luke waltzed into the living room. Jaxxon, sitting cross-legged on the sofa, grinned at him. "What's all this about?" he asked.

"Ah, I think he thought she'd come here to shag him," said Dane as he and Connor covered the doorway of the room, blocking Luke's path should his flight instinct kick in.

Connor shook his head. "Nah, I'm sure his intentions were totally honourable when he invited her inside."

"Do you do a lot of jogging, Luke?" asked Jaxxon.

The question took him by surprise. His shrug was small. "Not a lot, no."

"How often would you say you do?"

"What? I don't know. I just do it sometimes, if I feel like it."

"And you felt like going jogging on that morning that we first met, didn't you?"

He swallowed hard. "Yeah."

"Sorry again about Bronty growling at you like that. But as you said, he was just protecting me. Odd choice of words, wouldn't you say?"

He laughed nervously. "You're saying you think I was going to hurt you?"

"You tell me."

"A lone man jogging in the park has to have dodgy intentions these days, is that it?"

"I never saw you do much jogging. As I recall it, you just *appeared* out of the woods."

"Because I'd just spent the past half hour jogging through those woods, taking the short cut to the lake."

"And yet, there wasn't an ounce of sweat on you." She gave her head a little shake and shrugged. "What a phenomenon." She smiled as she assessed his posture. "You're looking a little nervous. You were looking a little nervous that morning too. And that night in the bar. Funny that you should turn up in the same place like that. It wasn't so funny that you did your best to get me drunk to bring me here." Her brows rose. "Nothing to say to that? How about a subject change then? Let's talk about Anita Donovan."

He didn't bother denying that he knew her. Why make the hole he was in even deeper? Besides, technically he hadn't done anything wrong. Well, maybe by Connor McKenzie's rule book he had. "I haven't seen her in a while."

"When did you last see her?" asked Connor.

"The night that I was talking to Jaxxon at the bar."

"So you two were seeing each other," said Jaxxon – not a question, a statement. When it was mentioned that she might have a stalker, she had tried thinking of anyone who might have acted strange around her, which brought her to think of Luke. But it didn't make any sense to her that someone like him – gorgeous, rich, always had girls throwing themselves at him – would bother following her around.

Then she had remembered when they were in the bar and Connor had appeared; Jaxxon had watched surprise and betrayal and, finally, understanding flash on Luke's face. But she had been positive that they weren't directed at her or Connor – he had been thinking of someone else. So she'd asked herself, assuming someone else *was* involved, who could possibly be connected to both her and Connor that would want to play games?

Luke rubbed his chin and sighed. "Only for a couple of weeks. There wasn't much going on other than shagging. To be honest, I thought she was a bit weird, but she was good in bed so that was overlooked; she was adventurous and imaginative when it came to games—"

Jaxxon held up a hand. "Too much information, Luke."

"Not sex games. I mean, well, they were sex games, but not like what you're thinking. We'd go out to a bar and she would pick out a bloke and I would pick out a girl, and then we would dare each other to go after them. We'd try to get their phone numbers, a kiss, an invite back to their place…We never used to go – it was just a game we played. Whichever one of us got the farthest had control in the bedroom that night."

"But you didn't try to get my number, or a kiss, or an invite to mine. You wanted me to go with you."

"Anita turned round one day and said, 'Hey, I dare you to go after Jaxxon Carter.' I said if we were ever out one night and you were there, I'd approach you." Connor growled, but Luke ignored it, even though the sound chilled him. "But she said, 'No, I'm changing the rules; you've got to approach her *out* of a bar and then get her to come back here.'"

"Hence, the pretend-jog incident?"

"She told me you walked your dog in the park on Saturday mornings."

The fact that Anita knew that didn't sound good to Connor, but he didn't interrupt; he wanted every detail.

"I had it all in my head what I was going to say to you," said Luke, sighing. "But when I got up close, it just all left me. I was just, well, mesmerised by you." He was surprised when she looked confused about that. He wasn't surprised that Connor growled. "Anyway, she teased me for hours when I came back here without you, and she wouldn't let the dare drop. But, well, my ego was sore and I didn't fancy getting brain freeze and making an idiot of myself in front of you again, so I told her to forget it. Then she said—" Here was where he suspected Connor wouldn't be too pleased.

Jaxxon arched a brow. "She said…?"

"She said she had it on good authority that you were into threesomes." As he anticipated, Connor growled again and spat a curse. "She said if I managed to get you back here then the three of us could…I mean, *come on*, I'm only bloody human." He turned to Connor and Dane. "Don't tell me you two wouldn't have been intrigued by the idea."

"I'm married," said Dane.

"I never would have shared her, no matter who it was with," stated Connor honestly.

"Whatever." Luke turned back to Jaxxon. "I'd heard you and your mate talking about going to Frankie's bar that night, so I went. And, well, you weren't easy to charm and then *he* showed up. That was when everything clicked into place. I remembered that Anita had been engaged to him 'til recently, and I thought about how weird it was that she had seemed so determined to get you here where she'd be waiting. When I went back home without you, she was fuming. I asked if it had all been some revenge game for McKenzie, and she flipped her lid – ranting about men and commitments and models and babies. Then she stormed out, and I haven't seen her or heard from her since."

Dane exchanged a look with Connor before he informed Jaxxon and Luke, "That was the night Anita turned up at my house in tears, looking for somewhere to stay."

"So you know where she is?" asked Luke, not that he really cared.

Nodding, Jaxxon smiled. "She's at Dane's house, she's absolutely fine, and she's very pregnant."

Luke gaped. "She's what? Wait a minute, it's not mine. We used protection."

"Did she ever try to get you to go bareback?" asked Connor, now seeing where Jaxxon's thoughts had taken her.

He shook his head. "No, never." Then a memory came to him. "We did go bareback once in the car because I had no condoms, but she said she was on the pill." Three sympathetic looks were directed his way. "You think this baby she's having is mine?"

Jaxxon sighed. She couldn't help feeling sorry for him. "The facts are that Anita was *planning* to 'accidentally' get pregnant with Connor's baby, but he found out and we were presuming he'd ended it before she had a chance to get the plan live and kicking. Then she told me a week ago that she was pregnant, but I can tell you right now Luke she *was* lying her arse off. Or, as it turns out, she was under the impression that she was.

"Yesterday she did a test and it was positive. I don't think she would have waited this long to do a test if it was Connor's baby, it makes no sense. So if she hasn't been able to come up with a positive until now, then she must only be in the early stages of pregnancy. If that's true, the baby can't be Connor's. But it could be yours," she added more sensitively. "I think she thought she could pass off your baby as his; you have dark hair and dark eyes like him."

Luke clenched his fists. 'Information overload' didn't even begin to describe this right now. He switched his attention to Connor. The man's face was blank. "I'm not just going to presume this kid's mine; I'll be arranging a paternity test."

"Same here," said Connor.

He turned back to Jaxxon then. He felt so mixed up; he wanted to kill Anita for her deviousness and how she could play with people's lives like this, but a part of him kept going over the fact that soon he might be a dad, and he couldn't find it in him to hate that idea. "I'm not going to say this is great news. But still, I'm glad you told me. I wouldn't want to have a kid somewhere and not know anything about it or be there for it."

She nodded. "Good. At least the poor little thing will have one parent who'll care for it."

"And if it's Connor's...?"

She shrugged. "That'll be his business." He didn't even want her to be part of *his* life, he would hardly want her to know his kid if he did have one. She thought it was sad that Connor had resigned himself to a life totally marriage-free, love-free, and children-free. Connor would make a good dad, he was protective and caring, though he didn't seem to see it. Maybe one day he would, like Dane, meet someone who meant enough to him to stop him from boxing himself away from all that stuff.

It was while Dane was driving Connor and Jaxxon back to Connor's apartment that he finally asked, "Do you want kids one day, Jaxx?" Quickly he corrected, "Jaxx*on*?" Connor still growled.

She nodded. "Yeah, I do. I never had much by way of family. I'd like to start my own someday. And I need to keep the Carter blood going. The world wouldn't be the same without us Carters."

Dane laughed.

"I think you might be right there," said Connor, smiling. It was a smile that covered the pain he felt knowing that one day she would have that family...but it would be with someone else.

"What about marriage?" asked Dane.

She shrugged again. "Maybe."

Connor gawped unattractively. "You always said you would never get married."

"I know, but that's because I never saw a marriage that worked. Every relationship I'd ever seen was a mess. But after seeing Lily and Tony together, it made me realise what it *can* be like. I suppose, like everything else, it's what you make of it."

"You're right there," said Dane, nodding. "It's not easy; you've got to work at it. But it's worth it." He smiled as a thought occurred to him. "I'd be interested to see what kind of wedding you have. I just know it wouldn't be anything traditional, or even *normal*."

"Probably not. I couldn't have a big princess wedding in a huge church surrounded by a load of people I don't even know. I don't think I could cope with the serious atmosphere either, I'd end up laughing."

"What about an Elvis wedding?"

"Now *that* might be fun."

"That big hound of yours, Bronty, could give you away."

"That would save me from having to choose between Ollie, Richie, and Tony." All of whom she thought would probably vie for the position...but only after they had lectured her on her choice of husband. She got the impression that they had no problem with the blokes around her until it looked as though some bedroom action might get going.

"You could have Anna and Warren as your witnesses. All that's missing is the groom. Although I don't think you'll have much trouble finding one."

"Ah, but not all blokes are comfortable with having their bollocks at risk on a daily basis. As Anna said, I'd need a *man*-man."

"A *man*-man?" echoed Connor, not enjoying this conversation *what*soever.

"Someone who won't be intimidated by me or be all submissive. Oh and who'll have a healthy sex-drive."

Feeling suddenly defensive, as if needing to compete with this hypothetical bloke, Connor very nearly pointed out that *he* wasn't intimidated by her, or submissive, and *he* had a healthy sex-drive. Then he realised that if he had, then he would have – in effect – been calling himself a perfect match for her. He'd like to think that he was but, in the end, it didn't matter because he couldn't offer her anything. Again, he found himself wishing he could.

Something else that had his stomach knotting was that, since there was no way of being around her without wanting her, they couldn't even keep in touch when things were over. There would be no way he could be in the same room and not touch her, and there was no way he could hear her voice over the phone and have a purely platonic conversation. At some point the words 'I need to fuck you' would come out, and then the call would be abruptly put to an end by Jaxx. No, there was no way he could fit her into his life after this was over, but how could he *not* have her in his life to some extent?

He really had had enough of the bollocks that went through his head.

Anita was glad when Connor answered the door to his apartment with a beer in his hand. Maybe Connor being under the influence of alcohol would make the seduction easier. But she wasn't going to play the injured soul or the in-need-of-a-rescue-princess this time. No, because now she had something she could hold over him, something that made *her* the one in control. That idea brought her confidence and gave her the spunk she needed to face him and his abruptness. "Aren't you going to invite me in?"

Connor made a thoughtful, 'hmmm' sound. "No, I don't think I will." Although Dane had warned him she was coming, he hadn't been able to work up the patience to deal with her.

"You should. This is important, Connor."

"Then you better spill it – and quickly, because you're letting in a draft."

She placed a hand on her hip and arched a perfectly plucked blonde brow. "I suppose, if you really do want your private business aired before your neighbours, we could just have this conversation here in the hallway. But I think you'll want to be sitting down for this."

He sighed and then strolled inside, leaving her to let herself in and close the door behind her. He squeezed onto the sofa next to Bronty. "Alright, I'm sitting down. Tell me what this is all about."

"You're not even going to offer me a drink? And when did you get a dog?" It was more like a donkey. And it didn't appear to like her. Well that was a mutual feeling. Come to think of it, the creature was a bit familiar—

"Anita, get on with it."

"If you insist," she said cockily. The idea that soon she would have him right where she wanted him made her smirk. She relaxed into one of his armchairs and crossed her legs.

"Did I say you could sit down?"

"You know what, Connor, you're going to have to grow out of this immaturity. And soon."

"Why's that?" His tone made it clear that he was absolutely bored.

She leaned forward, flashing him her cleavage. "I'm pregnant, that's why." She waited for that 'I'm going to be a dad?' smile. This was a guy who had grown up without a family – of course he would be overjoyed to now have one! But the smile didn't come.

"What does that have to do with me?"

"Don't be an idiot, Connor. You know this baby's yours."

"Do I? We weren't exclusive or anything."

"So now you're accusing me of sleeping around on you?" She should have expected that he might have a brief moment of denial. "How could you say something like that?"

"As I've just said, we weren't exclusive."

"Maybe not to you, but we were to me. I loved you. Still do."

Connor gulped down more beer. This woman was one of a crazy kind. "Oh and you're willing to take me back, I suppose."

"For the baby's sake," she finally said, "I'm willing to try again. But no more 'I don't do marriage' idiocy, Connor; you'll do right by us. And there's to be no other women, do you hear me?"

Connor whistled to himself, shaking his head. "Can't I even keep Jaxx?"

"*Especially* not her."

"Why *especially* not her? You don't like her?"

"She's not important," she snapped. Softening her tone, she added, "Only we are – you, me, and the baby." She flashed him her innocent smile.

"You're certain this baby, if you're even having one, is mine?"

"Of course I'm having one, and yes I'm certain."

He let a good twenty seconds pass before responding. "You know what, I'm just not convinced. I'll have my solicitor arrange a paternity test."

Anita kept the panic from manifesting on her face. "How can you be so hurtful, Connor?" She wrapped a protective arm around her stomach. "This *is* your child."

"Tell me, Anita, why would you think that being pregnant would make any difference to how things are? Maybe in your little world of fantasies a bloke marries a woman who's having his baby, but in the real world, it just doesn't always work that way. Would I want my kid to grow up watching its parents in a meaningless, loveless relationship? No, that would only make it miserable."

"It wouldn't be meaningless," she said through her teeth. "This is because of *her*, isn't it? You care about her, don't you?"

"I wouldn't have her staying with me if I didn't."

"And here was me thinking you were just being hospitable, Connor," said Jaxxon as she entered the room and strolled over to him.

Connor curled an arm around her waist and brought her onto his lap. Feeling her calmed him and he needed that. What he didn't need was his dick coming to life, but, in his defence, her hair was still wet from her shower and she was in that black, silk robe and quite possibly nothing else.

"Anita, isn't it?" said Jaxxon. The beautiful crackpot seemed frozen with shock. "Ah, pregnant again?" There was still no reaction at all from her. "You look surprised to see me here. I would have thought you'd have worked it out when you saw Bronty. Didn't you recognise him?"

Anita's gaze flicked to the dog who, looking very disgruntled about having to share the sofa, was now trotting out of the room. "Why would I?"

"I thought you might, since you've watched me walking him in the park, haven't you."

Anita was beginning to really hate this girl. "I don't know what you're talking about."

"Well then it's a good thing that Luke Winston was such a wealth of information."

"He's interested in seeing the results of the paternity test too," Connor told Anita.

Shit, shit, shit. Anita kept her expression blank. "Who?"

Jaxxon cocked her head as she continued. "One thing he couldn't help me out with is why you wanted him to get me back to his house. Oh, I know you told him it was because I was into threesomes, but as for the *real* reason…Would I be right in assuming you were going to take some snapshots of me and Luke – the father of your baby – together to give to the papers or maybe even Connor?"

Oh yes, Anita officially hated her. Fury like she'd never before known was whizzing through Anita's system and burning her from the inside out. She could feel her cheeks reddening. Her acrylic nails were digging deep into the skin of her palms, but she couldn't relax her balled-up hands.

"If I thought you cared about Connor, I'd feel sorry for you – only to a small extent, but still – but you don't at all. You just don't know how to handle not getting what you want. You got desperate. And somewhere along the line, you got this insane idea that you have the right to meddle with people's lives. Even to make a baby with one person and then pass it off as someone else's."

Twirling a chocolate-brown curl around his index finger, Connor gave a disapproving tut. "Something tells me Luke won't be up for that, he'll want access to his kid. You might want to think about handing over custody of the baby to him because, to be frank, I'm not convinced you're one hundred percent sane."

Anita knew there was nothing innocent about her expression now as she glared at Jaxxon Carter. "I suppose you're very pleased with yourself. I pity you if you are. You think you have him, but you don't. He's too closed off to belong to anyone. And when he's all done, he'll wash his hands of you and move on to another tart, just like he did me."

"Yeah, your good mate Lotti already explained. Good of you to warn me, though."

"You think you'll be an exception?" she scoffed.

"That's the thing, Anita: I *know* I won't be. I don't live in a fantasy world like some of us do, so I'm under no illusions."

Stuck, that was what Connor was. Hearing Anita's poisonous words, he had the same urge he'd had when it was Bruno being a twat; he wanted to deny the words, override them, and insist that it was different with Jaxx. But to do that would imply something more could happen, and he refused to give Jaxx false hope; he refused to make the mistake he made when he was sixteen of telling her what he thought she'd want to hear. "You know what, I think you might just be bitter because your devious little plan hasn't worked."

"Remember *this* for the future, Anita." Jaxxon's tone was grave. "You're not clever, you're cunning – there's a big difference, and that's what your downfall was. Now get out of my sight."

"Throwing me out?" She snickered then switched her focus to Connor. "Sounds to me like she's getting a bit too comfortable, talking like this is her apartment. You might want to watch out there."

"She'd have her own if you hadn't trashed it." Anita looked genuinely shocked, he thought. But then he had to remember that she didn't get an Oscar for nothing.

Anita snorted. "Is that what she told you? Oh, Connor, she's even better at games than I am. Don't you see? She obviously had it ransacked so that you would have to take her in, if it *was* even ransacked at all. You actually fell for that?"

Jaxxon rolled her eyes. "That's you judging others by your own standards."

"Maybe it was the other way around; maybe he trashed the apartment so you would have nowhere to go and he could get you to move in here."

"Divide and conquer…A very old trick." Connor gestured toward the door with his head. "Get out of our sight."

Sharply Anita rose to her feet and gave them both a fierce snarl. "I hope you're very happy together, but you won't be, will you." Then she stormed to the door, hissing and wishing them an early death.

"Delightful woman," said Jaxxon as the door slammed so hard she was surprised the plaster surrounding the frame didn't crack.

"I always thought so."

Cunning, devious, manipulative – Anita was all those things, but did that make her an apartment-attacker? Would those delicate little fingers have any idea how to pick a lock? Would she ever be prepared to dirty herself in corn syrup? After a minute of thinking about it, Jaxxon sighed. "I don't think it was her who strafed my apartment."

Connor twirled Jaxx on his lap to face him and positioned her so she was straddling him. "Forget about her," he muttered against her lips before kissing her softly. "Forget about that apartment." He did what he had been dying to do since she walked into the room. He loosened the tie of her robe and slid his hands inside, shaping her waist. Christ, she was totally naked under it. "You're here with me now." He slid a hand over the flat of her stomach, loving the velvety feel of her. Then he snaked his hand up and along her ribs.

"It's a bit hard to forget the 'Die Bitch' part, and I'm not thrilled about the 'slag' or 'slut'—" She broke off as his teeth grazed the column of her throat and one of his hands closed around her breast.

"You are a slut, you're *my* slut." He pinched her nipple and then bit the curve of her breast.

"Bastard," she said breathlessly.

He explored her neck with hot, open-mouthed kisses while moulding and clutching each of her breasts, wringing moans from her. She was about to make a protesting sound when his lips left her neck, but then his tongue curled around a taut nipple and flicked it. His mouth then closed over it and sucked hard. Moaning again, she ground herself against his hard, jeans clad dick. Oddly enough, she enjoyed the friction that came from the feel of the denim against her clit. She supposed she *was* sort of slutty with him at times.

"You've had such a shit day, haven't you, babe. Just relax for me. Let me give you something else to think about. Let me make you forget everything."

And then he worked her body like the master he was.

CHAPTER SIXTEEN

Jaxxon woke up to a lash of a tongue to her clit. The tip of that same tongue flicked the bud repeatedly, teasing it and sending zinging sensations through her. Then a long, cool breath blew over her clit and between her folds. She moaned and bucked.

"Morning," said Connor against her clit. When he suckled on it, she bucked again. He pinned her hips to the bed with his arm. "I woke up starving." As he took to swiping his tongue through the slick folds, her moans grew in volume. He couldn't help moaning along with her as the taste of her increasingly ate at his control. Then he thrust his tongue into her, getting a more thorough tasting of her. He could happily do this for hours.

After approximately fifteen minutes of utter torture, during which she must have plucked over a dozen hairs from his head while her fingers were threaded through it, Jaxxon couldn't take anymore. "Connor," she rasped.

"What is it, babe?"

Instead of words, a loud groan escaped her. "Connor." Being reduced to one word sentences was pissing her off. She mentally thumped herself. "I'm going to come."

"I don't want you to come until I'm inside you."

"Then you better get inside me very fast."

"Hold on for me a little longer."

"Can't." She was very close to sobbing. She hated it when that happened. "Now, Connor." Suddenly her hips were tilted and his cock plunged into her as he seated himself deep. Over the edge she went, crying out and shaking. What a way to wake up.

Connor held himself immobile until her little aftershocks slipped away. Then he urged her to curl her legs around his hips and began to move, keeping his thrusts leisurely and sensual. He buried his face in the crook of her neck, groaning at how hot and tight and wet she was.

The feel of Jaxx's tight muscles gripping and stretching around him was his own personal definition of heaven.

Jaxxon had been waiting for the deliciousness of having him inside her to wane with time, but if anything, it only got better. She loved that sensation as he first entered her. She loved how each deliberate movement was powerful and masterful and dominant, no matter how gentle or rough he was. She loved how he filled her *so* deeply, making her feel as though she could burst. And the smoothness of his flesh against her own was amazing. Wait a minute…His flesh against her own? She *knew* something felt different. "Connor—"

"I know, babe, I know I'm bareback; I'll put a condom on in a minute, I swear, I just want to feel you around me. Just for a minute." He'd never taken a woman without a condom before. Naturally he'd always wondered what it was like without them. But with Jaxx, he needed to know. He would put on a condom in a minute, he really would. He just needed to know how it felt to take her skin-to-skin. The feel of her come coating his cock was amazing.

Although his movements were slow, it fired her desire having the feel of him inside her like this. She tried not to arch into him and beat at his control, but while she was caught up in the thrall of the pleasure that he could give her, she didn't have a lot of control herself. His touch was rekindling the giddy tingles from her last orgasm.

"I'll pull out in a sec, I promise I will."

She wasn't sure who he was trying to reassure more: her or himself. She recalled the conversation they'd had one night when she had been teasing him about the slutty life he'd led – he had sworn that he had always worn a condom and he still got himself checked out regularly. "You don't have to stop if you don't want to, I'm on the pill." She had been since she was fourteen to regulate her heavy periods. Instantly Connor stilled. "If you want to use a condom then get it on quickly because I'm close and these slow thrusts of yours are—" She broke off as he abruptly slammed into her, dragging a loud groan from her which mingled with his.

"Harder?" he gritted out.

"Yes."

This time, he slammed into her so hard she hit the headboard. "Faster?"

"A lot faster."

He smiled at the frustration in her voice. Then he firmly caught her hips, dragged her to him away from the headboard, and hammered into her the way she loved. Jesus Christ, it was a million times better with nothing to keep his skin from hers. "Look at me, Jaxx."

She opened her eyes to find his face a mask of intensity; his lips were set into a hard line, his jaw was so tense she would bet his teeth hurt, and his eyes had that merciless glint to them and had darkened to flint. He cupped her arse and shifted her slightly so that he was now hitting her G-spot with every thrust. "God, Connor."

"Now, Jaxx," he demanded in a harsh voice. "Come for me right now, come with me." Then he slammed into her even harder than before and they both came together, her screaming, and him groaning her name.

Jaxxon closed her eyes as she waited for him to roll off her, and sigh, and mutter about how he shouldn't have done that. Any other bloke would see no need to panic, but this was someone who didn't want kids. Instead, he did something that took her completely by surprise. He gave her a soft, lingering kiss and then took her with him as he rolled onto his side. "What time is it?"

"Well, my alarm went off at half past six, so it must be about seven now."

"How is it that I didn't hear your alarm?" She had always been a light sleeper.

"You were obviously so satiated after I fucked you to sleep that you were halfway to comatose."

Hearing the self-satisfaction in his tone, she pinched his bicep. "No one likes a smug bastard. What time are you leaving for the gym?"

"Same time you're leaving for the studio, half past seven. So I suppose we better get up." He swatted her arse and then jumped out of bed before she could return the favour. One thing Connor adored Jaxx for was that she didn't take ages in the bathroom. Also, she didn't mind sharing it while she used it. This morning, though, she made him agree not to join her in the shower as they had learned during their stay in France that there was no way they could be together in the shower without something sexual happening. This morning, they didn't have time.

As usual, Jaxx was washed and dressed within twenty minutes. He was glad she wasn't someone who lathered herself in make-up – except when working, of course. In his opinion, she didn't need it and looked more stunning without it. Another thing he liked was that despite the industry she worked in, she didn't skip breakfast. Even if all she had time for was a slice of toast, she didn't start her day on an empty stomach.

What Connor *didn't* like about this morning was that he was leaving a humungous animal in his apartment for the day. Jaxx assured him that he wouldn't get back to find that Bronty had done a Turner and Hooch to the place – mostly because she didn't believe he knew he was a dog, which was something she was going to look into. Connor also didn't like the thought of her being away from him while the person responsible for trashing her own apartment was waltzing around and so far had gone undetected. He still believed it was Anita, but Jaxx still wasn't convinced.

Hoping to avoid Anita's watchful eye, he took Jaxx out the side door of the building; telling the guard, Chino, that she would be using this as an entrance and exit from now on. But Connor still couldn't relax. "Maybe I should drive you to the studio and then pick you up once you're done," he said as they approached her Audi.

"You are kidding, aren't you? No of course you're not," she grumbled. "I'll be alright. It's not like anyone has tried to hurt me. It was my apartment that they went after."

Yeah, but they had both pissed Anita off badly last night, so it wouldn't surprise him if she took things a step further after that. He shackled Jaxx's wrist with his hand and tugged her to him so sharply she dropped her handbag. "Look, I know that I can go over the top and be way too overprotective when it comes to you—"

"Did you honestly just admit that?"

"—but I feel uneasy and I can't shake it off."

"Now you're just being paranoid."

"It doesn't mean Anita's not following you. Luke said she knew what day you walked Bronty, so—"

"Maybe you're right and I'm being tailed by Anita the Vengeful but, in that case, won't I *need* my car so I can ram the thing into her?" When she pulled her hand free and bent to pick up the handbag, she heard him groan. "What?" she asked as she straightened.

"How great thou arse."

"Ah, so my randy bastard's back. I like him better than the paranoid one." Just as she was about to unlock the car, she was caged against it from behind. Yep, randy bastard was definitely back. He cupped and shaped her arse – then spanked it. Of course he spanked it. Why wouldn't he spank it? "Alright, this S and M shite stops now."

He whispered into her ear, "Deny it if you want, but you like getting your arse spanked. You get wet as hell every time I do it. Oh and I haven't even started with the kinky stuff, babe. One night, I'm going to tie you to my bed and have my wicked way with you, and you know what? You'll love every second of it. I bet you're getting wet just thinking about it, aren't you?"

She was. "Do you really want to get me all horny and then send me off to a studio full of male models?" She was spun around so fast, she stumbled. A chuckle burst out of her. "You are so easy to wind up, McKenzie."

"And you are such a tease, Carter." He merged his lips with hers. The kiss was punishing and possessive. "Remember: take a different route to the studio and be alert, alright."

"Sir, yes, sir."

"Sir? I actually like the sound of that. Lord and Master might be better, though."

Chuckling again, she shoved him away and got into her Audi. At the same time, he jumped into his Aston Martin convertible and beeped at her as they went their separate ways. Jaxxon sighed as it occurred to her that when they literally went their separate ways in every sense of the phrase, it wouldn't be anything like the easy, playful manner of just now. Or, at least, it wouldn't be for her.

First thing on her schedule was a conference call with the fashion designer and his team from Milan, who were still trying to negotiate some sort of deal for Jaxxon to model a special clothes line, which they wanted to brand with her name. Apparently they weren't fazed by her decision not to go to Milan to meet with them and, after some hounding on their part, a conference call was arranged. Sadly for the designer, this kind of thing wasn't for her, and she told him as much in the most frank way possible.

Next on her schedule was the shoot for the Allure line of the new season. It didn't escape her notice that Tony wasn't barking at her to move this way and that way like he usually did, so she guessed he was worried about her after what happened to the apartment. She was surprised that he wasn't sulking because she was staying with Connor rather than in his annexe, and just when she thought he was being mature about it, he made a snide comment. So she flipped him off. And he laughed.

When it was time for the next set of shots, which were to mostly concentrate on the eye products, Jaxxon went to have her make-up re-done into a different look. Kieran used a lot of smoky colours this time, making her seem like some sort of dark seductress. She didn't like it, but of course he saw that as a positive because it meant that she would have on her 'frustrated look' by the time she got back to Tony.

"Ooh, maybe this will cheer you up," said another of the make-up artists, Lorna. She placed a vase filled with burgundy-red roses and a black box with a black lacy bow – which she guessed contained chocolates – in front of Jaxxon.

"Who are they from?" asked Kieran.

She plucked out the envelope that sat within the bouquet and tore it open. The card read: 'They won't taste better than you, C'.

"C? *Oh*, they're from Connor McKenzie. You know you haven't told me much about him."

"I can tell you that he doesn't do flowers and chocolates."

"Luv, they all revert to the traditions when the right girl comes along. The two of you really do suit. And I don't just mean 'cause of how crazy you both are. I mean you *look* good together as well. That's always a bonus."

"What's that noise?" asked Lorna, flicking aside her purple hair to cup her ear. "Sounds like bells ringing. Church bells."

"Stop taking the piss, there will be *no* wedding," stated Jaxxon.

"Did someone say wedding? Who's getting married?" Louisa strutted over to Jaxxon and examined her ringlets. "They don't need touching up."

Lorna nodded in agreement. "We were just asking when the big date is for Jaxxon and Connor McKenzie."

"He proposed?"

Jaxxon held up the hand that Louisa was trying to snatch. "See – no ring. They're just trying to wind me up. And they're succeeding." She briefly contemplated ragging out Kieran's spiky hair and shoving it down Lorna's throat.

"Is that who the flowers and chocolates are from?"

"Yes," verified Kieran. "You know what, Jaxxon, you should make sure your wedding bouquet looks something like that – it'll be like a tribute to the first time he sent you flowers." He knew he was pushing it, but it wouldn't be a normal day if Jaxxon didn't tell him to sod off. It was part of his routine.

"*Wedding* bouquet?" echoed an extremely aggravated Ollie as he paced to Jaxxon. "McKenzie asked you to marry him? And you said yes?" Oh, he'd skin the prat.

Jaxxon put her hand over her heart and said her speech in a rush. "How could I say no? You were right when you said it was about more than just sex, I love him. I don't want to be without him." At the sight of his blazing-red cheeks, she burst into laughter and everyone joined in, other than Ollie who looked a mixture of relieved and annoyed.

"Bloody hell girl, you had me panicking then."

"Don't you like Connor?" asked Kieran.

"Oh don't get him started on Connor," groaned Jaxxon.

"It's not that I don't like him," said Ollie.

"So am I the *only* one who doesn't like him then?" Bruno winked at Jaxxon as he came to stand beside Ollie.

Kieran snorted. "Your opinion of Connor doesn't count, it's biased." He gestured for Ollie to continue, but the man was struggling for words. "Oh, I get it," chortled Kieran. "Daddy doesn't like his little girl having a sex life."

"Is it a good sex life?" Lorna asked Jaxxon, waggling her eyebrows.

"With the sexual tension those two throw about when they're in the same room, it must be." Louisa turned to Jaxxon. "Aren't you going to open those chocs, luv?"

Jaxxon didn't answer – there was no point as Louisa already had the box in her hands and was now opening it.

"Mmmm, dark chocolate."

"Ew, I don't like dark choc." Jaxxon shook her head in distaste.

"Dark chocolate's the healthy chocolate option," said Kieran. "The cocoa level's—"

"Kieran, will you sod off with that mascara and eyeliner before I end up looking like a bloody panda!"

He chuckled. "That's you done, luv."

"The details of the tour are all finalized," Ollie announced as he escorted Jaxxon down the hallway, en-route back to Tony. "As I already told you, we're going to New York first. It's an evening flight. I knew you would prefer one of them."

"What day do you leave?" asked Bruno, now walking on Jaxxon's other side.

"Monday," replied Ollie.

Bruno smiled when he managed to catch Jaxxon's eye. "I bet you'll be glad to leave that apartment behind after what happened."

She frowned. "How do you know about that?"

"I was eavesdropping when Ollie and Richie were talking about it, sorry. So how are you?"

"Alright. It's just stuff at the end of the day, isn't it?"

"There hasn't been anything else odd going on?" checked Ollie. She shook her head. "The place is still in the process of being cleaned. The mess was unreal."

"I've seen worse."

Ollie knew that, and the idea of it got on his wick. He'd hoped that her new life would get her away from that crap, give her security. He was so thankful that it hadn't made her take a step backwards in her progress with her transition from having nothing to everything she wanted.

It would have cut him up if she had withdrawn from it just because of some nut, but he'd seen it happen many times with other people. They couldn't deal with the lack of privacy, or being under the microscope of the media, or the sudden and massive amount of attention – the like of which they could never have imagined. He'd seen grown men cry when that attention suddenly became bad attention and there were criticisms, and wicked rumours, and the appearance of nutcases. But this twenty-two year old woman had taken it better than most he'd known in the past to have done.

As much as he didn't like that she was staying with McKenzie – the bloke looked at Jaxxon like she belonged to him – Ollie didn't want her to be alone, and Ollie knew McKenzie wouldn't hesitate in wiping the floor with anyone who tried to lay a finger on her. That was assuming the bugger wasn't dealt with by Jaxxon herself first.

Bruno snickered. "Is that why McKenzie was sending you the flowers and chocolates? Is he trying to coddle you through what's been going on? Or is he trying to dig himself out of the doghouse? I'll bet it's the second. He's so cocky and overbearing—"

At the end of her tether and feeling an inexplicably big need to defend Connor, Jaxxon spun on Bruno. "Do you know what, Bruno? I'm getting sick of your remarks about him."

"Whoa, whoa, I was just joking around."

"Jokes are funny." And it was never just what he said; it was the spite and bitterness that was always in his tone.

"Ah, come on, Jaxx."

"*Don't* call me that." Her voice was deadly. She could tolerate Dane doing it because she knew he was trying to wind Connor up. But the way Bruno had said it so intimately, as if he had that same level of familiarity and closeness with her that Connor did, ticked her right off. Wisely, he didn't follow her any further. Ollie was also wise – he didn't comment.

As Connor pulled up next to Jaxx's Audi in the car park outside of his apartment building later that day, he smiled. He had liked the idea that when he got home it would be to find Jaxx there, waiting. He liked that idea even better now that he was finally back. So did his dick.

"I come bearing gifts," he announced as he entered his apartment with a giant-sized pizza. Yeah, it seemed counterproductive to spend hours on his fitness levels and then devour a pizza at the end of it, but sod it. When Jaxx – who was watching T.V on the sofa – turned her head and smiled sweetly at him over her shoulder, something twisted in his chest.

"Mmmm, pizza. Good thinking, McKenzie."

Having dumped his gym bag on the floor, he went straight to the living area and kissed her. He'd only meant for it to be a brief, greeting-type kiss, but his control around her was as piss-poor as ever. "You're dessert, Carter."

"Please tell me that's Deep Pan Margarita," she said when he finally released her lips.

"Of course it is. I know it's your favourite." He sat on the armchair near the sofa and placed the pizza on the table in front of them, liking how it felt to lounge around while eating pizza out of the box like they used to – no plates, no cutlery, no prim crap.

"Good memory."

"I could hardly forget that, it was all you ate back then. How you could eat something that often and not get sick of it always amazed me."

"Well you forgot that I didn't like dark chocolate." Seeing the confused expression on his face, she slapped her leg. "I knew it wasn't you."

"What?"

"I told Kieran that's just not the kind of thing you'd do." She was torn between being pleased with herself for being right, and being agitated that someone else had sent them and she didn't know who.

"Jaxx, elaborate."

"Today I got a bunch of red roses and a box of dark chocolates sent to me."

The slice of pizza in his hand slipped from his fingers and dropped back into the box. "You what?"

"The card was signed 'C', so everyone assumed you had sent them. But it just seemed out of character for you."

"Where are they?"

She shrugged as she finished chewing on the food in her mouth. "I left them in the studio, so no doubt someone's took them home."

"I bet you would have felt like a right bitch if it had turned out that I *had* sent them then, wouldn't you?"

"No, I'd have told you it served you right for sending me corny crap."

"Christ, Jaxx." He shook his head. "I don't like this stalker stuff."

"You telling me you've never had some kind of obsessed fan? God, if you saw some of the fan mail I get, you wouldn't be so bothered. Anna spends hours reading it, either laughing her head off or blushing purple. There are some really odd people out there and, for some reason I've yet to understand, I seem to draw them to me."

He snorted. "Wrong, babe, you draw everyone to you, always have. It's just that it's mostly the odd ones who have the nerve to do something about it."

"It makes me shiver thinking someone might be obsessed with me, though. I don't get it."

"*I'm* obsessed with you. You're obsessed with me, though, so I can cope."

She laughed. "You tell yourself that if it's your coping mechanism."

"You deny it to yourself if that's *your* coping mechanism." He cringed when Bronty slobbered all over the sofa at the sight of the pizza. "Does he eat this sort of stuff? I thought dogs were more meat-eaters."

"Ah, but like I've said, I'm not convinced he's aware he's of the canine line. Bronty will eat just about anything, but I think it's because before I found him he was living off whatever scraps he could find out of people's bins. For the first week of him living with me, he was eating out of my kitchen bin; I had to train him to stop it. Observe and note that your apartment is in tip-top shape despite Scooby Doo here having spent the day in it."

"Observed. Noted. Appreciated." What he didn't appreciate was the knock on his apartment door mere seconds later. Cautious for Jaxx, he glimpsed through the peephole. He shot Dane a frustrated look as he opened the door, but his mate only smiled in response as he walked past him.

"Alright, Con. Mmm, what's that smell?"

"Smells like junk food," said Niki as she waltzed in behind Dane with Little Dane hanging off her neck. Quick as anything, he threw himself at Connor.

"Alright little man," said Connor as he perched the toddler on his arm so he could cling to him like a chimp, the way he always did. "You been a good boy for your mum and dad?"

Chewing on his thumb, he asked shyly, "Who'z that gwirl?"

Dane was already in the living room. "Hey Jaxx — sorry, Jaxx*on*, this is my wife, Niki, and my boy, Little Dane."

Although all she did in response was smile and offer a 'hi', Niki thought it was so warmly delivered, it was like an embrace. Niki had expected to feel threatened as a woman while being around someone so stunning, but there was something reassuring about Jaxxon Carter. "Sorry we didn't get a chance to meet 'til now, but I didn't want to risk seeing you when Anita might have found out."

Waving away the unnecessary apology, Jaxxon smiled. "Thanks for keeping an eye on her for Connor. She's a witch."

After chasing a very put-out Bronty off the sofa, Connor plonked himself next to Jaxx while Dane and Niki each claimed an armchair. "This is my very good friend, Jaxx," he told Little Dane. "Jaxx, this is—"

"Let me guess," she drawled. "Are you the Fat Controller who's friends with Thomas the Tank Engine and all his friends?"

He giggled and shook his head while Connor, Niki, and Dane all exchanged a look that said 'How did she guess he loved that programme?'

"Really? You look so much like him," continued Jaxxon. "Have you ever met Thomas?" Little Dane shook his head again. "I know a place where you can." His eyes bulged. "Tell your mummy and daddy to take you to a place called Wales in August and he'll be there. You can *ride* on him, and, Annie and Clarabel."

"And Percy?"

"Oh yeah, definitely him." Seeing the questioning look on Connor's face she said, "All little boys love Thomas. I learned about the Wales thing years ago when I was helping the local nursery teacher find excursions; she was a sister of a mate of mine." She didn't elaborate that this mate had been coming off drugs and both Jaxxon and the young teacher had been taking shifts helping her get through it. Filled with excitement, Little Dane hit her with one question after another about this August event until, eventually, he'd crawled onto her lap while she gave him all the details.

As Connor watched Jaxx win shy Little Dane over so effortlessly, he was overcome with a contradictory mixture of awe and anxiety. Awe at her naturalness with children, and anxiety at the idea that she would be a great mum and he wouldn't be around to see it. There was no way he could watch her being a mum to a kid that belonged to another bloke.

"You'll be pleased to know that Anita's gone," announced Dane before biting into the slice of pizza that he had helped himself to. "Left for L.A. this morning, fully admitting that the baby she's having isn't yours, Con."

Thank God for that. Then something occurred to him: if Anita was gone but Jaxx was still being tailed, it had to be someone else. But then, maybe Jaxx was right and she wasn't being followed. Maybe he was just being paranoid as she'd said. Stuck in his thoughts, he didn't realise Jaxx's phone was ringing until she gently placed Little Dane on his lap before hurrying to the bedroom to take the call. A few minutes later she reappeared, her olive skin pale. Immediately he was on his feet. "Jaxx, what is it?" She said nothing, just stared at him. "What's wrong? Who was it on the phone?"

"Richie," she replied. "Louisa's in hospital."

"Louisa?"

"She's one of the hairstylists. He was with her, going over some things, when she started vomiting; he said it was like something off the Exorcist."

"But she's alright?"

She nodded. "She stopped spewing about half an hour ago, and the doctor in the hospital gave her something to settle her stomach. They're keeping her in for the night."

"Hey, don't look so freaked out." But then Jaxx held his gaze with such intensity, he felt rooted to the spot.

"They think it was food poisoning. The thing is…she's the one who took those chocolates that someone sent me."

CHAPTER SEVENTEEN

The next morning, Connor's apartment was packed with people. Ollie was cursing with frustration because he hadn't been able to track down who sent the flowers and chocolates. Richie was exploring the theory that the sender may have been someone who was already in the studio building. Tony was relaying stories he had heard about past fanatic fans in an attempt to pre-empt what might come next and decide how best to deal with things. Lily was making everyone coffee, constantly signalling to her husband to shut up when his stories became creepy. Anna was again insisting that the police were brought into the matter, especially after what had happened to Louisa. Warren was trying to calm Anna, reminding her that Louisa herself didn't want anyone to know what had happened; she had seen enough obsessed fan situations to know that giving them attention was often counterproductive. Dane was offering his theory that maybe all this had been Anita's doing and she either hadn't left L.A. at all or had sent the flowers and chocolates before leaving.

Connor, however, was unusually mute as he witnessed the torment that an equally mute Jaxx was subjecting herself to as she sat on the sofa with her legs hugged to her chest, staring at the floor. Nothing he or anyone else had said had made any difference. Not even the fact that Louisa – who was now home under the care of her sister – had phoned and spoken to Jaxx, assuring her she was fine, had helped. He sat next to her and wrapped an arm around her as he spoke softly into her ear. "Babe, don't do this to yourself. It wasn't your fault."

Oh she knew that. Jaxxon wasn't assuming all blame for Louisa having been ill; to do that would be to relieve the oddball poisoner of the blame they were due. The reason Jaxxon was feeling sick to her stomach was that she hadn't listened to Connor and taken this matter seriously enough. If she had, maybe she would have been as vigilant and alert as he had advised her to be, and then she wouldn't have ignored her instincts that something wasn't quite right about those gifts appearing.

Also, if she was now to assume that this oddball would happily see her severely ill, was it such a stretch to wonder if this crackpot was going to do something similar again once they realised their plan hadn't worked?

It was horrible to think that there was someone out there who might actually hate her so deeply. She knew she was a moody cow, but was she really hate-worthy? Or was she dealing with one of those bizarre people who thought along the lines of 'I love you so much I have to kill you'? One thing she could deduce from all this was that, no matter the motive of the oddball in question, she couldn't be sure that the people around her were safe.

Hearing Tony and Lily propose that she would be better moving back into their annexe, Jaxxon closed her eyes and braced herself for Connor — who had stiffened beside her — to turn into a raging bull. Therefore, his reaction surprised her.

Gently Connor turned her face to his and softly asked, "Would you feel safer staying with them?" No one would ever convince him that they could protect her better than he could. Even though he had — without her knowledge — had GPS trackers planted on her phone and car by his mate, who was a security expert, Connor was still worried as hell about her. He wanted her to stay with him more than he wanted anything, but it was important to him that she felt safe. He had let her down once before when she needed him, though he still didn't know what he hadn't protected her from, whereas the three 'uncles' had more or less saved her from her old life.

The fact that Connor — someone who, by nature, didn't accept an answer that didn't cohere with his own — was actually putting what she wanted before his own wants almost put a lump in her throat, and Jaxxon wasn't an emotional person. Connor being self-sacrificing…Well that was new. In any case, he was what she needed right now. She shook her head.

He rested his forehead against hers. "Good." He kissed her gently then raised his head and announced, "She's staying here with me, and anyone who doesn't like it can talk to me in the other room, but note that I'll just tell you to shove your opinion up your arse." He felt her body shake with silent laughter, and noticed that Dane and Warren also seemed amused.

"Fine then," relented Tony begrudgingly, "but you make sure you keep watch over her. That means staying here with her, being—"

"Whoa there, Tone," interrupted Jaxxon, "no one is putting me on lock-down."

"It won't be for long, you're going to New York in a few days."

"I don't care. I'm not going to let some nutter turn me into a prisoner."

Suspecting that, just for once, he and the overprotective McKenzie would be singing from the same hymn sheet, Tony appealed to him with a look. To his utter shock, the bloke shook his head.

"As much as I'd love to keep her here where no one can get to her, it won't happen. She'll crack up. When we were teenagers and she was confined to her room for the weekend, she got so bad that, with a fractured wrist, she climbed down the drainpipe just to get out into the fresh air. That feeling of being trapped sends her over the edge." He heard her chuckle at the memory and looked back at her. "It wasn't funny, Jaxx. I had a panic attack, thinking you were going to fall to your death." She smiled unrepentantly.

Tony half-sighed half-growled, which made Lily elbow him in the ribcage. After scowling at her, he turned back to Jaxxon. "Luv, you can't deny that you'll be a lot safer just lying low for a couple of days. Look what happened to Louisa—"

"Not the right thing to say, gobshite," condemned Lily.

He scowled at his wife again. "Jaxxon, luv, I just want you to be safe."

"And she will be," stated Connor, cuddling her to him.

"No way am I hiding, Tony. Anna and I are supposed to be going out tonight; we've had it planned for ages. I won't see her for months once I go on tour."

When Tony switched his attention to her, Anna knew that he wanted her to support his argument and say that Jaxxon should hide. She couldn't do that. As Connor said, it would drive Jaxxon mental, and she had to agree with Jaxxon that it wasn't fair for her to be made into a prisoner. It would give the sicko a hard-on. Besides, she really had been looking forward to tonight; the invite from one of the models she worked with to come to her house party had come months ago.

"Where are you both going?" Connor asked Jaxx as he played with her hair. He didn't like the idea of the girls being out alone, but if he tried to suffocate Jaxx, she'd likely leave.

"It's an Ann Summers Party."

His eyebrows shot upwards. "Ann Summers?" Ann Summers as in the company specialising in kinky lingerie? he didn't say aloud but knew would be in his expression.

With a wicked smile, she nodded. "It's kind of like a social event that takes place in someone's living room where we all drink Champagne and look at a new line of lingerie. Oh and we get a goody-bag of funky toys to bring back."

Suddenly swallowing was difficult for Connor. He considered that maybe she was just winding him up but, as if she'd read his mind or he was completely transparent right now, she shook her head. Jesus Christ. He pointed a finger at her. "I get to drive you and pick you up afterwards." Deal made, his mind relaxed. His body, however…it wasn't going to relax until after he'd got to use those sex toys on that luscious body.

Anna, Warren, Dane, and Lily all exchanged knowing smiles. Ollie, Richie, and Tony shuddered, intending to expel the past fifteen seconds from their minds.

It wasn't until forty minutes later that Ollie got the opportunity he'd been waiting for. While Connor was in his bedroom taking a call, Ollie took the newly vacated spot next to Jaxxon. His expression made it clear to her that he wanted this to be private between them. "I've been thinking…What if we leave for New York early? I know it's not the ideal—"

"Alright."

"What?" He'd been expecting a dramatic argument.

"How much earlier do you want to leave?"

"You're not going to fight me on this?"

No, she wasn't, because she was terribly conscious that being around others put them at risk, and she was worried sick that something could happen to Connor while she was staying with him. If she had moved into Tony and Lily's annexe, she would have had them to worry about. The same rule would have applied no matter who she stayed with. "How much earlier?"

"We can leave as early as tomorrow afternoon if you want." His mouth dropped open when she nodded her consent. "Are you taking the Mick or something?"

"Let's see how the sick sod gets on following me round the world," she snickered.

"He might."

"He didn't follow me to France, though, did he? So I'm thinking maybe his financial situation won't permit it." That was something which was concerning her all the more – the nutter would know that her tour started soon. With the knowledge that after that he wouldn't be able to get to her, he might make a desperate attempt to do so in the next few days. Yeah, the sooner she left the better. Tomorrow sounded like a good idea. "Don't tell Connor." Not just because he would likely hit the roof, insisting she didn't need to change her schedule for some nutcase, but because it would get him in a sulk and she wanted their last night together to be fun, not gloomy.

"I won't be telling anyone other than Richie and Tony. You do the same. You can always phone Anna after you've left; she'll understand. So will McKenzie." Actually, he wasn't so sure about the latter – the last time she went off somewhere without telling him, the bugger followed her. But Ollie had to admit that McKenzie had been as sensitive as she had needed him to be today rather than a stampeding, seething elephant.

It was a while before everyone left, so she was surprised Connor was still sane, let alone not red in the face. "Sorry about all that, I know you don't like having people in here."

"Oi, don't be daft," he said as he handed her the coffee that Lily had made her before leaving. He searched her face as he settled next to her. "You alright?"

She nodded, smiling. She actually felt a bit better knowing that she was acting on what was happening, but she also felt like utter crap knowing that this was her last evening with Connor. "Louisa's alright; that's the main thing."

"Exactly. We grew up around nutcases, what's one more to add to the mix?"

She laughed. "I count you as one of those nutcases."

"So you should. But, in my defence, I'm pretty much normal when you're not around. It's you who drives me mental."

"Then I bet you can't wait for me to go on this tour."

He rained kisses along her neck. "Actually, I'm dreading it."

"Dreading it?"

"I've told you, I'm totally addicted to you. I can't get enough of you." He was beginning to think he would always feel like that, which meant that the decision of when this was over all rested on her. She literally had his soul in the palm of her hand and didn't even know it.

If it hadn't been for the fact that this was her career they were talking about and not simply a holiday, Connor would have asked her not to go. In fact, if he thought he could get away with it, he'd go along with her. However, not only would she tell him to sod off, but by that he would be implying that things were getting serious. "Don't be surprised when I fly out to see you now and then."

She snorted. "You'll have a new bed buddy within a week."

"Oi, what have I told you? Don't make out that I think that little of you."

She might have argued the point with him if she wasn't conscious of making the most of their last night. "I apologise oh Lord and Master."

He chuckled. "You really shouldn't say that unless you want to be tied to my bed with me fucking you senseless."

"Maybe I'll let you do that later when I've got my new toys."

He groaned against her neck. "You do know that I've been hard as a rock ever since you mentioned that goody bag you'll be bringing back, don't you? Take pity on me and don't be too long."

"The party's only on for two hours."

"Too long."

A smile crept onto her face as the temptation to tease him overcame her. "Anna was telling me that she's heard they give out edible body creams." He groaned again. "I said as long as it's chocolate flavoured, I don't mind using it. And you know what? Turns out that they do have that flavour."

"Jaxx," he groaned.

"I was wondering whether they would put some in the bag, or maybe they'll put in some kind of dildo. Or maybe they'll put in both."

He bit her neck. "Keep teasing me and I'll end up shoving my painfully hard dick in your mouth, I won't be able to help it."

"Maybe later," she whispered. That didn't seem to help him settle. If anything, it made him worse. He looked so highly strung by the evening that it was a struggle not to laugh. This didn't go unnoticed by Anna when they collected her on the way to the party. Jaxxon saw her mouth twitching in an effort not to laugh.

"Remember," said Connor gravely when he stopped the car outside their host's house, "don't come outside until I've phoned to say I'm here."

"Yes, oh Lord and Master," she said in a voice just as serious. Anna chuckled quietly.

"You're so lucky Anna's in the back of the car or I'd be fucking you right now just for teasing me like this again."

"We'll be late if you do that." Anna hopped out of the car and went to the passenger door to haul Jaxxon out of the car. Connor was kissing her; it was a sweet yet deep kiss, and it made Anna sigh. Why was he such an idiot? She had thought that over time he'd come to realise how much he cared for Jaxxon and then he would shape up. But whatever was holding Connor back had a tight rein on him, and he wasn't going to offer Jaxxon anything more. Anna could see that now. He would never have asked Jaxxon to stay in his apartment if he had thought it might lead to something permanent, just like he would moan about her going on this tour without him if he really wanted there to be more between them. Dane and Warren had agreed with her on that.

Oh Connor would acknowledge his mistake eventually, but Anna suspected that by then it would be too late; Jaxxon wouldn't let him barge back into her life a second time. He might not mean to, but he was going to hurt her in a big way when he waved her off at the airport, which was why Anna intended for the next few months to be utter torture for Connor.

Anna was going to make sure that Jaxxon left this party with plenty of toys and lingerie, and Anna was going to encourage her to use them all Sunday night – her and Connor's final night together. She wanted Jaxxon to be so stuck in Connor's mind that he wouldn't be able to be with another woman without thinking of Jaxxon. If Anna got her way, the torture would be so bad that he would have to buy a new bed if he was ever to get a good night's sleep again. Well, she had warned him not to hurt Jaxxon, hadn't she?

The host, Nina, ushered them inside the second she opened the door. She was so excited that her words were coming out in a high-pitched voice. Jaxxon had only met Nina a few times, but she liked the extremely tall auburn-haired girl. She reminded her a lot of Anna, only she was a very confident creature – but not to the point of having a swollen sense of self-importance. Jaxxon liked that.

As Jaxxon expected, the gathering of fifteen was females only and all were eighteen or over. It soon became very apparent why. Not only was some seriously kinky lingerie and nightwear from the Ann Summers catalogue being passed around by the party organiser, but they were also encouraged to play a number of games that made even Jaxxon blush.

During one game, so innocently named 'Blind Chocolate', two pairs got up; one from each pair was blindfolded while the other lay down. Then the blindfolded woman had to find and eat the chocolates that had been laid over the body of their friend, who was lying still on the floor. Some of the people who had been placing the chocolates over the women had rested them on some questionable places.

The party organiser also put a whole new spin on the game 'Pass the Parcel'. Not only were there forfeit slips within some of the layers, but there were also occasionally mini gifts, like little tubes of lube. The main prize was one of the newest in the range of vibrators. And guess who won it?! Jaxxon blushed purple when Anna read aloud the product details of this touch sensitive, hands-free vibrator, repeatedly insisting Connor was going to love it.

With all this craziness in mind, Jaxxon had to give full credit to Nina for having her mother present. Even more credit for having her little old grandmother there – who won a tube of lube.

And when the party organiser started passing around the newest vibrators and butt plugs…well Nina's poor little grandmother didn't know where to look. Nina's mum was tanked up on as much Champagne as Anna, so she had completely lost her inhibitions and even tried to put one of the vibrators into her mouth. The grandmother shook her head and tutted in disapproval, but it only made Nina's mum worse – she tried to cuff the poor woman.

"I want Nina's mum to be my mum," slurred Anna as she slouched in the chair next to Jaxxon while they were having refreshments in the dining room. "My mum's all prissy and uptight. What was your mum like?"

"I don't really know because she was always doped up, so I never saw the real her – just a dozy, often comatose, melodramatic addict. She was funny, though."

"I think you're funny, and I am going to miss you so much." She threw her arm around Jaxxon's shoulders and gave her a little squeeze before dropping her arm again. "You will phone me and stuff, won't you?"

The doubt in Anna's voice made Jaxxon remember that day that Leah had left. Jaxxon gripped Anna by the chin. "I promise I'll phone, text, and email you as much as I can, alright?"

"You never promise anything unless you mean it."

"Well there you go then. You can rest your mind now."

"Will you miss me?"

"Of course I will." She wasn't just saying that either, she honestly would.

"You won't miss me more than you'll miss Connor, though. Don't worry, I don't mind. You're bound to miss the bloke you love like crazy."

Jaxxon turned to her sharply, forgetting that Anna had been leaning her head lightly on Jaxxon's shoulder – the poor girl practically fell across Jaxxon's lap. She pulled her upright. "I don't love Connor."

An ugly snort erupted from Anna. "Oh please don't join him in The Land of Denial."

"I'm not saying I won't miss him a bit or that I don't care about him, but I don't love him."

"Are you sure about that? Think about it: why else would you have tolerated his crap? Why else would you have been glad to see him when he turned up in France? Why else would you be staying with him until you leave for the tour? And you've never kicked him in the bollocks – that should speak volumes to you."

More words of denial gathered on Jaxxon's tongue, but they never came out of her mouth. The truth hit her so hard, she felt as though she had been poleaxed. Anna was right. She loved the soft twat. Even worse, she always had. Although inside she was panicking, her body was shock still.

"I wish you could have fallen for someone who wasn't demented."

"I wish I hadn't fallen at all."

"You don't know how to face him now, do you," Anna surmised. When Jaxxon didn't deny it, she sighed. "Well, there's no getting around that. He's got your stuff and your dog at his apartment. And he won't accept you suddenly ending things without a reason."

Why does she have to be right? Oddly enough, the one thing that would make him let go of Jaxxon without a fight would be the truth. If he knew she loved him, he'd run a mile.

"Want my advice? I actually don't care if you don't, here it is: have at least just tonight with him; go play with your new toys and make it one to remember, and then you can stay at my place 'til Monday."

"I don't know if I can do that. I don't know if I can look him in the eye now that I know this. It really doesn't help that I know he doesn't feel the same."

Anna gave her a sly smile. "I know how to make sure you can face him. It's really a very simple, tried-and-tested technique. I've done it myself millions of times."

"What?"

"Get smashed."

CHAPTER EIGHTEEN

'*Give me ten minutes*' she had said when she flitted off all carefree into the bedroom twenty minutes ago. Connor was still sat, waiting. He wondered if he should go and check on her. Jaxx wasn't a big Champagne drinker yet, for some reason, she had gulped down the stuff tonight. At least she wasn't talking slurry or stumbling everywhere like Anna.

He rose and paced out of the living room but stopped abruptly, shaking his head. Oh who was he kidding! The reason he wanted to check on her was that he couldn't wait much longer to be inside her. Needing a distraction, he went into the kitchen and grabbed himself a beer. He leaned back against the counter, guzzling his drink as he strived to ignore the erotic images that had been dancing around his head all day.

She should never have said the word 'dildo' – he hadn't been able to get the thought of fucking her with one out of his mind. The wicked little witch hadn't even let him peek in that goody bag. No, she'd held it against her chest like it was a life jacket and she was in the middle of the Pacific Ocean.

"You're looking very fierce," said Jaxxon, leaning against the doorway. His scowl of sexual frustration was hilarious. She hadn't been purposely making him wait. She had just needed time to quickly pack her stuff so that she wouldn't have to do it in the morning. The last thing she wanted when she told him she was leaving was to then have to stick around while she packed. All done, she'd slipped into her brand new little nightie.

Connor's mouth went dry at the sight of her in that thin, white thing that was all lace and silk. It clung to her while giving him the most fantastic view of her incredible breasts. Jesus, it was shorter than mid-thigh. All he would have to do was raise it a few inches and there would be another fantastic view. "Come here." Wearing a cheeky smile, she shook her head. "I've waited long enough. Come here. Now." As she strolled to him with that feline grace of hers, he appraised her repeatedly from head to toe, riveted by the vision of her. *Mine.*

She pressed her body to his and ground herself against him. Then she put her mouth to his ear as she said, determined to blast his shaky control to nothing, "I'm wet just thinking about using those toys. Feel." She took his free hand and guided it under her nightie, letting him know that she was Commando. He skimmed a finger through her slick folds and groaned.

"I need you to fuck me real hard tonight, Connor. Hard. Fast. Rough. Deep." In one swift movement, he lifted and laid her on her back on the counter. This time, it was his tongue that skimmed through her folds and they were both groaning.

"You shouldn't have teased me, Jaxx," he admonished before taking another long lick. "I was already too close to losing it." He kept her pinned to the counter as he toyed with her clit with his tongue. "You know what that means, don't you?" He slid her to him, hooked her legs over his shoulders, and then released his cock from his pants. "It means I'm going to have to take the edge off."

Abruptly he drove into her and it felt *so* fucking good. He took her roughly the way she loved it. He was wound so tight that he could have come after three strokes, but he wouldn't let go until she had found her own release. He shifted his angle, zeroing in on her G-spot. Four hard thrusts later, she shattered, screaming. He was right behind her.

No sooner had Jaxxon's wits returned than she felt herself sinking into a mattress. Then there were clicking and jingling sounds. She brushed her curls from her face – well, she *tried* to. Cuffs? He hadn't wasted any time searching that bag, had he? She smiled as she thought of how he must have been desperate to rummage through it since the second he saw her carrying it out to the car. Opening her eyes, she spotted him at the foot of the bed examining something in his hand with a very wide smile on his face. Her brand new vibrator.

"Seven different intensities…Can be used hands-free…Interesting. I do believe we'll be having fun with this."

If Jaxxon wasn't still a little dazed, she might have laughed at the way he dropped his hand into the bag, blindly seeking something. He looked like a little kid playing Lucky Dip.

"Batteries. Not so interesting, but we'll need them."

"Hey, why am I naked?"

"Sorry, Jaxx, but as much as I loved that little creation you were wearing, it had to come off so I could have complete access to this body." He loved that he could get her so high on bliss that she hadn't even noticed him whipping her nightie off or washing his come from between her legs. He dug deeper into the bag and came out with a small box that contained a pink slightly curved mini vibrator. "Hmm. Recommended for use on the clitoris, but can be used to seek out other sensitive zones. I like the sound of that."

Another dip. "A box of flavoured condoms." He slung them over his shoulder across the room. He wanted nothing between her skin and his. "Chocolate flavoured body spread. Two bottles of lubricants, each designed to enhance sensitivity. Oh I think we'll have to try that. And last but definitely not least…" He wiggled the jingling toy in his hand. "Ankle cuffs."

Her legs were suddenly shifted and then there was more clicking. It instantly occurred to Jaxxon that she was practically helpless. "McKenzie, you try any freaky shit and I swear I'll shove my brand new vibrator up your arse."

"Hmm, I'm curious, how will you do that if you're cuffed to my bed? You know, Carter, I quite like you all at my mercy like this." He walked slowly around the bed, examining her from all angles and making her frustrated with anticipation. He didn't think there was anyone else who he actually liked while they were frustrated. There was definitely no one else who turned him on while they were frustrated. "What to play with first…"

As a sly smile played around the edges of his mouth, Jaxxon narrowed her eyes. "No freaky shit," she repeated. If there was even a *whisper* of a whip or a gag or a collar, she would kill him. If it wasn't for the effects of the Champagne, she might not have let him cuff her ankles as well as her wrists.

He knew he should reassure her that he wouldn't do anything that she didn't like, but he couldn't resist winding her up. "Or what?"

She mirrored his sly smile. "Or I won't suck you off."

"You really shouldn't have said that. Now I can't get rid of the picture of my dick in your mouth." Why should he try to? He watched hunger flare in her eyes as he removed his shirt and pants and, finally, his boxers. He moved close to her, letting his once-again-hard cock bob in front of her face. "Lick it."

There was only one reason Jaxxon was letting him get away with the dominant display – she had come to learn that there was power in being submissive. Not just because the safe word could end it all, just like that. In Jaxxon's experience, nothing seemed to turn on a male more than a woman doing what he told her. Before long, he lost control and then it was the woman holding the power. Locking their gazes, she ran her tongue from base to tip and then circled the head.

Connor sucked in a big gasp of air and his stomach quivered. "Can you taste us both on me, babe?" She nodded and then licked him again, this time starting at his balls. He groaned. "Open your mouth." When she did, he surged inside and his eyelids drifted shut at the amazing feeling of her sucking him and gliding her tongue around him. He knew he'd have to pull out now or he would reach the point of no return and spill in her mouth. "Stop."

Jaxxon successfully contained her smile as she watched him almost lose it. She doubted she'd manage the submissive act for long – his bossiness would drive her mental. He held up the mini curved vibrator and switched it on. It surprised her that it was practically noiseless. Maybe it was weak or—

Oh. No, definitely not weak. Jaxxon's leg quivered as he trailed the tip up her inner thigh. Instead of wandering anywhere interesting, he trailed it up her other inner thigh. Then he crawled over her and captured her lips with his, thrusting his tongue into her mouth and gliding it against her own. At the same time, he trailed the tip of the vibrator along her neck and dug his hips into hers. She moaned into his mouth and replicated the movement with her own hips.

When he broke the kiss, there was a sneaky expression on his face as he again appraised her body – it was one she'd seen before. "Oh no, *no way* am I lying here for like half an hour while you kiss and bite me from head to toe again." It had been torture having her climax so close for so long when he wouldn't let her go over the edge.

"I think you'll find that that's *exactly* what I'm going to do…only this time, I'll be using my new toy here as well. You know, I quite like it."

"Bastard," she hissed.

"Now that wasn't very nice, Jaxx. I think I might just take a little longer than half an hour now." She gaped in outrage. "Don't worry, if at any time you can't take anymore, just say 'please' and I'll—"

"I. Don't. Beg."

Oh he knew that. No matter how much he'd teased her, he had never been able to get her to beg. That was going to change tonight. The woman was a walking challenge and he couldn't help but rise to it.

"I can't believe—"

"Sorry, can't chat, I'm off to have some fun with this gorgeous body and my new toy." Using his arsenal of tongue, teeth, mouth, hands, and vibrator, he teased the hell out of her. First he explored her neck and along her collarbone. Next he teased her shoulders and arms. Then he moved onto the slope of her breasts. "Had enough yet?" he asked the shaking, moaning woman beneath him. She gave him a mutinous look. He skipped her breasts and worked along her ribs, stomach, and navel. By then, she was juddering and whimpering, and constantly bucking in an effort to grind herself against him, but he had raised his body over her so he was out of reach.

Again and again she neared her peak, but he backed off each time and waited while she came down from her mini high before he got to work again. "Shall I stop?" Another mutinous look. This time, he worshipped her legs from thigh to foot and then back up again. He licked along the creases where her hips met her groin, and she twisted and arched in an effort to get some relief from his mouth. Even though it nearly killed him, he resisted. "It's only a word, Jaxx. Just one."

"Yeah? Well here are two: Fuck. You."

He had to smile. Even though her body was completely restless and she was gasping for release, she fought him. She wouldn't be Jaxx if she didn't. "Wouldn't you like it better if *I* fucked *you*?" When she squeezed her eyes shut, he knew she was fighting herself. So close to begging. "You know what to do if you change your mind."

Again he licked the creases, again ignoring her body's pleas for release, and worked his way upwards. He made his bites harder and used more pressure as his hands kneaded her skin. With the vibrator, he paid particular attention to the erogenous zones he'd previously found, and occasionally he teasingly dug his hips into hers before elevating his body again.

"Connor, stop being a twat!" She had meant to shout but her voice was so hoarse and unsteady that the words sounded pitiful.

He seized those feral eyes. "I'm not giving in this time, babe."

"I don't beg."

He brushed his lips against hers. "I'm not trying to eat at your pride, it's not about that."

"Then why?"

"I need to know that you want me so much, you'd beg." He moved his mouth to her ear and whispered persuasively, "Say it, Jaxx. Say it and I'll shove my fingers inside you and fuck you with them until you come. Don't you want that?"

"Do it," she demanded through her teeth.

"*Say it.*"

She might have cursed him to hell, but then the crafty bastard lashed her nipple with his tongue and suckled on it, making her arch off the bed. "Please."

"Good girl," he whispered as he plunged two fingers into her. Kneeling over her, he used his other hand to tease her clit with the vibrator as he roughly thrust his fingers in and out of her, targeting her G-spot. She lasted all of about eight seconds before her climax crashed into her and she gave a loud cry. While he waited for the aftershocks to ease, Connor softly kissed her face and neck. "You have no idea how gorgeous you look when you come." When she just laid there limp, he smiled a very boyish smile. "You alright?"

All she managed was an intelligible sound. She felt the loss of his body heat and then the mattress bounced slightly as he got up. She wanted to open her eyes but her lids weren't cooperating. Her ears picked up on a cracking sound, like the plastic seal on a lid opening. She tried to remember what in that bag had a lid on it, but nothing came to her very dreamy mind. Then the bed dipped again and there was a very familiar smell that she adored.

Jaxxon's lids finally lifted, and there was Connor kneeling over her with his dick up close, smeared with chocolate spread. She didn't hesitate on lapping up a little. Then she lapped up more and swiped her tongue up the solid length of him before licking along the slit.

Connor groaned. She smiled up at him and his dick seemed to swell. "Again." He watched, riveted, as over and over she licked his dick like it was an ice cream. Whoever put this spread in her bag had his utmost thanks. Then she closed her mouth over the head and sucked vigorously, occasionally running the tip of her tongue along the slit. "Jesus, babe." She chuckled and the vibrations shot all the way to his balls. "You are a witch." He pulled out and backed away, settling himself between her legs where he had left two items waiting. Her eyes widened as he lathered the vibrator in one of the lubricants – not that she'd really need the lube, but it was supposed to enhance sensitivity. "Just relax for me."

Jaxxon did her best to relax, but as she felt the cold, lube-covered head of the vibrator breach her opening, the strangeness of it made her tense.

"It's alright, babe, relax, it'll feel really good in a minute when I switch it on." The sight was practically hypnotic as he pushed it in an inch and then withdrew, then another inch and he withdrew again. Then he worked it in deeper until he had it lodged as he wanted it. Seeing that the tension had left her, he pressed the switch. She bucked and moaned. God bless hands-free vibrators.

Connor positioned his cock near her mouth again and fisted his hands tight in her hair. She gasped at the sudden pain and he took advantage, surging into her mouth. Bliss. Keeping her head still, he fucked her mouth, loving the feel of her groaning around his cock. "Fuck, yeah." He'd been dying to know what it would be like to have her plush mouth wrapped around him while she came, and now he was going to find out.

When he sensed that her climax was looming, he reached behind him and pinched her clit. She cried out around him, sending vibrations shooting down his cock to his balls and up his spine. "Jesus Christ, Jaxx." Jets of come spurted out of him and into her mouth as his own intense climax hit. She'd kill him one day.

Again Jaxxon found herself in a dreamy state where her eyelids were on strike. She felt as Connor withdrew from her mouth and pressed a lingering kiss to her forehead. He switched off and pulled out the vibrator and then collapsed beside her.

It could have been minutes or hours later when the mattress bounced as he left the bed. Then there was rattling and jingling. More cuffs? No, her ankles were free. The mattress dipped again and then a mouth latched onto one of her nipples and suckled. How could she be groaning? Shouldn't her body be too satiated for this? It was like it was stuck in Shag Mode. The mouth was gone and then there was more jingling. Her wrists were free. She was about to mutter a thanks when she was flipped onto her stomach and her arse was raised. "Let me just have a minute."

"No rest for the wicked, babe."

"Shouldn't you be spent by now?"

"It turns out you're my own personal brand of Viagra." He ran his hand from the nape of her neck down the length of her spine and then drove a finger inside her. Her muscles gripped it tight and moisture drenched it. "Seems to me like your body doesn't need a minute."

"My body's a slut like you said."

"No, I said you're *my* slut. And do you know what I want my slut to do?" He curled his body over hers and whispered into her ear, "I want you to scream my name when you come." He slammed into her, groaning at how her muscles constricted around him. Then he was pounding into her like a man possessed.

Jaxxon fisted her hands in the bed sheet as he held her still and ferociously hammered into her. At that moment, Connor was sheer male domination. It was like that ravenous appetite he had for her had taken over and was manifesting itself in this frenzied pounding. The combination of the pressure of his size filling her and his feverish movements was the ultimate in bliss. Considering that she had already had three unbelievably intense orgasms, it was no surprise that the friction was already building again. Startling her, a hand came down sharply on her arse. The bloke was obsessed with spanking!

He did it again, harder this time, and her muscles clamped tight around his dick. "That's what I like, babe – your body gripping me like it never wants to let go." He spanked her again and she jerked at the impact but groaned; her muscles clutched him again and more moisture swamped his dick. "I told you that you loved it, didn't I?"

Jaxxon wouldn't have thought it was possible, but his pounding actually became more frantic. She was groaning feverishly, restlessly squirming in his grip as the friction inside her intensified. "I'm going to come."

He drove his fingers into her hair and wrenched her head back. "I want you to scream my name, Jaxx. I want to hear you scream it." He raised one knee and tilted her hips slightly, allowing him to go that much deeper, and then he was hammering into her again. "Come for me *right now*."

Her climax spiked and rippled through her shuddering body, completely fragmenting her. She screamed his name, and a second later he was growling hers as he slammed home one last time and pulsed deep inside her. Then they both collapsed.

In that state where 'awake' wasn't far away but opening your eyes felt like too much effort, Connor rolled over in bed to snuggle against Jaxx. His arm found nothing. The surprise of it made him frown — strange how waking up with her for a few mornings in France and then a couple here in his bed felt more familiar than a lifetime of waking up alone. Opening his eyes, he confirmed that, no, she wasn't there. Her side of the bed was cold.

He lifted his head, intending to call her name, but movement in the corner of the room caught his eye. There she sat on the stool that was usually kept in the bathroom. Two things registered: she was fully dressed, and she had a strange glint in her eyes. He lifted enough to support himself on one elbow. "Jaxx?"

"You once said that you nearly came to see me on my fifteenth birthday. If you had gone to the Glennons', I wouldn't have been there. And if you had asked them where I was and then gone there to see me, you wouldn't have seen me with some boy. You'd have seen a police car."

Aware that she was now about to open up to him, he sat up straight and gave her his full attention. Then what she said sunk in: she wouldn't have been at the Glennons'? Police car?

Jaxxon clasped her hands together. "The night after you left, Nick Crawley's gang turned up at the Glennons' house. They wanted to know where you were and figured you wouldn't have gone anywhere without telling me where. I guessed by the bruises and cuts that Nick was covered in that you'd beat him senseless. A couple of his mates were in a similar shape — especially Sean Beckett." Who was still a sick shit and she could only hope he hadn't found Celia and their little girl.

"They knew I wouldn't lie about where you were, because they knew you wouldn't have cared if they found you. So when I told them I didn't know but that you'd be coming to see me, they believed it." So had she. "They kept cornering me outside school, wanting to know if you had been in touch. I always had Leah with me and whatever boyfriend she had at the time, so they never did much."

Connor wanted to know what exactly she meant by 'never did much', but he didn't want to interrupt her flow.

"But then, six months after you had gone, she left. The day after that, Nick — who had reached the conclusion that if you hadn't been in touch yet then you weren't going to — cornered me outside school. I was on my own. He said that if he couldn't give you the beating you had given him, he'd settle on using me. Their plan was to take turns on me.

"What Nick wasn't expecting was for me to fight. When I got a good opening, I booted him in the bollocks and ran. You remember how fast I was. When I ran into the house with my hair looking like a bird's nest, my clothes ripped, and bruises already forming, the Glennons were concerned. Until I mentioned Nick's name. He was their nephew, remember. They didn't phone the police. They phoned social services, made me out to be some Jezebel and said they wanted me moved."

"Jaxx," he said in a quiet voice, shaking his head. "I'm so sorry."

She smiled a sad smile. "Why, are you a god? Did you make all that happen?"

"You know what I mean."

"And you know I'm right. Anyway," she paused and took a deep breath, aware that what she told him now might forever change how he looked at her, "I was supposed to go into a home – it's not easy finding placements for troubled teenagers – but instead, I ended up with this family who were religious fanatics. Other than taking their religion a little too far, they were alright. It was their son who was the problem. Obviously Matthew was the perfect Christian boy when his parents were around."

The disgust as she talked about the boy said enough for him to guess what had happened. "He raped you," he whispered.

She shook her head. "No. I let him do it."

"But, Jaxx, why?"

"Because it was either I was a good girl and did what I was told, or he'd use the five year old girl who moved there the same day as me. And he *would* have done that. It wasn't about sex, it was about control and power. Teenager, kid, boy, girl – those details didn't matter. To him, the foster kids in his house were toys. As long as I let him use me, he left the others alone."

"Didn't you tell anyone?"

"You think anyone would have believed me after what the Glennons had said about me? And like I said, the parents only saw a good Christian boy. If you said anything about him, you were punished."

"But you told the police eventually? That's why they came?"

"For the weeks running up to my fifteenth, he kept saying he had a nice surprise for me; he was going to make sure it was a special night. I didn't know what he meant, didn't want to."

Connor gritted his teeth. His fists were clenched so tight, his knuckles were white.

"The night before my fifteenth, I set my alarm for 2:30am to go meet him in the shed like he told me. But I just couldn't do it. I couldn't bring my hand to even touch the bedroom door handle. It was about 3am when he finally came looking for me. I was in bed, pretending to be asleep. I could smell Vodka on him, so he must have got trashed while he was waiting." Even now the smell of Vodka triggered flashbacks. "It wasn't 'til he got close that I saw the big knife. I honestly don't remember thinking *anything*, I just reacted. I grabbed my art scissors from the desk near the bed and stabbed him in his side.

"His parents phoned the plod, wanting me arrested. I didn't tell the police everything; just that I saw someone breaking into my room with a knife and acted on instinct. But they smelled the Vodka on Matthew, and the good Christian boy couldn't come up with an acceptable reason why he'd have a knife and be coming into my room at 3am. It turned out that some of the kids who had been there before me had made complaints about him, so he'd already been on the plod's radar. A case was built and he was eventually prosecuted. I'd left foster care by then."

"God, Jaxx." He couldn't even look at her – the guilt was swarming him. If he hadn't been so stupid as to beat up Crawley or if he had at least come to see her, he would have known and could have dealt with him. Then Jaxx wouldn't have gone through all that.

"The blame isn't yours, Connor. You didn't put a gun to Nick's head and make him try to rape me, or put a gun to Matthew's and make him do all that sick shit. If you take any of that blame, you're relieving Nick and Matthew of it. I won't let you do that, I want them to have that blame like they should."

"Do you know why I beat Crawley to a pulp? He asked if my leaving meant you were fair game. I lost it. But if I hadn't—"

"He would probably still have done something like that because he was a perv, always had been, just like Sean." She sighed. "The way I always thought of it was that if I'd stayed with the Glennons then Matthew would have done what he did to me to little Annie. She was just *five*. I could never wish that on her or anyone else. As sad as it is, this kind of thing happens a lot when you're in care. And when you're not in care. There are people who have been, who still are, going through way worse than me."

"How can you not blame me?"

For a while she had been angry with him, but it was only last night that she realised why: not because he hadn't helped her, but because he hadn't loved her like she loved him. "There are so many 'ifs', Connor. *If* the Glennons had done something about Nick, I wouldn't have had to be moved. *If* the social worker had sent me to a different foster home, I'd never have met Matthew. *If* Matthew's parents hadn't been blind to what their son was like and ignored all the complaints made about him, he would've been prosecuted before I came along."

He knew she was right, but still it was eating at him. He got out of bed and went to her. Squatting in front of her, he took her hands in his. "Whether you blame me or not, I'm still sorry. You're such an amazing person to get through something like that and come out of it the person you are." And he had every intention of twatting the life out of this Matthew, if he could find him. "Thank you for telling me. It can't have been easy for you to talk about. You're a stronger and bigger person than I could ever hope to be, do you know that?"

The gentle contact was killing her. She would have preferred for him to be repelled by her and not want to touch her. It would make what was coming next so much easier. "Connor—"

"Shh." He circled her with his arms and gently held her to him.

It wasn't an embrace filled with sympathy or Jaxxon would have ended it. It wasn't to comfort her either. It was as though he was holding her to reassure himself that she was okay, that she was away from all that. Her eyes closed when he started doodling circles on her back with his finger.

Never before him had she liked gentle touches. And why? Because it meant relaxing into someone, letting down her guard enough to trust that that touch wouldn't change into something else; to trust that they wouldn't hurt her physically or emotionally. Connor had actually penetrated that shield she had erected around herself, and now she was about to leave him. Made no sense when you put it like that, but all she would be signing herself up for with Connor would be something that would forever be casual.

"You really don't hate me?"

Her laugh was silent. "I don't hate you." It would be easier if she did. "I love you, actually." He pulled back and his eyes shot to hers. "I was angry that you never came back, but that was because I loved you and was missing you and was hurt that you didn't feel the same." She made sure she sounded reassuring. "I'm not expecting you to say you love me. I'm not expecting you to give me more. I'm just telling you so that you know why I'm ending this now. I can't be involved with someone I love who doesn't love me back, Connor."

Speechless. Connor was actually speechless. It had been the last thing in the world he had expected her to say. He hadn't believed that she could ever feel like that for him. Ever. He wasn't exactly a lovable person or the type to give her the things she wanted from life...which was why she was leaving. He was losing her for good. He'd probably never see her again. And just like that, he was panicking. When she started to stand, he held her in place. "Jaxx." He didn't know what to say. "Jaxx, you know I care about you."

She did know that, she finally believed it. "It's not enough, Connor. I'm not condemning you for that, alright, I'm not. I knew going into this that there could be nothing more, I wasn't expecting anything more. God, I wasn't expecting to *want* anything more." With a half-smile, she stood. "It had to end sometime, right? I'm just ending it sooner rather than later."

Feeling like he was in some sort of daze, Connor followed her out of the room. She was leaving. Leaving. And he didn't know what to do. He didn't even know what he was feeling. Different conflicting emotions were swirling inside him and fogging his thoughts to the extent that he couldn't tell what those emotions were. His chest ached and burned. All he knew for sure was that he didn't want her to go. Everything inside him rebelled against it.

When he saw her suitcase and handbag positioned near the door, he frowned. There was no way she could have packed without him hearing her fumbling around, which could only mean that she had packed last night. "You knew last night that you would be ending this today," he surmised. How had he not seen it in her eyes? "Where are you going to be staying?"

Wanting to dodge that question, she asked, "Would it be alright if I left Bronty with you and have Tony get him later?" Tony had moved her car and parked it outside his house to confuse whoever was following her. Connor had known, even gave Tony her keys, agreeing it was a good idea. "I won't be allowed to put him in a taxi with me." Ollie was outside right now waiting for her; they would be going straight to the airport from here.

"Yeah, sure." His voice was low and rough. He watched as she made a fuss of Bronty and then went to her case and handbag. Panic welled up again inside him. "Jaxx."

Jaxxon was surprised by the torment she saw on his face. She shouldn't have told him about what had happened with Nick and Matthew. Now he was feeling guilty and probably thinking that she was really leaving because she blamed him for everything. She went to where he stood – for once he was naked in front of her without an erection – and looped her arms around his neck and rested her head on his shoulder. She wasn't good at affectionate touches, but she wanted to give him a sort of 'bye hug', wanted him to know there were no ill feelings. He crushed her to him and buried his face in her hair.

"Stay."

The whispered plea had her eyes snapping open. In spite of the fact that she didn't want it to, hope was blossoming inside her.

"You're not leaving for New York 'til Monday, stay 'til then."

And just like that, the hope withered away. There was a spike of anger inside her. Here he was asking her to stay, even though he knew she'd be hurting the entire time. And all just to feed his addiction. Taking a deep breath, she returned to her case and bag. She gave him one final look as she held open the front door. "Take care, Connor."

CHAPTER NINETEEN

The second the door clicked shut behind Jaxxon, her oesophagus began to ache and a pressure began to build in her chest. With each step she made toward the elevator, the pressure became heavier – a pressure that had nowhere to go and was expanding inside her like a balloon. It was destined to burst and she knew it, and she found herself distantly wondering if it would manifest itself in tears. She was only 'distantly wondering' because it was so hard to care. She had just walked away from the bloke she loved, who cared if she cried?

The very moment she stepped into the empty elevator, her eyes began to sting and her throat felt swollen. Yep, she was going to cry alright, and it seemed that her body was fighting it because her jaw had hardened and her lungs were insisting on steady breaths. The feeling of descending as the elevator began to lower only made the whole thing worse – the distance between her and Connor was increasing too quickly for her to deal with.

A part of her regretted ever letting him back into her life, but another part of her couldn't bring herself to wish away the good laughs they'd had. Of course the infatuated teenager in her couldn't understand why she was leaving him; she believed that she should be wherever he was, and she was heading for a breakdown. But the mature side of her, who had moved past what Nick and his gang and Matthew had done, was resolute that she would get past this too; was reminding her that, sure, it was painful but pain was part of life.

She hadn't taken more than four steps out of the elevator when her mobile phone began chiming. She dug it out of her bag and frowned at the screen. Tony. She really didn't want to speak to anyone right now. She wasn't even sure that any words would come out – at least not without her sounding like she had a frog jammed in her throat. The tears were so close. But this was *Tony* – someone who had done so much for her, rented out his annexe to her, and was even going to take care of her dog for her…She'd phone him back in a minute when she was feeling more composed.

Cancelling the call, she switched off her phone, flung it into her bag, and made her way to the Emergency Exit. Chino was there as usual and gave her a curious look as he spotted the suitcase. Still he politely held open the door and did his usual 'bye' salute. Only this time, as if he knew it was a permanent goodbye, he added a smile and a wave.

She returned the smile and then continued through the alleyway, striving to ignore that the ache in her oesophagus was now amazingly more prominent and that the pressure in her chest was so heavy she could hardly breathe. It just felt so wrong to walk away from him. Her brain told her it was the smart thing to do, but her soul was crying out for her to retrace her steps until she was back in Connor's apartment.

Shaking her head at herself, she picked up her pace and swerved sharply around the corner, passing the garbage bins. Then she abruptly stopped dead at the sight in front of her.

Ant.

A curved blade.

"Sorry to interrupt your quick getaway, but it sort of clashes with my agenda," said the scratchy, pitiless voice that belonged to the twat holding a blade to Ant's throat.

"*You.*"

"Yes, you really should have guessed it was me. I can see by your face that you didn't. What, you thought I wouldn't be clever enough to go around undetected like that? I'm offended."

Seething, she had to grind her teeth to stop herself from barking a string of curses. She spared a few fleeting glimpses at Ant, not wanting to take her eyes off her stalker for very long. The poor kid was sweating, shaking, and biting on his trembling lower lip. Yeah, she could well relate to the fear of having the decision of whether you live or die in the hands of someone else – this wasn't a first time for her, but if her stalker's expression was anything to go by, the plan was that this would be her last. She wanted to tell Ant it was going to be alright, that she wouldn't let him be hurt, but she couldn't show too much concern for him in front of the twat.

"Nice kid," said the stalker. "Bugging his house helped a lot with keeping track of what you were up to. As soon as I heard his dad talking about you leaving early, I knew I'd have to make my move. I predicted that you wouldn't cooperate, so I brought along a damsel for you to save — you never could resist them, could you? You know, I was hoping that you would go back to his annexe after I'd strafed your place — that would have made it a lot easier to get to you, and there wouldn't have been any nice CCTV footage of me hurling you out. Not like with your apartment building.

"But…you went and stayed with *him* — at least you've been so kind as to use the side exit where no one's around. The camera's no longer functional, in case you were wondering. You know, I don't get why women flock around that bastard. Is it the *danger* vibe that you like?" The malicious smile widened. "I've got a *danger* vibe myself, and you're about to find out just how bad it is. First, I need you to make your way to that navy Ford Escort car just behind the other set of bins. Bring your stuff with you. Don't worry, me and Ant will be right behind you."

Jaxxon shook her head. "Not a chance. I've seen this film: the victim does as she's told but the hostage still gets hurt once his role's up. I'll go with you, but only if you let him go first. Before you ask, no I'm not expecting you to just let him run crying for help. Tie him up or knock him unconscious if you must, but his role ends now." She knew she was taking a chance here, but she could see how eager the stalker was to get hold of her — she was the objective in all this and she was so close — the thing that the stalker had been building up to was so close to fruition.

Her stalker laughed. "How is it that *you're* the one making demands when *I'm* the one with the knife?"

"Anyone can pick up a knife — that doesn't make you terrifying to me. Having said that, I want to live, so for as long as you're pointing it at me I'll have to do as I'm told. But you're not pointing it at me, are you?"

The stalker hissed. She had a point — the bitch. Besides, placing this knife against *her* throat was the fantasy. It wasn't so surprising that she'd guessed that the plan hadn't been for the kid to run along home unharmed. In fact, the plan had been for the hostage to stick around a lot longer just to ensure she was a good girl.

Seeing how torn the stalker was over the idea of giving up a tool in the plan, she asked, "Do you want me to do as I'm told because he's in danger? That'll only mean that most of my attention is on him. I would've thought you would want my full attention." She shrugged. "Up to you."

"Yes, it *is* up to me. And you'll do as you're told because *I'm* the one in control."

"Then control me. Or do you need to use a teenage boy to have that dominance over me?"

Knowing time was of the essence, the stalker made a quick decision. "You try to run and I'll slit his throat."

So abruptly that she almost jumped, the stalker used the butt of the knife to whack Ant over his head. He fell in an unconscious heap on the floor. She resisted the urge to sigh in relief. A bad headache and a lump would beat a slit throat any day of the week. Knowing better than to test her stalker, she didn't run nor did she fight when she was roughly grabbed and the knife was then put to her own throat.

"*Now* we go for a little drive. Are you ready for this?"

"Yes."

"Yes, what?"

"Yes, Sean."

He smiled approvingly. "That's my good girl. I have a feeling today's going to make up for what I missed out on eight years ago. Let's find out, shall we."

If it had been any other woman, Ollie wouldn't be surprised by the fact that he had been waiting twenty-five minutes instead of the fifteen she'd said she would need. But Jaxxon didn't dilly dally or spend ages colour coordinating her stuff, and nor was she the type who would pack everything with the utmost precision. That could only mean that she and McKenzie were having some kind of row. Maybe she'd told him she was leaving for New York and he had lost the plot over her jetting off again. Or maybe he was dumping her and she was putting his bollocks through some serious pain. On the other hand, maybe they were shagging like rabbits.

Whatever the reason, he was tired of waiting. Sighing, he fished out his mobile phone from the pocket of his jeans and tried calling her. No answer – her phone was switched off. He was just about to jump out of the car and go fetch her personally when something collided into the side of the car. His eyes insisted what he was seeing wasn't real: Ant with blood trickling down one side of his face pressed against the window, banging his fist on it and mumbling something too fast for Ollie to understand in a somewhat hysterical voice.

Ollie leaned over and unlocked the door, and Ant slid in beside him, panting. "What the hell happened to you?" And why was he even there?

"Someone has Jaxxon."

"*What?*"

"Her stalker, he has her." It all came out in a rush. "He took me from outside my house and brought me here to use as a hostage, but she wouldn't go with him unless he let me go first. He thought he'd knocked me unconscious but he hadn't, I faked it, and now he has her."

Panic like nothing Ollie had ever before experienced blast through his system. "I'm gonna kill the bastard."

The hammering on the front door snapped Connor out of his reverie. Jaxx? Was she back? Lightning-fast he was at the door, swinging it open...only to find Ollie and Tony's son looking back at him. It wasn't until the kid quickly looked away, red in the face, that Connor realised he was still naked. *And* that the kid was holding a bloody tissue to his head. "What the—"

"You still have the bugs on Jaxxon?" asked Ollie as he barged in, uncaring of McKenzie's indecent state. Ollie was the one who had kept Jaxxon distracted while McKenzie and his mate planted the trackers.

"What's happened?" He was already searching out his phone to get in touch with his mate and find out her location.

"It's her stalker. He had Ant at first but he doesn't know much about him except that he drives a navy Ford Escort and that Jaxxon called him Sean."

The bottom fell out of Connor's stomach. "What did this Sean look like?"

Ant shrugged. "Mousey hair. His face had acne scars all over it. They already knew each other. He said something about finally getting to do what he tried to do eight years ago."

"*Fuck.*"

As the boot door flew open and the dim morning light met her eyes again, Jaxxon squinted. The bastard had kept her squashed in the stuffy, oily space, whistling away like he didn't have a woman curled up in the rear of his car with tape across her mouth and a thin rope pinning her wrists behind her back. He also had rope for her ankles but hadn't tied them up; he said he'd wasted enough time already and needed to get her away quickly. And now here they were...at an old warehouse?

Oh, how original.

Yes, she should be taking this more seriously as opposed to rolling her eyes as though she was dealing with a toddler who was having an extremely bad tantrum, but she had been the victim *how* many times before? She was just so tired of it now. So tired of being played with like she was some toy. So tired of being a vessel for someone else to practice their dominance levels on. So tired of people wanting to have control or power over her.

It was all so familiar and mentally draining that she couldn't find it in herself to panic. It was anger, infuriation, and loathing that was prevailing over all else. Besides, the bastard wanted her to be a quivering wreck, and if he thought she would give him what he wanted, he was very mistaken.

"I was going to take you to the alleyway where we almost had our fun last time," he told her as he peeled the tape from her mouth, giving her a quick kiss. Before she could spit at him, he twirled her around and, knife at her throat again, roughly guided her into the musty, dull building. "But I figured you'd be a noisy one, and there was *no* chance I was letting anything stop me this time around."

Jaxxon managed not to gag at the way he was sniffing her hair and licking her neck. "So that's what all this is about? One act of sexual rape that you never got a chance to commit?"

He roughly grabbed her breast, just like he had last time. "Oh there's plenty more to it than that."

"Oh do tell."

He sniggered at her attitude. Even in a situation like this, she came out with smart remarks. "Do you know how old I was when I first decided I was going to have you? Twelve. You and your sister turned up with a social worker at Nick's uncle's house. I said to Nick, 'That one's mine.' You hardly even *looked* at me."

And that was because she had felt the callousness pouring off him and Nick in waves. So had Leah – a girl who was never one to stay away from a boy had stayed well clear of those two and the rest of their little gang. "You know, when I was twelve and I was in a pet shop with

Leah, I pointed to a big white rabbit at the back and said 'I want that'. I never got it. Do you see me chasing after the sodding thing eight years later?"

"Always the comedian," he grumbled as he urged her quickly up a flight of stairs. "I can promise you that you won't be laughing or making jokes in a minute when I've got you underneath me. You know, I'm not sure what will turn me on more: you screaming in pleasure, or in pain. Probably pain."

"You haven't got the equipment to make me scream," she scoffed. Yes, she was pushing his buttons. What was the point in behaving herself? The result would be the same no matter how she behaved.

He tugged painfully on her hair. "What was that?"

"I got a glimpse of your jimmy that day in the alley. You're about as well hung as a gerbil."

"You cheeky bitch!" On finally reaching the second floor where he kept a mattress for when he brought any girls here, he shoved her toward it. Unfortunately she didn't stumble and fall like he'd expected. *Always so bloody awkward.*

"That's why you have to use a knife to get a girl to go with you. You've got nothing to offer her that'll make her come to you."

He snickered. "Trying to make me snap Jaxxon so I'll slit your throat in a fury and then this will all be over?"

She frowned. "That's actually not a bad plan. Why is it that I hadn't thought of that *but* you did with your two brain cells?"

"You make out like I'm stupid and yet I've managed to follow you around and mess with your life without being spotted. Did you know that I'm not the only one who follows you about? I saw quite a few 'watchers' while I was tailing you. They weren't so discrete. Even that Ant kid is obsessed with you. I used to always see him peeking into the windows of the annexe of a night, trying to catch you getting undressed. I could have saved him the bother and told him how you always close the curtains. Why do you think I kept robbing them when you were living in the flat?"

"That was you?"

"Oh yeah. But then you had to go and get yourself famous, and I had to hunt you down when I wanted to see you. I had to hunt down what's mine. Can you believe that?"

"I'm yours because you claimed me with your eyes when you were twelve?" she asked incredulously, but he ignored her.

"You were off in a different world then – me forgotten. You had your money and your new car and your designer gear and your celebrity friends. Me? I had nothing. Not even Celia and that kid of mine to keep me entertained."

"Best news I've heard all week."

"Then you had the nerve to actually leave the country. You went on your big posh holiday and even had McKenzie join you." He growled. "McKenzie…Now *that* is a man I hate. You always ran to him, always gave him that big smile. Never once did you look at me like that."

He honestly found that confusing?

"But him, you looked at him like the sun shone out of his arse."

Shit, he was starting to advance on her with baby steps now. She didn't want to back away from him – that would take her closer to the blood-stained mattress. But to go to the side would take her dangerously close to the gaping hole in the floorboards.

"Yeah, you shagged him over and over like the little slut you are. I watched you that time in the woods, you know." He smirked at her gasp. "I even kept that thong you left behind."

Somehow, that seemed like one of the worst things he'd done. "You perverted bastard."

"I wanted to kill him that day. Both of you, actually. It shocked me that – wanting to kill you. I'd never wanted to hurt you before."

Her mouth fell open. "*You tried to rape me.*" He shrugged and waved a hand, as if that was somehow different. Now it was her who was feeling homicidal. "I'm pretty sure even the Devil himself would be disgusted by you."

"I'd have thought you would be calling *me* the Antichrist."

"I wouldn't give you that much credit. You're not all big and powerful, Sean, which you already know otherwise you wouldn't have that knife in your hand."

"You don't like my knife?" He held it up and admired it lovingly. "I enjoy caressing my girls from head to toe with it. I think you might like it. You did in my fantasies, anyway."

"If you really had this big plan to have your wicked way with me, why try to poison me with those chocolates?"

"I just wanted you ill so that you couldn't go on tour. Then I found out that not only had you not eaten them, but you were sneaking off early. Did you honestly think I'd let that happen? That I'd let you get away from me again?"

He seemed to genuinely want an answer. "Going by the fact that you kidnapped me and brought me here, I'm going to say 'no'."

"I had planned to have this place set up all nice, but you went and forced my hand. I had to act quickly before you were halfway across the world. I wasn't ready yet."

"Sorry, I know the feeling of people messing about with your schedule." She took slow, subtle steps toward the hole.

"This bravado won't wash with me, Jaxxon. I know you're scared."

"Sean, I'd like you to consider this for a minute: you've been following me without showing your face, you've been leaving notes like some juvenile, you broke into my apartment but then scuttled off into your little hole, you've been acting like some sort of peeping Tom, and then not only did you use a kid to try to get me to do what you wanted, but you've tied my wrists so I can't defend myself. The picture I'm getting from that is of one bloody big coward. Forgive me for not feeling the need to quiver."

"You *should* be quivering. Not only do I intend to force my way inside you and plough into you while you fight me and scream, but I'm going to do it over and over. Until you bleed." A malicious grin dominated his face. "Ever taken it up the arse, Jaxxon? You will tonight. I can guarantee you'll bleed then. Maybe I'll invite Nick round when I've had my fill of you."

"I think you better had just to make up for your gerbil dick."

"Maybe I'll even invite the other lads too. What do you think? Would you like a nice, big reunion?"

"You just can't move past that failed rape in the alleyway, can you?"

"That afternoon would never have happened anyway if you had just chosen me in the beginning over McKenzie."

Anger and disbelief swirled through Jaxxon. "What?"

"You knew I wanted you, you knew—"

"Hang on a minute, at what point did our roles reverse and *you* became the victim?"

"You chose him!" he shouted, spittle shooting out of his mouth. "You looked down on me!"

"Oh you can stop right there with that talk! No *way* am I letting you blame me for what you tried to do to me back then. You did that because you *wanted* to. It was never that you wanted me. No, you didn't want a girlfriend. You wanted me crying in pain while you forced me to do whatever you wanted. And that's because you're a sick twat."

A smirk spread across Sean's face as he watched her steady herself at the edge of the hole. She'd be able to see now what he already knew: there was an almost identical hole in the floor below, as if something extremely heavy had once crashed through both floors. She wasn't going anywhere, and she knew it. He cracked his knuckles. "Just think, I'm about to finally get what I've been wanting." He was expecting a snarl, he got a smile. "Something amusing about that?"

"It's just that I haven't the faintest idea why you would think you're getting what you want."

When she peered down at the drop, he understood. "You wouldn't do that. You wouldn't pick the coward's way out."

"It's not about being a coward. It's about bringing a dramatic early end to your plan. If falling to my death means I get to stop you from having what you want, I'll happily do it."

No, it couldn't be happening again. He couldn't stand this feeling of being so close but so bloody far. She was right there…He finally had her. No, he wasn't going to let her rob him of this. Not a chance would he let her.

He abruptly reached out to grab Jaxxon, but he hadn't known a few things. He hadn't known that she was expecting this; that this was what she wanted him to do; that she in fact had no intention of leaping to her death.

And there was something else: Sean hadn't known what had happened with Matthew. Every time Matthew had touched her, he'd tied her hands behind her back first. She had never been able to figure out whether that was a precaution or if he'd just liked it that way, but Jaxxon had hated that feeling of being totally helpless. She'd learned over time how to untie that knot, but never had she freed her hands. It hadn't been that she intended to fight back. It had been so she then had that small knowledge that she wasn't helpless. It helped remind her that she was *allowing* it to happen; she was doing it for Annie. But right now, the only person she had to protect was herself.

Her movements were just as quick as his: she flung out her arms like they were wings and sharply sprung to the side. As she'd hoped, he lost his balance and fell flat on his stomach – leaving from his head to halfway down his torso dangling over the hole. He dropped the knife and it fell through the hole, hitting the floor below with a clang.

He could have easily slid himself backwards out of harm's way...if Jaxxon hadn't sat on his legs, keeping a firm grip on him.

"Now I haven't seen *this* film," she said. "Usually the victim makes a run for it when she gets her opening, doesn't she? Then the killer chases her and eventually closes in on her, delivering the killing blow."

Sean attempted to struggle, trying to buck her off him, but then stopped abruptly when the floorboards beneath him creaked.

"I don't feel like running, Sean. I ran last time and look what happened. You came after me. How old was I back then, fourteen? Is that how old all the other girls were? Or were they even younger like your *daughter*?"

He grunted when she dug her fingers into his legs. "Get off me!"

"Hurting any kid is vile, but your own daughter, Sean...How could you do it?"

"*Get off me!*"

"Shall I tell you how? Because you're certifiably evil. Oh, I'm not saying you were born evil. No, because that would be the same as saying that you can't help the things you do and that it's part of your make-up. No, you're evil because you *choose* to do such cruel, disgusting things."

He gritted his teeth against the pain of the cracked floorboard digging into his chest. "Get off me, you bitch!"

"Are you sure you want me to do that? There's a good chance that if I do, you'll topple to your death."

"*Get off me!*"

"Doesn't feel good being helpless, does it?" she growled. "It turns out you're not so big and bad without your knife."

"You bitch! I'm going to fucking kill you!"

"You know, that's really not the way to get in my good books and make me consider letting you up and, thereby, live. I could so easily shove you down that hole, and you know it."

He sniggered. "You wouldn't kill me. You're a lot of things, Jaxxon—"

"Oh you mean like a slut, a bitch, a slag—"

"—but you haven't got it in you to take someone's life."

"Maybe you're right. But then, maybe you're not."

"If I were you, I'd run so far so fast—"

"How can you not realise how ridiculous you sound threatening me right now?" She dug her fingers into his legs again, wrenching another grunt from him. She could tell he was in some serious pain. He was shaking from the effort to keep his upper body from dangling, and his hands were bleeding from where he was clinging to the broken, spikey boards. "Would you like me to move off you so you can get up? I'll want something from you."

"Oh yeah?" he snickered.

"Yeah, I'll need you to apologise to me for everything you've done."

"Fuck you."

"Sorry, that plan's already been foiled. Let's instead hear you say a great, big sorry."

His words came out through gritted teeth. "Get off me, bitch!"

Jaxxon sighed loudly. "This is very disappointing. But you know, Sean, even if you were sorry and I genuinely believed that you'd never, ever, ever hurt another kid ever again, that you'd never take another girl's innocence away, that you'd never beat up or rape another woman or hurt any human being ever again...*it just wouldn't be bloody good enough.*" She punctuated that by digging her fingers into his legs again.

"You want a promise? I'll make you a promise! I swear I'm going to fuck every hole you have in your body and then I'm going to slit your throat! Now get the hell off me!"

"If you insist." With that, she sharply stood to her feet and moved away. Having lost her bodyweight he toppled over, hoarsely crying out. There was then a loud thud. Jaxxon walked carefully to the edge and peeked over. Sean was perfectly still, sprawled on his back. She couldn't tell whether he was still alive or unconscious. She should care, but she didn't. How many lives had he ruined? How much innocence had he stolen? It had been a case of her life or his, and she'd choose her own over a bastard's like that any day.

As her body sagged in relief, she backed up a few steps and lowered herself to the ground. There she sat, breathing through the madness in her mind and regaining her sense of composure. It could have been seconds or minutes or hours later when she became distantly aware of noises and voices. And then a set of arms wrapped around her, and she was hurled to her feet and crushed against someone's chest. She knew who it was, and she hugged him back just as fiercely.

The next few minutes passed in sort of a blur. Connor and Ollie both fussed around her before being pushed aside by a paramedic. He examined her and, satisfied she was fine but might need a needle for the shock, handed her back to Connor. A team of police officers and paramedics went into the warehouse, and an unconscious and badly injured Sean was brought out on a stretcher. Connor and Ollie both expressed their wish that he died before reaching the hospital.

While she remained in the area cordoned off with tape from the public, she was asked dozens of questions by different people until she finally reached her limit and told the male officer who was now in front of her that if he liked his bollocks, he should consider shutting his trap and moving out of her way.

"That means she's fine," said Ollie. He'd make sure she stayed that way, just as he would next time. Because, sadly, there would be a next time. Many next times. It was, unfortunately, the price that came with this life. He knew from the business he was in just how much power people believed came with beauty. They seemed to believe that if you were beautiful, things could come easy. More often, you had to put up with bitterness, envy, pettiness, and even obsessions. As such, celebs were often stalking targets. He wouldn't be surprised if Jaxxon had more than just Sean stalking her. "I'm going to call Richie, let him know you're alright."

Connor ran his hand through her hair as he held her to him. Just the thought that she could be dead right now…He felt sick. "You sure you're alright?" He felt her nod against his chest. "Come on, I don't want you standing round here any longer. Will you come back to my apartment with me?" He held his breath as he waited for her answer.

She peered up into his eyes. "I can't," she whispered. She knew nothing had changed for him. Why would it? Maybe if this was a Hollywood film, Connor would now be declaring something corny like coming so close to losing her had made him see exactly how much he cared for her, and now he wasn't prepared to let her go blah, blah, blah. But Connor's decision to not have his own family had been made before they even met; it was a decision that she didn't know the real reason behind, but she knew enough to know that it would take someone very special to him to get past whatever it was, and that person wasn't her.

He dropped his forehead to hers and sighed. "Jaxx, I do care about you."

"I know." She tried to leave his arms, but he tightened his hold and mashed his lips with hers. For once, it wasn't a kiss of hunger. It was a kiss filled with *feeling* and adoration and a hint of desperation. But that affection was just like a slap in the face because it was nowhere near enough. The verbal equivalent of this moment would have been for her to say 'I love you' and for him to say 'thank you' or 'and *I* love spending time with *you*.'

Jaxxon tore her lips free and stepped away. "Will you promise me something?" He said nothing, but she continued, "I want you to promise me you won't get in touch. No texts, no calls, no surprise visits."

"Jaxx—"

"I want to get on with my life, Connor. I want to face this head-on like I'm going to do with what happened with Sean and like I do with everything else. But I can't do that if you're popping in and out of my life whenever your 'addiction' gets too much."

"You honestly think we can cut each other out of our lives just like that?" He'd always known it would have to be this way, always. But now that it was actually happening, his mind, body, and soul were fighting it.

"Are you saying you can give me more than casual?" It was a rhetorical question but when he didn't say 'no', she was surprised. She refused to let hope well up inside her this time, though. "Well?"

The words came out hoarse. "I can't."

"Then yes, I can just cut you out." And for the second time that day, she walked away from the bloke she loved.

CHAPTER TWENTY

Connor had never actually talked to a dog before, not like this. It turned out that they were good listeners. Bronty had lay on the sofa, peering up at him with an almost worshipping look as if every word that came from Connor's mouth was a pearl of perfect wisdom. Even better, there was no judgmental crap. He could easily tell the dog how he was missing Jaxx, how he couldn't look at his kitchen counter without thinking about the time he'd lain her on it and shagged her senseless; how a shower was no longer relaxing because it only made him think of the mornings they had spent in it; how every time he sat on the sofa, he remembered the time she'd rode him on it so hard his dick should have snapped.

Worse, Connor couldn't stop dreaming about her night after night. He would wake up sweating and aching for her, and hard as a rock. Christ, she had only been staying here a few days, and the whole place was marked by her and memories of her.

Anyone else would have told him to shut the hell up moaning, but not Bronty. What the dog couldn't help him with was the answer to the question of whether this was normal: Was this what it was like when you were trying to get over someone? At first, he'd thought that this all must just be part and parcel of it. But it had been five weeks now and, if anything, he felt worse. It was like he was grieving, and no matter what he did, he couldn't make peace with the fact that she'd gone. He couldn't find it in himself to accept the situation and move on.

Only one thing in his life was separate enough from her that it didn't make him think of her: racing. Or so he had thought until he arrived at the test track and, all of a sudden, he remembered how cute she had looked that time when he'd sat her in an old sports car that was perched outside of a car museum.

He couldn't even go to the gym without talking to someone who eventually asked, 'You still seeing Jaxxon Carter?' Not once had he said no. The word never came out. He couldn't bring himself to disclaim her, to say she wasn't his, to face the fact that it was over. Somehow, there was comfort in thinking that no one yet really knew the truth; it was nice to be around people who thought the status quo hadn't changed because then he could pretend for just a while. Jesus, this really was like grieving. But was it normal?

He also wanted to know if this was how Jaxx was feeling. Or had she moved on like she'd said she would? Did she think about him? Did she miss him? Did she still love him? Was she happy? As much of a bastard as it made him, he hoped she wasn't happy without him. He wanted her to be missing him as much as he was her. He knew that was cold and selfish, but he didn't want to believe she could cut him out as effortlessly as she'd made out that she could.

So many times he'd had her number up on his BlackBerry screen with his thumb hovering over the call button, but he hadn't been able to pluck up the courage. Then one night he'd finally pressed it…only to discover that she had changed her number. That just made him feel even more like crap. Knowing that she genuinely didn't want to hear from him hurt.

On top of all that, he had the knowledge that she was as far away as Australia right now. The other side of the world from him. He was sorry he'd asked Warren to find out her location from Anna. He had thought it would make him feel better to at least know where she was, but he'd come to the conclusion that nothing could make him feel better short of having her there in front of him.

The knock on the door had him groaning. As per usual, Bronty didn't bark. Weren't dogs supposed to go mental when someone invaded their territory? Shrug. The dog could do what the bloody hell he liked for being such a good listener. It wasn't a surprise that his visitor was Dane. His judgmental frown wasn't a shock either. And this was why Connor liked Bronty better.

"I didn't see you at the gym, so I thought I'd pop round, see if you were alright."

"Why wouldn't I be alright?"

"Oh I dunno," said Dane as he lounged in one of the chairs and Connor returned to the sofa. "Maybe because you're spiralling into a state of depression, all because you haven't got the bollocks to go to the land down under and see her."

"Oh don't start, Dane."

"I only speak the truth."

"I've already told you, she told me not to go see her anyway."

"What's that got to do with anything? And why is there a brown stain on the leg of your pants? Don't tell me that's dog shit."

"Oh it's, um, chocolate spread. I dropped the tub and some went on my pants." Or, more accurately, he'd thrown it in a rage when he found it under the bed and some of it splashed him as the tub burst.

"Why's the dog still here?"

"Tony turned up the day Jaxx left, but I said I'd keep him here."

"And why would you do that?"

Maybe it would make sense for him to get rid of Bronty and anything else that reminded him of Jaxx, but even though having it all around him was torture, he didn't want to let go of her. He didn't want to forget her or the laughs they'd had.

"You do know Jaxx will want him back, don't you?"

Connor's voice was like a whip. "Don't call her that."

"Really bothers you that, doesn't it? Soon enough she'll be someone else's Jaxx, so get yourself ready for it."

Slapping his hand over his face, Connor groaned. "Dane, if you've come here to try to wind me up then just—"

Dane ignored him. "It's not like you'll get to enjoy the bliss of ignorance. It'll be all over the papers, magazines."

"*Dane.*"

"And if she does have that Elvis wedding, the photos will be everywhere."

"Just out of interest, what did I do to you to deserve to listen to this?"

Luring him into a false sense of security, Dane quieted for a moment, letting Connor think the torture was over. "What are you going to do if you hear she's pregnant?"

Connor's eyes shot to his. "I'll support the kid, obviously."

"I never meant with *your* baby, you dumb dick. I meant with whoever she walks down the Elvis aisle with." As Connor took a long guzzle of his beer, Dane saw just how much the idea of that pained him. "Why haven't you flown out to see her? Don't tell me it's because she asked you not to. You jetted off to the Alps without hesitation, why not now?"

In a low, toneless voice, he replied, "She said she loved me."

"Let me guess, you still wouldn't take things beyond casual."

"You guessed right."

"Relationships are such frightening things, are they?"

They were to him. "I'm not made for all that."

"And just what exactly did you think it was that you and Jaxxon had? You were faithful to her, you went on holiday with her – although, granted, it was a holiday you gate crashed – and for Christ's sake, you even had her living with you. It might have only been for a few days, but still. Was all that really that scary?"

"Why the hell are you here, Dane?"

"To hammer the truth home, mate. Why else?"

"The truth?" he echoed with a snicker.

"Be honest with yourself, Connor. This is about you being worried you'll turn out anything like your parents." When Connor's gaze whizzed sharply at him, Dane nodded. "Oh yeah, there were a lot of things you told me that night when you got rat-arsed on Jaxxon's fifteenth birthday. You're nothing like your dad. You haven't got it in you to hurt a woman or a kid. If I didn't fully believe that, I would never have made you godfather of my son."

"I'm like him, Dane."

"No. Being a bad-tempered bastard does not make you anything like him. Just like being able to drop people from your life doesn't make you like your mum. Does Jaxxon know all about him and what he did?"

He shook his head. He might have told her after she revealed all that stuff about Crawley and Matthew if she hadn't followed the story up with *and now I'm leaving*.

"Go see her, Con. Not just because you want to see her, not just because you miss her, but because you genuinely can't function without her here, can you?"

Connor buried his face in his hands, groaning. "No," he admitted. The feeling that he *needed* another person wasn't something he'd ever thought would happen. But Connor really did need Jaxx. He had always seen her as his Achilles' heel, but now that he thought about what the past five weeks had been like without her, he realised she was also his biggest strength.

"It wouldn't be because you love her, would it?" Dane's voice was heavy with sarcasm.

"Yeah, I love her," he said in the quietest voice.

At last, thought Dane. "It strikes me that you can, either, carry on believing what you've always believed about yourself and let your parents mess this up for you…Or you can stop being a dick, get off your arse, and go get her. Maybe you'll end up like me and Niki, and you'll get married one day and have some sprogs. On the other hand, maybe you'll bugger it up. But ask yourself: Do you want to go through life not knowing? Do you always want to have that 'what if' hanging there? More to the point, do you want to go through life without her?"

He shook his head. "No."

"Then what are you going to do about it, you daft prick?"

Ticked off, Jaxxon was totally and utterly ticked off. She hadn't slept one bit last night. The guests sleeping in the hotel suite above her had humped all night long. No matter what she jammed over her ears, all she could hear was 'harder', 'faster', 'say my name', 'who's your daddy', and 'I love you, David!' It turned out her suite was below the Honeymoon Suite. The newly-weds' activities only served to remind her that her own body was crying out for sex.

If only seeing to that problem was simple. But Jaxxon didn't do one night stands; she just wasn't built that way, and she didn't trust people easily enough to hand her body over to a perfect stranger. At the same time, however, she didn't want a relationship. Not right now, anyway. That only left her with the option of a casual fling.

Oh wonderful, more casual crap.

The biggest problem of all was that her body just didn't seem in the slightest bit interested in anyone she met. Oh it was as horny as all hell, but it just didn't respond to anyone. Anna said some crap about Jaxxon currently going through a transitional phase. In other words, her body was having withdrawal symptoms from her once pretty active sex life of a month ago.

So here she was, half asleep and moody, in a large drugstore in Perth, Australia – a place that was fantastic, apart from the fact that it was roasting hot and so she was in a dress. Yes, a dress. She still wasn't a big fan of those things. Of course Ollie didn't care that she was irritated, it made her eyes feral the way he liked.

Just as they did in every All-Sorts store they stopped in – the store that the Allure products were exclusively available at internationally – as part of the tour, she stood on a platform with Ollie while he rambled on to the frighteningly big crowd about the essentials of skin-care and big tips on make-up. Naturally his every solution included the use of one of the Allure products, and the crowd were swallowing up every word like he was the king, just as the crowds did wherever they went.

Once his mini lesson was over, Jaxxon had to say a few words as the face of the campaign, and then it was question time while some small Allure samples were passed around. Once it was done, they were bombarded with people who wanted photos or autographs. Both she and Ollie obliged anyone who was within easy reach as they made their way down the cordoned off area that led them behind the shop floor. Minutes later, they were sneaking out of a private entrance/exit and jumping into their black limousine, returning to their hotel.

Jaxxon snuggled back into the seat and closed her eyes. A little doze would do her the world of good right now.

"Are you and Anna going to spend your last day in Perth tomorrow going off to see the sights?" asked Ollie. "I can arrange a driver for you."

"I don't know yet," she replied tiredly. Anna had been flying to and from London to see Jaxxon every couple of weeks for a few days. Richie probably wouldn't have allowed the disturbance to Anna's schedule if he and Ollie hadn't been concerned about Jaxxon after the whole Sean thing. Apparently the fact that she hadn't had some sort of breakdown was worrying the hell out of them. The Sean thing she could move on from without being tempted to dwell. In fact, instead of it feeling like a terrible event, it all actually gave her a sense of peace. Maybe that was because she finally felt that she'd fought back against bastards like him, or maybe it was because now she could relax knowing that he wouldn't be terrorizing any of the people she cared about while she was gone.

"I noticed you and Anna talking to that rock band last night who's staying in our hotel. They're on their own tour, right?" At her nod, he continued, "The lead singer has taken a shine to you." A real shine to her, but much to the bloke's disappointment, she hadn't been responsive. The singer had attributed it to her being with McKenzie – the world hadn't yet realised that their 'relationship' was over, which was good because it was giving her time to heal.

But what concerned Ollie was that she wasn't healing. She was still her normal blunt, rude, playful self…but something was missing. He wasn't sure if he most wanted to pummel McKenzie, or demand that he come and fix what he'd broken. "Oi, did you see the most recent FHM magazine addition?"

"I can't say one of my pastimes is reading men's mags."

"You got the top spot on the Hottest 100 Women."

She shot him a sceptical look. "You're taking the Mick."

He chuckled at her incredulity. "Luv, may God strike me down dead now if I'm lying. You've heard of the actor who seems to be Hollywood's favourite right now, Aiden Roberts, haven't you? Well, when he was asked in an interview what celebrity he would love to date, he said you."

She sighed. "Ollie, stop with the Cupid crap. I'll bother with a bloke when I can be arsed."

"If this was Anna, you'd be just as—"

"Oh for the love of God, Ollie, will you shut your gob so I can sleep!"

He fought the urge to laugh. "Shutting up right now."

But Jaxxon didn't sleep. Most of the time, she managed not to think about Connor. She had accepted it was over and knew that spending time thinking about him was counterproductive to healing. Her mind understood that and was clear about moving on. Her body and soul were lagging behind.

Was it possible to force yourself to stop loving someone? She wasn't optimistic, considering that she had spent the past eight years in that state over him. Would it take eight years to dig herself back out of it? *Could* she?

Realising what she was doing, she gave herself a mental slap. Hadn't she promised herself that she wouldn't pine over him, that instead of treating it as an ending she'd look at it as the beginning of something new? In so many words, that was what Ollie was hinting at, wasn't he – move on, make a fresh start with someone else. It was the 'someone else' part of his solution that she had trouble with.

In spite of the fact that every bone in her body was exhausted, she was strides ahead of Ollie as they exited the limo and headed into the hotel. *Bed.* She was going to go to her room, munch on chocolate, then collapse into bed. And if her upstairs neighbours decided to talk a bit more about who the daddy was or cry again about how much David was loved, she'd go up there and give them something to really bloody cry about.

Jaxxon abruptly stopped in her tracks in the reception area as a tingle spread down her spine and the hairs on the back of her neck rose. Someone was staring. It didn't feel *wrong* the way it had when Sean had watched her, but there was something intense about the gaze locked onto her. Like the time at the charity event. Like the time in the restaurant at the Alps.

Slowly she turned…and hitched in a breath. There Connor stood about ten feet away from her in a simple get up of a dark blue t-shirt and blue jeans. He was still so gorgeous, masculine, and tempting that it hurt. A rush of heat and hunger assailed her as her body leaped to attention.

So long, it had been so long since Connor had last been able to soak up just the mere sight of her. His pulse was racing; not just with the cravings he had for her, or the anticipation he was feeling at the prospect of touching her, but with just being near her again and breathing the same air as her. He wanted to go to her and touch her, but she was looking pretty cheesed off. In fact, she'd looked like that before she even saw him. Now…it was bad. Her eyes were more feral than he'd ever seen them, but it only made his dick jerk.

As she watched him advance on her, Jaxxon's heart went into hyper-drive. It was pulsing just as wildly as her clit. Her entire body throbbed and ached for him, which just made her want to kill him. She despised herself for the fact that she was happy to see him and tempted to feel his hands on her. Fortunately for her, she had enough anger curdling inside to fuel a decent rejection. She could do this; she could think past her need for him and her jolt of happiness at seeing him, could tell him to sod off and walk away a third time. She had to.

"Hi babe," he whispered as he dropped his forehead to hers and inhaled the scent of her. She was wearing her usual perfume, and it was playing with his senses and triggering memories that were only increasing his hunger for her. He didn't dare kiss her – she would probably slap him. Worse still, it wouldn't make him stop ravaging her lips; if he started, he would not stop.

"You promised me no contact," she hissed.

"Actually, if you think back, you'll find that I didn't promise anything." He twirled a chocolate-brown curl around his finger. God, he'd missed these wild ringlets. "I'd known deep down that I'd never be able to keep that promise."

So he'd just stayed quiet and let her believe what she wanted? "You devious little—"

"Not devious, babe, just someone who won't give my word on something unless I'm positive I can keep it. Just someone who really needed to see you."

She bit back a growl. "I'm not one of your women who'll hop, skip, and shag you whenever you turn up. Go home, Connor."

Seeing that she was about to walk away, he sighed. "I had a feeling you wouldn't be reasonable." He shrugged. "You only have yourself to blame for this." With that, he scooped her up and threw her over his shoulder.

"What the hell are you doing?! Put me down!"

"Can't, Jaxx, sorry. We need to talk." As he headed for the elevator, he noticed Ollie gawping at them. Connor raised an eyebrow, daring him to intervene. But Ollie just shrugged and sighed as if defeated.

"If I wanted to talk to you, I'd have phoned!"

He smiled when he felt her reaching under the waistline of his jeans, searching for his boxers. "You're wasting your time on that one, I'm going Commando. You'll also notice that I fastened a belt around my jeans so you couldn't pull them up the crack of my arse." Cursing him, she kicked her legs and beat his back with her fists. "As much as I love feeling you rubbing against me like this, you should know that the more you squirm, the higher your dress is riding up your thighs. I don't mind getting a flash, but I'm not sure you'll want everyone else to get a good look at your Brazilian."

She growled as he stepped into an elevator – an elevator that wasn't empty! Although she stopped squirming, she resumed punching his lower back and then took to scratching him under his t-shirt.

"Mmmm. That's it, babe, I love it when you scratch me."

"We'll see if you love it when I ram the heel of my shoe up your rusty bullet hole!"

"Dirty talk already, Jaxx?"

She continued to struggle. "Connor Lee McKenzie—"

"I'm getting my full title? You must really be fuming with me right now."

Growling, she got to work on his lower back again. Then she jerked and gasped in shock as a hand came down hard on her arse. "You just spanked me!" she said disbelievingly. And in an elevator in front of people! Oh she was so going to kill him.

"God, I've missed doing that."

"You'll be missing your balls as well!"

Exiting the elevator on the fourth floor, he took long, quick strides to the luxurious suite he'd checked into only minutes ago. Once inside, he advanced straight to the bedroom and plonked a still struggling and cursing Jaxx on the huge double bed. Before she had a chance to launch herself at him, he flipped her onto her stomach and pressed his body weight down on her while he secured her wrists with the cuffs he had waiting on the headboard.

"Ohhhhhhhhhhhh, you sadistic twat!"

He slid down her body, keeping his weight over her, until he reached her ankles which he then also cuffed to the bed – leaving her in a fantastic starfish pose. "Sorry, Jaxx, but I had to be prepared in case you wouldn't listen to me."

"You think *this* will make me want to listen?"

"Well, no, but it does mean you'll have to." He settled down beside her, but she turned her head away. Propping himself up on one elbow, he drew circles on her back through her dress – a dress that had a long zip that stopped at her pelvis, begging to be lowered.

"Don't touch me!"

"I'm just trying to relax you, babe."

"Just tell me what you want. Oh hang on, let me guess, you were passing by and thought you'd drop in for a quickie."

"Actually, I've just got off a very long flight from London to see you."

"Why? Haven't you got over that addiction yet?" She snickered, trying to veil how her body was responding to his touch. "Or was it that you heard some rumour about me being with another bloke and felt compelled to come and scare him off with the caveman routine?"

"I'll be honest and say that it has been playing on my mind that you might be with someone, and I just can't have that, Jaxx."

"Oh, so you get to have as many bed buddies as you like while I have to live the life of a bleeding nun?"

"I haven't been with anyone since you." Needing to taste her skin again, he kissed her shoulder.

She snorted. "Like I'd believe that."

"It's true." He trailed kisses along her shoulder to her nape. Her answering shudder relieved him. She was still responsive to him, even if she wished she wasn't.

"Stop kissing and touching me."

"I can't, babe, I've missed you so fucking much. Everything in that apartment reminds me of you, and having the dog didn't help."

"I told Tony to take him."

"I kept him."

Shocked, she almost laughed. "Why?"

He buried his face in her soft, silky hair, loving the scent of her strawberry shampoo. "He was all I had left of you and I didn't know how to let go. I didn't want to either."

That had her backpedalling. The combination of his words and his relaxing touches – that were, unfortunately, still managing to feed her craving for him – had her melting into the mattress and calming. It was nice to know she wasn't turning frigid. "It's not enough that you missed me, Connor."

"I know, I know." Unable to stop himself, he slowly lowered the zipper on her dress.

"Connor, no—"

"Please, babe, I need this, I need to touch you." Lightly he ran his fingertips along her back.

"If you know it's not enough then why are you here? On the off-chance that I might be up for a one-off shag?"

After a deep, preparatory breath, he spoke. "You remember I told you that my sister died? What I didn't tell you was that my dad killed her." Her head instantly whipped round to face him, her expression one of shock. "He used to knock my mum, me, and Selina about all the time. One day, when she was eleven, he took it too far. My mum and I walked in as he was finishing her off. He was so smashed, he didn't even realise how much damage he'd done."

"That's why you hate him so much," she whispered, recalling the times she'd tried to get him to stop wasting energy on hating him.

He nodded. "The reason my mum found it so easy to dump me onto social services when her boyfriend asked was because she couldn't bear the sight of me. She said I looked too much like him, I reminded her of him. And I had his temper. You know what? Before that, she was a good mum, a good person. What he did just messed her up. He messed up her life and mine and, worse, ended Selina's. I was terrified she was right and I was like him; that I might have it in me to hurt a kid or a woman or mess up people's lives."

"So you decided not to have a family."

"I didn't cry when Selina died, you know. Or when my mum dumped me. I came close, but never did. I don't ever remember crying much as a kid. I thought if I couldn't even cry when my own sister died then I couldn't have really loved her, and if I couldn't love my own sister then I was someone who just couldn't love at all. That was what I reasoned."

She really wanted to say something. He had just told her some major stuff, had just confided in her to an extent that he never had before. But nothing came to mind.

"I'm not telling you so you'll feel sorry for me or to soften you up," he stated as he kissed his way along her spine. "I just want you to understand that the reason I tried to keep things casual wasn't because I didn't care about you. I honestly didn't think I could give you anything more or feel anything more." He slid his hand under her dress and palmed her arse. "But as it turns out, I've been a blind prick."

She couldn't help but close her eyes and moan as he clutched and massaged her arse. She'd missed him and missed his hands on her. Then his words filtered through. "Blind prick?"

He glided his hand along her inner thigh, loving the way she quivered, and slid his finger past her thong and between her slippery folds. "Jesus, babe, you're already wet for me."

"Stop." The protest was so weak, she might have slapped herself for sounding so pathetic if she wasn't cuffed to the bed. So caught up in the sensations, she couldn't even open her eyes. "Connor, don't. I told you I can't move on if you walk in and out like this."

"I don't want you to move on. You're mine, Jaxx. You always were."

"I belong to no one."

"Wrong." He slipped his finger inside her; her walls gripped him and moisture coated his finger. He thrust his finger in and out at a leisurely, teasing pace. Her low moans were eating at his control. "I worked it out, Jaxx – the way I hate you being away from me, the way I can't stomach the thought of anyone else touching you, the way sex is so different with you…" He draped himself over her and peeled up her dress. "I'd convinced myself I was just addicted to you, but you know what Jaxx?" He snapped her thong, ragged off his belt, and shoved down his pants. "The truth of it is, I love you." Then he slammed himself home, groaning at that blissful, familiar feeling of her muscles clasping him like a vice.

She'd forgotten just how much he stretched her, forgotten how good the burning and stinging felt. The bliss of it all almost distracted her from the conversation. "You, what?"

"I love you." Thrust. "You're mine." Thrust. "And you're not leaving me ever again." Thrust. "I really am *so* sick and tired of trying to live without you." *Thrust.* He then raked a hand in her hair, brought her face to his and began roughly pounding into her as he ravaged those sensual lips. His longing for her, everything he felt for her, spilled out of him in a furious, manic pace that was punctuating everything he'd said. "I've missed this."

"Oh my God," she moaned into his mouth. She couldn't keep quiet: she was moaning, groaning, whimpering, and coming dangerously close to crying with the perfection of it all. She probably should have been doubtful about a bloke suddenly claiming that he loved her, but she knew Connor well enough to know that if there was one thing he would never lie to her about, it was that. And the knowledge that he loved her just made this all the more amazing. Every ruthless thrust was a stab of pure bliss. She was burning from the inside out, heading closer and closer to her orgasm.

Her noises were killing Connor. He wouldn't last much longer, not when he'd been starved of her for so long. He slid a hand beneath her and palmed her breast before sliding it down to her clit. He teased and circled it with his finger and she sobbed into his mouth. "That's it, babe, isn't it? That's what you like. Tell me you love me. Tell me, Jaxx, I need to hear it."

"I love you," she rasped.

"Tell me again."

"I love you." Feeling her climax closing in on her, she cried, "Connor, I'm going to come."

He roughened his pace and pounded harder. "Scream my name for me, babe. Now."

He pinched her clit and Jaxxon was gone; a violent climax like nothing she'd ever known before crashed into her and rippled through her reverberating, frenzied body.

The combination of her walls closing in on him and his name escaping her lips in a scream had his dick practically detonating: his come fiercely jetted out of him. "*Fuck*." It wouldn't stop, his cock seemed to just keep pulsing inside her, filling her with every last drop he had. Then, totally and completely sated, he collapsed beside her and nuzzled his face in her hair.

When he could finally form a sentence again, he murmured, "I'm sorry I took so long to sort my head out."

"Mm," was all she managed in response. She heard him chuckle and then there was a lot of fidgeting and bouncing of the mattress. Then her arms were free and next her legs. She still hadn't moved when he joined her on the bed, not even to retract her arms; she was utterly spent and had no real intention of moving just yet. Connor snuggled against her side and played with her hand, kissing it and fiddling with her fingers.

"I knew it would fit."

She frowned. "Mm?"

"It fits."

Lazily opening one eye, she gazed at the hand that he was still fiddling with…and the white-gold diamond ring that now surrounded her third finger. Instantly both her eyes were wide open. "Connor." She swallowed hard. "What're you doing?"

Connor's lips twitched in amusement at the way she spoke to him in a calming tone like he was an insane person who might need to be talked down from a frenzied state. "I picked white gold because I know you like it better than yellow. I wanted to get you a big, bulky diamond, but I know you'd never wear it. But no chance was I going to get anything as understated as you would have chosen, so I'd say that's a good compromise."

What the hell was the mental bugger doing? "Um, Connor—"

"I wanted to ask you while I was in my favourite place." He slipped a finger inside her, indicating what he meant. "But I figured that if I did that, you would think I'd only asked you because I got carried away while we were shagging." He brushed his lips against hers. "I admit I do get carried away when I'm inside you."

"If this is some sort of gesture—"

"No, no gesture. I'm one hundred percent serious."

"But you just told me about why you never wanted any of this."

"I also told you I've been a blind prick." He manoeuvred her so she was fitted against him; face to face, chest to chest. "I love you, Jaxx," – kiss – "and I want to marry you" – kiss – "and I want my kids to grow right here." He stroked her stomach gently. "And if you say no, I'll put the cuffs back on and keep them on 'til I can get you to change your mind." He wasn't kidding.

"I didn't end this because I wanted you to ask me to marry you. All I wanted was to know that it could happen one day."

"Good. We're ahead of schedule then."

She was so tempted to relax into him and the moment, but she couldn't quite get her head around his complete change of intentions for the future from permanent bachelor to committed husband and dad. "I don't want you to force yourself to do this and then end up changing your mind later."

"If I wasn't sure, I wouldn't ask you, would I?"

"Technically, you haven't asked at all."

Realising she was right, he smiled. "Marry me, Jaxx." Not that she really had a choice. He wasn't living without her, he couldn't.

"You're sure this is what you want?"

"Positive. The question is: Is it what you want as well?" As the seconds dragged on and she remained silent, he was about ready to panic. But then her lips curled into a cute, little smile that plucked at his heart.

"Yes, you dick," she whispered. Without missing a beat, his lips landed on hers and he took her mouth in a soul-wrenching kiss. In record time, both their clothes were off and he was inside her again. It had started off slow and sensual, but the fact was they just weren't 'slow' people. Before long he was hammering into her at his usual feverish pace that they both revelled in, and then she was screaming his name while he was growling hers.

They were still panting and shuddering with the aftershocks when her mobile began ringing. As she was comfy sprawled over Connor with him still inside her, she didn't bother getting it. But then it rang again. And again. Huffing she reached over the bed to where he had dumped her bag and dug out the still chiming phone. It was Ollie. "Hello."

"Jaxxon, there's, er, someone here who says you know them and wants to, er, see you."

"Who?" Her mouth dropped open wide at his answer. She sat up abruptly. "Where?"

"In the reception area, but if you want to do this and you want some privacy, we can meet you in my room."

"Alright. I'll be five minutes."

"What is it?" asked Connor the second she finished the call. She didn't shout her answer until she was in the bathroom. He swore at the news and jumped up. As she'd locked the door, he stood outside it. "Why wasn't your response 'fuck off'?"

Little more than twenty seconds later, she was back in the bedroom redressing with Connor following her about the room like a lost kitten. "What happened to my shoes?"

"Jaxx, you don't have to do this," he said as he quickly threw on his own clothes.

"Stop panicking."

"I don't want you upset."

"Who says I'll be upset?"

"Her pastime was upsetting you."

"I'll be fine." Finding her shoes under the bed, she slipped them on. Now fully dressed – bar her thong, which Connor had destroyed – she made her way to the door.

"Babe, you don't owe her this," he told her as he followed her out of the suite toward the elevator. "She left you—"

"So did you," she said softly and non-judgementally. "And I've just said I'll marry you. If I can do that, then I can give my sister two minutes of my time, can't I?"

He supposed that was a fair comment. He *hated* that it was a fair comment. He was still tormenting himself over leaving her. But this was Leah they were talking about – the one who had spent years picking at Jaxx's self-esteem until she didn't even see herself as the beautiful person she was, inside or out. What's more, she was the one who had let Jaxx think for the past eight years that he'd spent their time in foster care shagging Leah, that he'd loved Leah. What he knew now was that, even back then, he'd loved Jaxx. It still ticked him off knowing that she'd spent all that time they'd been apart angry with him and believing that of him. And it was all Leah's fault.

He wasn't exactly surprised that she had reappeared now that Jaxx was a celeb. Nor was he all that surprised that she hadn't come earlier – she had probably spent the past few months resenting Jaxx and being bitter as hell. Obviously she had now calmed down and was ready to use emotional blackmail or some other technique to get herself money or something. And he absolutely despised the thought of Jaxx being manipulated or used. He just wanted to sweep her up and take her back to his suite.

As they reached the door to Ollie's suite, Connor sighed. "If it was the other way around, she'd tell you to sling your hook. You know that, right?"

"Connor, calm down before you hyperventilate. I'll be fine, I'm not fourteen anymore."

He combed his hands into her hair. "Are you sure you want to do this?"

"I'm sure. Now move." It was only seconds after she knocked on the door that Ollie opened it, looking as awkward as he'd sounded on the phone.

"Er, why don't you go in. McKenzie and I will wait out here."

Connor huffed. "Oh no, I'm going in with—"

"No, you're not." And with that, Jaxxon swung the door shut. Taking calming, steady breaths, she strolled leisurely through the suite. She found Leah in the small kitchenette, washing out a coffee mug. She looked *so* different. It shouldn't have been such a shock, considering it had been years, but the transformation was pretty dramatic.

Her long, straight blonde hair had faded to a mousey shade and was just above shoulder-length. She'd put a little weight on and actually had boobs. Jaxxon never thought she would ever see Leah look smart, but she did in that black pencil skirt and lavender blouse. Not like a business woman, but like…a housewife. Jaxxon flicked a glance at Leah's left hand and there was both an engagement and wedding ring. Whatever she'd expected, it hadn't been this.

"Oh my God," said Leah as she turned. Usually when you saw a celeb up close without the abundance of make-up or camera tricks to hide the blemishes, they weren't as stunning. But Jaxxon was even more-so. She could see the apprehension and hesitation in Jaxxon's eyes and it broke her heart. Leah knew it was only what she deserved, though. "Hi."

"Alright," Jaxxon greeted quietly. "How've you been?"

"Good, actually. You?"

Jaxxon nodded. "Yeah, great."

"You look really well."

"What are doing in Australia?"

"I live here. My husband and I migrated here a few years ago. I couldn't believe it when I first saw you in a magazine. My baby sister."

If there was one thing that Leah had never referred to Jaxxon as before, it was that. 'My sister', yeah. But the affectionate, 'my baby sister'…Never. "What do you want, Leah?"

A fond smile crept up onto her face. "Still blunt as anything. I think you were born blunt." She drew in a long breath and exhaled slowly. "I'm not here to ask you for anything, but I don't blame you for thinking I might be. Actually, I want to show you something." She dug into her pocket where she'd placed the item she was anxious to show Jaxxon.

Still apprehensive, Jaxxon took what was a photograph from Leah's outstretched hand and looked at it. Whoa.

"He's the image of you. He's got my nose and Alan's eyes. Alan's his dad, my husband. But the rest – those chocolate curls, the olive skin…it's just you."

She was right. This little toddler looked exactly as Jaxxon had when she was that young.

"His name's Riley. He's adorable, but he's going through the terrible twos right now, so he's driving me up the wall. You know, he's got so many of your expressions. He really looks like you when he's upset. And it makes me think of all the times I put that look on your face." Tears welled up then. "Jaxxon, I'm here to say sorry."

Instantly Jaxxon's head snapped up. This was unexpected, to say the least, and she couldn't help but feel suspicious. Her instincts told her she didn't need to be, but still she was a little.

"I know you probably couldn't give a damn. But I am. I was messed up over what mum did. I know that's no excuse – she was your mum too, and you didn't let it turn you into a bitter cow. But I was nowhere near as strong as you and, I'll admit, I was jealous of you for that. And for how people seemed to automatically like you. It always amazed and frustrated me that you could have been the most popular girl in school, but you didn't want any of that whereas me…I wanted it so badly. I needed to feel *liked*, I can't explain why. I envied you so much and I hated myself so much and…well I was a bitch.

"You might not believe it, but I hate myself for it, Jaxxon. I really do. Because I did and do love you. Every time I look at my son, I think of you and how I treated you…" She trailed off as the tears finally flowed over.

Words failed Jaxxon. First Connor's appearance followed by the 'I love you' and then the proposal. Now this. Hearing her sister had come here had been surprising enough.

"What I said about Connor…Again, I was jealous. He never showed any interest in me…but you, he'd have done anything for you. I'm glad that you two got together." She gestured to the beautiful ring on the hand that was holding the photo. "I take it he gave you that."

Jaxxon, still utterly speechless, just nodded.

"Congratulations." And she meant it. "I won't lie and say I planned to come and see you. It wasn't until I knew you were in Australia that I really thought about it. I was just so ashamed of myself. I hadn't even told Alan you were my sister. I didn't want to have to tell him why we'd lost touch and why I was too scared to try to see you. But then I broke down one day and told him everything. He convinced me to come, said if you were anything like the person I'd made you out to be then you wouldn't turn me away without letting me talk to you."

"How long have you been married?"

"Four years now. He's kind of a handy man – electrician, plumber, computer expert. Geeky, really." She laughed. "Never thought I'd fall for a geek."

"No, I didn't see that coming. But then, I never would have thought I'd have gotten into modelling either. I'd always thought that if either one of us was going to be a celeb, it would be you."

Smiling, Leah waved away the comment. "I was never going to be famous. I just craved attention so badly. It was pathetic really. I'd never have been secure enough to survive that world – one critical comment and I'm thrown. Not like you." She braced herself for a snort. "This might sound stupid, but I'm proud of you. It must be weird for you to hear something like that from me – or any kind of compliment."

"I'm glad everything's worked out for you. I can't believe you're a mum."

"I panicked when I found out, whining to Alan that I didn't have a maternal bone in my body. But I'd like to think I'm doing a good job. Not making any of the mistakes our mum made. Keep that photo, I've got thousands. I can't stop taking pictures of the little bugger." Bracing herself for the rejection she deserved, Leah went to Jaxxon and offered her a slip of paper. "That's my address and phone number. Just in case you ever feel like getting in touch. I know you'll probably be too busy to visit but…" She literally sighed in relief when Jaxxon took it. "My email address is on there too, just in case you use email more than phones..."

"I'll want more pictures of Riley emailed to me," said Jaxxon with a smile.

She laughed – it was dripping with relief. "Like I said, I have thousands, I can send you loads." She squeezed her sister's hand tight, hoping this wasn't the last she ever saw of her. "Take care of yourself, Jaxxon."

Jaxxon nodded. "You too." At that, Leah grabbed her handbag and left the suite. Jaxxon just stood there staring at the photo, engrossed by the sight of her nephew, who could easily pass as her son.

"Jaxx."

She turned toward the voice; it was soft, cautious, concerned. As was Connor's face. He had no need to be. She felt a million times lighter. She hadn't realised how much her strained relationship with her sister and her lack of answers as to why it had ever been strained had affected her until now. That fourteen year old girl in her was as high as a kite; Connor McKenzie loved her and had proposed; Leah did love her and was happy for her. And that was why Jaxxon could do something she'd never been able to do before. She flung himself into his arms, wrapping her legs around his waist, like the young girl in her wanted.

EPILOGUE

Five years later

She was going to kill him. Jaxxon was going to kill him. Maybe one day she would be able to understand why her husband liked to ignore her, but that definitely wasn't today. She stormed through the kitchen of their house and out the back door. Then she trekked through the grassy land toward where Connor was darting round crazily on his mini racing track on a quad. Wisely, he slowed his speed when he saw her nearing and then parked the quad, but she could see his body shaking with a muted laugh.

"Something funny?" she asked through her teeth, hating the fact that even while she was planning how to murder him and hide the body, she couldn't help admiring and desperately wanting said body.

Seeing that frustration was practically steaming from the woman he loved, making her look as provocative as ever, Connor decided it might be in his best interests to remain sitting on the quad for just a minute. "Now Jaxx, babe—"

"Oh no, do *not* think that will work with me. Not only are you supposed to be helping me get everything ready, but I've asked you time and time again not to put her on that thing if you're going to go all kamikaze!"

"But Mummy," whined three and a half year old Isabel, who sat snug between her daddy's legs. "I've got on my helmet, and Daddy wasn't going *that* fast."

"Not going that fast," echoed Jaxxon in a quiet voice filled with disbelief.

"Maybe we were going a bit fast," admitted Connor sheepishly, "but do you honestly think I'd drive at a speed like that if I didn't think

I could control it?" He knew that wasn't the point, and her facial expression said just that. But the fact was that their daughter loved a good adrenalin rush and had absolutely no fear – something which concerned Jaxx but made him proud as all hell. "I remember when it was you I used to drive around, and we went a lot faster than that."

"Oh yes, I remember your misspent youth and how petrified I was that you would crash."

"It's alright, Mummy, I'm fine. You don't have to shout at Daddy."

Jaxxon shot her a sweet smile. "I'm not shouting at him, angel, I'm just helping him hear." Knowing there was only one thing Isabel loved more than the quad, Jaxxon asked, "Aren't you coming to give Ferrari his dinner? I can do it if you want." The little girl practically leaped off the quad. Jaxxon had tried to get Isabel to name the puppy something normal, but as she was as obsessed with cars as Connor, there was no changing her mind. She skipped ahead of Jaxxon and Connor toward the house, her dark curls bobbing all over the place.

Connor wrapped his arm around Jaxx's shoulders and kissed her cheek. "Yes, I'm sucking up to you because I don't like being in your bad books." He trailed seductive kisses along the curve of her neck. "I like it better when you do the sucking, though."

She laughed. "You say that with such desperation as if I didn't do that just last night."

"It was torture when I smelled that coffee this morning. It just reminded me of last night. I love it when you suck me off while you're having a hot drink. Maybe once Izzy's in bed, I can make you another coffee."

"I liked it better when I cuffed you to the bedframe." She began shaking with giggles.

"That wasn't funny. How would you like waking up to find that you can't move?"

"Just a little payback." She'd teased him for a full half hour from head to toe before making him come. "You should be thankful I didn't spank you as well."

"One day you'll admit you like that." No sooner had they stepped inside than the doorbell rang. He swatted Jaxx's arse. "You get that. I'll help Izzy with the dog food."

Jaxxon opened the door to find a very pregnant Anna and a flustered Warren on her doorstep. Clearly they'd had a tumble just before leaving their apartment. "Hi, get your arses inside. You're the first ones here. Anna, sit down. Warren, make yourself useful and help Connor set the barbeque up."

Warren saluted her. "Yes, ma'am."

"He hasn't done it yet?" asked Anna.

"The race track was more interesting," grumbled Jaxxon.

Anna smiled at the stunning little girl who was emptying dog food into two bowls. One for Bronty, one for Ferrari. "Hello Iz, are you helping your mummy like a big girl?" She responded with a solemn nod. Although she looked uncannily like Jaxxon, she had her dad's serious expressions. She also had Jaxxon's entrancing eyes, which meant that she could wrap just about everybody around her little finger – especially Connor. He worshipped the ground the child walked on, just as he did Jaxxon.

Next to arrive was Dane, Niki, their six month old baby boy Lewis, and Little Dane who told Jaxxon that he didn't want to be called 'Little Dane' anymore because he was 'five and three quarters'. As usual, he followed Isabel around like she was a guiding light. As usual, Isabel didn't seem to notice.

Ten minutes or so later, Ollie and Louisa, who had been seeing each other for the past five months, arrived. Then shortly after that came Richie, Tony, Lily, and Ant. They all made a humungous fuss of Isabel.

"You know," began Ollie to Jaxxon, who was in the kitchen getting the salads and pastas ready, "most kids would lap up that kind of attention, but your Izzy always shrugs it off. I wonder who she gets that from."

"I can't imagine."

"I asked her what she wants for her birthday this year. You should probably know she wants a baby brother."

Jaxxon nearly choked on the slice of cucumber she was munching. "Well that's a big progression. Last time I asked her, she said a goldfish."

"When did you get the puppy?"

"When she reached exactly three and a half. You know what Connor's like. Any excuse to buy her something."

Ollie never thought when they first met that he would ever be of the opinion that McKenzie was good enough for Jaxxon. But the bloke had proven himself again and again, and he had even won over Richie and Tony. The world followed their relationship even more closely than before, and the rate of celebrity Elvis weddings rocketed after

Jaxxon and Connor married in Vegas. The only complaint Ollie had was that the pair still threw too much sexual tension around. They were even doing it right now with their heated gazes while they stood at the barbeque grill.

Dane inhaled the dreamy smell of the burgers, kebabs, sausages, and steaks as they sizzled on the barbeque rack. "I'm famished. So famished that Ferrari's dinner is starting to look real nice."

"Blame Connor about the delay," said Jaxxon.

He looked at Connor. "Does that mean you were too busy playing on your track with Izzy? I still can't get Dane anywhere near a bike or quad. He's not into cars either. He likes golf, DVDs, and chocolate; that's the extent of his world."

Jaxxon smiled. "He's got very good taste in food." What she wouldn't give for some chocolates right now. "And girls." She gestured toward Little Dane, who was chasing Isabel round the garden while Ferrari and Bronty yapped playfully at their heels.

"Just like her mother," sighed Connor. "Always got males chasing her." He received a scowl from Jaxx for that.

"She's going to break hearts when she's older," said Dane. The kid really was a little stunner, which was hardly surprising considering her gene pool. He couldn't help smiling as he turned to see Connor curling his arms around Jaxxon's front and kissing her nape. Dane was feeling very chuffed with himself – he'd played an extremely big part in his mate having all he had now. He'd even helped organise the wedding well before Connor even knew he was going to propose.

Their Vegas wedding had to have been the most hilarious experience of Dane's life. Nothing normal about it, not even for Vegas. And now Connor no longer stood all alone when they were at a party. Looking at him now, no one would have thought he was a bloke who hadn't wanted marriage or kids; he was in his element, more settled than Dane had ever seen him. The only time there had ever been any anxiety was when they were told Sean Beckett was being released from prison. But then he violated his parole conditions by coming near Jaxxon, and was now back in prison, where he belonged.

"Only three more people left to come," said Jaxxon.

"I don't even know why you invited them," grumbled Connor.

"Don't be a D-I-C-K," she said with a smile. "And try not to snarl this time."

"I didn't snarl last time."

"Yes, you did. Just like you did at our wedding, and Izzy's Christening, and Izzy's first birthday party, and Izzy's second birthday party, and—"

"Alright, I'll *try* not to snarl."

Dane chuckled. "I wouldn't get your hopes up if I were you, Jaxx."

Connor looked at him, brows raised. "You'll have to remind me when it was that I said you could call her Jaxx."

"Oh for God's sake, Connor," she groaned.

He twirled her around, pulled her tight against him and spoke against her lips, "You're my Jaxx, no one else's." It was definitely a mistake aligning her body to his, but he doubted it was a mistake he'd learn from.

"Why not just pee in a circle right around me."

"I might have to, actually, just to stop Ferrari from doing it anymore." At the sound of the doorbell and the puppy barking – Bronty still didn't bother with barking – Connor had to swallow back a sigh. "Go on, go let them in."

The second she opened the front door, Riley dashed in and hugged her legs. "Auntie Jaxxon!"

She scooped him up and kissed his cheek. "You're getting so big."

"I know. I'm the biggest boy ever," he added as he spread out his arms.

"Hi," Jaxxon said to Leah and her husband Alan – who *was* very geeky – as she gestured for them to follow her inside. "How was the flight?" And then she heard a squeal. "Oh bugger, what's she done?" Jaxxon raced to the garden to find Isabel laughing hysterically on the ground.

"She tried to ride Bronty again," said Connor with a sigh. The dog had bucked all over the place like a rodeo bull, just as Isabel had known he would. He held his daughter up high above his head and tickled her sides, wrenching delighted squeals of laughter from her. "You. Have. To. Stop. Giving. Me. Heart. Attacks."

"So she's still got no fear then," giggled Leah.

"None," confirmed Jaxxon.

Leah nodded at Connor. "Alright, Connor." He simply nodded back and gave a similar greeting to Alan. Jaxxon rolled her eyes while Leah hid a smile at his attempt at civility. She doubted he'd ever forgive her for the fact that Jaxxon had spent eight years of her life despising him, and Leah could understand it. That was why, although Jaxxon's home – and what a gorgeous home it was; spacious but modest and cosy – had room for them to stay, Leah, Alan, and Riley always stayed in a hotel when they came to London. She didn't think it would be fair to make Connor feel uncomfortable in his own home.

Leah preferred that Connor was so protective of her sister – that was the way it should be. Looking at them both now, cuddling – though it was obvious that Connor was making lewd suggestions into Jaxxon's ear – she didn't think she'd seen a couple so well-suited.

After giving Isabel a big cuddle and kiss, Leah approached Jaxxon and handed her a little gift wrapped box. "I know you didn't want us to bring you anything, but there was no way I couldn't get my baby sister a present."

"I told you not to," groaned Jaxxon.

"Actually," said Anna, "we did too. I stashed it in the living room."

"So did we," admitted Dane.

Ollie, Louisa, Richie, Tony, Lily, and Ant all nodded guiltily.

Jaxxon gaped and shook her head. "I said the only way I was having a birthday party was if it was nothing big and fancy, if there were only a few people, and if there were no gifts."

Connor had to smile at the look on her face. She'd always felt awkward accepting presents from anyone. She was great at giving them, just not receiving them; it made her feel uncomfortable. He was just relieved that she was actually celebrating her birthday properly again. Although he'd been able to get her to privately celebrate her birthday over the past few years, she hadn't had an actual party before now. If she had thought about Matthew at all today, she'd never once shown it.

"We don't have you a secret birthday present upstairs hiding under my bed wrapped in silver paper, Mummy," declared Isabel, shaking her head.

Connor groaned at the little girl balanced on his arm.

"We don't have an even bigger secret one hidden under yours and Daddy's bed either."

"Alright, Iz, you can stop now before that big vein in Mummy's head bursts."

"And we didn't buy you a big, massive, secret cake either."

As Connor watched Jaxx's face slowly become a disturbing shade of purple, he didn't know whether to laugh or wince.

"And it's not a secret chocolate cake, Mummy, I promise."

Jaxxon raised a brow. "Chocolate?"

He nodded. "But if you don't want the chocolate cake—"

"Let's not be unreasonable," said Jaxxon, "you've obviously gone to a lot of trouble getting me a cake, so I don't see why—" His tight, one-armed hug and firm kiss cut her off.

Isabel's face scrunched up. "Yuck."

"I love you, you mental bitch," he whispered into Jaxx's ear.

"And I love you, you dick," she whispered back.

"Shall we sing 'Happy Birthday' then," called out Lily as she brought out the huge cake lit with candles.

"No, *no* singing!" insisted Jaxxon. But they sang. Bloody sods.

ACKNOWLEDGMENTS

A huge thank you to my husband and children – they're really too fabulous for words and I'll always adore and be thankful for them.

Big thanks to Andrea Ashby, my much-appreciated Beta reader, for her proofreading skills and the time and effort she puts in to helping me.

Thank you so much to my son for creating the 10th Anniversary Edition cover, you are so talented it is intimidating.

And finally, a massive thank you to all my readers for taking the chance on a self-published author. Thanks so much for both buying and taking the time to read my book. Hope you enjoyed it.

If for any reason you would like to contact me, whether it's about the book or you're considering self-publishing and have any questions, please feel free to email me at suzanne_e_wright@live.co.uk.

Take care,
Suzanne Wright, Author

Read on for a glimpse of the first chapter of Izzy McKenzie's story, ACHE FOR ME, which will be featured in the upcoming anthology WEAR SOMETHING RED.

CHAPTER ONE

Should I find it amusing that the man sitting opposite me was an absolute bag of nerves? Probably not but, much like my mother, I wasn't the most forgiving of people. And this bloke here had scribbled his name on my shit list.

I hadn't thought he knew that I'd been made aware of his ... indiscretion, but I could think of no other reason that would explain his current behavior. Ryland had confidence in spades. He ordinarily didn't struggle to make eye-contact, nor did he make nervous gestures. But over the past fifteen minutes he'd repeatedly adjusted his tie, cleared his throat, averted his gaze, drummed his fingers on the table, and repositioned his glass of wine.

Three of my friends, who were sat at a neighboring table intent on ensuring things didn't get ugly, were casting me *well go on, tell him it's over* looks.

I couldn't really blame them for keeping an eye on the proceedings, since they were aware that I longed to fiercely rip him a new one. I wasn't the type to bite back words when I was pissed. In that, I was also my mother's daughter. But causing a scene would risk me getting banned from the club, which I really didn't want.

The Vault, one of the most popular hotspots in Redwater City, was an exclusive 24-hour club that was well worth its membership price. If you fancied an average night out, you could head to the main floor where there were DJs, loud music, spotlights, and fog machines. If you preferred to be entertained, you could either make your way to the Burlesque floor or go up to the rooftop and enjoy the comedians and Dueling Pianos shows.

I was a fan of each and every floor, but I mostly came down here to the basement. It catered to people who were looking for something a little ... different. Sexual. Raw.

It wasn't like a fetish club. Wasn't dark or dingy. Didn't play heavy metal music or feature medieval-looking machines.

In essence, it was a safe place to explore your fantasies.

The themed private rooms were extremely popular. You also could indulge in public displays of sexual affection either right here in the lounge or in the dome, which was the basement's dance floor—no one would bat an eyelid about it.

Some people who were intrigued by BDSM but not entirely sure they wanted to explore it used this very floor as a means to seek out like-minded people and dip their toe in the pool.

You needed an additional membership fee to access the basement, and that fee wasn't at all cheap. But that clearly didn't bother the many high-profile people who came here. A huge reason for that was simple—it often suited them to have the typical 'arrangements' that existed in the basement.

In sum, they could enter into a sort-of-relationship that only existed within the confines of the Vault ... allowing them to not only keep their business private from the outside world but to keep their personal life separate from that of the person they'd claimed here. In that sense, it was a great place to come if you wanted something light and fun rather than impersonal hookups.

Of course, some *did* meet and have fun outside of the club as well. Each couple—or threesome or foursome or whatever—had their own rules and boundaries.

I wasn't a submissive in the typical sense of the word. I didn't want to be collared or whipped or anything like that. I simply wanted to give up control in the bedroom. After living a life where I'd always had to be mindful of my words and actions due to the public scrutiny my family as a whole was subjected to, it was almost a relief to simply *let go*. Having no power was the only time I really felt free.

Being a dominant character but not *a* Dom, Ryland was the type of bloke I went for. The gorgeous and globally desired model knew what he was about. Still, I'd held back from him, even in the bedroom. I didn't find it easy to trust, and I would need to fully trust someone before I could really let go.

He'd sensed that I was holding back. I knew he had. And I also knew he didn't much like it. But that didn't justify his actions.

"We have to talk," Ryland abruptly blurted out.

Why yes, yes we did.

He put his fist to his mouth and let out a quiet cough that seemed forced. "I like what we have. I like it a lot." He cricked his neck. "But I want more."

I blinked. He, what?

"I want us to go public. I want us to be an actual couple. I don't want you to only be mine *here*. It's not enough for me anymore."

He couldn't be bloody serious. Here I'd thought he was a nervous wreck because he'd learned that I knew he was a traitorous twat. Apparently, he'd simply been gearing himself up to make this little announcement. "Ryland—"

"I know you're a private person and don't much like the limelight, but we can't go on like this forever. We would have gone public sooner or later. I'm all for sooner."

I was all for slapping him silly. He had the nerve to ask this of me after what he'd done? Did he feel no guilt at all?

I felt my upper lip begin to curl. It wasn't that I was terribly hurt by his betrayal. We weren't serious. But he'd made me pretty promises when we agreed to an arrangement, and he'd gone ahead and broken them. *That* stung. As did the fact that I'd evidently been wrong in thinking he might be 'different' from the blokes in my past.

He'd never questioned why I'd chosen to be a sports photographer when, given I looked uncannily like my mother, it was thought I'd be just as successful at modelling as her. He hadn't ever dumbed down conversation around me like I had no brain in my head—an assumption people often made, as if a person couldn't possibly be any better than average looking in order to be smart. He hadn't ever suggested I should credit my success to having great connections or to being a sort-of-celebrity as the child of two famous people.

"You weren't expecting this, I can see that," he finished. "But don't overthink it. Don't hem and haw."

"You're not—"

"We fit, Izzy. You know we do. I care about you. That's not a one-way street. I know it isn't."

Uh, it absolutely was. And if he interrupted me one more time …

"I can't be happy with only having parts of you. Not anymore. I want everything." He took a deep breath. "It's all or nothing." His mouth curling into a soft smile, he rested his hand on the table, palm up in a silent invitation. "So, we take this to the next level, yeah?"

It was plain to see that he expected me to excitedly *jump* at that invitation. Unreal. "I'm not comfortable with that."

His face fell. "Jesus Christ, Izzy, why the hell not? We've been together for three months."

"We've *known* each other for three months—a period during which we met here for sex. That's it."

"Don't you belittle what we have."

"Why? You did it when you kissed Genevieve Martin."

His eyes flashing with shock, he went completely rigid. Seconds of silence ticked by before he spoke. "Th-that wasn't real. As part of the shoot—"

"It had *nothing* to do with the photo shoot. You kissed her in a bloody alleyway where you thought no one would see you."

"I don't know where you heard that, but it isn't true. Whoever said it twisted the whole thing."

"You're calling my mum a liar?"

His head jerked back. "Your mom? How could she possibly hear about something like that?"

"You both have the same agent, dickhead. She was able to learn *plenty* about you." I hadn't wanted to explain the ins and outs of the Vault to my mum, so I'd merely told her I was very casually seeing someone. She'd badgered me for his name, and I'd known that she—being incredibly overprotective—intended to take a peek in his closet in search of any skeletons.

I *hadn't* known she'd phone me back and break such shitty news to me before adding, "*I am going to ram a plunger up that cheating bastard's rusty bullet hole.*"

Ryland leaned forward. "I'm sorry, Izzy. More sorry than I can say. The kiss meant nothing. *Genevieve* meant nothing."

"Then she should have been easy for you to resist."

"It wasn't planned, it was a moment of madness. I don't even know how it happened."

"I can give you a recap. You pushed her against the wall, played tonsil tennis with her, and then said that you couldn't wait until later because you needed to fuck her 'again.' As such, I'd say it was way more than a single moment of madness. More like several."

He spluttered. "I hadn't seen you in weeks, I missed you, I was lonely."

"How is that justification for betraying me?" It was the most ridiculous defense *ever*.

"To be fair, it's not like we're in a real relationship."

"It was still a betrayal. *You* requested that we be exclusive, not me. You gave me your word that there'd be no other women in or out of the club. You went back on said word even though you expected me to stick to mine. If you can't keep any promises you made regarding a simple arrangement, why in the fuck would I trust you to be faithful in a serious relationship?"

He squeezed his eyes shut, sighing. "Izzy." His eyes popped open when I slipped out of the booth. "Wait, don't go."

"There's no reason to stay." And there was a genuine risk that I'd pour my wine over his head if I did. Just to be on the safe side, I drank the last of it and set the glass on the table. "We're done."

He shot to his feet. "There's more to say, more to discuss."

"All you'll do is try to convince me to let this go and forgive you, and all I'll do is tell you to shove your excuses and apologies right up your arse."

"Don't do this, Izzy. Don't give up on us. We can work through this."

"Why would I want to? You proved that you're not worth shit. Quite frankly, Ryland, I can do better. I *deserve* better. Now if you'll excuse me ..." I went to pass.

He gripped my arm tight, something cruel rippling across his face. "We're not finished here."

I snarled, keeping my voice low as I warned, "Let go of my arm or I'll snap your fucking fingers."

"Everything okay over here?" a voice chirpily asked. A voice that belonged to one of my friends who'd been watching the entire scene.

Ryland tensed, his scowl melting away. Dropping his arm to his side, he cleared his throat—*again*—and turned to Inaya. "Yes, fine."

She gave him one of her trademark bright smiles that could light up a room. "Great. I just need to borrow Izzy. For, like, ever. You have a good night." Slipping her arm through mine, Inaya led me away. "Well that looked unpleasant. I couldn't hear everything that got said."

"I'll bet that near devastated you," I said.

"It's not my fault that I'm nosy, you can't hold it against me."

Reaching the table where our other friends sat, I took an empty seat as I blew out a breath. "My hand actually tingles with the urge to slap him."

"We ordered you a shot of Tequila," Briar told me, her slanted blue-green eyes glinting with sympathy. With hair the color of pink champagne and all the curves a man could want, she was a woman who made an impact. "We figured you'd need it," she added as she slid a small glass toward me.

I knocked back the shot, enjoying the burn. "You weren't wrong."

It was Briar, who was also my neighbor, that first brought me to the Vault. Well, she wasn't technically *my* neighbor. Not exactly. The apartment I was currently staying at belonged to my parents—they had various houses and apartments but were based in London like me.

I enjoyed my job, and I was good at it—even if I did say so myself. I'd covered a lot of big sports events over the years. It was both challenging and exciting. But it wasn't what anyone would call relaxing, so there were times I sought a break. Whenever I needed downtime, I headed to the apartment here in Redwater. I'd been here for the past four months and wasn't yet feeling a tug to leave. Each visit had been longer than the last, in truth.

"I got the impression that he tried defending his actions," said Briar.

"I suspected he would," I told her. "But the absolute last thing I expected him to do was declare that he wanted us to go public and have something real."

Inaya's lips parted. "He honestly said that?"

"Yep. Of course, at that point, he had no idea I'd heard about him and Genevieve. He also insisted he cared about me. What a load of ole shit."

Crossing one sun-kissed, long leg over the other, Cat tossed her platinum blonde beach waves over her shoulder. "I'm not sure I'd agree that he cares for you. What he feels is more like an obsession. Not a creepy kind. I just mean it's more like he's fixated on *owning* you than on actually building something with you. And while I have nothing against a guy wanting to own his woman in some sense—it's actually kind of a turn-on at times—it's not so great if you're no more than arm candy to him."

"Agreed." Sighing, I glanced around the lounge. The tasteful and stylish bar-slash-restaurant boasted dim lighting, dark walls, and shiny black marble flooring. Sensual background music played low.

Some people sat at tables and booths. Others congregated at the bar or relaxed on the leather sofas. For most people, a meal or drink at the lounge was a prelude to a night of 'play.'

There'd sadly be no 'playing' for me tonight.

I turned back to my friends. "Why is it that I always seem to fall into bad relationships? I don't get it. It's not like I have the sort of emotional baggage that would make me subconsciously seek out arseholes or anything. The blokes I get involved with are always so nice to me in the beginning. Little by little, they change. They do occasional mean shit or try to put me down. I know that nobody's perfect. I'm not expecting perfection. I just … it would simply be nice to break the pattern, that's all."

"You have the same issue as Inaya," said Briar. "Men feel intimidated by you. You're not only astonishingly beautiful, you're talented and successful. More, you're fiercely self-reliant and don't *need* people. I think the dudes in your past were kind of daunted by it all. They probably didn't feel secure in their hold on you and might have even resented you for it—hence the attempts to peck at your confidence and shit. When they couldn't convince you that you were lucky to have them, they struck out at you to soothe their ego."

I frowned. "You and Cat are beautiful and talented and all that other stuff."

"But while our families are well-known, our faces aren't. We're generally not recognized on sight, unlike you and Inaya. Also, I'm a costume designer. Cat is a freelance book editor. Neither are thought of as manly professions. Sports photography is, though it shouldn't be."

"Inaya's a singer and lyricist. They're not considered masculine professions."

"But we can all agree that the rock music industry is male-dominated. She belts out rock music like a boss. She's spoken of in the same sentences as legends like Freddie Mercury and Bruce Springsteen. She's collaborated with dudes like Jon Bon Jovi and Elton John. All her albums went platinum, and she's won God knows how many awards.

"More, when she didn't win a particular music award—I still say that was fixed—both Steven Tyler *and* Bono complained on social media while singing her praises. No pun intended. That level of fame and recognition can be intimidating to any guys who are interested in her, especially if that level tops *theirs*."

I looked at Inaya. "Even with all that, I still don't understand how you could possibly be single."

Warm and authentic with an indomitable spirit, Inaya was always moving and doing and singing ... like a hummingbird. She was also incredibly beautiful with her heavy-lidded Nordic blue eyes, golden skin, slender build, and her ruby red hair that was lightly streaked with black and various shades of purple.

Inaya smiled. "Why, thank you. The reality is that the dating scene is hard for everyone. Hence why I like coming here and keeping shit simple. Most arrangements don't last very long, but they can be a whole lot of fun and involve no heartache. I mean, look at you—you're pissed at Ryland, but you're not devastated. You can easily carry on with your evening, feeling no need to dwell. Right?"

I nodded. "Absolutely." It wasn't so much as a ping on my radar.

"Well then, on that note, we should all go dance." Inaya stood. "Let's head to the dome."

"I'm up for it." Cat drained her glass and then pushed to her feet.

"You're not waiting for Danton?" I asked the blonde, referring to the bloke she'd been in an arrangement with for quite a few months.

She shook her head. "He's not coming tonight. He had to cancel." A long sigh slipped out of her.

Briar poked her arm. "What's that sigh for?"

Cat shrugged. "It's just never nice when someone isn't quite as into you as you are into them."

Standing, I felt my brows draw together. "You sure that's the case?" Because *I* wasn't. I'd seen how Danton looked at her. It was intense and hot and *all* male possession.

"Oh, I'm positive," said Cat. With that, she strode off, every inch the haughty princess—a look she'd mastered and used as a *don't come too close* shield. It often worked.

Not that she needed said shield while at the Vault, considering she wore a red dress—anyone who was part of an arrangement wore something red to indicate they were claimed, ensuring others let them be. And anyone who'd seen *who* she'd been claimed by would never dare attempt to trespass in any case.

Danton Quintero might call himself a businessman, but everyone knew that most of his businesses weren't exactly above board. Just as they knew he was a merciless bastard who suffered no fools. None of that much bothered Cat. But then, her father was into shady shit, so ...

Briar and I fell into step behind Cat and Inaya as we made our way to the door at the other side of the lounge.

Briar gently elbowed me. "You need to take off the red bracelet. You're back on the market."

I felt my nose wrinkle. "I might keep it on for the rest of the night. I'm not in the mood to be approached, and this will warn men away."

She snorted. "Your glare will do that just fine. You might look like your mom with your huge brown eyes, olive skin, big boobs, and that head of dark curls, but you have your dad's *don't fucking test me* glares. I've never known anyone not to heed them."

She had a point. I took off the bracelet and dropped it into my purse.

As we stepped into a long dimly lit hall, I could hear the thumping music coming from the dome up ahead; could see strobe lights flickering through its ornate glass doors.

Clusters of people stood here and there, talking and laughing or engaging in a little foreplay. Recognizing a few, I flashed them brief smiles as I strode along the hall, passing door after door—all of which led to themed rooms.

Glancing over her shoulder at Briar and I, Inaya subtly tipped her head toward two exceptionally good-looking blokes. "Don't judge me, but I'd *totally* spend a few hours stuck between them."

"You'll get no judgement from my corner," I told her.

Trace and Kaleb were regulars at the club, but I'd recognize them anyway—one was a famous actor, and the other was a voice actor who female readers everywhere *adored* due to his deep, rumbly voice alone. The two close friends enjoyed sharing women but never claimed any. A lot of females who frequented the basement were determined to 'bag' them, but the boys were anti-arrangement for some reason.

Briar hummed. "It's rumored that they know their way around a woman's body. I heard they don't fuck around; that it can get intense, I mean. Not whips and canes intense. Just, you know, they like to give a girl a rough ride."

"Even better," said Inaya.

"I don't know if I could enjoy a threesome," said Cat. "I think I'd always worry someone was feeling left out."

"I would have thought you'd totally be up for it," Inaya told her. "There's not much you haven't tried."

"Yeah, well, no amount of games or scenes or whatever really did it for me," said Cat. "I *enjoyed* them, but I'd only want that stuff as an occasional added spice."

"So are you and Danton pretty much vanilla or do you just keep things light?" asked Briar.

"I wouldn't say we keep things light, but he doesn't use toys," replied Cat. "The way he sees it, *I'm* his toy."

Inaya let out a dreamy sigh. "I wouldn't mind being someone's toy. Maybe even Trace and Kaleb's for a night. But they're more interested in Briar."

Briar's head jerked. "What?"

Inaya smiled, dropping back to sidle up to her. "They watch you. A lot. They're discreet about it, but I see all."

Flushing, Briar glanced away. "I have an arrangement with Grover."

"Who you hardly ever see, since he's always away for work. Yeah, I know you two are only exclusive *inside* the club so you can still get laid elsewhere, but that's not the point."

"I like him."

Cat snorted. "You like solitude, so it suits you that he's not around much—that's not the same thing."

Briar shrugged. "He gives good head."

Cat gave her a droll look. "And that's what's important." Reaching the dome, she pushed one door open. The interior was as dark as any bar, but it was *nothing* like an average bar. More like a large, fancy, sensual ballroom. Dome shaped—hence its name—it had black marble walls and a shiny checkered floor. There were fluted columns, long mirrors, tiered chandeliers, and also French windows that were framed by red velvet drapes.

A door on the opposite side of the space led to more private themed rooms. Also, there were some additions near the rear of the dome. Five tall, boxes with mirrored walls. Boxes that were big enough to fit two people. And while said people would be able to look *out* at the dance floor, no one from the outside could see what was happening within the boxes.

As usual, the dome was packed with people dancing, talking, drinking, and even getting up to some raunchy stuff in the arched hollows barely out of sight.

"So who's getting the drinks while the rest of us go hit the dance floor?" asked Cat.

"I'll get the first round," I said. "Who wants what?" Once I had their orders, I headed to the long bar.

I didn't make it there.

Because a bunch of people moved aside, and suddenly another person was in my line of sight. One I recognized. One I'd had very filthy thoughts about on several occasions. One who right then pinned me with a predatory gaze that seemed to plant my feet to the floor.

Well now. Things were looking up.

SUZANNE WRIGHT

ABOUT THE AUTHOR

Suzanne Wright lives in England with her husband and her two children. When she's not spending time with her family, she's writing, reading, or doing her version of housework – sweeping the house with a look.

TITLES BY SUZANNE WRIGHT:

The Deep in Your Veins Series

Here Be Sexist Vampires
The Bite That Binds
Taste of Torment
Consumed
Fractured
Captivated
Touch of Rapture

The Phoenix Pack Series

Feral Sins
Wicked Cravings
Carnal Secrets
Dark Instincts
Savage Urges
Fierce Obsessions
Wild Hunger
Untamed Delights

FROM RAGS

The Mercury Pack Series

Spiral of Need
Force of Temptation
Lure of Oblivion
Echoes of Fire
Shards of Frost

The Olympus Pride Series

When He's Dark
When He's An Alpha
When He's Sinful
When He's Ruthless

The Dark in You Series

Burn
Blaze
Ashes
Embers
Shadows
Omens
Fallen
Reaper

Standalones

From Rags
Shiver
The Favor
Wear Something Red (Anthology)

Printed in Great Britain
by Amazon